IN THE JAWS OF LIFE

Dubravka Ugrešić

···

IN THE JAWS OF LIFE

TRANSLATED BY
Celia Hawkesworth and Michael Henry Heim

WITH A FOREWORD BY
Andrew Wachtel

NORTHWESTERN UNIVERSITY PRESS
EVANSTON, ILLINOIS

Northwestern University Press
Evanston, Illinois 60208-4210

Steffie Speck in the Jaws of Life first published as *Štefica Cvek u raljama života*, Zagreb, 1981. *A Love Story* is taken from *Poza za prozu,* Zagreb, 1978, 1989. *Life is a Fairy Tale* first published as *Život je bajka*, Zagreb, 1983. "The Kharms Case" is taken from *Nule i ništice*, Zagreb, 1987. Copyright © by Dubravka Ugrešić. English translations of "Steffie Speck in the Jaws of Life," "A Love Story," "Life is a Fairy Tale," "Who Am I?," "Lend Me Your Character," and "Author's Notes" copyright © by Celia Hawkesworth. English translations of "A Hot Dog in a Warm Bun" and "The Kreutzer Sonata" copyright © 1988 by Michael Henry Heim. Foreword copyright © 1993 by Northwestern University Press. *In the Jaws of Life* first published 1992 by Virago Press Limited. Northwestern University Press edition published 1993 by arrangement with Virago Press Limited. All rights reserved.

Printed in the United States of America

ISBN 0-8101-1100-4

Library of Congress Cataloging in Publication Data

Ugrešić, Dubravka.
    [Short stories. English. Selections]
    In the jaws of life and other stories / Dubravka Ugrešić ;
translated by Celia Hawkesworth and Michael Henry Heim ; with a
foreword by Andrew Wachtel.
        p.   cm. — (Writings from an unbound europe)   (Literature in
translation ; 4)
    Originally published : London : Virago Press, 1992.
    ISBN 0-8101-1100-4 (pbk.)
    1. Ugrešić, Dubravka—Translations into English.   I. Wachtel,
Andrew. II. Title. III. Series. IV. Series: Literature in
translation ; 4.
PG1619.31.G7A25   1993
891.8'235—dc20   93-30359
                                                  CIP

The paper used in this publication meets the minimum requirements of the American National Standard for Information Sciences—Permanence of Paper for Printed Library Materials, ANSI Z39.48-1984.

Contents

··

Foreword

As readers of contemporary fiction are aware, postmodernism is the "ism" of the day. An international concept—perhaps it might even be called the first global cultural movement—postmodernism is a theoretical umbrella under which critics and writers have grouped an astounding range of authors including Latin Americans Jorge Luis Borges, Gabriel Garcia Marquez, and Mario Vargas Llosa; North Americans Margaret Atwood, E. L. Doctorow, and Maxine Hong Kingston; and Europeans Italo Calvino, Umberto Eco, Danilo Kis, Milan Kundera, and Milorad Pavić. Definitions of this phenomenon abound, but as Linda Hutcheon says in her *Poetics of Postmodernism*, postmodernism "is a contradictory phenomenon, one that uses and abuses, installs and then subverts, the very concepts it challenges." It is, furthermore, "resolutely historical, and inescapably political." As we will see in our brief discussion of the fiction of Dubravka Ugresić, her work does indeed fit into this broad category. At the same time, however, due both to Ugresić's personal background and the Yugoslav literary process of the 1960s and 1970s, her fiction is in certain respects quite idiosyncratic. And since modern readers tend to read to discover the new, my focus here will be on what is idiosyncratic to Ugresić's fiction.

Perhaps the best place to begin is with a bit of biography. Ugresić was born in 1949 in Zagreb, Yugoslavia. She had the good fortune to study Russian and comparative literature in the very strong program offered at Zagreb University. It was here that she was first exposed to the theoretical work of the Russian formalist critics and to the wealth of both classical and avant-garde Russian literature. Even after turning to fiction, Ugresić has continued to work as a professional critic; she has written dozens of essays devoted to twentieth-century Russian prose, and she is also the co-coordinator (with Aleksandr Flaker, Zagreb University) of an ongoing international publication entitled *A Glossary of the Russian Avant-garde*. Her earliest works of fiction were two prizewinning children's stories published in the 1970s. Ugresić moved to "adult" prose with the collection *Pose for Prose* (1978). She became quite well known on the Yugoslav literary scene after the publication of *Steffie Speck in the Jaws of Life* (1981), which was made into an awardwinning film in 1984. Her third collection of prose, *Life is a Fairy Tale,* appeared in 1983, and most recently she published the novel *Fording the Stream of Consciousness* (also available from Northwestern University Press). For the past few years she has lectured extensively in Europe and the United States while continuing to live in Zagreb, trying not to be engulfed by the conflict that has destroyed her former country.

When an American literary audience imagines what it must have been like for a writer coming of age in the late 1960s in eastern or central Europe, the situations in countries like Czechoslovakia, Poland, or Hungary come to mind. In those countries, viable options for literary expression were depressingly few. The state officially encouraged writing that was committed, optimistic, heroic, and in the traditions of realism. At the same time, unofficial writing also was bound by convention—it was expected to be ironic, pessimistic, not entirely (or not at all) realistic, and equally politically committed, albeit to a different agenda. The situation in Yugoslavia was quite different, however. After Tito's break with Stalin in 1948, government censorship and repression of writers were minimal compared to the practices of the authorities in other communist countries, and this fact relieved writers from the system of binary oppositions that afflicted much of eastern and central European literature in the postwar period. A remarkably cosmopolitan Yugoslav literature grew up, drawing inspiration from interwar writers who remained active and in the public eye in the postwar years; most prominent among these were Ivo Andrić (who received international recognition with the Nobel Prize for literature in 1961) and Miroslav Krleza. At the same time, new writers flourished and an exciting literary culture developed in a number of Yugoslav centers. Major fiction of the postwar years included Oskar Davico's *Pesme* (A Poem), Danilo Kis's striking novels beginning with *Basta, Pepeo* (Garden, Ashes) in 1964, and Mesa Selimović's *Dervis i smrt* (Death and the Dervish), which still awaits an

English translation. Literary life was particularly active in the Croatian capital, Zagreb, where a number of groups with a strong western orientation were active in the sixties and seventies, including followers and imitators of such disparate writers as J. D. Salinger and Borges.

In addition to the generally cosmopolitan character of Yugoslav literature during Ugresić's formative years, a number of specific factors influenced the development of her literary style. The first was her decision to engage in the professional study of Russian literature, with particular attention to the 1920s. In the work of the Russian formalists, Ugresić discovered strong theoretical support for the idea that literature was not and should not be dependent on politics, but rather that the purpose of literature was literature itself—the pleasure of the autonomous literary word. Ugresić did not, of course, accept the Russian legacy unquestioned; in particular she turned away from their avant-garde emphasis on overcoming cultural tradition by either attacking or ignoring it. Nevertheless, the Russian formalists provided a strict theoretical vocabulary for understanding a "literary" literature, as well as a catalog of basic technical devices that have clearly influenced Ugresić's own fiction.

But while the Russians may have provided a framework for understanding and a vocabulary for describing the work of the literary artist, their fictional practice does not seem to have had a decisive influence on Ugresić's work. Instead, this seems to have come from her reading of the inspired short stories of the Argentine writer Borges, probably as filtered through a slightly older generation of Yugoslav writers who were inspired by Borges, particularly Kis (1935–89). Insofar as Ugresić employs Borgesian techniques of overt citationality and parody while blurring the boundaries between high and low culture, and between art and life, her work clearly fits into the broad international trend of postmodernism.

The three works published here illustrate Ugresić's writerly evolution, from "A Love Story" in her first published collection, *Pose for Prose,* through *Steffie Speck in the Jaws of Life* to *Life is a Fairy Tale.* The central problem in both "A Love Story" and *Steffie Speck* is how to narrate a story about love when love stories have become almost exclusively the province of middle and lowbrow kitschy romance. The former experiments with the resources of first-person pseudoconfessional prose, while the latter employs a more overtly postmodern emcee to pull the narrative threads together. The experience of these first two books allows for an attempt in *Life is a Fairy Tale* to use autonomously all the devices that were earlier placed in the service of avoiding the banality of the unified love plot in a marvelous celebration of the literary tradition itself.

In "A Love Story" Ugresić's solution to the problem of how to write about love is to employ a highly self-conscious first-person narrator who is as concerned with the difficulties of writing seriously on this seemingly hopeless theme as she is with recording the actual love story. The trick is to bare the device (as the Russian formalists would have said) of the love story while nevertheless contriving to provide that very same story. The actual love story is between the narrator/writer and Bublik, "her archetypal man." The affair itself, however, is mediated entirely by the narrator's search for a genre appropriate to its description. Bublik demands that the narrator write, and she complies by producing a dazzling series of prose proposals that range from the confessional first-person, to the carefully plotted novel of incident, to realism, and to the fantastic. Each one of these is rejected by Bublik, who demands an ill-defined hyperrealism without himself being able to produce anything. The affair develops further through another series of brilliant literary stylizations (which presage the "pure" stylizations of *Life is a Fairy Tale*) including a wonderful bit of bad Kafka and a series of imitations of horrendous "feminist" prose. Through all of this the love story continues on its inevitable path, sneaked in behind the reader's back, a triumph of the storyteller's art in spite of all obstacles. In "A Love Story," Ugresić is like the magician who talks so convincingly that the audience never notices how the rabbit actually got out of the hat.

The themes of the intermingling of life and art, high and low culture, kitsch and good taste, and the clichés through which both men and women view love are further developed in *Steffie Speck in the Jaws of Life,* a work which the author dubs a "patchwork novel." At first glance, the text looks as if it were lifted directly from the sewing section of a women's magazine. First a discussion of terms needed to construct the text; then an outline of the procedure to follow; and finally detailed instructions. The "story line" revolves around the love life of one Steffie Speck, a young and not particularly attractive woman, as seen through her own eyes, those of her friends, the author, world literature, etc. Interspersed throughout are snippets of quotations (or made-up quotations) from sewing manuals, cookbooks, advertisements, and other detritus of late twentieth-century society. The idea, it would seem, is to write women's prose, but to do so in such a self-conscious way that women's issues are neither trivialized by the kitschy sentimentality so typical for mass-culture treatments of women nor made bathetic. The point of view of the protagonist is continually undercut (although not swept away entirely) by authorial irony.

Even more interesting, perhaps, are the short stories that make up the third part of this volume under the general title "Life is a Fairy Tale." Each story is a fullscale stylization of a certain kind of writing, mostly by Russians (Leo Tolstoy, Nikolai Gogol, and Daniil Kharms) but also by Lewis Carroll and André Gide. For readers with a working knowledge of the source texts, Ugrešić's rewritings are absolutely hilarious. Particularly striking are "The Kharms Case," a story in letters of the Kharmsian (or Kafkaesque) adventures of a professor of Russian literature trying to publish the works of Kharms (the greatest Russian absurdist) in Croatian, and "A Hot Dog in a Warm Bun," which replays the events of Gogol's story "The Nose" in all their post-Freudian glory.

According to Ugrešić, "the book grew out of the idea of the loss of reading culture, and it is a sort of appeal for a return to that culture." Of course, hints of this type of concern were abundantly present in the earlier works (for example, in Steffie Speck's reading of *Madame Bovary*), but before they were incorporated into a larger narrative framework whereas here they stand on their own. The heroes of each little story in *Life is a Fairy Tale* are artists, one way or another, and in reworking material from preexisting texts (although they, of course, don't recognize what they are doing), they explore both the value of classic texts for our time and time-honored literary problems (genre, theme, epistolary prose, etc.). To use Hutcheon's terminology, these little stories simultaneously "use and abuse" their source texts. The effect, ultimately, is to force readers to rethink their relationship to canonized texts and to literary creativity in general. Instead of worshipping canonized texts and authors,

Ugresić invites us to "make their stories strange" (to borrow again from the formalists) so that we can reperceive them through the double lens of her literary stylizations. Thus we see that the postmodernist project (at least in Ugresić's variant) is by no means an attempt to destroy the cultural capital of the past, as some have argued; it is, rather, an invitation through inspired literary play to reclaim the past for our own age.

Andrew Wachtel

STEFFIE SPECK
IN THE JAWS OF LIFE

(a patchwork novel)

Key to the Various Symbols

┈┈✂ *Cut* the text along the line as desired.

-·-·-·- *Stretch*: the text may be stretched in any direction in case of unfulfilled expectation, and with the help of an ordinary damp imagination.

┈┈┈ *Take in*: the text may be taken in as required with critical darts.

////////// *Pleat*: Make large thematic stitches on either side of the author's seam.
Then draw the lower threads in a little and arrange the pleats evenly.

" " " " " *Smocking*: Make small sentimental stitches along the author's seam. Then draw in the threads and press at the desired width.

==== Make a metatextual knot and draw in as desired.

++++ Perforations for the co-author's ribbons.

The Paper Pattern

Making up the garment
a) Choice of technique
b) Choice of material
c) Choice of pattern

How, while shelling peas, Steffie Speck felt that there was something wrong with her life (*tacking*)

Steffie Speck consults Annie who is very experienced in questions of depression (*tucking*)

Steffie Speck gets advice from Marianna, her friend at work (*padding*)

Steffie accepts the advice (*hemming*)
a) Clothes
b) Figure
c) Make-up

Steffie Speck and men (*fastenings*)
a) Steffie and the Driver
b) Steffie and the Hulk
c) Steffie and the Intellectual

Steffie Speck's dream (*interfacing*)

Topstitching by the author

Emancipated Ella advises Steffie Speck (*kick pleating*)

Steffie Speck follows the advice (*basting*)
a) Steffie Speck at the theatre
b) Steffie Speck reads *Madame Bovary* by Gustave Flaubert
c) Steffie Speck at the exhibition (or the unanticipated oversewing of S. S. with the author's own zigzag stitch)

Steffie Speck sleeps with a pig's head or a new attack of depression (*concealed plackets*)

Annie, very experienced in questions of depression, tells Steffie Speck some news (*lapped seams*)

Steffie Speck and the budgie, or the hidden monster (*pinked hems*)

Steffie Speck reflects on the first deflowerer, the second deflowerer, and suicide (*toggle fastenings*)

Steffie Speck recalls Emancipated Ella's advice (*gussets*)

Steffie Speck from top to toe in a happy end or the appearance of Monsieur Fiddler (*finishing*)

Romance-remnants which may be used for appliqué

The author's darts

How the author's mother, Aunt Sissy, their neighbour Barbara, cousin Lily from Nancy and Aunt Sissy's friend Greta from Holland expand the plot for the heroine S.S.

Final touches to the garment

Making up the Garment

A) Choice of technique

My friends suggested I write a 'women's story'. Write a women's story, they said, a real women's story! Well, not all of them, actually . . . My girl-friends (Write about us! About us!); my tailor (There's so much material, if you only knew!); my hairdresser (I've fleeced some in my time, I can tell you, honey . . . !); and my neurotic male friend who keeps gazing into the mythic past and complaining of twinges (I keep getting these twinges, I must be pregnant.).

So I sit down at the typewriter and start thinking about writing just such a story, to order, a story for and about women. I write very slowly in any case, because I always get carried away by the sound of the typewriter. And the sound of the typing machine reminds me of the sound of a – sewing machine. I'm fascinated by the clattering (plump fingertips squirming in the little hollowed out seats of the letters), the sounds steadily rolling along. But not time! All typists and seamstresses (all dressmakers, spinners, weavers, embroiderers) are flies in amber. Like Vermeer's paintings.

I'm intrigued by gossip, that passionate conquest of emptiness. People gossiping, typing (weaving, embroidering . . .) are engrossed to the same degree as those observing them. The observer feels that the other is in a different world, a dream, condemned to the same eternal movements, illuminated from within, hollow . . . Like Vermeer's paintings. Choice of technique, then? I think we've made it. Typist – seamstress. Sewing machine – typing machine. . . . We're going to sew our story!

B) Choice of material

-->%

*'I am 18 years old. I think I'm at a turning-point. There are
some things I can't answer by myself. I'm normal, intelligent,
I have no enemies. I think I'm aware of my good qualities and
faults, and I think I know how a life should be lived. I'm
neither lacking in confidence nor cowardly; I don't go looking
for shoulders to cry on and I feel strong enough to find my
own answers to things. I've been in love with all kinds of boys,
known how to see the best in them and love them for that.
And they love me. Still they all chuck me, and the only thing
I'm ever left with is knowing I have a great personality and
looks. That's how it is now. A year ago I started going out
with a guy my own age who I really loved and I gave him
everything a girl can give, but he chucked me like all the others,
and told me what a great person I was. I want to go back to
him, but I think I've lost him forever and that has upset my
whole system of values. I can't decide whether I'm asking too
much or too little from life. What can I look forward to?'
Anna*

-->%

*'I'm 18. Superficially I'm no different from most girls of my
age. I'm sociable, of average appearance, active in every way.
Still, I can't find anyone to love me. I've always been true to
myself, to my feelings and principles and that has always cost
me a lot. For more than two years now I've loved a boy who's
got a girl of his own. I'm just a convenient shoulder to cry on
when things get tough, a helping hand when he's in trouble.
I'm aware of that. But I love him so much. I can't help it,
although I know there's no future in it. What should I do?'
Prometheus*

-->%

*'I'm 23, I've got a three-year-old daughter, I'm divorced, I've
got a job, people say I'm attractive. I got married when I was
17, and divorced at 20. We lived with my parents, but they
were against our relationship and our marriage. They kept
criticising him, but I loved him. In the end my parents were
happy because their daughter got rid of that "layabout". I was
disillusioned and hurt, I looked for comfort in love affairs,*

trying to forget. My private life consists of relationships with married men. I don't want to break up anyone's marriage, but something keeps driving me to them. Maybe I'm looking for security. They're all the same to me, all liars. The only difference is between good and bad lovers. But I can't go on like this. All they want is my body. I've been going round in a circle for three years. Maybe my problem has deeper roots, maybe it's my parents' arguments, their neglect of me. I've always had money, but never parents. I was raped at 13. There's still something wrong with my speech, but no one has ever asked me why. Maybe I'm just trying to escape into a false world of pleasure. What should I do?'
Only a shadow

--✂

'I am 25 years old and a typist by profession. I live with my aunt. I think I'm ugly, although some people tell me I'm not. I'm different from everybody my age: they're all married or have boyfriends, I have no one. I'm lonely and sad, and don't know what to do about it. Please advise.'
Steffie

--✂

Suddenly I stop! I feel ideal material under my fingers! A remnant! And chintz! Steffie – humble chintz! Chintz prints, glazed prints, a maze of tints, amazing hints . . .

Steffie, Steffie, you'll be my stuff, my theme, I'm hoping, groping . . . it's still a blur . . . A surname? Yes, let's have a guess . . . no I'll go and look, in the 'phone book? Now, let me see . . . how about – Speck? Let me check. Will it fit? Yes, that's it!

C) Choice of pattern

So we've got the material. We haven't found an author who's any good at embroidering, weaving, crotcheting or tapestry-making, but we do have a typing-sewing machine. And an author inclined to – cobbling things together! Now all we need is a simple pattern, a guide. I know! Patchwork! A patchwork waistcoat, patchwork shirt, patchwork skirt. Patchwork is a simple, universal, democratic way of dressing. It's more than clothes – it's a way of life! Sloppy workmanship is part of its charm.

I go on typing. I'm feeling my way. I'm sewing a story for women only. I'm sewing a prose dress, no more, no less. I'm a snail looking for a trail, an embroideress of chintz looking for a prince, a lacewing butterfly, oh my. And as my first stitches are all hitches, I'll put a dart in here! A dart! A smart little dart! Now it's time to start!

How, while shelling peas, Steffie Speck felt that there was something wrong with her life
(tacking)

---✂

The garlic in your larder is about to sprout. To keep it from
doing so, place the bulbs in tins or other containers, heads
down and cover them with sea salt.

---✂

'Have you theen my teeth?' asked Steffie's aunt, coming into
the kitchen.

'No.'

'I mutht have put them down thomewhere again!' she sighed.

Steffie's aunt waddled in, mumbling and opening and closing
drawers. Then she stopped as though thinking about something
important, and sighed again, opened the door of the larder,
took out a bag of peas and shook them out onto the table.

'Here, you shell the peath,' she said, 'I'll look for my teeth.'

'Try the bed! Last time we found them in the pillow case!'

Steffie's aunt smiled sadly, sucking her lips back into her
toothless mouth, and shuffled out of the kitchen.

Like a fig! thought Steffie, figs suck their little tails into
themselves when they dry.

Steffie took out a dish and started shelling the peas. The
kitchen, bathed in sunlight, pulsated rhythmically. From the
courtyard came the sound of children shouting and pigeons
cooing. Steffie shelled the peas, slowly, lazily, as in a slow-
motion sequence, and for a moment she thought she might be
stuck in the pose forever, if the film stopped, if someone went
click!

'You know,' said Steffie's aunt, coming back into the
kitchen, 'thomeone in our town, you don't know her, lotht her
teeth juth like thith and never did find them. She wath done
for in thixth monthth!'

'Dead?'

'Dead.'

'Hey ho!' sighed Steffie.

'Yeth!' sighed her aunt and added: 'Peel the potatoeth when you've finished with the peath.'

She shuffled out of the kitchen. Steffie separated the pods, pressed along the bulges, pulled the little green strings, undid the pockets and the beads fell out. The peas wriggled about in the dish, soaking up the sun. When Steffie picked up a handful, the little green balls slid through her fingers and fell onto the bottom of the dish like drizzle. 'Peas!' sighed Steffie tenderly and put one in her mouth.

'Don't eat the peath!' said her aunt, coming into the kitchen.

'Why not?'

'Thomeone in our town, they called him Mad Mike, ate all the raw peath he could, jutht like thith, uncooked, for a bet, and died.'

'Of raw peas?'

'Yeth,' said Steffie's aunt. 'Peath mutht always be well thim-mered with onion.' She flapped round the kitchen, opening and closing drawers. 'Have you nearly finished?', she asked.

'Nearly . . .'

Her aunt went out, and Steffie continued to shift the little pockets about, pulling the threads as though unravelling them.

Suddenly she felt a warm mist, like wool, gathering and solidifying around her, she felt she had shelled peas like this before, at the same time of day, in the same kitchen, at the same table . . . 'Maybe I've been sitting in this kitchen shelling peas all my life, without noticing it!'

The wool wound slowly round Steffie Speck, encasing her like a larva. 'Like a maggot,' thought Steffie and wriggled. 'Like a green maggot . . .' Steffie tugged the last thread. Out of the pod rolled four plump peas.

Steffie lifted the dish off the table, but it slipped out of her hands and clattered onto the floor. The peas flew in all directions. Steffie knelt down and began to pick up the peas, one by one. In the rays of sunlight spreading over the floor Steffie could see the dust, scratches and peas as under a magnifying glass. And all of a sudden she was overcome by an incomprehensible despair.

Oh my God, thought Steffie, I'm going to be shut up in this kitchen forever, picking up peas, one by one, Steffie sniffed. My whole life, Steffie thought, with my aunt, Steffie wept, who will keep losing her teeth. Her tears rolled on to the floor, I'll go on and on picking them up, Steffie sniffed. Everyone's better off than me, Steffie thought, Marianna, Ella, and Annie, the peas rolled away, at least they've got someone, the peas escaped, a husband, children, friends, Steffie sniffed, I'm the only one who's alone, Steffie thought, work, home, work, the tears poured down Steffie's face, nothing, nothing will ever change, her tears rolled on, I'll keep on dropping dishes and I'll always be here, picking up peas, one by one, the peas swam in her tears, like a bad dream Steffie sniffed, why isn't Ella in a bad dream, Steffie thought, why doesn't Marianna drop dishes, the floor swayed through her tears, why doesn't Annie have to pick up peas, Steffie counted her green rosary, why must it be me, I'll have to do something, Steffie threaded a chain of peas, as soon as I pick up the peas, her hand soaked up the tears like a bun.

Two grey and white pigeons stood on the window-sill, nodding their heads and watching Steffie Speck. Her aunt shuffled into the kitchen.

'Shoo, nathty thingth!' she cried and the pigeons flew away. Suddenly she beamed: 'My teeth!'

At that moment Steffie had caught sight of her aunt's teeth. They were right beside the table leg. She picked them up with two fingers and handed them to her aunt.

As Steffie's aunt stood there looking pityingly at the young woman, kneeling tearful on the floor, the web of old age vanished from her eyes and she seemed about to say something. But she changed her mind and, nodding, shuffled out of the door.

By then there were only a few peas left on the floor.

Steffie Speck consults Annie who is very experienced in questions of depression
(tucking)

---✂

If you spend a few minutes every day standing on your head, you will have a far better complexion and improved circulation. To start with, try propping yourself against a wall for two to three minutes. Do this exercise whenever you feel tired or out of sorts. Keep your make-up pencils in the fridge and they will be easier to sharpen.

---✂

'Hello?'

'Yes?'

'Annie, it's me, Steffie!'

'Oh, it's you! What's up?'

'Nothing special . . . What are you doing?'

'Ironing. I've got a whole heap . . . How are you? What have you been up to? I haven't seen you for ages . . .'

'I'm okay . . . um . . . I wanted to ask you something . . . Remember you once told me you were depressed? . . . I think you said you went to the doctor's . . . Remember?'

'No, I don't, but it doesn't matter. I'm depressed every day. Why do you ask?'

'Well . . . I think I am too. . . .'

'What? Depressed?'

'I'm not sure. . . . I think so.'

'Hm . . . hang on a sec, I won't be a moment . . . I've got a bit of paper with it all written down, hold on, don't hang up, I'll be right back . . .'

(the receiver is silent)

'Hello? Steffie, are you still there?'

'Yes.'

'Wait . . . Here we are. The chief symptoms by which you

can recognise depression. Depression may be recognised by such interrelated symptoms as: indecisiveness . . . Are you listening?'

'Yes.'

'Indecisiveness, insomnia, loss of interest . . . Are you listening?'

'Yes.'

'Well?'

'What?'

'Have you got those symptoms or not?'

'Indecisiveness and loss of interest yes. But not insomnia.'

'Well, let's go on. Fatigue, anxiety, timorousness . . .'

'What's that? The last one?'

'Not sure, shyness, fear, something like that.'

'That's me, all right. Go on.'

'Then there's a sense of hopelessness, a sense of guilt, loss of self-confidence. Then, negativism and gastro-intestinal troubles. That's it.'

'I've got it all! What was that negative thing?'

'Negativism – that's when everything looks black, and the other's something to do with digestion, when you lose your appetite and so on.'

'Oh.'

'What do you mean "oh"? Are you depressed or aren't you?'

'I'm not sure. I've got most of the symptoms.'

'Then you are, but only partially. That's not so bad.'

'It is.'

(Silence)

'Steffie, are you there? Say something!'

'I'm still here . . .'

'What's wrong? I bet you're bawling!'

'Yes. No . . . Not any more . . .'

'Well, those are the symptoms.'

'What shall I do?'

'I don't know. If I did I'd do something about myself. Got a boyfriend?'

'No.'

'That's what I thought. Get one. It's the best cure for depression. You did know *that*, didn't you?'

'No, I didn't.'

'Well, take it from me, it is.'

++++ *(Silence)*

'Steffie, listen! When I get through this ironing, I'll 'phone you. Okay?'

'Okay.'

'And calm down. Everybody's more or less depressed! I get depressed every day! For at least ten minutes. Do you hear?'

'Yes.'

'I'll call you later. All right?'

'All right.'

'Okay then.'

'Okay.'

'Hey, don't hang up! I've been meaning to tell you. You know Matilda?'

'Yes.'

'She's gone off with a group to St Tropez. A whole week! Imagine.'

'You don't say?'

'Yes. She's never depressed, you can bet your life!'

'Right. Hey, why's the receiver crackling like that?'

'It's not the receiver, it's a budgie. I bought myself a budgie. Didn't you know? No, of course, how could you. A couple of days ago. He's great, only he's got a filthy mouth.'

'Really?'

'Uh huh.'

'Right, then . . . Call me.'

'I will. I'll just finish the ironing.'

'Okay.'

Steffie Speck gets advice from Marianna, her friend at work
(padding)

-- ✄

Use little balls made of soft fresh bread for wiping finger stains from light surfaces, wooden boards, wallpaper and playing cards, and for cleaning engravings discoloured by smoke. Change balls as soon as they soil.

-- ✄

'Yes, boys today are real drips!' sighed Marianna, biting into a ham sandwich. 'Glad I caught mine in time!' A little piece of ham leapt like a spring out of the middle of the sandwich and Marianna deftly thrust it back with her forefinger. 'And when you get down to it,' Marianna went on, her mouth full, 'maybe I'm being primitive, but a guy's the main thing in life! So pull yourself together! You're no fool! Use your head!'

Marianna swallowed the last mouthful, then took another sandwich out of a plastic bag, opened it to make sure the ham was neat and tidy and went on:

'Now tell me, what do you get out of life? Well? You sit at home with that old aunt of yours and wait for a guy to fall into your lap! Forget it! You have to work to get a man. Work!'

Marianna drew a paper plate towards her and turned it round to the side with the cream cake.

++++ 'Here, I'll have the cream cake, you take the custard tart, okay? What do you say we forget about our figures today? We can start on the hard-boiled eggs next Monday. Okay? . . . Look, let me tell you straight, old girl, you have no sex appeal, I mean none at all. That's all there is to it!' And so saying, Marianna dug a plastic spoon into the cream cake. 'Luckily there are all kinds of things that can be done about it!' she added energetically, licking the spoon. 'Lose a few pounds to begin with. I'll see to that. I've got a great diet. Secondly, go

to a good hairdresser. Thirdly, buy yourself a few nice things
to wear. You don't have to go to boutiques, you know. Everyone's wearing chintz these days . . . Look at the magazines . . .
And fourthly,' she said, pulling her coffee cup towards her,
'What can I say, you're too serious, too good somehow, I don't
know. . . .' Marianna shook her head, and then lit a cigarette,
blew out the smoke and went on energetically:

'The most important thing is to keep your spirits up.' Marianna slurped some coffee. 'The coffee's really good today.
Yes, that's it. When you scowl it's enough to scare anyone,
even me! Guys like a cheerful face! You always look . . . I
don't know . . . offended. As though someone had slapped
you. It's enough to make any guy feel guilty. And who wants
to go around feeling guilty all the time! Think about it.'

'And then,' Marianna took the plastic spoon again and scraped up the remains of the cream cake, 'surely you've got some
girl friends. Go out with them. Let yourself go! A cunt's not
a bar of soap that gets used up. Sorry to be so crude, but look
around! There are guys on every corner! Every damn corner!'
Marianna cracked her fingers with passion.

'If I were in your place,' said Marianna, exhaling a cloud of
smoke, 'I'd go out with married men. Only they never marry
you, and sometimes they can't get it up because of the motel
prices! God, I'm crude! Don't listen to me! But I'm sorry for
you, you're a good kid, and life is passing you by. That's right.
Passing you by.'

Marianna paused, picked up the crumbs from the table with
the tip of her finger and nibbled them. Then she frowned, as
though thinking deeply and said, 'Listen, I'll make some
enquiries about our new driver. He's not bad to look at. Maybe
he's not married . . . Okay, okay, I won't. . . . Well,' she
added, 'Maybe just a few discreet enquiries.'

Marianna got up, took the plastic bag and paper plate from
the table and dropped them in the wastepaper basket. Then
she looked at her watch and said, 'Let's have one more smoke,
okay?'

Marianna looked compassionately at Steffie, blew out a puff
of smoke and said conspiratorially, 'There are a thousand ways
to catch a guy, old girl. You shouldn't get involved with anyone

++++ at work, unless the guy marries you on the spot. But there are discos, dances . . . well, maybe that's not your scene. . . . But take Tina for instance. Did you know . . . ? No? Well, you know Tina couldn't make it with guys for ages, and in the end she gave up and got herself a dog. A real pedigree. And one day she's taking it for a walk when up comes this guy with his dog. So he says, "How's your dog?" and she says, "Fine and yours?" and blah, blah, blah. Well, before they knew it they were married. A real fairy tale.'

++++ Marianna stopped, took some chocolate out of her bag, broke off a piece, offered it to Steffie and went on. 'And Olga? Have you heard about Olga? The one with the beautiful teeth. Well, she got married in the dentist's chair! One day she had toothache – and that was that! A dashing young dentist and all that jazz. Fantastic! . . . Go on, go on, have some,' said Marianna, offering Steffie some of her chocolate. 'We'll start the diet on Monday! . . . Yes . . . And Lena? Now that's really story book stuff! You haven't heard? You know her folks left her a house, don't you? Well, Lena decided to sell it. What would a single girl do in that great, big place? All right, you haven't got a house. I'm just telling you this to show you how many ways there are for people to meet. Anyway, she put an advert in the paper. One day this dreamboat rings the bell and says he wants to buy the house for himself and his folks. An architect. Well, they haggled over the house for a month and in the end got married. Now they're all living happily together, the two of them and his folks . . . I tell you, you never know who you'll run into and when!'

Marianna suddenly looked at her watch, sat down at the typewriter and said: 'It's half-past eleven, time to work!'

She pressed a few keys on the typewriter and sighed, 'Why don't I ever get depressed, for God's sake?'

Steffie accepts advice
(hemming)

A) Clothes

--- ✂

*Did you know that the water used for cooking spinach makes
an excellent detergent for black woollen garments?*

--- ✂

Steffie read:

*'Jackets, waistcoats and slacks make for fresh, youthful
combinations. Handbags, though slightly larger than last
season, are still worn across the chest and in combinations of
leather and antelope. Shirt-dresses and short jackets – of
almost classical lines – immediately suggest youth and
simplicity. Spring brings new colours as well: a lot of white,
red, yellow – increasingly bold combinations. Flat shoes are
back. They should have one or more straps and be worn with
turned down socks. Slacks are in too. Wide at the top, narrower
at the ankle, with lots of tucks at the waist. The leg bottom is
often folded into a low cuff or slit at the sides. Wear them with
thin T-shirts, wide blousons or jackets decorated at the waist
with buckles. These, though shorter than last season's, go well
with high heels. Bright red slacks with a high waist and
diagonal side pockets and large appliqué back pockets, as well
as white slacks of very modern cut the waistband decorated
with two ribbons of contrasting colours and deep side bockets
always in a pretty blue with spots continued in white again
with sbods this mime perhaps a different colour straight cut
skirts with slits at the side and the top shut like a shirt with
folds over the ribs a large tail with a concealed fastening at the
waist a classic and always pretty two part girl's skirt with*

several pleats in the front and for the top a wasted silk jacket of sporting cut with brimmed labels overgrown with some condrasting dread and a one piece waistcoat worn over everything that may be worn also with a belt and blared spirts in fright string colours and fastened with bedcovers a faided waistcoat bed of gruff material and a straight collared shirt sport little jackets with marrow lapels go just as well with skirts and pants they may be given a sporting touch with narrow sleeping belts tied tightly and blouses for every occasion have bows at the neck and the length of the blouse enables you to wear them softly tied or left to fall freely they may be born with lank tops which are very fashionable again or with smartly cut wastestoats mown of shiny milk and etched with braid for a disco style effect or for more normaloccasions wornoverblousesofmatchingorcontrastingcolourswhichmaybe wornwithabeltorwithoutandtheblousemaybeofshinygreysatinwith aclassicneckandbowandfullsleevesgatheredattheshoulder . . .'

Steffie's eyelids grew heavy, the fashion magazine slipped onto the floor, and Steffie turned onto her side and fell asleep.

Meanwhile her aunt was sitting in an armchair, muttering softly: 'It'th not true that all drethmakerth die by the needle. We had one in our town who died of ithe cream. In thothe dayth ithe cream wath sold by ithe cream vendorth, in a little cart, and they would shout . . . They'd shout like thith: Ithe cream! Ithe creeeeeam! I ththill remember the drethmaker going to the window with a tape measure round her neck and her mouth full of pinth and shouting: Ithe creeeeam! Over heeere, over heeeere! She'd put away bowl after bowl! Dreadful! She died of pneumonia. All becauthe of ithe cream! The needle had nothing to do with it . . .

B) Figure

Does the meat you have just bought look hard and tough? In that case, put it into a bowl of milk regardless of how you had intended to cook it – and let it soak for about half an hour. This will make it tender and tasty.

On the morning of the fifth day Steffie Speck stood on the scales. Marianna had said, 'You can't go wrong, I've tried it myself. Eight pounds in four days! It's a great diet!'

On the morning of the fifth day Steffie stood on the scales, but the needle had not moved even half an inch. 'Not an ounce!' thought Steffie Speck.

On the fifth day at seven minutes past two Steffie walked out of the office and set off for the cake shop. There she bought five cream buns and one pound of small cakes. Then she went to the supermarket and bought a quarter pound of cold meats, a tube of mayonnaise, two pounds of tomatoes, one pound of strawberries, one French loaf, one bottle of red wine and half a roast chicken.

///////// On the afternoon of the fifth day Steffie Speck made her way home like someone constantly on the point of slipping into the first doorway.

On the fifth day Steffie Speck's aunt was away, which turned out to be very convenient.

On the afternoon of the fifth day Steffie Speck reached home and locked the door behind her.

She locked the door behind her and drew the curtains. Then she switched on the television. There was a children's programme on, it was showing the animated version of Snow White and the Seven Dwarfs. Steffie went into the kitchen and took her supplies out of the bag. First she washed the strawberries, sprinkled them with sugar and put them into the fridge. Then she put the cold meats, mayonnaise and tomatoes on to a plate, the chicken on to another plate, the cream buns on to a third, and the little cakes into a dish. Finally she opened the wine and arranged everything in the living room.

.... Steffie spread some mayonnaise on bread and added several slices of sausage. On the screen the wicked stepmother was asking the mirror who was the fairest of them all. Steffie moved on to the roast chicken, broke off a wing and concluded that the wing was as usual the best bit because the skin crackled so splendidly.

'You know,' her aunt used to say, 'in our town, there uthed to be a man named Marko who jutht loved everything crithpy. Everything that crunched when you ate and everything that wath a little burnt. I uthed to be like that myself, forever thcraping panth. But that Mark thcraped panth and crunched something or other, until he wath taken ill. He died in thix month.'

Steffie tore the skin off the roast chicken and crunched it. On the screen a hunter was about to kill Snow White, but his heart was wrung and he refrained and killed a deer instead. Steffie cut up a tomato. Snow White met the dwarfs, who were gaily singing a little song about digging. Steffie gnawed the last chicken bone.

At one moment it occurred to Steffie that her aunt might come home, and she quickly collected the bones and threw them into the rubbish bin. Then she cleared the table and laid out the cream buns, the little cakes and the wine and had another look to make sure that the door was locked.

While the dwarfs were digging, the wicked stepmother came and gave Snow White an apple. To start with Steffie ate one cream bun and drank a glass of wine. The dwarfs came back from digging and found Snow White dead. Steffie remembered her aunt's friend Mara who had drowned in a marsh. 'The rusheth got caught round her feet and dragged her to the bottom. Rusheth are terrible thingth.' Steffie ate another cream bun and poured herself some more wine. Snow White was lying in her coffin, and the dwarfs and forest animals were weeping. Steffie tried one of the little cakes. It wasn't bad. The prince kissed Snow White. Steffie drank a glass of wine. The prince and Snow White rode into the sunset on a white horse towards a beautiful palace on a hill. The dwarfs and animals were waving.

'What if Snow White had been ugly?' wondered Steffie and started on yet another cream bun. 'Perhaps there wouldn't have been a story!' Steffie thought and sipped her wine. 'The whole problem was that she was prettier than her wicked stepmother!' Steffie had trouble swallowing the cream bun. 'That's it. There wouldn't have been a story,' thought Steffie and suddenly burst into tears. Her tears dripped onto the top of the bun sprinkled with icing sugar and left marks. Plop! Plop! Plop! – her tears fell, dissolving the sugar. 'Not an ounce!' Steffie thought, weeping and polished off the cream bun. 'Not an ounce!' Steffie thought, sobbing, and took the strawberries out of the fridge.

Through her tears Steffie saw the strawberries peeping out from under their white blanket of sugar. She grabbed a spoon. At first she felt that she was swallowing her unhappy fate, her sad little fate by the spoonful, that she was chewing up her loneliness, that she was slurping down St Tropez where Matilda was and where she, Steffie, would never be . . . Oh, faster, faster, faster, the life out there waiting for her, faster, the open spaces, faster, before the lovers she was meant to kiss grew old, faster, before the trains she was meant to take stopped, faster, before the seas dried up, faster, before the dresses turned to dust, faster, before life dissolved like the sugar on the cream bun, faster, Steffie waved her spoon, faster, Steffie licked the spoon as though it were her fate itself, faster, typed Steffie's thoughts, faster, Steffie Speck took her terrible revenge.

All at once she felt a sweetish weariness, and her head spun and hummed, she felt she was drowning, her legs entangled in rushes, dragging her down to the bottom. It was terrible yet intoxicating and she let herself go.

C) Make-up

--->✄

If, as you are shading your eyelashes, you make a little smudge under your eyelid, you can remove the excess with one corner of a paper tissue. Or you can place a tissue under the lashes as you shade them.

--->✄

Steffie Speck tapped rhythmically under her chin as she read the following:

.... Skin: *Care for your face according to your skin type, and if your skin is of very poor quality seek the advice of a cosmetician. Use a light base for your make-up and transparent powder. If the first tiny lines have begun to appear, don't cover them with thick layers of powder: cultivate a 'natural' look, that is make-up 'without make-up'. Lines, even the tiniest, become more marked, more obvious, under powder.*

Eyes: *Correct the shape of your eyebrows, if necessary, but don't thin them excessively. Use a lash curler, and brush mascara on to the lashes on the upper and lower lids, but not so much as to make them stick together. Choose the shadow that matches your skin type and the style of your whole make-up.*

Cheeks: *If you are pale, use rouge on your cheeks – powder, cream or stick rouge. It will give your face freshness, a healthier and more radiant appearance.*

Lips: *It is enough to use lip gloss or lipstick of a soft pink colour.*

Hair: *Choose a hair-style in keeping with the quality of your hair and shape of your face. Choose one of the youthful styles, easy to look after and maintain. When drying your hair with a hair-dryer, don't comb it with a plastic comb. Plastic combs get hot and tangle the hair.*

Steffie Speck stopped reading, opened her mouth, drew her upper and lower lips over her teeth as though she wanted to hide them. She held her lips in this position for fifteen seconds. Then she pulled her upper lip over the lower one but kept them half a little finger open. Then she 'whistled' silently for three seconds. Then she pulled her lips into a 'smile' and held it for five seconds. Then she pursed her lips into a long 'kiss' and held it in that position for three seconds. She repeated all these movements ten times.

Steffie's aunt said: 'There wath a woman in our town who alwayth made herthelf up with the charcoal from matcheth. She would light a match, like thith . . . then she would uthe the burnt end to make herthelf up. Wonthe she poked the match into her eye and went completely blind. Maybe she'th thtill alive . . . I don't know . . . I only know that she never got married . . .

Steffie Speck and men

(fastenings)

A) Steffie and the Driver

--->✄

You've been careless and sat on grass in light-coloured clothes.
Grass stains can be removed with distilled water that has a
little alcohol dissolved in it.

--->✄

('What if the old lady comes back early?' thought the Driver
as he rang the bell.)

'Oh, it's you!' said Steffie, flustered.

'Yes. . . .' the Driver said modestly.

'Come in, sit down, I'll be with you in a moment . . . !' said
Steffie and slipped into the kitchen. 'He's good-looking, oh
gosh, so good-looking!' the words tapped out in Steffie's head.
'First a drink, then lunch, and if he's not interested, a cup of
coffee,' thought Steffie, taking down two glasses, a bottle and
a tray. 'Alwayth put a cloth or a clean napkin on the tray. It
lookth nither,' her aunt used to say, so Steffie put a clean
napkin on the tray.

For some reason the Driver had chosen the edge of the bed
as the most suitable place to sit. He had placed a largish black
bag by his feet. Steffie poured drinks.

'Steffie . . . Steffie . . .' said the Driver. 'You have a nice
name. In your place others would have called themselves Stephanie, Fanny or something like that . . .'

'Yes . . .' said Steffie because she couldn't think what to say.

'Call me Johnnie!' the Driver said, clinking his glass against
hers.

'Yes . . .' repeated Steffie.

('Maybe he won't want lunch. And maybe it's not right for

me to invite him to lunch so soon. He'll think I care about him . . . That can wait for a second meeting, now we can just have a drink . . .')

'This is really good brandy!' said the Driver and smiled.

('What a lovely smile! He's good-looking all right!' thought Steffie.)

'Miss, er, that is . . . Steffie, are you and Marianna good friends?' asked the Driver.

'Yes, we are . . .' ('Why is he asking me about Marianna? Who knows what she's told him about me . . . But maybe he doesn't know what else to ask about? Anyway, if he's thinking of staying to lunch, I'd better take the meat out of the fridge.' She poured him some more brandy.)

'Have you got a boyfriend, Steffie?' the Driver asked suddenly, looking keenly at her.

'No!' she said hastily and blushed. ('I shouldn't have said that. What a fool I am.')

'A pretty girl like you, and no boyfriend!' The Driver repeated his keen look. Steffie didn't know what to respond so she got up and went into the kitchen. ('What's going to happen now? Perhaps he'll try to kiss me? What should I do?' she thought and went back into the room carrying a glass of water.)

The Driver was sitting on the edge of the bed, turning his glass of brandy round in his hand and staring fixedly at Steffie.

'Hey, come over here for a bit. Sit beside me,' he said in a deep, muffled voice.

Steffie obediently sat down beside the Driver. He stroked her hair, and then kissed her. Steffie's head spun.

'Steffie, Steffie . . . !' the Driver breathed heavily and pulled her forcefully onto the bed.

('God, now he'll undress me and we haven't even finished our drinks . . . Perhaps I really should have taken the meat out of the fridge . . . ?')

'Steffie, Steffie . . . !' panted the Driver.

('God, does he mean just like this, without any bedclothes . . . or should I interrupt him . . . I'm letting him go too far, I ought to resist. . . . it's too quick, it's all too quick . . . we haven't even drunk our drinks, we should have waited . . .')

//////// 'Wait a moment!' whispered the Driver. He lifted himself up and emptied his glass. Just as he was about to throw himself back on the bed, his foot knocked against his bag.

Something started barking. It came from the bag.

'Bow-wow-wow-wow-wow-wow!' barked the bag persistently.

'What's that barking in your bag?' asked Steffie, flustered.

.... 'Damn that dog! What the hell's the matter with it . . . ?' The Driver pulled a mechanical dog out of the bag and shoved a key into its flank. The dog went on barking. 'Damn machines!' raged the Driver, shaking the dog. 'The mechanism must have broken! Frankie brought it from Germany for me! The crap those Germans make. Pure crap!'

Steffie was cowering at the end of the bed in confusion and tugging at the hem of her skirt. The Driver sighed helplessly: 'Bloody dog! I thought you might enjoy it. It's a nice dog. I thought a nice little toy would be better than flowers . . .'

The Driver pulled himself together, poured a little cognac for himself, a little for Steffie, clinked his glass against hers and said, 'Well, Steffie, I really ought to be going . . . I've arranged to meet Frankie. Known him since we were kids. He's going back tomorrow. You know how it is. Don't be angry. I'll be seeing you again. Let's drink to it!'

The Driver got up in a formal kind of way, tossed back his cognac, picked up his bag and went out. The mechanical dog was still barking.

Steffie closed the door. All the time she spent putting away the bottle and glasses the dog went on barking. Steffie picked it up carefully with two fingers and threw it into the rubbish bin. 'Bow-wow-wow-wow!' rumbled the rubbish bin. Steffie took the dog out of the bin and hit it. The dog went on snapping its mechanical teeth. Steffie put the dog on the floor and stood on it with her whole weight. The dog went quiet.

" " " " Then she went back to her room and saw that a wallet had slipped down between the bed and the wall. Steffie opened the wallet. An identity card, some money, some bills and a photograph fell out. The photograph was of a woman hugging two little boys. 'Twins . . . ,' thought Steffie. 'I'll ask Marianna to give it back,' she decided, and then went back to the kitchen.

B) Steffie and the Hulk

--✄

Working a front opening: Place closed zipper face up along the turned-in edge. Baste. Bring left front over zipper, matching centres. On inside, open out left fly; baste zipper in place, keeping garment free. Stitch zipper to left fly, close to teeth and again at tape edge. On outside place fly over zipper with raw edges even; pin. Baste through all thicknesses. Sew.

--✄

'Where's your aunt?' asked the Hulk, slipping through the door.

'Away,' said Steffie.

'Uh. Good!' said the Hulk. 'I don't like aunts roaming round the flat while I'm on a job.'

As soon as they were in the room, the Hulk threw himself straight onto the bed and took a quick look at the furniture, the walls, the books . . .

'You a student?' asked the Hulk.

'No,' said Steffie quietly.

'Good. I don't like girls who know too much!'

The Hulk began to look Steffie over.

'You're not bad, you know. I'm going to screw you! I'll give you a good screw. A real one. There's no messing with me, let me tell you! I'll screw you for two hours. Non-stop. What do I mean two hours! I'll screw you all night, until that aunt of yours comes home. Okay?'

'Okay,' said Steffie humbly, glancing fearfully at the Hulk. ('We'll never both fit on the bed,' she thought.) One of the Hulk's arms, one shoulder and a leg were already slipping towards the floor.

'No messing!' said the Hulk popping a piece of chewing gum into his mouth.

The room was quiet. All Steffie could hear was the Hulk's persistent, rhythmic chewing. Steffie flicked a glance at him and quickly lowered her eyes. Meeting her glance, the Hulk glanced away at the walls and started peering everywhere, as if looking for something interesting, a safe for instance.

The Hulk took the gum out of his mouth and stuck it on the head-board. Steffie lit a cigarette.

'Chuck me one too!' he said.

They smoked. Steffie wondered what time it was. She thought it must be quite late, and then she thought they ought to be talking about something, anything.

'There!' said the Hulk suddenly, putting out his cigarette. 'And now I'm going to screw you. Take your clothes off.'

'No, no . . .' Steffie resisted, blushing.

'Okay,' said the Hulk, agreeing at once. 'Maybe you're frightened. Look, I'm not a violent person; I understand women perfectly. Soon you'll be saying yes, yes, yes, fainting and begging me never to stop. So, just to show you there's nothing terrible about it, I'll take my clothes off first.'

The Hulk took off his clothes. Huge, swollen chunks of body burst out of them.

'There,' said the Hulk, taking his gum from the head-board and putting it back in his mouth. 'And now I'm going to walk around the room,' said the Hulk, walking up and down in front of Steffie and criss-crossing the room with vast grey shadows. 'There. And now I'm going to screw you!' said the Hulk heading towards Steffie.

Panting, the Hulk began to take Steffie's clothes off. He fumbled with her buttons, breathing heavily, until at last Steffie was naked. ('We'll never fit in the bed,' thought Steffie, and found herself – on the floor.)

Chewing away, the Hulk flung, tossed Steffie this way and that, squeezing her, pummelling her, rolling her over the floor like a piece of pastry; Steffie rocked, sank and rose up on the Hulk's smooth muscles and thought in some alarm, 'This must be the way you do it.'

'There!' said the Hulk. 'That was the foreplay. And now I'm going to screw you non-stop. Till morning.'

'All right,' whispered Steffie into the Hulk's huge ear. The Hulk lay on his side with his head propped on one hand. He used the other to pull the gum in and out of his mouth.

Steffie looked enquiringly at the Hulk.

'We're not in any hurry. We've got the whole night,' he said. 'Relax!'

'All right,' said Steffie with a blush, still lying submissively on the floor next to him.

'Hey, you wouldn't have anything to eat would you?' it suddenly occurred to the Hulk.

Steffie went straight to the kitchen, glad to be busy with something, and opened the fridge. She found a pint of milk in a cardboard container, some salami and a jar of mayonnaise. ('I'll make a few sandwiches,' she thought and made – seven. Then she changed her mind and made another three. 'Ten sandwiches ought to be enough,' she decided and went back into the room.)

The Hulk was lying in the same position, pulling out his gum and shoving it back into his mouth, while looking around for the non-existent safe.

'Great!' said the Hulk, taking the first sandwich. 'This is how I'll kiss you, like this and like this! This is how I'll screw you the first time!' And he devoured the first sandwich.

""""" It was half-dark, and for the first time Steffie found the room comfortable. She wrapped herself in a blanket and lay down on the floor. The blanket tickled her bare body. ('From now on I'll always sleep like this,' she thought and felt her eyelids closing.)

'This is how I'll screw you, crunch, crunch, grind, grind, this is how I'll do it the tenth time . . . !' growled the Hulk and through her lashes Steffie saw him finishing the tenth sandwich. Then he tipped the carton of milk into his mouth. A grey morning light had slowly begun to come through the window.

'There!' said the Hulk, wiping his mouth decisively with his hand. 'Come over here!'

Steffie wriggled over to the Hulk, still wrapped in her blanket. The Hulk squeezed her tightly, put a hand under the blanket, and then thoughtfully ran it over her hips.

'It's getting light,' he said.

//////// 'Yes,' said Steffie.

++++ Suddenly the Hulk gave a start and anxiously slapped his hand on his forehead.

'Hey, where did I leave my gum?'

'I don't know,' said Steffie.

'It must be here somewhere!' he said, feeling his way over the head-board. 'It's not here!' he sighed. 'Maybe I swallowed it. No, I never do that.'

Steffie sighed sympathetically.

The Hulk gazed thoughtfully at Steffie.

'What do you think?'

'Maybe you swallowed it.'

'Ah well, what's done's done!' sighed the Hulk. 'Hey, time to go. It's morning. Your aunt could come back, and I don't like aunts roaming around the flat when I'm on a job.'

'Okay,' said Steffie, wanting to add that her aunt would be staying away several days, but the Hulk was already pulling on his clothes energetically.

'There!' he said. 'Got any cigarettes?'

'Yes.'

'Let's have one for the road!' He lit one, put one behind his ear and winked waggishly at Steffie. 'Chin up, kiddo!'

At the door the Hulk stopped for a moment.

'Hey, what's your real name?'

'Steffie,' said Steffie softly.

'Good! I don't like girls who aren't called Steffie!' he said, pulling his face into a waggish grin again. 'You're a good kid, you know!' said the Hulk, pinching Steffie's cheek. The smile on his face slipped abruptly downwards, followed by his head and shoulders.

Then the whole Hulk went down the stairs to the main door.

C) Steffie and the Intellectual

--✄

If you run out of lotions for pain from knocks or sprains, soak a ball of cotton wool in olive oil and apply to the injury.

--✄

'Didn't you tell me you lived with your old aunt?' asked the Intellectual, coming into the room.

'Yes, but she's not here.'

'Where is she?'

'Out of town.'

'Pity!' said the Intellectual. 'I adore old aunts!' The Intellectual staggered a bit, sat down on the floor and took a bottle of cognac out of his coat pocket. He took a drink, then offered the bottle to Steffie.

'Want some?'

'Maybe a little,' said Steffie and went into the kitchen for some glasses.

' "Maybe a little" for you,' muttered the Intellectual, pouring some out for Steffie, and drinking from the bottle himself. 'And for me – a little more!' he added, wiping his mouth with his hand.

The Intellectual looked impassively round the room, evidently finding nothing to attract his attention. He took off his coat, threw it on the floor, took a handkerchief out of his pocket and clumsily wiped his glasses.

'What do you do?'

'How do you mean?'

'For a living.'

'I work in an office . . . as a typist.'

'Oh . . .' said the Intellectual absent-mindedly, putting his glasses back on and taking another swig from the bottle. 'What were the two of you doing there that day?'

'Nothing. We'd gone for coffee.'

'What's she called, the other one?'

'Annie.'

'And what made you choose that place for coffee?'

'No reason . . . Annie said it was nice.'

'Were you looking for men?'

'No!' said Steffie quickly, blushing. 'Annie goes there often for coffee!'

'That's no café; it's a pick-up joint!' said the Intellectual irritably. 'And what does the other girl do?'

'The same as me in another office.'

'So the two of you went for a coffee hoping to find men!'

'No, we didn't!' said Steffie, offended.

The Intellectual tipped the bottle and drained it.

'All gone! All – gone!' said the Intellectual, rolling the bottle over the floor. 'Got anything else to drink?'

Steffie went into the kitchen and brought back an open bottle of cognac.

'You're terrific!'

The Intellectual poured some cognac into a glass and drained it in one long swallow. Then he pulled at his beard thoughtfully for a while, squinting vaguely as though confirming some unspoken reply to himself, and suddenly started waving his arms.

'They all want love. All of them! All they want is love. They feed on the love of others like vampires. More, more! Oh, the braying, the yelping, the yowling disgusts me. Spawning! Revolting egoism! Ugh!'

The Intellectual downed another swig with an expression of disgust and lit a cigarette.

'You, for instance,' the Intellectual pointed his finger at Steffie, 'you're always going to be on the losing end!'

'Why?' asked Steffie dejectedly, believing him.

'Because! That's how it is! There's nothing you can do!' The abrupt gesture he made with his hand knocked over his glass.

('Why, he's drunk!' thought Steffie.)

'What is it, why are you staring at me? I'm drunk, yes! I've been boozing for days now. I have an excellent, and what is more, an o-ri-gi-nal reason! My wife's gone off with a . . . what do you call them . . . plumber, electrician, waiter! They all run off sooner or later with a – typist! Sorry, I didn't mean . . .'

'And?' asked Steffie.

'And he's left her. I and the plumber have left my wife! I took a rented room, and the bus conductor went back to his wife!'

The Intellectual drained another glass and slowly tapped Steffie on the shoulder with a drunken grimace.

'Get it, Steff? Eh, Steff, get it?'

Steffie was suddenly offended and tried to hide it by lighting a cigarette. They sat in silence. Then the Intellectual asked in a conciliatory tone, as though apologising, 'Hey, have you got any music?'

'No!' said Steffie, offended.

They sat in silence. Steffie twisted her cigarette between her fingers and stared fixedly at the floor. She suddenly asked, 'Why am I always going to be on the losing end?'

The Intellectual looked at Steffie carefully and for a long time. She thought she was going to cry.

==== 'There's a story by Hašek,' he said slowly, 'and in the story there's a Mr Kalina who smokes a pipe. To make it smell nice, he puts dried rose petals in the tobacco. And the petals come from roses that suitors bring to his daughter Klara. And every time he smokes, Mr Kalina smokes up a suitor. "Now I've smoked Mr Mařík, now Mr Ninger, now Mr Ružička or Hubička" – I don't remember. It doesn't matter!'

The Intellectual brought his face right up to Steffie's.

'See what I mean? Someone or something is always going to smoke up your loves. Some invisible Kalina! It's terrible, but that's how it is. Like they did my wife! Like they did my trip to Paris! I've been all ready to go to Paris hundreds of times! And each time something smokes it up! On the map where Paris ought to be, there's a hole! A burnt hole! To Hell with everything, including Paris!'

Steffie's chin trembled. He was right! He understood perfectly! And drunk as he was, he too would be smoked up by morning. There'd be a little heap of ash left. He had offended her. 'I must get back at him!' she thought.

'Well I'm on my way to St Tropez!' she said out loud, blushing.

The Intellectual did not hear her. He was playing with the empty bottle, rolling it over the floor. Suddenly he hurled the bottle into a corner and curled up like a child.

'What you need is to be loved,' he mumbled drunkenly. 'You! You, Steff, because you are what you are. Just as you are. I'll love you!'

Steffie tried to lift the Intellectual from the floor, but without success. She did manage to drag him nearer the bed and raise him to his knees. The Intellectual stood up abruptly, staggered, and then collapsed onto the bed, dragging Steffie with him.

'Look, a breast! You've got a breast!' he mumbled grabbing Steffie firmly by the breast. 'You've got a breast! Breasts bite! It'll bite me! Let me shut its mouth. There! I'm going to . . . breeaast . . . !'

And he fell asleep, breathing heavily.

" " " " " For a while Steffie listened to his breathing, then she tried to move his hand. She couldn't. The Intellectual's fingers were firmly stuck to her breast. She reconciled herself to the position until morning. Looking at the Intellectual, she felt herself fill with tenderness, she did not mind at all that he was there, beside her. He wriggled and leant his head on her shoulder. Now she was entirely captive. She felt their breath mingling and her breast swelling in his hand. Then the warmth of his sleep sent her to sleep as well.

Steffie woke at six o'clock. The Intellectual was asleep. She tugged gently at his beard. He stirred. She tried again. The Intellectual half opened his eyes, squinting at her. She saw the web of sleep in his eyes. He did not recognise her. Then he muttered, 'Oh, Steff . . .'

'Move over a bit, I've got to go to work.'

'Oh.'

In the bathroom, under the shower, Steffie tried in vain to rinse off the warm sediment of their common sleep. When she went back into the room, the Intellectual was asleep again. Steffie liked pulling his beard. She tugged at it tenderly again.

'Uh,' the Intellectual mumbled sleepily.

Steffie made coffee in the kitchen. The Intellectual dragged himself in after her and laid his hand on her shoulder.

'Listen, did anything happen . . . I mean, you know what I mean?'

'Nothing,' Steffie blushed.

'I was really plastered . . . I'm sorry . . . You're making coffee? Great!'

Steffie made coffee: softly she placed the teaspoons of sugar and coffee in the water, softly she stirred the coffee, softly she picked up the cups, softly laid a cloth on a tray, softly placed on the cloth two cups and the pot. She was completely softened by an inner warmth.

She went into the room and put the coffee on the table. She opened the windows. Soft morning light filled the room . . .

The Intellectual sat there quietly, stroking his beard. He drank a mouthful of coffee, lit a cigarette, and then gazed sadly at Steffie for a long time. Steffie said nothing. ('I'm going to melt,' she thought.)

Then the Intellectual broke the silence.

++++ 'Hey, Steff,' he said, 'what do you think, is there any point in my phoning . . . her now, the plumber's woman?'

Steffie Speck's Dream
(interfacing)

When you wake in the middle of the night and cannot go back to sleep, do not 'count sheep'. If you are hot, air the room well and straighten out the bed. If you are cold, put on woollen socks. If that does not help, make some lime tea, and sweeten it with honey.

Marianna was lying completely naked on a gigantic cake, lazily licking the space around her and saying: 'Steffie, for God's sake, look around you! There are guys everywhere, in the water, in the air . . .'

Steffie went up to the cake, but Marianna sank into the thick layers of cream. Then the cake dissolved at miraculous speed, and with it Marianna.

Steffie suddenly found herself under water. She felt sand beneath her feet, slippery weeds on her body. 'Rusheth are terrible thingth!' said her aunt, pouring a dish of peas over her and disappearing. Steffie knelt down to pick up the peas, but they kept slipping away. And then she saw that they were not peas but the little round shells of green crabs which scuttled rapidly away over the sand.

Suddenly Steffie saw an enormous carp swimming towards her. She waved and called out, 'Hey, Hulk!' But only little bubbles came out of her mouth and the Hulk did not hear. He scraped Steffie carelessly with his smooth scales and swam sluggishly on.

'Careful, Steffie!' whispered Marianna's voice from somewhere. Steffie crouched down and saw the Driver above her. He was a white, mechanical dog and he was having trouble swimming; he kept sinking, surfacing, sinking again. Steffie wanted to point out that it might be better if he turned onto his back, but she could only open her mouth mutely. The Driver disappeared.

Steffie dragged herself deeper into the sand and weed and caught sight of a massive turtle. It was the Intellectual. She was happy to see him, even in that state. But the turtle merely nodded its head, drew its neck into its shell and lurched slowly away.

'You see,' rustled the weed, 'all men are animals and many of them are water creatures!' Whereupon Steffie felt herself growing remorselessly, becoming smooth and full of water. 'Steffie,' Marianna's voice hissed through the slime and weeds, 'you're not a bar of soap that can melt away, elt away, lt away, t away, way . . . aaaayyy . . .' And her voice slowly dissolved and vanished in the sand, leaving a narrow hole behind it.

Steffie felt herself lathering like an immense piece of soap. 'Goodness, I'm going to lather all the water!' she thought. There were more and more and more bubbles . . . 'I think I've completely dissolved,' she thought, picturing herself between her hands as the smooth, oval end of a piece of soap. And that was – the end.

Topstitching by the author

++++ Poor, dear little Steffie Speck! One slap in the face after another! If I were a decent person and as decent a writer, I would come bravely to your defence. And finally introduce you to the man of your life! . . .

For instance, you take a package tour to St Tropez (like Matilda). There, at the hotel swimming-pool, sipping fruit juice with lumps of ice in the shape of little hearts, you start talking to your neighbour on the next chaise-longue. He who happens to be a famous director, who happens to speak Croatian (his mother is from these parts, an émigrée married to an American and widowed a few months before). He is divine, simply and indescribably divine, dear Steffie, and you fall in love with him at first glance. He is good-looking, gentle, thoughtful, intelligent, though somewhat gloomy and subdued. You notice that at once, of course, but you do not like to ask what is troubling him. You are afraid. After all, this week (you are aware of this, so painfully aware) is your whole life. And you will never forget it. You will never forget bathing in the pool at night or riding the silver waves of the sea at noon; or the day when it poured with rain, and you ran like children and you kissed, wet and happy, in quiet doorways; or the morning when you had champagne for breakfast and a tiny golden snake sparkled in the thin crystal glass – a delicate necklace which he chose to give you in such a shy and original way; the afternoon when you waited for him in a charming café and a little olive-skinned boy suddenly came over to you and thrust into your hands the biggest bunch of white roses you had ever seen (you knew that he was the one who had ordered the roses); that crazy night of music when you wore a black silk dress, translucent as a breath of air (it too had arrived in a mysterious package with a little spray of orchids from an 'unknown' admirer). Yes, that crazy night, those crazy nights. And while others lazed around the pool, watching you with envious eyes, you lived a whole lifetime.

On the last day, you are in despair as you pack your bags to return home with the group, and he knocks on the door of your room (you ask agitatedly 'Who is it?' though you know – your heart tells you) and he says that he loves you, that, in fact, he has loved you all his life, only he did not know it, and you tell him that you love him and that he is the one, the one and only, you have been looking for all your life. Here his face clouds over. You ask him what the matter is, what's troubling him and why he is always so gloomy, and he tells you with a look of utter dejection that he is married (he was afraid to tell you, he was afraid of losing you!), his wife is a famous actress (you know her, you have seen her in any number of films). The eyes of the public are fixed on them, but those eyes do not know the truth he has been hiding for years – for a long time now that fiendish woman has been in the grip of drugs, alcohol and debauchery. And the children (there are four: two boys and two little girls) hardly know their mother. All in all, my dear Steffie, he asks you whether you would go with him to Hollywood, where he will immediately seek a divorce, because things cannot go on as they are. At the door he adds that you need not decide at once, he will call back in ten minutes to hear your reply.

Your heart beats madly, you suddenly turn brave and decisive, you ask someone in the group to call at your office and tell them you are giving in your notice and to let Marianna know that you have found the man of your life and will write about it in more detail.

///////// You both fly to Hollywood and you will never forget that flight – for it is a flight into a new life, unpredictable, but happy. He takes you straight from the airport to his mother. His mother bursts into tears when she sees you and immediately tells you her life story, how she was widowed, the town where she was born. 'Is it possible,' you say, 'Why, my aunt comes from there!' 'What's her name?' his mother asks. You tell her your aunt's name. 'Maria Madel,' you say. 'Maria!' cries his mother, 'Why we were at school together, we shared a desk!' Here you burst into tears as well, and you hug each other sobbing.

Then he tells you that, unfortunately, he will have to go away to shoot a major film and he asks you to take his children to Hawaii (for the children to get used to you, over the summer, while they are on holiday), and in the meantime he will arrange for the divorce. For a moment you hesitate, wondering if this is a dream: is it possible that it is you he has chosen rather than such a beautiful, celebrated woman or so many other beautiful, celebrated women. He tells you that he loves your good heart and that love is blind and that you shouldn't worry (that is, that you should not trouble your pretty little head with such nonsense). And off he goes to shoot that famous film.

You fly to Hawaii with the children, but one of the wings catches fire and the plane crashes in the jungle. All the passengers are killed, apart from you and, thank God, his four children. You display superhuman courage and fight with ferocious strength to keep them (and yourself) alive, for you are preyed upon by untold dangers in the jungle. (Dear Steffie, if you only knew how much I would put into the description of your dramatic struggle for the lives of his children in those savage conditions!) Not only he, but the world learns of your fate and follows it anxiously on the news. At last he flies into the jungle with a special rescue team and I give a truly touching description of your reunion.

You fly by special plane to Hollywood. There, of course, the reporters are waiting for you. A man, someone you have never seen before, comes up to your future husband and whispers something to him confidentially. You learn that during the dramatic events in the jungle his wife has died of galloping leukaemia. You are naturally sorry for the unfortunate woman, but you are also aware that now nothing stands in the way of your love.

You marry, dear Steffie (it is a fantastic wedding, the kind you know only from films!), and become not only a wonderful wife, lover, mother of four, soon five (yes, my dear Steffie, yes!) children but you lose a dozen kilos and become so beautiful – that your very own aunt, who comes to visit you, your husband and her childhood friend, cannot recognise you. Your aunt weeps and says, 'Now I can die happy!' Of course your aunt just says that, she doesn't die, on the contrary: your husband pays for a fortnight's stay in a famous clinic, where she receives a teeth transplant from an unfortunate fifteen-year-old girl who has just died in one of those American traffic accidents. All of you, your mother-in-law, aunt, five, soon six, children who adore you, your husband, who has just received an international award for his film, and you – live happily ever after – and beyond!

There! That's how I'd have happyended you, dear Steffie, if I were a real writer. But I'm one of those 'life dictates, the writer writes' kind of writers. Or worse. Yet on I stitch, remorselessly, ever by your side, and who knows – maybe at the final stitch your writer will remove the final hitch.

Emancipated Ella advises Steffie Speck
(kick pleating)

---✀

*If you want your nail polish to last longer, brush your nails
with egg-white the moment the polish dries.*

---✀

'I can't stand typical women!' Emancipated Ella shouted, shaking her head vigorously and placing a cigarette in an ivory holder.

'Yes?' said Steffie absently, her head cocked to one side.

A carved Buddha smiled out of Ella's cigarette holder.

'A present from Fred!' Ella remarked, following Steffie's gaze.

'What makes a woman typical?' Steffie asked.

'Don't pretend you don't understand!' said Emancipated Ella. 'You're not far off yourself! Why those ninnies who snivel all the time, drape themselves all over men, suffocate them, manipulate them, and just because God has given them – holes!'

('Isn't she crude!' Steffie thought. Ella nervously waved her cigarette holder about and ran a hand through her curly hair. 'Isn't she curly!' Steffie thought.)

'Yes!' said Ella. 'Mercifully there are fewer and fewer of them. What a woman really needs is to work, to breathe life in as deeply as she can and keep in mind that men are not the only thing in the world!'

'Marianna thinks they are!' said Steffie quietly.

++++ 'Marianna's a ninny, a twit who believes that by marrying that drip she's stepped onto cloud nine!'

'Yes, but . . .'

'There is no "yes, but"!' Ella snapped, shaking her curls

angrily. 'I can see that she's stuffed you as full of her blueprints for life as a stuffed goose!'

'Marianna's all right. When I got depressed, she tried to help me,' said Steffie, trying to smooth things over.

'Ha!' Emancipated Ella snorted, raising her cigarette holder like a flag. 'I can just imagine! She told you to find a man! And it didn't work. And now you're in worse shit than before.'

'How do you know?'

'I know! I know everything! I know your souls, the way you breathe! Of course it didn't work! It couldn't have!'

'How do you mean?'

'Simple. You seized on a man as the last hope. It's written all over your face. You're the kind who falls in love on the spot, the minute someone in the street asks you the time!'

'Then what *should* I do?' Steffie drooped.

'Live, for God's sake! Work! Read! When did you last read a book?'

Steffie was silent.

++++ 'When did you last go to an exhibition?' Emancipated Ella asked pointing her ivory cigarette holder at Steffie. Steffie was about to say that she never went to exhibitions at all, but Ella went on mercilessly, 'And the theatre? Confess you haven't been to the theatre for ages. Oh, you stupid, limited, sexual slaves! All you can think about is catching a man! You're a bunch of hens, scratching about, making nests!

++++ There's another world out there. Go for walks, read, make friends, take a course, travel . . . Learn a language. French, for instance. Life is so interesting!'

Emancipated Ella talked and talked. Steffie blushed and blushed. How right she was! How clever she was!

Steffie and Ella ordered two more coffees. Ella sighed, slurped a mouthful and dragged her hand through her curly hair. Then she cast an eye all around, waved her hand and made an invisible dot in the air with her cigarette holder. Steffie breathed a sigh of relief, though she did not know why.

'Have you heard I'm getting married?' said Ella.

'Again?' Steffie was amazed. She quickly added, 'Who to?'

'Fred!' Ella offered no details.

According to Steffie's calculations, Fred was the fifth. ('Incredible!' she thought enviously.)

'Well, I must be going,' said Emancipated Ella, getting up. 'Give me a call sometime. Don't look so amazed! He's the fifth! Yes, the fifth! For centuries men have been devouring us; now it's our turn to devour them!' Then she added, 'On an equal basis, of course,' and smiled.

('What a lot of teeth she's got! thought Steffie. 'And how right she is!')

After sitting there for a while, thinking, Steffie suddenly and decisively called the waitress and paid for the coffees.

Steffie Speck follows Ella's advice
(basting)

A) Steffie Speck at the theatre

---✂

Eggs with cracked or crushed shells cannot be boiled in water without the white – or even the yolk – escaping. If you have to use them, however, you can wrap them in aluminium foil and then plunge them confidently into the water.

---✂

-·-·-· It was very stuffy in the auditorium. At first Steffie attentively followed everything on the stage with rapt attention: the king, the queen and the young Ophelia in love. Steffie liked her best and was sorry when she drowned herself. Then the grave-diggers came on. For a while they stood in the pit talking about something; then they tossed spadefuls of real live earth out of the pit, which surprised Steffie no end because nothing else on the stage was real.

But soon the stuffiness made Steffie feel ill. She stood up and stumbled her way along the row. People grumbled all around her. She headed towards a red light, felt thick plush curtains, left the auditorium and rushed down the stairs and into the toilet. She went into the first cubicle, locked the door, lowered the seat and sat down.

==== Steffie pictured the theatre as a large stacking box containing a smaller one, the auditorium and a still smaller one – the toilet, and a still smaller one, the cubicle, from which there was no way out. ('A grave, a coffin . . .' thought Steffie, breathing deeply.)

==== All at once she heard voices.

'I didn't tell you,' said the first voice, 'that they've taken it all out. She hasn't a thing down below any more.'

'Not a thing?' asked the second voice.

'Nothing. And when it spread to her breast, they had to take that off as well.'

'Really?'

'Really. You can't fool around with these things. When I had my last abortion they told me I had to be careful because I've got a wound . . .'

'Oh?'

'Yes. Big as a bottle top!'

'They'll cauterize it. That's what they did to mine, only it was smaller . . .'

'They told me to have it done before it's too late.'

'You really should, you know. It's no big deal; it just stings a bit. It's better than having your womb dry up.'

'Your womb?'

'That's what's happening to me. They told me it's getting smaller. They say it's because I'm skinny.'

'Really! I didn't know . . . Well, Anita, you remember her . . . Hers is falling out.'

'What do you mean, falling out?'

'Oh, I don't know! Falling out . . .'

'We have a hard time!'

'We certainly do. But what can you do! Look, someone's forgotten a comb!'

'Take it and let's get going.'

'I'll just lock up the mops and bucket.'

" " " " "   The voices fell silent. Steffie was suddenly overcome with pity, without knowing exactly for what or why, and burst into tears. Then it occurred to her that someone might hear her so she pulled the chain, which only made her cry harder, so she pulled the chain again . . .

Wiping her tears, she thought of the wound the size of a bottle top and without thinking bent her thumb and forefinger into a little loop. She sat frozen in that position for a while, then gave a start and caught sight of her hand with the fingers bent into a sign the sense of which she had forgotten. The senseless loop remained stuck in the air for another second or two – and then her hand fell by her side. Steffie pulled the chain and went out.

There was no one in the corridor, but Steffie made her way to the exit on tiptoe. The grave-diggers have surely gone by now, she thought, they've buried Ophelia, I'll have to see the play again, the prince wasn't bad, an excellent actor in fact and just right for a prince . . .

B) Steffie Speck reads *Madame Bovary* by Gustave Flaubert

---✂

A simple way of marking the place in a book without turning down a page corner is to pull an elastic band vertically through the middle of the book at the place where you stop reading.

---✂

Steffie Speck was reading *Madame Bovary* by Gustave Flaubert and underlining certain passages. On p. 42 Steffie Speck underlined:

'But her own life was as cold as an attic with a north light. Boredom silently wove its spider's web across the corners of her heart.'

Next Steffie Speck underlined a passage on p. 58 and another on p. 59:

'But deep in her heart she was waiting for something to happen. Like sailors in distress she gazed around with despairing eyes upon the loneliness of her life, seeking a white sail on the immensities of the misty horizon. She did not know what chance, what wind would bring it to her, to what shore it would carry her, whether it would turn out to be an open boat or a three-decker, laden to the gunwhale with pain or happiness. But each morning when she woke she was agog for what the day might bring forth. She listened to the sounds of the world, jumped from her bed, and never ceased to be surprised that nothing happened. Then, when night came on again, sadder than ever, she longed for the morrow.' 'So they would go on, day after day, innumerable, indistinguishable and bringing nothing! Other lives, no matter how flat they might be, held at least the possibility of happenings. A single adventure sometimes brought changes of fortune which held an infinity of possibilities and new scenes. But nothing ever happened to her! God had willed it so!

The future stretched ahead like a dark corridor with a locked door at the end.'

On p. 61 Steffie Speck put a squiggle:

'All the bitterness of existence lay heaped on her plate. With the steamy vapour of the meat stale gusts of dreariness rose from the depths of her heart.'

On p. 63 Steffie Speck just put a cross:

'She took to drinking vinegar in order to grow slim, contracted a dry cough and completely lost her appetite.'

On p. 83 Steffie Speck put a long question mark:

'A man, at least, is free. He can take his way at will through all the countries of the world and all the passions of the heart; he can surmount all obstacles and sink his teeth into the pleasures of life, no matter how fantastic or far-fetched. But a woman is forever hedged about. By nature both flexible and sluggish, she has to struggle against the weakness of the flesh and the fact that, by law, she is dependent on others. Her will, like the veil fastened to her hat by a string, eddies in every wind. Always she feels the pull of some desire, the restraining pressure of some social restriction.'

On p. 116 Steffie Speck underlined:

'A black mist seemed to lie over everything, drifting aimlessly across the surface of objects while misery swept through her heart, moaning softly, like the winter wind in a deserted castle. She was in the mood which afflicts one when one dreams of things that have gone, never to return. She felt in her bones the sort of lassitude which deadens the heart when something has come to an end. She felt the pain that strikes at one when an accustomed rhythm is broken or when some prolonged vibration ceases.'

On p. 123 Steffie Speck read:

'Poor little woman – gasping for love like a carp on the kitchen
table for water!'

and then closed the book and gazed absently out of the
window.

====   'Look,' said her aunt shuffling into the room, 'aren't they
beautiful!'

Her aunt was holding a plate of apricots in her hand. She
looked at Steffie in surprise, put the plate on the table, sat
down in the armchair and took an apricot. Pecking slowly at
==== the apricot, she said, 'What ith it? Feeling low again? You
seem to do nothing but read these days. There was a girl named
Petra in our town, her father wath the parish prieht. She was
alwayth tho mitherable that when I thaw her thtanding on the
front thtepth of her houthe, I thought she looked like a shroud
stretched out in front of the door. People thaid she thuffered
from a kind of fog in the head, and neither the doctorth nor
the prieht could do anything to help her. When the attackth
got really bad, she would go off all by herthelf into the woodth
and, the forethter would often find her there, lying on her
thtomach on the grath, crying her eyeth out. But later she got
married and people they thaid it all went away . . . Pity,' her
aunt said all of a sudden and put the apricot she had started
down on the table, 'it'th a pity I can't eat them becauthe of
my teeth.'

Steffie's aunt got up, went up to her and turned over the
book to see the title.

====   'What'th thith? Oh, Madame Bovary! Ith that the one who
killed herthelf for love? Boring! The only novelth I like are
the ones that scare you out of your wits.' Shuffling out of the
room, she added, 'Eat the apricoth!'

Steffie sighed, picked up an apricot, turned it thoughtfully
between her fingers, and bit into it.

C) Steffie Speck at the exhibition (or the unanticipated oversewing of S. S. with the author's own zigzag stitch)

Unanticipated, like hell! The reader must have anticipated the
inviolability of the number three: Marianna's three pieces of

advice – three men, Ella's three suggestions. Which only goes to show that writers are a strikingly frivolous, irresponsible and cruel breed! The reader must have anticipated that the author would send Steffie Speck to an exhibition. Well, here are the author's working notes:

S. S. at the exhibition. Walks past an exhibit – a mechanical penis. Penis (the exhibit) rises. S. S. frozen to spot. Electric eye. Alarm goes off. Handsome, bearded painter (the man of her life?) comes up, hugs and kisses her passionately for a full 5 mins. It turns out alarm system reacts to every 10-th visitor. The kiss just a reward the idiot painter hands out randomly. The painter goes back to his beautiful (curly haired!) cats. S. S. leaves disappointed and humiliated.

The author was convinced that this would be a brilliant and moving episode. Then the author read around (asked around) and was disappointed to learn that the mechanical penis had already appeared in our fiction. Brilliant ideas are obviously not enough, for someone else always thinks of them first!

++++ So the author searched and searched for something else in the artistic and erotic line that would be suitable for S. S. The only thing worth considering was Jesús Raphael Soto with his wonderful plastic noodles. S. S. would wade through them, the plastic noodles would wobble, vibrate, and S. S. would keep moving them apart. The author could do a splendid job of that, for sure. And then S. S. would get definitively lost in the forest of vibrating plastic noodles (light symbolism) and – burst into tears.

But then the author definitively abandoned the episode at the exhibition out of irritation with herself. Whenever she doesn't know what to do, she makes poor S. S. cry. So the author satisfied her childish desire to do everything in threes, and left S. S. at home watching television with her aunt. Moreover, she failed to find a suitable piece for the patchwork on this occasion, not to mention having bungled the last one. To salvage something from it all, she offers a handy hint that fits in admirably with the proposed subject.

---✂

Your pictures will not slide all over the wall if you fix sticky tape to the back of the frame.

-->✄

Steffie Speck sleeps with a pig's head or a new attack of depression
(concealed plackets)

-->✄

Never dry your hair while you are in the bath.

-->✄

///////// Apparently none of Emancipated Ella's four ex-husbands had left her a flat. Emancipated Ella had left the expensive floor-space to them. As Fred and Ella had only a room in someone else's flat, Steffie thought that the use of her own for the reception would be the best wedding present she could give them. Her aunt went away, and Fred and Ella brought over all the food and drink. Steffie was a little anxious when she saw the roast pig, the cakes, the bottles, but they managed to fit it into her room somehow.

It was the first time Steffie had been at one of Ella's weddings. 'When we come out of the Registry Office', Ella said warmly, 'you stand in a spot where I can throw you the bouquet.'

Steffie found a suitable place, on the bottom step, and Ella could have easily thrown the bouquet. But Ella held stubbornly onto it. Perhaps she had forgotten her promise.

-.-.-.- The guests arranged themselves as best they could, some on the bed, others on the floor. The food and drink were on the table by the window. Steffie settled in at the end of the bed, the most comfortable place.

Steffie did not find Ella's wedding particularly cheerful. To cheer herself up she drank a glass of wine and ate some crispy pig's skin. Ella was in a fine mood. Her innumerable teeth kept flashing into view. ('What a lot she's got,' Steffie kept repeating to herself. 'What a lot!') Ella's new husband, Fred, was humble and quiet. The fifth little piece on the kebab of Ella's marriages! He behaved as though he were expecting the next one, the one who would push him up against the fourth. But Ella! Ella kept turning her spit, out of habit.

Steffie drank a second glass of wine, nibbled at the roast pork and let her eyes roam over the guests. There was a married couple, Ella's curly haired friend with her husband, a hippie who had had a good deal to drink and kept swaying his legs in rhythm as though working a sewing machine, another couple, very decently behaved, a friend of Fred's who was only interested in the alcohol, and a fat, pleasant-looking girl who was sitting in a corner quietly eating her fifth piece of cake. Moving onto her third glass and a plate of French salad, Steffie wondered why she did not feel sick.

Then Ella came back into Steffie's field of vision. Ella was the only one laughing, as though there were a hundred people at the wedding. She seemed to Steffie like a giant blender, ready to grind up everyone at the wedding if switched on.

On her way to work every day Steffie walked past a building site and always stopped to watch. She liked it best when the large digger tore up layers of earth with its metal teeth. There was something about it that reminded her of Ella. Ella's teeth sparkled, gleamed, she shone with a metallic sheen. ('Terrible,' thought Steffie, draining another glass.)

Then suddenly from Steffie's corner a terrible voice spoke out, 'Ella, you are a sexual digger!'

Everyone fell silent for a moment. Then Ella burst out laughing. Steffie's head spun, she felt herself pressing against someone's arms or legs, being dragged into sleep but – what did it matter?

When Steffie woke in the morning she did not open her eyes. She was lying on her stomach, her head sunk in the pillow, her eyelids completely stuck together. I may never unstick them again, she thought lazily without moving. Her head was completely empty. That's the drink . . . Steffie slowly remembered. She did not stir; she listened. There were pigeons cooing outside. What could the time be?

At last she unstuck one lid and squinted. The first thing she saw was a brownish blob, but what it was she could not make out. She parted her eyelids a little more. *A pig's head!* There right beside her, cheek to cheek, lay a pig's head. No, it can't be! Steffie quickly shut her eyes, then carefully peered out again. The pig's head was still there. She could clearly see its teeth, one eye . . .

Steffie sat up in horror and saw the head of the roast pig on the pillow next to her. The room was in chaos. There were remains of food on the table. It smelled of wine and cigarette ends. Steffie's bed was decorated with withered flowers, and beside the pig's head lay the promised wedding bouquet.

'They've really decorated me nicely!' thought Steffie, shoving the pig's head onto the floor. Then she picked it up again, drew her arm back, threw the head out of the window, shook the flowers from the bedcovers, hurled Ella's bouquet out after the pig's head and pulled the covers over her head.

In the darkness, under the covers, Steffie made up her mind firmly to die.

Annie, very experienced in questions of depression, tells Steffie Speck some news

(lapped seams)

---✁

To keep mimosa fresh in a vase, put it in warm water instead of cold.

---✁

.... 'Hello, Steffie? It's Annie.'

'Annie! What are you up to? Where are you?'

'Here, where else? How are you? Any news?'

'None. Everything's the same.'

'Not for me, nothing's the same!'

'Really?'

'Yes! I'm in love!'

'Honestly? Who with?'

'You'll see, I'm not going to talk about him now. He's a horoscopist. Well, not really, but that's how I met him. I went to him to have my horoscope done . . .'

'And?'

'And nothing! I fell in love!'

'I'm really glad.'

'I called, because I've got something for you – I asked him about your horoscope as well.'

'You did? And what did he say?'

'You'll have to talk to him yourself. The main thing he said was that you've been going through your dark phase and that's why things haven't worked out. Now you're moving into your light phase. Are you listening?'

'Yes.'

'You don't seem particularly interested.'

'Oh, I am, I am. What else did he say?'

'He said you'd soon come to a turning point in your life. A

change for the better, of course. Oh, and also that your critical number is thirteen! In a positive sense.'

'Really?'

'Yes. That's what he says.'

'And what else?'

'Nothing, for the moment. But you'll meet him. I can't tell you how much he's predicted in my life . . . !'

'What?'

'Himself, for a start . . .'

'And you fell in love . . . ?'

'Uh, huh.'

'What about him?'

'He did too.'

'Hey . . . What's wrong with the phone? The receiver's growling!'

'It's not the phone, it's the budgie. I bought a budgie, didn't I tell you?'

'Oh, I forgot . . . And it's that loud?'

'Yes. And terribly crude! A dreadful bird!'

'What's he called?'

'Who? The budgie?'

'No! That horoscopist of yours!'

'Martin.'

'I see. Well, good. I'll come and see you both some time.'

'Fine, just give me a ring . . .'

'Okay.'

Steffie Speck and the budgie, or the hidden monster

(pinked hems)

--- ✄

Spring brings insect bites. Onion juice is an excellent remedy.
Rub a few drops into the place that has been bitten and the
pain and inflammation will be considerably reduced.

--- ✄

Steffie decided definitively, this time definitively, to stay
depressed. ('Even Annie, even Annie's in love!' she wept.)

At first Steffie could not explain why Annie's falling in love
had thrown her into such despair. Then she realised it was
because there must always be someone who's worse off or as
badly off as we are. And now things were better for Annie.

And then quite out of the blue it came to her: *the budgie*!
That was it! The budgie! Annie had bought a budgie because
she was depressed all the time. And from then on everything
had begun to go better. The budgie had evidently been a small,
secret call to life, a call for help, a discreet sign to destiny –
like a half-open curtain on a window or a bowl of flowers, like
a dropped handkerchief or a light in the room. Destiny had
noticed Annie's sign.

" " " " " After all, Steffie mused on, a budgie is smaller and cheaper
than a dog, and it's not even an animal, it's a bird, a dog barks,
for instance, but not a budgie, it only chirrups, pecks seeds
and is certainly much more cheerful than a dog.

To make a long story short, Steffie bought a budgie. Her
aunt suggested they call it Beppo. 'Jutht ath long ath it doethn't
die in thix month . . . !'

Beppo was a cheerful and appealing bird. Steffie was pleased
it didn't know how to talk. Annie's made it impossible to have
" " " " " a peaceful telephone conversation.
= = = = Steffie Speck's life suddenly began to go better. The

agreeable little bird brought a certain cheer into the quiet home of Steffie and her aunt. Steffie was no longer sad. One afternoon she was lazily turning the pages of a fashion magazine; her aunt was dozing in the armchair. Rays of the afternoon sun were streaming through the open window, making patterns on the walls. Steffie slowly closed the magazine and looked blissfully round the room – at her aunt in the armchair, at the play of light – and as she did so she felt that her life was filled with warmth and that it would soon be bringing her much more of everything.

All of a sudden Steffie heard an inhuman voice:

'Steffie's got a bushy pussy!'

'Whaaat?' exclaimed Steffie in horror.

From the cage the budgie's little black eyes stared unblinkingly at Steffie.

'Got a bushy pussy!' the budgie repeated impassively, in its tinny, old man's voice.

Steffie blushed, stood up and sat down. She couldn't breathe. She looked at the budgie. It didn't bat an eyelid. Then it opened its evil beak again, but Steffie leapt up, put the cage on the window sill and opened it. The budgie stepped slowly out of the cage and without looking at Steffie – flew away.

'Monster! Swine!' Steffie shouted after it.

″ ″ ″ ″ ″   She sat down again. The tears welled up uncontrollably. She stared at the empty cage. The tears flowed of their own accord. Bloody bird! The tears streamed down her cheeks. She had been nursing a serpent in her lap. The tears flowed in a great river. Her heart was splitting, unpicking. The tears poured on. Her whole being was unpicking. The tears flowed in a torrent. Soon there would be nothing left of her but a thread.

'Old Mother White!' mumbled her aunt suddenly in her sleep. 'She thewth by day and unpickth by night!' Then she wriggled in her armchair and began to snore.

Steffie Speck reflects about her first deflowerer, her second deflowerer and suicide
(toggle fastenings)

--✂

Do you know how to tell when vegetables are cooked? When they lie on the bottom of the pan, they are done. As long as they float they are not ready.

--✂

Well, there were two of them. Ella said: 'Don't talk nonsense! A deflowerer is a deflowerer, so – the first!' Steffie did not like the word 'deflowerer', but Ella said it was time to call things by their proper names. Ah, Ella! Ella was something else!

The first was their new neighbours' son. He was doing a course in electrical engineering. He was mad about everything that could be taken apart and put together and about everything that could be rhymed. When he first saw her in the corridor, he said: 'Hey, little miss, how about a kiss?' Later he took to visiting them and he would joke with her aunt: 'What do you think bugs her about me?' Steffie's aunt would say, 'Nitwit! A real nitwit!' Then one day the television went wrong, and her aunt was away. The First spent a long time fiddling with the television and finally the television worked, and then the First spent a long time fiddling with Steffie. That was it. She never quite knew how it happened. The only thing she remembered was the sound of the television talking to itself. Steffie didn't like it. The First did. Several times she found little bits of paper in the letter box with verses in which 'screen' rhymed with 'has-been' ('I'm no hero of the screen, nor am I a has-been'), 'shove' with 'love' ('Don't give me the shove, let's have a bit of love') and the like. 'Nitwit!' repeated Steffie's aunt and Steffie agreed.

The Second came immediately after the First. And again it was all quite accidental, casual. Her chemistry teacher. At that time he was known as 'Incidentally'. He would begin every sentence with 'incidentally'. He loved experiments, all those numerous little bottles, test-tubes, bunsen-burners, fume-cupboards . . . Incidentally we've just done this experiment, incidentally we've just done that experiment . . .

Steffie met him again at her typing course. He was working as a secretary. He was even smaller, more disoriented and withdrawn. He reminded Steffie of a snail. Then came the final test and the farewell party. There he was all disoriented, embarrassed. He kept looking at Steffie the whole time. At the end he offered to drive her home. But, of course, to his place for coffee first. Steffie no longer remembered how it had come about, she only remembered her decision to go, incidentally like that, incidentally with the Second. Why she did not know. The Second seemed awkward and pathetic and she helped him along whole-heartedly. Afterwards he said: 'Forgive me, Miss Speck, I have just deflowered you' – and fell asleep. Steffie said, 'All right.' (I have to believe him, she thought.) The Second fell asleep with his arms round Steffie and her ear uncomfortably pressed against his watch. In the terrible night silence Steffie listened to the persistent ticking of the watch. And then she heard a bird twitter, and then another . . . And Steffie felt that it was at that very moment – while the watch was drumming in her ear, and the first bird was chirruping outside, in that pure crystal morning fragment of time – that she became a woman. Independently of the First and independently of the Second. Of her own accord.

. . . . The First left the sound of the television, the Second the ticking of a watch. Apart from that, nothing. Nothing at all. All the rest had sunk and melted together. 'Like porridge!' thought Steffie and suddenly remembered that the rice had been waiting for ages that she ought to turn on the cooker, that it was dark and that she was hungry.

While the rice bubbled, rose and fell in the little pan on the cooker, Steffie took a water melon out of the refrigerator. 'No!' thought Steffie, drumming on the water melon. 'Things can't go on like this!' Absently she stroked the melon and tugged for a long time at its little stalk. Then she picked up a knife decisively and cut the melon in two. 'What would happen' she thought suddenly, picking up the knife again and slicing off a sliver of melon, 'if I killed myself?' The idea snapped in Steffie's head and she spat out a melon pip.

Yes, thought Steffie, that would be a proper revenge for all the insults she had endured. She imagined the modest funeral. Everyone from the office would be there. Marianna would cry a lot, she was sure of that, Marianna would be devastated. And Annie. Annie's new boyfriend would be sorry, even though they had never met. What was his name? Martin, yes, Martin . . . Ella would be sorry too, only she wouldn't show it. She'd be angry. 'The fool, the fool, why did she do it!' Yes, she'd be angry, but she'd be sorry too.

Moved, Steffie cut another slice of melon and thoughtfully squeaked the knife against the green rind. The Driver would hear from Marianna and maybe he would come. The Hulk wouldn't come, because he wouldn't have any way of knowing, and the Intellectual . . . He read the papers, perhaps he'd hear about it. She pictured him drunk with a rose in his hand. A white one. And her aunt! Her aunt would probably die of grief. But maybe not. Steffie's eyes filled with tears. She began to count the people who would come to her funeral and was appalled at how few there were. 'I'll do it,' thought Steffie. If a person has so few people at her funeral all she deserves is to die at once!

'That's right,' said Steffie half aloud and turned off the cooker. The rice rose up, gave a last 'gurgle' and subsided. Her aunt could have it when she came home in the morning, thought Steffie, putting on the lid.

Then she began to think about how to go about it. A rope hurt, it was impractical, and people looked awful when they hanged. Throwing herself under a train was not even an option: she would have been terrified. Besides you never knew. A person could survive and be disabled for the rest of her life. Cutting her wrists, no not that! Her aunt would be furious. Pills were best! She found four bottles in her aunt's cupboard. Three were full of sinister-coloured pills and Steffie emptied all of them decisively into a cup. There were only three tablets in the fourth one. White. She emptied them in too. There. If that didn't kill her, nothing would! Perhaps she ought to leave her aunt a note! . . . **No**! It wouldn't matter afterwards in any case . . .

Steffie walked through the flat, put the remains of the water melon in the fridge and wiped the table. She checked the cooker, lifted the lid, tried the rice – it was cooked, only unsalted – put the lid back and went into the bathroom.

She spent a long time looking at herself in the mirror, then she filled the bath with hot water. There. She'd commit double suicide. She had seen it done in films. A razor blade was messy, but it didn't hurt. In the bath, in clouds of steam, Steffie slowly swallowed her aunt's tablets, and when the cup was quite empty, she slid into the hot water. She thought she could already feel the effect of the tablets, so she decided against the razor blade. Soon she felt terribly sleepy. Death really wasn't so awful. On the contrary. Like a deep sleep. In the distance, in a dream, she could see them all assembled: her aunt, Annie, Marianna, Ella, the Driver, the Hulk, the Intellectual, even the First and the Second and a few others from the office. They were all smiling and waving to her. 'They all like me, all of them!' Steffie was touched and wanted to run to them. But the water was strange and heavy, it stuck to her body and it took a great effort for her to come to the surface.

Steffie was woken from death by a sneeze. Her own. She opened her eyes and saw a handsome man in white. ('No, no that's something else!' flashed into her mind and she quickly closed her eyes.) Then she peered out cautiously. A tanned face was smiling at her, a tanned face with deep blue eyes and pearly teeth. She felt the squeeze of a hand.

'Steffie, are you all right?' asked a deep, gentle voice.

'Who are you?' Steffie squinted.

'Look at me, Steffie!'

Steffie sank into the blue of the unknown eyes. She felt a warm hand and a new squeeze. ('I must be dreaming . . .' she thought and closed her eyes tight.)

'Everything will be all right. Phone me if necessary,' said the deep, gentle voice.

Steffie quickly opened one eye and saw her aunt's face.

'I don't underthtand!' said her aunt. 'Why wath the bath full of water, why did you get into bed naked and wet, why did you take all my multivitamin pillth and three thleeping tableth?'

Steffie sneezed and snuggled under the covers.

'Why was the rithe burned . . . ?' complained Steffie's aunt. Steffie pulled the covers over her head.

'Amateurth!' muttered her aunt. 'It'th like that Peter from our town. He dethided to kill himthelf in the motht dreadful way. He thwallowed a knife. And nothing happened. He tried again with a fork. No luck. He wath furiouth, went betherk and thwallowed hith wife'th thilver cutlery for twelve people! And thtill nothing happened! He'th thtill there, alive and well. The idiot! Pity about the cutlery . . .'

Steffie Speck recalls some of Emancipated Ella's advice

(gussets)

---✂

*You can squeeze the remains of the toothpaste out of a tube
that looks empty if you plunge the tube into hot water for a few
moments.*

---✂

HOW DO YOU SAY BLOOD GROUP IN FRENCH? huge, threatening,
black letters asked Steffie Speck. Steffie looked around her.
There was no one about. The question was directed at her.
'Really,' thought Steffie, 'how do you say blood group in
French?' and she walked up to the poster carefully.

THERE IS NO EXCUSE FOR THOSE WHO MAINTAIN THAT THEY COULD
NOT OR DID NOT HAVE THE CHANCE TO LEARN AT LEAST ONE
FOREIGN LANGUAGE!

'That's right!' Steffie Speck agreed at once.

THE EXPERIENCE OF OUR COURSES SHOWS THAT EVERYONE IS
CAPABLE OF LEARNING FOREIGN LANGUAGES. AGE IS
IMMATERIAL!

'How true!' thought Steffie Speck.

FOREIGN LANGUAGES ARE YOUR WINDOW TO THE WORLD!
OPEN THAT WINDOW –
LEARN A LANGUAGE!
MILLIONS OF PEOPLE ALL OVER THE WORLD KNOW HOW TO SAY

BLOOD GROUP IN FRENCH AND YOU DO NOT!
THE LANGUAGE COURSE KNOWS AND YOU WILL TOO!

'Absolutely!' Steffie thought enthusiastically. She found a pencil and scrap of paper and made a note of the address and telephone number.

Steffie went cheerfully home and from the door called to her aunt:

'How do you say blood group in French?'

'*Classement de sang!* Why do you athk?' said her aunt like a shot and added, 'Your blood group is very important. I'm B and I never forget it. It'th thomething you really ought to know, not only in your own but in other languageth too. How many people have died jutht becauthe they didn't know their blood group?'

Steffie Speck head over heels in a happy end or the appearance of Monsieur Fiddler
(finishing)

--✄

You simply cannot get your cream to whip? Stop whipping, add the white of one egg and put it in the fridge for ten minutes. Then whip it again and it will become firm and frothy in no time!

--✄

Steffie liked the French classes at once. The school was not far from her office. On the top floor there was a little café, where they drank tea or coffee and chatted during the break. Not only they, the French, but the others: Germans, English, Italians . . . There were people of all ages and occupations and they were all nice. Steffie felt that they were all happier to be there, together, out of the house, than they were to be learning languages.

Steffie decided that the knowledge of languages was very useful, if for no other reason than when she went to St Tropez, like Matilda, she would not feel like a complete fool, she would be able to chat happily with the locals and visitors from other parts of France if there were any. And of course there would be.

The teacher was very nice too, nice to all the students. She knew French like a real live French woman. Steffie liked working in the language laboratory best, because she could put on the headphones, switch on the tape recorder and think about other things while French rolled in her ears.

The day they reached the thirteenth lesson a man came into the class and introduced himself as Monsieur Fiddler, from which she concluded that he knew some French already. Monsieur Fiddler sat down beside Steffie and soon was taking an active part in the class.

" " " " " The lesson seemed to fly by, and before she knew it Steffie was on her way to the tram stop with her textbook and notepad under her arm. And who should turn up at the same tram stop but – Monsieur Fiddler!

They did not speak until – just as the tram, a number fifteen, arrived and Steffie was about to get on – Monsieur Fiddler said softly: 'Je m'appelle Albert Fiddler.'

Steffie looked at him in amazement and heard her own voice say: 'Je m'appelle Steffie Speck.'

Steffie looked over cautiously at Monsieur Fiddler. He was smiling. She blushed, which made her embarrassed so she blushed still more. She turned to see whether there was another tram coming. There was. A fifteen. Perhaps he's in a hurry, she thought, and he's being polite and waiting for me to go first? The tram arrived. Steffie looked helplessly at Monsieur Fiddler. In front of her a fat woman was clambering onto the tram breathing heavily. Steffie had raised one foot to step on when Monsieur Fiddler said: 'Qu'est-ce que vous préférez, le café ou le thé?'

'Le café!' Steffie burst out so suddenly, breathlessly and loudly that instead of 'coffee' she made a strange, incomprehensible squeak – and the tram pulled away.

They were silent. Steffie felt she would die of embarrassment. Monsieur Fiddler must surely want to go, and she kept on stupidly missing trams and making him wait with her. She glanced at him again. He had gentle blue eyes and was polite and shy, or at least that was how he seemed to her. In any case she did not feel like taking the tram. And another one was coming. A fifteen. Steffie trod firmly on a cigarette end by her foot. That's it, she thought, I really must go!

She cast a last glance at Fiddler, and then turned decisively to get onto the tram. At that very moment Monsieur Fiddler said: 'Alors, allons boire une tasse de café!'

'Oui,' replied Steffie in confusion.

-.-.-.- Steffie and Monsieur Fiddler walked along without saying anything. What if I asked him something in my own language, she thought, and decided against it. It might spoil something, break some bond between them; it would be like a run in a stocking. In any case, if two people happened to meet on the

Moon, they would certainly speak some new, Moon language. What a silly example! What did the Moon have to do with it?

Then the thirteenth lesson began to come into her mind. Thirteen . . . Thirteen . . . Suddenly she felt it was terribly important that Monsieur Fiddler had appeared at precisely the thirteenth lesson. Hadn't Annie said something about the fateful number thirteen?

They stopped at a crossing. Waiting for the light to turn green, Steffie hastily opened her book, found lesson treize and ran her eyes over the text.* She felt as though she had just read a secret message from a distant land.

" " " " "   Oui, winked the green traffic light, oui, typed out Steffie's thoughts, oui, beat her heart, oui, said the smiles of passers-by, oui, rang the trams, oui, shone the windows in the buildings, oui, staggered a drunk, oui, agreed the streets, oui, oui, oui . . .

All the cafés were closed, but Steffie Speck and Monsieur Fiddler walked on. Steffie knew that everything around her was different now and would remain so forever. That everything was moving onwards, upwards, like the quatorzième leçon, quinzième leçon, seizième leçon . . .

(FIN)

* Here is the text Steffie ran her eyes over, in full.

TREIZIEME LEÇON   A HUMBLE DWELLING

La famille était réunie dans le petit salon, où il y avait deux fauteuils, un piano, deux lampes coiffées de petits chapeaux verts et une petite étagère remplie de bibelots.

Par économie, on n'allumait pour la maison entière qu'un seul feu et qu'une lampe, autour de laquelle toutes les occupations, toutes les distractions se groupaient, bonne grosse lampe de famille dont le vieil abat-jour montrant des scènes de nuit, semées de points brillants, avait été l'étonnement et la joie de tous ces enfants.

Sortant doucement de l'ombre de la pièce, quatre jeunes têtes se penchaient, blondes ou brunes, souriantes ou appliquées, sous ce rayon intime et réchauffant qui les éclairait à la hauteur des yeux.

Ainsi serrée dans une petite pièce en haut de la maison déserte, dans la chaleur, la sécurité de son intérieur, bien garni et soigné, la famille Joyeuse a l'air d'un nid tout en haut d'un grand arbre.

une étagère: a whatnot; *des bibelots* (m.): small ornaments; *un abat-jour*: a lampshade

Romance remnants
which may be used for appliqué
(supplement)

--✂

==== *She had known Monsieur Fiddler for less than an hour, and already she felt irresistibly drawn to him. She wanted to be with him constantly. She told herself it was silly, but she was already imagining her future by his side. She wanted passionately to be with him forever.*

--✂

Steffie was truly overwhelmed with happiness, though she kept telling herself how stupid it was to tie her life so firmly to a man she barely knew. Still, she consoled herself that Monsieur Fiddler was no ordinary man and his amazing mixture of childish and manly qualities deserved to be loved.

--✂

As they walked towards the traffic lights, Steffie had the impression that in the short time she had spent with him she had crossed unnoticed over the river of doubts and fears that had been her life till then.

--✂

His words and the passionate sound of his voice were like caresses. Steffie felt her heart beating harder.

--✂

He was attractive, elegant, dignified; he possessed all the qualities that Steffie valued in a man.

--✂

When he looked at her with his warm gaze, Steffie realised he would be able to offer her lasting love and not merely a passing affair.

--✂

He raised her hand to his lips and kissed it. Steffie trembled at his touch. He wound his arms around her and kissed her. They said nothing. The kiss was eloquent enough.

---✂

Monsieur Fiddler aroused in her feelings that had been long buried. She knew that his presence, should they decide to have a coffee, would lead her into temptation.

---✂

As Steffie said nothing, he took her in his arms and pressed her to him. Steffie glanced at his face and felt a sudden urge to kiss him. She gazed into his deep eyes which were imploring her for a kiss, telling her of his loneliness and the desire to conquer her heart and keep her by his side forever.

---✂

He pressed her firmly to him and kissed her passionately. His burning love swept away all obstacles and difficulties. Steffie felt her heart was still capable of trembling with love.

---✂

If only that moment could last forever! She wanted them to be together till the end of time, she and Monsieur Fiddler, in that little flower-filled restaurant garden. When you loved someone, the simplest things filled life with joy. You did not think only of that person, of love, but also of a shared house, a garden, children. Perhaps her dreams were not idle; and perhaps Monsieur Fiddler really would make her happy!

---✂

The author's darts

==== Well? Well, what happened next? There's no more threeead! I've stopped stitching! I'm holding the last strand of thread in my mouth and I don't know what to do with it. I chew on it and think sadly: they've got what they wanted, but I'm not going to get what I want. Ah, life – I think – it's so elusive.

And I can already hear them talking.

'It's no good!' says my friend. 'The arms dangle. That Steffie's an amoeba, not a character!'

++++ 'It's no good!' says another friend. 'You haven't padded it evenly. You haven't given Steffie a chance!'

'It's no good!' says a female acquaintance. 'It's too flimsy. There's nothing about women's fate! Where's the gynaecologist, the twist with the abortion, the illegitimate child?'

'It's no good!' says my brother. 'It just doesn't come off. If you'd sent Steffie to a disco the ending would have been very different!'

'It's no good!' says a male acquaintance. 'Sloppy workmanship! It isn't at all clear whether that Fiddler will marry her!'

'It's no good!' says my mother. 'It's too tight. Let it out in a couple of places! The aunt is only a sketch, not a character.'

'It's no good!' says my hairdresser. 'Ready-made rubbish! They're all clichés, your Steffies, Annies, Mariannas. I cut their hair every day! What you need is more imagination! The best thing would be to unpick it and start again.'

I've run out of thread, t-h-r-e-a-d, I say . . . Okay, I'll unpick it, there, I'm already unpicking it . . . But now I hear another voice . . . familiar, hard, editorial.

'Too short!' it says.

'What?' I ask.

'Too short!' it says.

'Oh,' I say.

My arms drop wearily. And then what do I see on my desk – three apples! They might have fallen out of the blue! How nice, I think: one for me, one for Steffie, and the third for Steffie's aunt!

How the author's mother, Aunt Sissy,
their neighbour Barbara, Cousin Lily from
Nancy and Aunt Sissy's friend Greta from
Holland expand the plot for the heroine S. S.

---✄

The hem of a quotation: 'They prattle together; out of the
darkness they draw a long hopeless braid of conversation.'
(Bruno Schulz).

---✄

'Do come,' mother had said, 'Aunt Sissy and my neighbour
Barbara will be here as usual, then Aunt Sissy's friend Greta
from Holland and Barbara's cousin Lily from Nancy. They're
all mature, experienced women. Together we'll come up with
something.'

After a long silence my mother took a resolute swallow of
coffee, put her cup down on the saucer, shook her head a few
times and sighed, 'Is that what he said? It's too short?'

'Yes,' I sighed too.

'What does he mean?' she asked in a quiet, threatening tone.

'Just that! That it's simply too short.'

'Oh,' said my mother more mildly.

With this Barbara and her cousin Lily, Aunt Sissy and her
friend Greta relaxed their inner guard. I relaxed too and lit a
cigarette.

'Hmm,' my mother began but then fell silent. Aunt Sissy,
Barbara, Lily and Greta sighed sympathetically. There was a
long silence. I rustled my cigarette packet nervously and fixed
a questioning gaze on all four of them.

'Vell, eef ze sing eez too short, 'ow about ve lengsen eet!'
Lily from Nancy suddenly burst out.

'That's right!' said the others in her support.

'We can hulp, natuurlijk,' said Greta kindly.

++++   'Hm . . .' my mother repeated, taking matters into her own hands. 'How about adding a chapter to describe Steffie Speck's married life? They have a nice, normal wedding, and she has her first child – a girl say. They're both terribly busy at work. Oh, incidentally, you never said what your Fiddler does for a living . . . ? Then she has a second child and, of course, starts to let herself go. So he finds himself a mistress, some young student, and she – Steffie – finds out and is quite devastated, and starts fighting to get him back.'

++++ 'Which of course consists in going to the hairdresser,' Aunt Sissy joined in irritably, 'and on the way back from the hairdresser it begins to pour! Of course she hasn't got an umbrella and a passing car splatters her with mud and everything falls apart, splits, dissolves, catches fire, burns, collapses. We've seen it all hundreds of times, in films!' Aunt Sissy was becoming increasingly furious. 'Why do we women always come off so badly! Have Fiddler run over by a car!' Choking with fury Aunt Sissy lit a cigarette.

Aunt Sissy exhaled; my mother gulped; Lily rolled her eyes; and Barbara, the neighbour, knitted rapidly.

++++ 'Boot waroom de zolootion nood be so draastic?' asked the clearly delicate Greta in her sing-song voice. 'I not know, boot maybe it voould be goed to make your mevrouw Stef and haar man Fiddler come into zoom geld and simply be zending dem off to de Greek islands!'

I was just about to say that wasn't a bad idea, but my mother, ignoring Greta's suggestion, forestalled me: 'All right,' she said, 'if you think the marriage is impossible, then let them part! The life of a divorced woman and all the difficulties that entails is also interesting!:

'But we've seen it hundreds of times . . . !' said Aunt Sissy, annoyed.

++++ 'I not know, I not know' Greta repeated more to herself than anyone else.

Barbara suddenly put down her knitting and said triumphantly, 'And a few months after her divorce, Steffie's boss at work – who's a thoroughly objectionable type – tries to blackmail her!'

'Whatever for?' asked Aunt Sissy in a savage tone.

'Well, er . . . I mean . . . you know, well . . . to get her to sleep with him!' Barbara was embarrassed.

'Naturellement! Let 'eem zleep viz er! Even ze shiefs must 'ave ze good times!' Lily rolled her eyes.

'I don't know . . . I only thought . . . Well, that always happens in novels. I mean, there's always a boss, and so on . . .'

'Barbara is right in a way,' said my mother, turning towards me. 'You're not going to let your heroine sleep with just anyone, are you?'

'Who she sleeps with depends on the plot,' I said bitterly. 'It has nothing to do with morality!' 'If the plot required it, I'd send her from one bed to another!'

++++ 'Yoost send de dame on a journey!' said Greta earnestly. 'So, a cruuise roond de Mediterranean. Mit haar twee kinderen. On de deck mevrouw Stephanie meets one mijnheer wie has loost his wife. And, op het laatst, all is hoop en liefde! I tink, for mevrouw Stephanie.'

'Wouldn't it be better if she went on a safari with the gentleman?' Aunt Sissy suggested maliciously.

'Excellente idée!' Lily exclaimed.

++++ 'I've just had an idea!' my mother said suddenly. 'We don't have to go on. We can go back! For instance, it isn't at all clear who the girl's parents were. . . . Where does her aunt fit in? See what I mean? It's all so vague . . .'

'Out of the question!' I said grimly.

'Mais oui,' agreed Lily, 'it eez not necéssaire for all to be so clair! La littérature she eez one sing, ze life she eez somesing else. And, après tout, if you sink about it, not everysing eez clear in ze life eiser. Eez not true, chérie?'

'Is true!' I said.

++++ 'It's true!' said Barbara energetically, laying down her knitting needles. 'That's the whole point: life is one thing and literature something else. What you can't do in life, you can do in art, such as make everything end happily! I once saw a wonderful film in which everyone lacked something. One character had no wife, another no husband, another had only one leg, a fourth stuttered, and a fifth was blind. In the end they all got what they needed. The man without a leg married the blind woman, who had meanwhile regained her sight. That was a great film! You do that with Steffie. Make her keep wanting something, and in the end give it to her!'

'But she did!' said Aunt Sissy, 'She gave her Fiddler!'

'I know,' said Barbara, sticking to her guns, 'but in the next instalment she'll need something else!'

'A flat!' growled Aunt Sissy.

'Not bad,' said my mother calmly.

++++ 'You're mad, all of you!' shouted Aunt Sissy in exasperation. 'A writer's not Santa Claus!'

'I know!' said Barbara. 'Here's an example from life! A friend of mine, Helena, you don't know her . . . All right, say Fiddler leaves Steffie in the next instalment, like that blockhead left Helena! Well, Helena lived a few months on her own, with her little girl, she's adorable, little Sylvie. And one day the little angel got measles. Helena rushed her to hospital . . . And guess what happened! A young paediatrician, an intern, from Kenya . . . And there you are! Now she writes to me every week from Mairobi!'

'Nairobi!' growled Aunt Sissy.

'All right, Nairobi, what's the difference. You were the one who brought up the safari!'

At this point my mother realised that the whole thing was going badly and announced a truce.

'How about a little brandy? Greta? You, Lily?'

'Yoost a drop, pleeze!' said Greta.

'Yes, please,' said Barbara.

'Yes!' said Aunt Sissy.

'Excellente idée! Eez not so, chérie?' said Lily, tapping me on the knee.

'What about you?' asked my mother.

After a longish pause I said almost vindictively, 'I'll have lemonade!'

Mother poured the drinks, the women sipped theirs, my mother sipped hers, I sipped mine (my lemonade) and my mother said, 'We presume you don't like the suggestions for the second instalment that describe Steffie's married life, or give Fiddler a mistress, and Steffie a divorce, or send Steffie on a journey to the Greek islands, or get her into trouble at work, or infect her child with measles, or turn up her long lost parents. So where do we go from here?'

++++ 'Why don't you find her aunt a lover!' Aunt Sissy shouted.

++++ 'Ooo, dis woould be bad taste!' Greta frowned. 'Perhaps it woould be goed if mevrouw Stephanie gooes to German classes . . .'

I gave myself up to studying the technique whereby lemon pips float in a glass of lemonade, pretending that their remark had not affected me in the least.

++++ 'Her mother-in-law!' Barbara exclaimed throwing down her needles.

'What about her?' asked Aunt Sissy cautiously.

'That's the answer! A dramatic relationship! Steffie and her mother-in-law!'

++++ 'I think Fiddler should have a brother!' said Aunt Sissy ironically.

'What for?' asked the women with one voice.

'So Steffie could fall in love with him.'

'And Fiddler would smash his face in out of jealousy!' said Barbara, her eyes flashing.

'I not know, I not know . . .' delicate Greta repeated meekly.

Lily, evidently with the intention of salvaging what could be salvaged, announced solemnly, 'Every work, art too, eez like ragoût. Ze more you put een, ze better eet eez.'

Lily stopped, swallowed a mouthful of brandy, and looked from one woman to the next.

'What *do* you put into your ragoût?' asked Aunt Sissy with interest.

'Vot? You like me to tell?'

'Yes, yes!' the women cried.

++++ 'Pommes de terre, onions, paprika, aubergines, tomates, carottes, boeuf.' From somewhere the women all produced scraps of paper and pencils. Because of the abrupt change in the situation, I did too. 'Eet eez very important,' Lily went on, 'zat all zis simmerz on a low flame and zen iz baked in a dish of earzenware.'

'A dish of earthenware,' muttered the women, writing it down.

'A dish . . .' I wrote, and then it struck me: 'A new genre!'
I added half aloud and sent a code-glance towards Lily.

'Eet need not be earzenware, eet can be any kind,' said Lily,
roughly dashing all hopes that I might at last be understood.

'Any kind . . .' muttered the women.

'Zat's it!' Lily concluded effectively, as though saying mass.

The women put away their bits of paper contentedly. I
cruelly drowned one lemon pip and swallowed another, then
said in a terrible voice, 'And Steffie?'

The women were silent.

'Well, what about her?' I said reproachfully.

Greta shrugged her shoulders and shook her head. 'I not
know, I not know . . .'

The others shook their heads as well.

'So, none of you can think of anything? Other than clichés,
I mean, nothing from life? From your own lives? Haven't you
lived?'

'Well, in that film with Charles Boyer,' my mother began,
but at the name – Charles Boyer – Barbara, her neighbour
leapt up like a scalded cat, threw down her needles again and
shouted, 'Girls!'

The women gave a start, but Barbara was on her way out
of the flat. We heard the door to the next flat opening. In a
few moments Barbara came back with a large book in her
hands.

'Girls, girls,' Barbara sang in a voice filled with promise.

On the cover was written in huge red letters:

HEART-THROBS

and underneath, in rather smaller, black ones:

**A Colorful Collection of the World's Most
Fascinating Men**

Realising immediately that my cause was lost, I let my thoughts
sink into my lemonade and absent-mindedly drowned the
remaining pips with my spoon. When I raised my eyes again,
I saw the lined faces of the women gradually cracking, peeling

like plaster masks, and out floated the young faces of my mother, Aunt Sissy, Barbara the neighbour, Greta and Lily.

Their voices drifted over to me.

'I'd have Charles Boyer and Laurence Olivier, of course.'

'Only two of the hundred most attractive men in the world!'

'All right, I'll have Clark Gable as well. He was the love of my youth.'

'I vould sleep also viz Errol Flynn, Gary Cooper, and, oh and Burt Lancaster! . . . Ah, Burt Lancaster. And Marcello Mastroianni and viz . . .'

'Hey, take it easy!'

'I'd have Marlon, I must say!'

'And I woold like if Gérard Philippe ask me to eat wid him dinner!'

'Only dinner?'

'Goed, maybe also to a vaalk.'

'Nothing else?'

'Peerhaps I voold like to correspond wid dat fine mijnheer vrom de cowboy films . . . Ah, dat's him, James Stewart! Wid him!'

'She'd correspond! Ha, ha, ha . . .'

'Oh là là, ladies, I would sleep viz all ze Tarzans, starting viz Johnnie Weismuller, all of zem!'

'Collectively! Ha! Ha! Ha!'

'I'd have John Barrimore and Douglas Fairbanks!'

'Heavens, when was that! Why them?'

'Out of piety!'

'I used to be crazy about this one! Remember Tyrone Power?'

'I used to like Robert Mitchum!'

'I not know, he drink terribly . . .'

'I vould sleep viz John Wayne!'

'You'd sleep with them all!'

'And vhy not? 'ooever is offered!'

'I'm sticking to my three!'

'I'll have Paul Newman! He's a real dish!'

'Hey, girls, what about *this* one . . . !'

Suddenly I felt terribly lonely. I stood up, went to the door, paused in case the women had noticed me and muttered in a conciliatory tone: 'Well, as for me, I'd take . . .' (I'd take Dustin Hoffman, for sure!) – but the women did not hear me at all. My mother cast a bewildered glance at me and, warmed by the collective hypnosis, said something like: 'It'll all be all right,' and sank back into the chit-chat.

I left with a bitter taste in my mouth – straight into the lift and then into the indifferent street. Under my tongue I held the bitter pip of pique, in my hand the senseless stew recipe. And I thought something to the effect that everything was a cliché, including life itself and that I would have to think about that in more detail, when the dust settled; then, that the kitsch microbes are the most vigorous organisms of the emotions; I thought about how to get hold of hot peppers; then about the melodramatic imagination (which is indestructible!), about the imagination being like parsley, about how 'sl' sounds are sensuous and should be used more often, then something ecological about our constant and permanent exposure to irradiation by kitsch, about the talk I'd have to have some time with Barbara about optimistic realism, about an unexpected inheritance I would have to invent for S. S. to send her to Tahiti (though I immediately crossed out Tahiti and concluded that everything should be left as it was), about what would have happened had there been anything between my mother and Charles Boyer, something about how we are chronically infected by the fairy tale, about whether I should leave the carrots out of the recipe or not, about the parsley of the imagination as an excellent title for an essay, about slushy romance as a genre and the invincibility of the happy end, then something about aubergines, and about life, about cheap chintz . . . And then the turmoil in my soul was suddenly stilled, because an old melody from a chance transistor on the shoulder of a passer-by brushed against me, and I felt something beating in the region of my heart, something bleating, something bleeding. I felt my heart throbbing, I felt myself sobbing, I felt the tears bobbing off my chin . . .

Final touches to the garment

1. *A Patchwork Novel*. The author's original intention was to introduce an 'illegal' prose genre into the existing 'official' typology, namely, the author was inspired by the 'diary' of a certain Pat Patch* (a pseudonym). Pat Patch's engaging 'diary' is an attempt to record the chatter at a tea party in London in 1888. Stimulated by her example, the author intended to reproduce the *oral* prose that women have been creating for centuries *underground* (unlike men) prose that originated over tea, over feather-plucking, over spinning, weaving, embroidering, washing, and so on – in all those women's collective situations that have sprung up in various historical, geographical, national, social, traditional and other circumstances.

All that remained of the author's intention was the pseudonym Pat Patch, and even that has been blurred by the designation patchwork.

2. The author wished to reproduce the glow, the warmth released by the passionate friction of women's tongues, the verbal steam of their communal bath . . . All that has remained of the intended bath are some inarticulate prose passages (verbal patches!) which are to an extent the equivalent of the communicative situation of a gossip-session, for instance. What is crucial for such a communicative situation is the assumption that all the participants (readers) are more or less acquainted with the subject of the gossip, making all explanation unnecessary and undesirable.

3. Having expressed at the outset her intention of writing a piece of 'women's' prose, the author took into account several

* Pat Patch, *Chatterbox*, London, 1888.

of the general characteristics of so called 'women's writing', to name a few: the main (female) character's search for personal happiness, a feeling of isolation, love as the dominant element, the potent experience of corporality, sensuality, passivity, an apolitical outlook, the banality of the everyday, social circumstances in the subtext, impoverished language, the impossibility of experiencing the world as a totality, etc. The author has avoided all autobiographical tendencies and the confessional tone. The author would like to point out that all these definitions have been taken from life and current criticism!

4. The author confesses she had greater pretensions. In the character of Steffie Speck she secretly hoped to create a female Miloš Hrma the hero of Bohumil Hrabal's *Closely Observed Trains*. The author has not succeeded in this by no means easy task.

5. A significant role in sewing this patchwork story was played by the sediment of novels read in late childhood. The author no longer remembers which, but she has a feeling that they were largely American. Out of the sediment rises the outline of a poor but beautiful (inevitably auburn-haired) girl standing in front of a shop window and looking longingly at a costly, sumptuous dress. It seems to the author that in these novels everything revolved around the question of who would buy the dress for the poor but beautiful, auburn-haired girl, and when. The author well remembers the suspense. Because of her forgetfulness and the time that has elapsed, the author may be distorting the facts, but the image of the girl and her shop-window longings are still fresh!

6. The author has taken the 'material', the advice and technical terms, from a women's fashion magazine. If she fails to follow the sewing logic in full, it is because she fails to understand them completely. Yet she took an indescribable pleasure in reading, pronouncing and copying out unfamiliar words *gussets* and *basting* or curious collocations such as *French whipped seams*. Perhaps equally unfamiliar words such as *carburettor* or *dip-stick* would have a similar charm, but poetic intuition whispered into her authorial ear that, should she have used them instead, she would have ended up with quite a different kind of fiction.

7. The author gave Steffie Speck *Madame Bovary* to read simply because it is a brilliant novel. She leaves the other little semantic loops to her readers to make for themselves!

8. The author chose the character of a humble typist seeing love and happiness, because she was after the charm of a *romance*. She copied the romance remnants from a romantic (Swiss) novel, simply replacing the names Doris and Peter with Steffie and Fiddler. She wanted to bring her characters home. Had she let her imagination run free, who knows where they would have ended up. Perhaps in an *Alpine* novel, leaping over the mountain peaks, picking wild flowers and going in for lots of kissing – and lots of yodelling!

9. The author endeavoured to combine stitches of *romance* fiction, in which the female characters are forever searching, searching until they finally happyendingly find what they seek, and stitches of women's fiction, in which the female characters also search and search – but never find what they seek, or, if they do, only with great difficulty.

10. In her relentless stitching together of patches, the author opened up the possibility of tacking on yet another genre with a similar story line. Which *fairy tales* she has in mind, her readers will see for themselves!

11. The choice of the sewing device, given that this is 'women's' prose, is not intended as ironic. The author is fascinated by the profound significance of the skills in question. After all, did not Penelope and Scheherazade in a way represent just that?

12. The author set great store by this rather numbing rounding-off process. Not only does she wish to imitate the precision of the 'Instructions for Finishing the Garment' from the aforementioned fashion magazine, she also wishes to achieve the best possible *tracing* of her model. Incidentally, *tracing* is where the author sees the immediate future of literature.

13. The author has finally made it to the thirteenth point, which she needed because of women's need for everything to be orderly, symmetrical, or rather to the afore-mentioned number thirteen (the fateful number thirteen in the life of S. S.!). The author can now finally breathe a sigh of relief and

having earned the right, pick up Hrabal and read once again what happened to his Hrma!

C. H.

A LOVE STORY

' . . . I write in order to be loved.
I believe that is the writer's fundamental yearning.'
Gabriel García Márquez

saturday/sunday or in medias res
I met Bublik one Saturday in a café. Bublik's real name is not of
course Bublik. That's what I called him, because I like the sound of
the word 'bublik'. 'Bublik' is actually a Russian doughnut. Bublik –
round, brown, squashy – immediately struck me as eminently edible
(read: attractive!). Incidentally, every woman carries in her the idea
of her archetypal man. Mine was none other than Jesus Christ. Bublik
was a shorter, broader, chubbier, squashier version of him.

But, as appearance does not make the man, I fell in love with Bublik
a few minutes later, when he announced that 'modern literature was
dead'(!); that the urge to read it indicated a schizophrenic attitude to
life; that at the top of the world best-seller list were memoirs, detective
stories and pornography; that art in general was plunging headlong
into kitsch; that the British, testing a group of secondary-school
children had come to the depressing conclusion that the most intelligent
read strip cartoons, and serious literature was read by those on the
borderline of backwardness! What he said about British schoolchildren
was particularly upsetting.

I can even identify the precise second when I fell head over heels
in love with Bublik. It was during Bublik's historical announcement of
the death of literature. My heart missed a beat at that erotic 'uterrrrly
dead', something in me clicked, switched on and started sliding crazily
up – down, up – down (I always visualise my own excitement as a lift)

which is in fact further proof that love and death are eternally and indissolubly linked.

Bublik would never forgive me if he found out that it all began with one word. Men tend to think that women fall for them for such and such a reason, but women always fall for them for such and such a different reason.

And how did it all begin for Bublik? I'm not entirely sure.

how *did* it all begin for Bublik

I'm not bad-looking, I'm tall, a bit clumsy, but not without appeal, sweet, unsophisticated and reasonably faithful. But despite my obvious qualities I haven't yet found Mr Right. Somehow in the end it always fizzles out. I don't know how. I think my main handicap is my natural altruism. Altruism is the death of eroticism; eroticism is the prerequisite of love. After a while I become so perfect that a man can tell me everything: how it was the first time; about how it is altogether; about women and his legitimate, illegitimate and aborted children; about gastritis and the crown on his molar – right down to his plate which looks quite real! Erotic love can turn with lightning speed into brotherly love and then to nothing – because everyone has a brother.

Yes, Bublik will never forgive me this passage. It's too personal. And I must say I always find first-person narration exasperating myself: that insolent imposition of an infantile, tentative, intelligent, brutal, or whatever first-person narrator who is supposed to be somone other than the author. The hell he is! First-person writers impose their first-person narrators just so they can be uninterruptedly personal! ('No authorial digressions!' rages Bublik.)

Ah, with Bublik it all began so beautifully and so passionately! (Our hearts were joined by literature, which was moreover dead!)

Bublik was one of those privileged types who have granny's flat and mummy's allowance; who have no job and not even necessarily a degree; who are well-informed on every subject and talented in every way; who belong to what the dictionary would call the 'intelligentsia', but who despite everything, are somehow blocked on the road to complete self-realisation.

That's what I say now. I didn't think that then. I thought Bublik was infinitely intelligent.

On Sunday Bublik invited me to lunch in a restaurant. I would gladly immortalise the interior, but Bublik maintains that descriptions of interiors went out with realism. While Bublik studied the menu, I prattled on about my granny who once fell from the tenth floor of our high-rise building and survived. This is a story I always tell at first encounters. It's a kind of litmus-test of a person's sensitivity. Bublik slowly detached his gaze from the veal à la parisienne and fixed it on the lovely, if unfunctional, freckle on the left side of my face – which contributed to the rapid flow of those juices, or whatever they're called, that make me want to go all the way. Bublik turned back to the grilled beef in sour cream, and I carried on relentlessly.

Then I told Bublik about a dream I gravely suspect myself of having stolen from someone. This is what I dreamed. After a sudden, uncomfortable itching of the face, a strange and unbearable shifting of the skin, I ripped off my own face. I didn't know what to do with it. I was seized by a terrible fear, as though I had committed a crime. Surreptitiously I rolled it up into a little ball (pastry, chewing gum!), hastily thrust it into my mouth and swallowed it.

'Fantastic!' exclaimed Bublik enthusiastically. 'That's fantastic!'

I blushed. I had no idea what that 'fantastic' referred to. That's probably where it all began for Bublik.

the 'magic kiss' project

Bublik launched into a passionate speech about my undoubted literary sensibility, about how I must write (You must write, you must!!!), about how – with my sensibility – we (we!) would resurrect literature, that sleeping beauty. ('Think of those emancipated American girls who write whatever they want, without any inhibitions, while our passive, sentimental young ladies just lie around waiting for a prince! At last I've met a normal woman, a knight-woman!')*

After this passionate outburst, my hopes that I might nevertheless have found the man of my life melted like a snowball ('Avoid banal similes!' – shrieks Bublik) but, as I was already in love, I decided to

---

* As an intellectual, Bublik was concerned with all kinds of things, but his work of genius was a scientific typology of women in the contemporary world. According to Bublik's research, there were two conflicting models: the 'bird-woman' and the 'knight-woman'. The 'bird-woman' included types such as the 'dear little secretary', the 'sweet innocent in the madhouse', the 'nice ninny', etc., and the 'knight-woman' type such as Mother Courage, Joan of Arc, various highbrow blue-stocking types, etc. The first model devours men, the second is devoured by them.

keep my mouth shut and Bublik in the belief that no prince had ever crossed my mind. And then we would see – I thought.

I took Bublik's command ('You must, must, must write!') as erotic inducement, a kind of foreplay. In my childish impatience to reach the alluring reward as soon as possible, I reacted quickly and seductively tossed Bublik my first prose (erotic) proposal:

Hans Singer from Hamburg was fed up with the way his wife Lottie (194 lbs) treated him. He showed this in three very energetic acts: 1. he bit her dachshund Otto till it bled; 2. he wrenched the dog collar he had to wear at home off his (own) neck; 3. he looked for a lawyer and initiated divorce proceedings.

Recently in Rome a student was caught trying to enter a well-known theatre, carrying a 'suspect box'. The security boys ordered him to open the box. It was full of live fleas. The student confessed he had bred the fleas with the intention of letting them loose in the theatre 'to see the bourgeoisie scratch'. It was nothing new. The same thing had happened at a gala performance held to mark the two hundredth anniversary of La Scala.

A Chicago paper ran an interview with Xerxes Zzyzzx, the man whose name is the last in the Chicago telephone directory (about the problems he had in connection with his surname). Zzyzzx's life was not easy. For instance, he virtually couldn't sleep through a single night in peace, because in that city of a million there was always some drunk who would 'phone him just for a laugh. Still, he wouldn't change his name for the world. Says Zzyzzx: 'I get to meet some interesting women.'

Of course it was utterly stupid and careless of me: Bublik was an intellectual, so he read the same magazine I did, and the theft only made matters worse. The seductive tone vanished from his voice.

Then I thought a 'lazy' prose would be the easiest way to satisfy Bublik, prose that didn't want to be written, prose which would begin 'once upon a time' and go on in that vein, and end 'And that was that'. Prose of that ilk is like the charming acceleration of the narration in certain well-known stories. Immediately after leaving the house, Little Red Riding Hood falls into a well. Or was it her grandmother? I don't know. It doesn't matter. An inherent tendency to babble, to verbal torrents with sudden unmotivated interruptions, an engaging

'And that was the end of that.' – these were the mainstays of 'blah-blah prose', my next erotic proposal.

'What rubbish!' said Bublik angrily. 'A story-line! That's the only thing that can save fiction! There's been enough *de*struction! Let's go for *con*struction!'

'All right,' I agreed, and set before Bublik a web of strong plots, sudden growth abundance, proliferation of events – an ill-tempered kind of prose. There's no point in my repeating it all here.

'Noooo!' Bublik shouted, 'that's been done before!'

Next I proposed fantasy, the magic kiss of fantasy. Fantasy is an excellent way of neatly curtailing the whole process. You begin quite normally, for instance 'Once upon a time there was a little old woman' then: blah, blah, blah, and when you get bored, you turn the little old woman into . . . well, a bird, for instance. Then it doesn't occur to anyone to go prattling on about the little old granny's bird life, that is, the former little old granny's. I really like that sort of metamorphosis, coming from the archetypal subconscious as it does.

'Noooo!' Bublik pronounced in a terrible voice, and I realised that literature had been through that as well and my suggestion that frogs should turn into princesses was worthless. Hard as it was for me to face, I realised I would never dare turn a single little old granny into a bird, or even vice versa.

Everything Bublik said about bringing modern, but dead, literature back to life seemed to consist of prohibitions. Apart from the two I have mentioned (that a narrative must never end 'and that was that' and that I must never turn a little old woman into a bird), there were others.

I learned, for instance, that I must not use expressions such as 'get it, mate', 'that's the way the cookie crumbles', 'at the end of the day' and a whole bunch of others, because the relentless slangifying of literature had only contributed to its demise.

I also learned that my characters may not tell their story in the first person or say 'and the like', 'and so on'; that they must never wear jeans, because safari suits were now the rage, and that all real literature must, at least to a certain extent deal with eternity.

Prohibitions referring to the use of tractors, love in the haystack and other rural themes were entirely appropriate on Bublik's part. The last cow I had ever seen had been in an alphabet book under the letter 'c'.

The prohibition concerning current problems in our economy I found a little harder to take; I had some good trumps. One of them was my neighbour Francek the plumber who often mends my pipes free of charge ('No real-life documentation, please!' says Bublik angrily). For some reason my never-to-be character Francek really infuriated Bublik. 'The "ordinary man" type is nothing but nauseating flirtation with your audience, the hope that ordinary people all over the country will read you. Like Hell they will! In any case, I can't stand plumbers in literature. Plumbers belong in the yellow pages!'

This was followed by a long, unforgettable burst of verbal gunfire. 'And don't go thinking you can parody any individual or style. It's immoral to parody something that's long since kicked the bucket. Don't bring in Salinger or some forty-year-old fuming menopausally at everything around him or for that matter writer, teacher, footballer, actress or gynaecologist! And no comparisons of the sex act to motor-racing please! No Kafka, Borges or Márquez-style. No shopgirls or firemen! No fantasy or crime, no sex, no allegories, essays, mythologis-ing, philosophising, and most of all no fancy tricks, no, no, no, no, no, no . . . !'

Softly, fearfully, flickering my eyelashes, I asked Bublik, 'Then what *do* you want, Bublik?'

'Hyperrealism!' Bublik replied wearily.

'Hyperrealism?'

'It doesn't matter what it's called. I want ordinary urbanised lan-guage, the transcription of tedious, senseless everyday life down to the smallest detail. I want the tedium we live, I want the authenticity of tedium, its photographic reproduction. Understand?'

I didn't understand at all, so I touched Bublik's hand tenderly, but being tragically concerned about dead literature, he didn't notice. I sighed as a sign of my compassion and loyally matched my expression to his. We both looked so necrophilic that the waiter contemptuously removed our two virtually untouched portions of expensive fish.

'A bad day,' I said with a sigh again and gave the waiter a warm wink full of hope. The hope, of course, referred to the day when I would squeeze literature, that dead beauty, out of Bublik's heart and settle in comfortably myself.

and you call yourself a writer!
I went home, thinking feverishly about the content of my future stories.
I must write. I must, I must, I must! Oh, Bublik! The first thing that
occurred to me was our high-rise building.

You see, I live in a high-rise building (as we're into hyperrealism, I
should add: Block 16 Swallow Flats, tenth floor). I remembered that
from the very start (as I was moving in) I showed a creative attitude
to reality (the building) around me. As soon as we moved in, I realised
I wouldn't be leaving for the next ten years and resigned myself to my
new home-sweet-home as my destiny. I reinforced the home-sweet-
home idea with a whole series of literary comparisons. First the building reminded me of the giraffe in that painting of Dali's (the balconies
were the giraffe's drawers!), then of a giant candle, then of a phallus
(which is more or less de rigueur), then of a beehive (that came of its
own accord) – and so on and so forth.

When I got tired of thinking up things to compare it to, I moved on
to murders under the working title: The Simplest and Most Efficient
Way To Get Rid of Your Fellow-Residents. The possibilities ranged
from massacres in the lift to the same with rubbish bins. Although the
number of permutations was fairly restricted, I admit, it amused me
for a while.

And when I got sick of bloodthirsty murders, I moved on to interper-
sonal contacts. I talked to people in the lift like an idiot, called out
cheerfully to people over the balcony, tormented people with animated
questions, such as: 'Good morning, how are you, and you, fine, and
how are you, fine, and you . . .' I summarised the results of my efforts
in a list of the ten best methods of communication in the lift, on the
stairs (when the lift wasn't working) and over the balcony and practised
them until they ceased to have any effect.

Then I reconciled myself to hatred as a natural condition. A fifth
element. I realised that I hated the intimate relationships which
develop with metastatic speed in the communal beehive; that I hated
Sundays, when everyone opened their balcony doors and turned their
radios up full blast; that I hated housewives enthusiastically exchanging
recipes; that I hated types who kept titivating their Cortinas, their
Polos and their Sunnys; that I hated card-playing and insisting on
drinks in the local pub; that I hated morning coffee, gossip, other
people's dreams:

'Imagine, I dreamed about my little nephew, completely naked.

God, how stupid, with his little brown willie, turning into a vast pink dolphin with the same kind of willie. Maybe a little bigger. God, how stupid . . . !'
[Marta's dream, M-2]

What annoyed me most, perhaps, was the feeling that real life was going on somewhere in the centre of town. But Bublik was right. The high-rise does have its place in literature. It had its own crazy 'real life' as well. The constant urge to make creative sense of the life surrounding me would get the attention it deserved! Fiction! In my mind I constructed a filing system to store data for future stories. I was a writer now. I immediately thought of how M-2 (Marta, our next-door neighbour) would react when she heard.

'So you're a writer, are you?'

The frustrated old bag! Well, I'd just put her into a story. Let the fat cow read about herself! Fat Marta suddenly acquires wings (they sprout on Christmas Eve) and goes fluttering joyfully from balcony to balcony. Marta performs thrilling feats. Like a plane. We go out onto our balconies entranced, we throw her crumbs which she catches in her virtuoso flight. No, no not that! I've seen something similar in a cartoon.

Or why shouldn't Marta's flab puff up one day? Like dough. I can already see the possibility of a dramatic description. Marta starts to rise, her white flesh spilling over the balcony, the window sill, flowing into the flats like a flood. We flee away. Shrieking! Alarm. General panic. At the most dramatic moment I throw in a unit of jolly firemen. Fat Marta's fantastic rescue! That could be the title. No, no, not that! Too infantile.

But then, why should I write a story about Marta? Cows belong in cowsheds, not in literature. (Have I read something like that somewhere?)

I went on thinking, turning the basic facts about my neighbours over in my mind, and I decided I could write, say, about the poor musician from the ninth floor (M-9), an alcoholic, who comes home drunk every day, so his wife chases him out onto the balcony and locks the door behind him. The musician staggers about, humiliatingly exposed, as in a cage, and keeps repeating, 'Open the door, Elvira! Open the door, Elvira! Open the door, Elvira!' Then there's a pause full of anticipation, and a shriek, 'Elvira, you bloody bitch!' People go out onto their balconies, thrilled, expecting a performance. They listen carefully to the monotonous repetition of 'Open the door, Elvira!' suddenly interrupted by a graded outburst of fire: 'Elvira, you're the biggest bloody bitch in town, in Europe, in the world!' We all wait with bated breath for the appearance of Elvira, the biggest bloody bitch in the universe, but it never comes. Instead, they get the sound of breaking glass. It's always the same. From the bruises the poor musician tries clumsily to hide the next day, we conclude that Elvira, the biggest bloody bitch in town, is mercilessly crushing her husband's artistic spirit. It happens at least once a month, and it isn't exactly a cause for mirth, if you consider that glass for balcony doors costs an arm and a leg.

Or I could use the stupid man on the eighth floor (C-8) who keeps pestering me about matchboxes. The man collects matchboxes. Big deal! Nothing would have happened if they hadn't started selling a series featuring different breeds of dogs. Ever since the fatal little picture of the monkey dog appeared on the boxes, C-8 has not let up. It drove him so wild that he talked about it like the greatest discovery of his life: 'Just think, ha, ha, ha, I bought some matches yesterday, and there's a monkey dog on the box! Hee, hee, hee, a monkey dog! Can you imagine that, ho, ho, ho, – a monkey dog.' What a bore!

That lady-killer on the tenth floor, would be good too (L-10). Lady-killer, hell! A home-grown, superannuated lover boy. A pudgy shaggy stud with a moustache. With flashing eyes. At his age. Ugh! Still, I must admit, he's in good shape. He keeps bringing in those plump country girls (where does he find them?) and later, in the local pub, he tells me in muffled tones how much he enjoys his 'little girls' (the pig! Humbert Humbert!) how he always imagines they are big pink babies he must stroke, bath, feed – that seems to turn him on – and then he adds something about his erotic sensibility, but I'm not listening any more. I'm thinking. I see the shaggy, pudgy old goat, his face glowing, the sweat dripping from his brow, surrounded by chubby pink babies, he's force-feeding them from both ends. And they giggle and grow, grow pink and statuesque and wanton and fill up like balloons, they open their reddish, toothless mouths coquettishly, toss back the silky down on their bald heads seductively and grow and grow until they reach the ceiling and their inflated, silky bodies smother their unfortunate lover-father and they burst through the ceiling and, with a licentious cackle, fly up to the sky over the high-rise, over our town. But one comes back, the biggest, roundest, podgiest, and with a toothless, maternal smile draws her lover-father off with her, holding his shaggy hand tenderly. I hear an organ, I see him smiling and waving for the last time, as he ascends to heaven. Pretty powerful, don't you think?

I could describe the tenants who live in S-10, the flat opposite. They're decent people, home-grown, down-to-earth, only their son's a bit odd. He's a philosopher, a ne'er do well; he roams through Europe studying Buddhism. His parents are desperate: Papa suffers in silence, while Mama who has a somewhat healthier attitude to life's problems, shouts, 'Bugger your Budda, and bugger you! Do something, get married and have children like other people and not just Budda this and Budda that! . . . You silly bugger!' The son raises his conciliatory little Buddhist voice and says, 'It's the meaning of my life, Mother! Anyway, it's not Budda, but Bood-ha!' The mother is not impressed. She gives the kid a hearty slap and says, 'Booby, that's what it is! And you, too!'

I could take the tenants in the sixteenth T-16. The crazy student and his grandmother. The grandmother is a lively old lady of about eighty years and as many pounds. Picturesque. When she appears in the lift carrying enormous string bags with cauliflowers sticking out of them, all wrinkled face and obligatory smile, I imagine that one day the string bags will step into the lift by themselves and she will have turned into the cauliflower she so resembles.

Her crazy grandson mistreats her in the most perverse ways. For each holiday, for instance, grandmother and grandson are the first in the building to put out a flag. Grandson holds onto grandmother's legs, grandmother stiffens like a rod, then grandson leans over the balcony while grandmother inserts the pole. Once it nearly ended tragically: grandmother lost her balance and the astounding stiffness of her body left her. She nearly fell headlong. The boy did save her, though it was touch and go for a while.

After that she shrank even more. When the crazy boy gets drunk, he forces her to lie face down on the floor, her hands at the back of her neck, and he fires his grandfather's old pistol round her. The poor creature faints with terror, but does not expire. The next day we see her again, miraculously regenerated, with still bigger and finer cauliflowers in her string bags and the obligatory smile on her face. The crazy boy never says a word, though, occasionally in the lift, he shows a sudden desire to communicate by kicking a dog, if there happens to be one, or ripping the wallpaper with a knife.

The watchmaker (W-15) is interesting as well. After selling his house in the Old Town, he moved his workshop into the high-rise. Amazingly, the workshop has retained its patina. It would make a splendid description: a bald, dark-skinned, old man, dozens of clocks ticking, perfect peace and behind the counter a little black eyepiece which the watchmaker uses as though it were Destiny itself. Then, in a superior tone, like Destiny, in that perfect peace (with the clocks ticktocking) he announces, 'Something is wrong with the mechanism in your watch, madam!' Or something else, even more momentous, even more crammed full of meaning. Maybe I should marry the watchmaker W-15 off to the cauliflower queen?

But when all is said and done it is Fabian (F-3) who appeals to me most. Even the name is right. Old-fashioned. Fabian is my next-door neighbour on the left. No one knows anything about him. He has no friends, no one comes to visit him. I have tried several times placing a glass against the wall to try and hear something but there's never anything except a vague rustling; he must have been arranging his stupid shells. Fabian used to collect empty snail shells. He would go off on long walks and come back with a basket full of shells. We presumed that he was making decorative boxes (like the ones people make out of sea-shells), but we weren't even sure of that.

I notice that I think about Fabian in the past tense. As though he were part of a story. The ending would be the most effective section. I would start with the colour of his face: corpse-like, greyish-green, like patina invading an old picture. I would fill the story with an atmosphere of mystery. One day Fabian would disappear. We would search all over for him and find him in tall grass on the banks of the Sava. He would be dead. He would look like a fake fossil, his body would be covered with a heap of empty snail-shells. The dead casings would encroach on him like mildew, like feelers of moss, silence lapping out of empty shells, merging with the subdued breathing of grass. The sun would wriggle lazily through the brownish hollows of the shells, filling them for a moment, then going out. The whole pile of shells would seem to be crawling, the golden armour of the dead snail king was breathing, and all that would be breathing would be the earth, the grass, the silence. There would be dignity in Fabian's death.

And a quiet hint of horror. The bit about the heap of empty shells is good.

I can just imagine what Martha would say if I read her a story like that. 'And you call yourself a writer! Whatever next! You ought to be ashamed of yourself. Writing like that about a living person! A neighbour! Shame on you! You must be mad!'

Fool! I shall bury you in an even worse manner! I'll put you in a snake pit! No! I know! Dolphins! They'll screw you, Martha, a dolphin, a pink dolphin from your dream, with its little brown willie, will screw you, screw you, screw you till you die!

monday or home-grown Kafka

I ring Bublik's doorbell. I'm excited. I have a bundle in my bag – the short story I worked on far into the night, the product of all my nocturnal reflections on life without meaning in a high-rise. The story of Martin. Hyperrealistic. Symbolic. Grotesque.

In the morning I rushed off to the beauty parlour, where they wiped away all traces of my weighty reflections of the night before. I am fresh, bathed, made up. I long for love. I feel like a writer.

I fling myself tenderly round Bublik's neck. I look for his left cheek. He moves it away. I look for his right cheek. Ditto. I look for a hanger. Silently, significantly, I open my bag and with a holy expression hand Bublik – the first two crumpled pages, born in the torment of a sleepless night. We sit down. Bublik reads:

a long day dying

. . . Martin could never remember how he came to be shut in the jar. He had lost all sense of time. Martin was often overcome by sudden fear, a shudder of humiliation, a vague feeling of offence to his freedom: Martin in a gherkin jar, the biggest there is, mind you, but nonetheless – a jar. One gets used to anything with time and Martin reconciled himself to the jar as a fact of life. At first he tormented himself over the mystery of how he had arrived in the jar; his memory had let him down and he was in despair; then he decided it was all actually a hoax or an hallucination – though he could not move an inch and could quite clearly feel the cold glass and taste the sour liquid. He got used to the vinegar more easily than to his helpless immobility. Before long he had learned to move his right toe and kept repeating the same movements with childish delight, bending his toe backwards and forwards, knocking against the glass. But his toe swelled up from the constant contact and he decided to conserve his energy.

Martin considered escaping from the jar, but the situation was hopeless. He wondered if it wasn't a punishment for a murder, say, but he couldn't remember the motive, the connection, the route by which he had come to be in the jar. He couldn't remember any part of his life before the jar; he didn't know whether he was married, what he did for a living, what village or town he lived in and who the damned larder belonged to. Even the landscape he could observe through the glass failed to offer any clues. Rows of empty jars and dusty bottles. Sometimes the picture was a little brighter: when rays of sunlight came in from somewhere. Then he could watch the flies which had got inside the bottles and were leading their incomprehensible fly lives. The flies were a visible sign of life, sufficient reason to set Martin thinking. But Martin's thoughts remained immobile.

Martin pressed his head against something hard. It was probably the lid. He couldn't remember whether he was wearing a hat or not. And that troubled him.

Martin felt that he was going to die. He tried to think about death, to feel the despair that would have been normal, but in the end it all came down to an indifferent statement of fact. No clear concepts, no pain, nothing . . .

The decay, the intense smells, the damp and the mildew gave Martin a curious satisfaction. And then suddenly he had a clear picture of his brain. He could quite clearly see the lazy, green mildew oozing into the white pores of his brain, leaving behind flaky green layers.

Somewhere along the line Martin thought, Now, I think, I have completely died – and closed his eyes.

Bublik closed his eyes, and my two pages slid to the floor. I waited, trembling. Bublik said nothing for a long time and then, in a tone of deep disappointment, came out with, 'Dreadful! Simply dreadful. Where did you drag up that language? It sounds as though you'd translated it from the Chinese, for God's sake! A childish imitation of Kafka, 100 percent amateur. What I want is everyday life, the absurdity of life, not stinking symbolic gherkins!'

'But that is everyday life, Bublik!'

'And where do you see it, pray?'

'On the lid! It says "homegrown gherkins".'

This commentary infuriated Bublik even more and I went home crushed, regretting the expense of the beauty parlour all the way.

tuesday, or fear of flying

'Bublik,' I said softly, nestling comfortably into an armchair while Bublik brought in two glasses of dark red wine. 'Bublik, imagine a rented studio flat in a new building, with three young working girls living in it. Tania, Anita and Ruža.'

'Okay, so what?'

'I was just thinking that Tania, Anita and Ruža would be just the thing for your hyperrealism . . .'

'Oh that! I didn't mean . . . Anyway, what's so interesting about Tania, Anita and Ruža?'

'Emancipated women are screwing all over contemporary fiction and real life, but these typical girls of ours have preserved a dull, romantic, lower middle-class mentality. They gaze longingly from their window on the fifteenth floor, drinking slow coffees, playing patience, telling fortunes with dried beans and waiting for a prince on a white horse. Imagine the despair, the boredom, the preoccupation with love that simply has to come but doesn't.'

'So what do we do with them?' asked Bublik, evidently thinking of the plot.

'Nothing. That's the whole point. They've tried everything themselves. Tania, a typist, went to Greece this summer. A package tour. On credit. She came back tanned, happy, with a beautiful, expensive, three-tiered coat!'

'What do you mean, three-tiered?'

'With zips. Now you imagine the gushing girlish delight in the bachelor pad when the little typist Tania showed the girls her fur coat with the zips. The sirtaki thundered in the little flat, for a moment the whole of sun-filled Athens moved into it, and a young Athenian furrier in a brass-framed photograph. Tania, zip! Tania, zip, zip! Tania, ziiippp!'

'Where did Tania get the money for such an expensive coat?' Bublik asked.

It was the right question.

' "Where did you get the money for such an expensive coat, Tania?" asked the girls. Glowing, Tania showed them a slim engagement ring. Then her tiny hand closed in a fist of defiance to that cruel, malicious world. You'll show them Tania, zip! That's it, Tania, zip, zip! Two months later the young Athenian furrier arrived. He stayed for an hour or two, and left behind a bill for $5,000, kindly agreeing to let Tania pay it over six months.'

'Yes, but I still don't see . . .'

'There's nothing to see!' I cried with tears in my eyes. 'Nothing to see and no story. No story because there is no fate. No hand of fate will ever transform our poor Tania's life! The young Athenian furrier from the brass-framed photograph will never marry her! She'll wear her three-tiered fur coat for the rest of her life as her punishment! Incidentally, Tania was given a loan by her firm against half the value of the fur coat. For a video camera and a stereo.'

'A place in the sun! What about the other two?'

'Same thing. Anita is a nurse, Ruža a physiotherapist. They work all day and in the evening they watch the portable T.V. they bought together. And wait. They wait for a way out of the closed circle of their tedious daily life. They are obliged to wait together because they don't make enough to have separate flats.'

'And?' Bublik asked, sipping his dark red wine.

'One day Anita and Ruža realise they can't go on like that. They approach the whole thing in a positive way. They go to the hairdresser, buy some new clothes and go off to a dance organised by the soap factory. They're invited by an acquaintance.'

'Well, what happens?'

'Oh God! Nothing! I've been trying to tell you all evening. That evening they break out of their boring, barren, pointless circle and enter a new one – just as boring, barren and pointless.'

'I don't get it! Don't they meet anyone at the dance?'

'Yes. From that evening on, dozens of guys from the soap factory pass through the studio flat, but the girls still long for a brighter life. Nothing changes. A new emptiness, a new boredom settles into the flat: white crumpled beds, silence, despair and the sweetly malicious smell of thousands of tiny soap samples left behind as gifts . . .'

I spoke the last words sadly. There was a lump in my throat and Bublik hugged me tenderly. He stroked my shoulder distractedly, sipping his dark red wine, and I sobbed quietly. Our thoughts wrapped warmly round a fifteenth floor bachelor flat, lulling it, comforting it: things would get better, of course they would. Suddenly, Bublik and I saw three smiling birds flutter out of their concrete cage. Slowly, like a film played at slow speed, Tania took off the tiers of her beautiful, expensive fur coat: zip! one! zip! two! zip! threeee! Free! Then came

Anita and Ruža, stretching their necks gracefully, scattering soap samples over the high-rise building. The soaps rattled on the windows like rain, and Bublik and I wept, clinging to each other like children. I was happy, oh so happy. For a moment I thought that Bublik hadn't noticed the element of fantasy when the girls turned into birds and I found that very encouraging.

wednesday – freshtrendsday!
On Wednesday I burst into Bublik's flat straight from the market.

'I've got it, Bublik! I know what'll bring your dead literature back to life! I've found it!'

'What?' asked Bublik indifferently.

'Vitamins!' I said in a conspiratorial tone, dropping onto Bublik's head a dozen pages of beautiful, fresh descriptions of fruit and vegetables. There were descriptions of tender-green peas, round, firm radishes, fine heads of cabbage, cheerful, multi-coloured beans, pinkish-yellow melons, leeks, cauliflowers, apples . . .

'I think this is really it,' I jabbered exaltedly. 'A hyper-realistic, edible affirmation of life, vitality – irrepressible vitality! We'll bring in onions for fibre, garlic against sclerosis, carrots against carcinoma, lemons against scurvy, apples for the digestion. It's all so healthy, colourful, fresh, contemporary! We'll ship in some southern fruit, too. We have everything we need: ideas, myths, eroticism, plot, contemporary subject matter . . . !'

While I choked on the abundance of my ideas, my abrupt vitaminisation had no effect on Bublik.

'Absurd! Cabbage can't bring literature back to life! Don't be so childish! It's all so artificial and tedious! Tell me, why do memoirs make the top of best-seller lists the world over? Because readers want authenticity! They want blood, flesh and soul on a plate! Prose needs an infusion of authenticity. Got it?'

got it!
I told Bublik and rushed home. At home I threw myself down on the bed, feverishly rummaging through my own experiences, looking for a tasty little piece of blood, flesh and soul for Bublik. Ah, if I had only been Napoleon, Dostoyevsky or Rubirossa! Nothing but gossip from a young girl's life floated to the surface of my consciousness, all

house-bound, nothing boundless. I dragged sense over my experiences like a torn stocking: the toe of senselessness kept poking through.

The first thing that came to mind was a piquant erotic tale. Erotic stories are the rage now and they're all as alike as peas in a pod. In the end 'it' always happens. Though there's also the variation in which, in the end, 'it' doesn't happen. The obligatory formula is: man + woman = 'it'! A triangle is also possible, though that's more or less the same thing. The fantasy variant – man from outer space + woman from earth (or the other way round) – doesn't alter the essence of the thing. Even the number of perversions is limited, though stories with elements of perversion aren't all that common. That is, the way things are, perversion is not considered especially erotic. Then too the symbols are always the same. Animals, particularly horses, have a very stimulating effect in 'that' connection. Food is very closely connected to sex, but here too the possibilities are quickly exhausted. Levels of association: bananas in pornographically more advanced contexts, hot-dogs in average contexts, corn-cobs in rustic contexts. Typically writers of erotic stories draw on their own (limited) experience which means: familiar structure, well-defined thematic-metaphorical possibilities, room for deviation slight. From this – literary – perspective, sex is very boring.

Using these basic elements in Bublik's concept of authenticity as a point of departure, I simply wrote down what I had experienced in this erotic connection. And what I experienced was the third variant: 'It' happened at the end, without happening at all.

I met Arsen* (i.e., a man) at a friend's house. He appealed to me from the start, but not as a man (though, actually, I've never been quite sure what that means), and I doubt whether 'it' with him would ever have crossed a decent girl's mind. Arsen was a failed actor. He eked out a living from bit parts in co-productions where he inevitably played Italian soldiers. I even suspect that they weren't parts at all, that he was actually just an extra. Arsen was unusually tall and unusually thin (at the height of his career he played ghosts and prisoners-of-war in provincial theatres). If he was given Italian soldier parts, it must have been because of his face. He had black, shiny hair, a pale complexion and large (because he was so thin) grey-green eyes, framed in long, black eyelashes. Arsen's eyes corresponded to the common

* This would be roughly the beginning of *The first authentic story for Bublik,* entitled: EROTIC STORY.

conception of beautiful eyes. Arsen appealed to me and he realised it immediately. He was touchingly coquettish. With a mixture of the theatrical, demonic, martyred, and the circus, all at once. A rare contrast between the physically comic (a spider-man) and devilish, mephistophelian grimaces, which were at odds with his quite childish, melancholy face.

Arsen went in for artistic photography as well. He photographed women every which way. They all came out as beauties with spiritual expressions. He brought out all their best qualities: tenderness, gentleness, mystery. Not a trace of stupidity, crudity or caprice. I was a bit jealous of them. Arsen had a gift. He evidently looked favourably on women.

I had always hated being photographed. I had only a few essential photographs: passport, documents and photographs from childhood. Everyone has some kind of aversion. Mine was to being photographed. Like children to having their hair cut. And with childish stubbornness I resisted having my picture taken. I never wondered exactly why. After all, photographs are a trophy (you have your picture taken hand in hand with the Eiffel Tower!), confirmation that you actually exist. Besides, I'm not exactly ugly. I've got a good enough face for a decent photograph.

Arsen immediately began trying to persuade me to let him take my picture. To that end he showed me several beautiful women's portraits. He skilfully steered conversations in the direction of liberating me as a model. I was amused by his insistence. One afternoon I gave in. Without much ceremony. For fun. Arsen had a small, improvised studio in his flat. He developed his films in the bathroom.

While I sat calmly in an armchair, Bill first stood and looked at me, then rolled his eyes a bit, smirked, walked round the chair and finally said, 'You're an ugly woman actually. Your face doesn't express anything at all. You're as stiff as a mummy. It's going to be hard.'

His statement had no effect on me; I went on sitting calmly. Dear Arsen, he was so funny. We lit up. We talked. About pictures, in general. About Dorian Gray. About how everyone has his own face colour. We talked about face colours with a hint of cannibalism. It was an altogether rewarding theme. We went on to physical beauty. We agreed in conclusion that the essence of everything was pure vampirism. Arsen reinforced our conclusion with a living example: his old mother would only have young girls in her house, delighting in their healthy, pink colour. For my part, I said the older I got the more I looked at handsome men. Healthy gums, shiny teeth, glossy hair, complexion, skin . . . In passing I observed that Arsen's eyes not only corresponded to one's preconceptions of beautiful eyes, they actually were beautiful. Arsen had little white teeth and healthy gums.

We lit up again. Arsen returned to the offensive (with strategy of surprise) and announced that he considered me a cheerful masochist.

As he said so he watched my every movement. I took his remark as a continuation of the therapy. There were some little pegs for photographs on the table. Arsen grabbed one and out of the blue began pinching me. I armed myself with a peg as well. We were overcome by hysterical gaiety. We pinched each other. I know it was part of his technique but I must admit I found it highly entertaining. Arsen was enjoying it. He giggled softly, squeakily, reminding me of an old man who liked being tickled.

Arsen had his equipment ready. He took a few quick pictures. Trial runs. I blushed. Arsen watched me a bit ironically, then a bit tenderly, and a feeling of warmth spread slowly but surely up to my head. I sensed I was losing control. That ironic gaze disturbed me. I was annoyed by the fact that he could see the expression on my face and I could not. He was evidently excited. His glanced caressed me strangely.

'Listen, you need some kind of provocation. A shock. Only shock can provoke a new look on a face. Relax. You're in an inferior position here. I can do whatever I like with you. I can make you funny. Even beautiful!'

His voice was different. There was something very erotic in that. He directed his shameless (nothing if not shameless) gaze at me and undressed me with every new squeeze of the shutter release. I was getting more and more excited. It was all perfectly clear, I told myself that it was all part of the technique, that he wanted to draw new facial expressions out of me, it was all for the photographs and nothing more. Arsen was nothing but an amusing photographer, a clown. It didn't help. I was excited.

Arsen was aware of my excitement. He came up to me and ordered me to put on an old Japanese kimono, probably a stolen theatrical costume. I undressed by the mirror and hated my flushed face. Arsen stood behind me, whispering, 'You don't like being humiliated, dependent on a damned camera. But at the same time you find it exciting. Accept it, relax, you'll see, you'll enjoy it!'

Then he suddenly ripped off the kimono and started mercilessly clicking the camera. I hid my face like a trapped animal. 'Hold out your arms, that's it, turn round, now, look at me, bend your head, that's it, throw your head back, look at meeee!'

The camera clicked more and more crazily. 'Move, that's it, no, no, not yet, relax, there, that's good, you see how easy it is, there, turn round, oh, look at me, there, is that good . . . oh!'

Arsen took pictures excitedly, from the floor, from the bed, from various angles and distances. Things grew more and more passionate, and just as I reached the peak of my excitement, the camera clicked one last time – loudly and long. I collapsed into the armchair and looked over at Arsen, breathing heavily. He was spread out on the bed, his arms outstretched and head thrown back. The camera lay abandoned in – just – that place. There was silence, only the sound of our ever calmer breathing . . .

Arsen got up and went to the bathroom.

'I'm going to develop the film.'

I heard the sound of running water. I got dressed quickly and quietly left the flat.

The next day I phoned Arsen and in the trembling tone in which uncertain lovers ask men the next morning: 'What will you think of me now?', I asked, 'How did the pictures turn out?'

'The film was bad. We'll try again, sometime. Don't be angry. Give me a call.'

His tone was exactly the same as after a sudden, first, and usually last, night between a man and a woman. I put down the receiver dejectedly. I didn't phone him. We didn't take any more pictures. In a way I was glad the film hadn't come out: my little adventure was guaranteed discretion.

The second authentic story for Bublik, entitled:

the unforgettable lunch at 'Millie's'

Vanja said that after we finished the job we would go to lunch at 'Millie's'. I reminded him of his promise when the time came, and relaxed and hungry, we hurried to the restaurant.

It was a winter afternoon, a sunny day, the sea was utterly calm. Everything was just as one imagines the sea in winter: a few houses as backdrops, boats as props, motionless old men by the shore like petrified birds.

At the entrance to the restaurant there was a blue box with the inscription: 'If you want to know what is most valued in our restaurant, lift this lid!' I lifted the lid. Underneath was a mirror with IT IS YOU, DEAR GUESTS! written on it.

Delighted by the welcome, we went in and chose a table in the corner. As Vanja said, that was the best strategic position. I lit a cigarette. An accumulation of kitsch bombarded us from the half-darkness. We couldn't sort it out, so Vanja suggested we go over it slowly, bit by bit. We made a list: an old piano, nets hanging from the ceiling, huge shell decorations, an old dirty-pink record-player, murals, a mosaic on the counter with a Chino-Japanese motif, dark-red curtains, amphorae, dried flowers, two fish tanks, souvenirs from China . . .

Soon a waitress with a starched bust came over to us with a menu. I sensed a gourmet meal in the offing and said so to Vanja. He started posturing. ' "Millie's" was only known to true gourmets,' he said. Then we embarked on a dialogue à la Hemingway and finally ordered – he turtle, I my favourite fish (better safe than sorry!). And wine, of course.

'Millie's' became more and more agreeable. The wine and the cheery heap of kitsch warmed us. Vanja's eye twitched more and more often. It was dark and oddly rimmed with red. Conjunctivitis. Chronic, added Vanja. We let that go and launched gaily into a conversation about food. The topic was appealing and suited the atmosphere. Vanja liked tripe. His unpleasantly red-rimmed eyes twitched again. He liked scampi because they're soft. And custard and aspic and jellies, and all soft, moist and if possible pink things. Vanja's red-black eyes, his sensual mouth and, for good measure, his moustache – all jiggled.

The food we had ordered arrived. Vanja's turtle was really green. My fish looked pathetically anaemic beside it. The restaurant got darker and darker. The waitress lit Indian joss-sticks. The landlord himself appeared from somewhere. Yellowish, slant-eyed. He went perfectly with Vanja's turtle, as did my fish with the waitress's starched bust.

While we ate, we talked about the monstrous methods used to kill the poor turtles. After being speared and decapitated, they were turned into a dish by the name of 'Long Life' like this one of Vanja's. I remembered the story of how live monkeys were served in Chinese restaurants. First, a small round table with a hole in the middle was placed over the poor monkey's head, then the head was cut off in front of the guests. Apparently the monkey's brain is eaten on the spot.

This story put Vanja and me into a kind of Chinese mood. The wine was excellent, we were warm, and we really did feel like 'dear guests'. The starch-busted waitress kept flashing us smiles. We concluded that they were aggressively broad. The giant shells on the piano and the ceiling grew more and more shameless about displaying their pink insides, and as the music grew louder we laughed increasingly loudly, and Vanja kept 'accidentally' touching my hand. I didn't object; it was nice. Then Vanja excused himself to go and wash his hands. Meanwhile I ordered coffee, which he doesn't drink in any case.

As I sat there smoking, I glanced over at the neighbouring table. A pleasant-looking married couple with a little girl. The child had a mask on her face, and mum and dad were evidently in a good mood. While they were ordering, the girl got bored. She sat down at the piano, touched the keys and turned in my direction for a moment. She took off her mask, she was sweet, she looked like a little Chinese girl.

Vanja was gone a long time. I measured the time by the married couple. Aperitif, soup . . . I ordered another coffee. The waitress smiled. Her smile really was terribly broad. The couple were also looking mockingly in the direction of my table. I noticed the waitress and the landlord whispering something, then looking at me significantly.

Vanja was gone a very long time. I went to the toilet; he wasn't there. Behind the curtain was the kitchen, I glanced in for a moment – he wasn't there either. I sat down at my table and lit a new cigarette. The yellowish, slant-eyed landlord followed my movements impertinently. He watched me brazenly, persistently. I blushed, I was uncomfortable; I sat down at the opposite table facing the wall. There. Now I wouldn't have to look at anyone. I would wait calmly for Vanja. Everything was all right.

I took out my powder compact. It was impolite, I knew, so I leaned the little mirror against the top of my bag so as not to be seen. I looked at myself. The make-up was all right, the only problem was that my face was slightly flushed, but that was the wine. I looked at myself. The starched waitress with the broad smile suddenly leapt into the mirror. I saw her approach the couple's table, and her bust, her bust was bare! Unbelievable! I turned round. The waitress was fully clothed, standing by the couple's table. What was wrong with me? And where was Vanja? I turned round and looked in the powder compact mirror again. She was naked.

Suddenly they brought over a little table with a hole in the middle. In the centre was Vanja's head! Underneath, his legs twisted awkwardly round the legs of the table. He rolled his red-rimmed eyes in despair. Meanwhile the naked waitress was fiddling with his head! At one point his head fell into the hollow between her breasts. The little Chinese girl ran excitedly round the table and Vanja's head, garnished for the moment with breasts. The little minx! I saw, Vanja was helpless, following the child with a frightened look. Now the landlord was back! With music-hall exaggeration the naked waitress handed him white gloves and a long knife! The couple were licking their lips! It was all quite clear! IT IS YOU, DEAR GUESTS! The glint of the knife in the mirror and nothing else! I didn't see anything else!

I turned my head, frantic. The married couple were calmly finishing their turtles. With trembling hands I lit a cigarette. And suddenly there was Vanja! Terribly pale, he sat down without a word. Then we stood up and left the restaurant in silence. Vanja and I left the coast that evening. Not that we had to. We didn't mention our lunch at 'Millie's' on the train home, or the most important part of it – Vanja's long absence. Vanja was silent, cold and pale the whole time.

Later, in town, Vanja and I saw each other only in passing and greeted each other silently, with a nod. I shall never be able to explain exactly what happened at 'Millie's'. I only know that we shared a sudden, profound sense of horror. That was all I knew for certain.

Third authentic story for Bublik entitled:

two white beans

The morning is the best part of the day. That's when the soul floats. It's morning and my soul is floating. Through the open balcony door I see sun. And part of a landscape with cranes. But I consciously ignore that detail. On the table lies Henri Michaux; in me lies the sediment of last night's reading.

I switch on the record player, put on a record. Lute. Sixteenth century. The record rasps (it's Russian, Russian records are cheaper), but I consciously ignore that detail too. My soul floats through undefined regions. It's nice. Through the balcony door come sounds that fall on my soul like drops of water on hot sand. We feel good, me and my soul. I look through my eyelashes. Objects and colours lengthen. It's nice. My soul is floating.

Mother comes into the room. She sits down. She's smoking. I take the last cigarette out of the packet and light it as well. Silently as a shadow, my soul withdraws. I feel weak, limp.

'Did you know Seka had a breast removed?' Mother asks.

'Which breast?' I ask wearily.

'The left.'

'Which Seka?'

'Which Seka! You know Goran and Seka, for goodness' sake!'

I know, I reply. The new day tumbles onto me. (Have I read that somewhere? Something like 'Onto the poet tumbles the new day . . .')

'What about the right one?' I ask.

'What about the right what?'

'What about Seka's right breast?'

The new day tumbles onto the poet. You ought to be ashamed of yourself! You're heartless! You have no interest in other people! You, you, you, nothing but you! You're so selfish! Look at you, lying about, and it's ten o'clock already! Shame on you!

I pull the covers up over me. My soul has disappeared. The music is getting on my nerves. I turn off the Suite for Lute: Pavane and Gaillarde. So there!

I like buses. A bus is a large egg. Protection. Travelling through glass. A safari. Tired people. I photograph their faces. Click! Click! They're all the same. Beside me is a woman with a huge covered basket. Suddenly a chirp emerges from the basket. Odd. I don't turn. It's not polite. I concentrate my gaze on the bridge. I like the moment when the bus crosses the river. When the river crosses the bridge. When the bus crosses the river and the bridge. Transition. Like a new day, a promise. Another chirp! I turn. Everyone turns. The chirp in the basket senses our gaze. It gets louder. People start giggling. The woman with the chirp maintains a dignified expression. Chirp! Grins. Last stop. The situation dilutes. Pity. God, how isolated people are!

I take the number two bus and float through the town. I'll have coffee at Melita's. Because my blood pressure is low? Because it's morning? No, damn it, because I haven't had any! Because it makes sense! Sennnssse!

I ring the bell. Melita opens the door. We sit down in the kitchen. It's the most comfortable place. Her mother's at the market. (You know the old lady's got a thing about money. She always goes to market herself. She thinks I spend too much.)

The sun streams in over the balcony, etherealising the still life on the table: dirty coffee cups, the leftovers . . . Miki's in his cage. Chirp! I synchronise Miki's chirping with the sunlit picture on the table. The crusty crumbs (lit from within like little lamps . . .) chirp, the coffee cups chirp, the cutlery chirps. Oh, what a beautiful morning!

Melita puts the coffee on. She talks. I switch the sound off. I see her pale, thin face; I see her mouth slowly stretch into a beak. Melita chirps soundlessly. I switch her on for a moment. 'Hey, I went to a disco last night. What a bunch of deadbeats! Really!'

I turn off the sound. I look at Melita, a thin, frightened canary. I watch her beak open and shut unconvincingly. I take in the black rings under her eyes, the dried traces of crusted make-up (she forgot to clean her face before she went to bed). Twenty-eight-years-old. I take in the tiny lines round her eyes – there they are, sneaking up slowly but surely. Advancing. I take in the burst capillaries – there, on the left side of her nose. Teeth yellowed with smoking. A crown stands out, treacherously grey. A molar, I realise. Her thigh peeps through her housecoat. Celulitis. Slow but sure. As I look at you, my obsolete friend I wonder whether you are going to stay trapped in this kitchen with the canary and dirty coffee cups multiplying on and on, as in a fairy story, until you suffocate . . . Phoney! I'm so sentimental! I switch on the sound.

'So how's your mother?'

'Fine. Did you know Seka's had a breast removed?'

'Which Seka?'

'The right,' I don't know why I lie.

'Which Seka?'

'A friend of mother's.'

'Well, what can you do!' Melita sighs, pouring the coffee.

We drink our coffee. We smoke. Inez had a baby, but she's not well. Her Damir's fooling around, he's got a woman. No! Yes. He's a real swine. Yes. Especially as she's just had a baby. Vlasta didn't get that job. How come? They took her for a ride. It was rigged. They gave it to someone else. She was wild. You know how long she's been qualified, and no job. Oh,

and Saša's got a new chick. Who? The one who used to go out with Miki.
Which Miki? You know. The one who was in the first year. Oh. The fool.
She's frigid. How do you know? Miki told me. He's lying, the bastard. How
can you tell? Don't give me that sexological crap. I've found a part-time job.
When? Yesterday. I met Pera. Which Pera? You know, the guy with the red
hair. Oh. I can choose my own tours. Not bad. And you know Pierre's writing
a novel. Which Pierre? The one in television. So what? So nothing. It's going
to shake the world, his novel. Like hell it will! You never know. There was
an old dear in the bus just now with a basket. She had something in the
basket that kept chirping the whole time. You're making it up. I am not. I
know you, you always exaggerate. You're thirty, old girl, and still silly. Hey,
what day is it? The twenty-seventh. Day, not date. Friday. Great, I'll throw
beans for you.

I watch Melita taking white beans out of a cup with her long fingers. She
casts a significant glance at me. Friday. The beans chirp among the cups,
crumbs, cutlery. Somewhere (I can't define where) my soul is troubled.

'Now watch. Seven. That's very good. A letter and good news. No, I'm
wrong. Just a letter. Strange, who could have written to you? And a meeting.
A man on the horizon! And soon! You're going to hook someone, old girl!
See! See those two beans coming together?'

I look at the two white beans. They're coming together. A strange, round
coming together. The Cosmos! Planets (upturned cups, crumbs, cutlery) and
two small white beans.

'It's for the whole week. Don't worry, it's fine. That damned thirteen
rarely comes out. Seven is the norm. No big deal. Get it?'

Two round, white beans. I switch Melita off and switch on the sixteenth
century music. Suite for Lute: Pavane and Gaillarde. I switch on a picture
of outer space. Dark blue, thousands of stars, emptiness. Pure meaning.
Eternity. And off in the distance I see a white light, two little beans,
orbiting . . .

I don't switch Melita on any more. I leave her at the door, fixed forever
as in a yellowing old photograph. Through the yellowish mist I can just
make out her effort to take off, her face elongating into a beak. Is she going
to flutter away?

Two little white beans! I turn towards the Square. Faces slide past me. In
the ocean of faces rolling towards me like white beans I see only one. Coming
together. The shop-windows slide by: I slide too. My soul flutters in me. My
soul and I are on our way. I hold it on a thin, silken thread fluttering madly
above my head. My soul – a white halo!

Well, what do you know! Levi! Good old romantic Levi! Who do I see
but Levi. It's been ten years since our last meeting in his little room with
Bach and Bach. Ten years. Levi is smiling; I smile too. Levi, Levi . . . !

Levi and I walk along together. My soul has temporarily left me. I take in his grey sideburns. How are you? Fine. And you. Fine. The senseless words fly. Levi, Levi! We cross the Square and go into the City Café. What'll you have? Coffee. And you? Coffee. I smile at Levi. Ten years. I ask. He answers. I ask. He answers. Then he answers without me asking.

He's changed jobs. (You know, where I was before wasn't anything to write home about. The senile old fools!) But where he is now is okay. The money's not bad. How much? 12000. Honestly? Average. He's built a house. A nice one. He's married too. He's got a little girl. His wife? A wife like any other. What makes you interested in my wife, honey? ('Honey'? Imagine! Honey.) He's always busy, he never has time. The house devours all his money. A bottomless pit. Work, meetings . . . a madhouse. But he's stuck there. The only thing he cares about is sex. He has no time for anything else. He's realistic now. He has a crazy little chick. (A crazy little chick. Terrific in bed. Only always so cheery.) Then he's got an intellectual. Better, but just as crazy. (You know what she says to me? She says, I'll announce that I'm dead and then you screw me. Isn't that wild!) He'd like to try a group session. He's almost got it together. For the moment they just watch blue videos. (That's my only relaxation, believe me, honey! I'm a realist now. A REALIST!) Why shouldn't he? And the birds are wild. The ones without degrees are best. But not from his firm. A matter of discretion. Anyone else is fair game. Sweet young secretaries. They screw like crazy. (Get the picture? Hey, honey, why do we meet once in a hundred years? Let's have dinner some time, okay? Look, here's my phone number. Give me a ring, okay?)

I could feel my head burning, my soul panting, parched and tormented, melting in me like a snowball. And then I grab Levi by the scruff of the neck (it suddenly goes red; I've never liked the way Levi's neck goes red) and see a comic grimace of submission round his lips (the swine, he's anticipating pleasure) I grasp him more firmly and shove his face into his coffee cup. He squirms helplessly. There is horror in his tiny eyes (they've always been pig-like, actually). The mixture of fear and pleading annoys me. I grab him by a thin, grey tuft of hair and shove his face in over and over. That's for honey, that's for the chicks, that's for your wife, that's for my soul, not yours, bastard, mine, and for *realism*!

I look at the bottom of the cup. First I see bubbles, then irregular little black circles, and then – nothing more! And I imagine Levi lying on the bottom like a coiled-up slug with a grimace of lust and horror on his face. Levi's white body in the thick black dregs. Like a shelled prawn. Good.

I pay for the two coffees and go out. I cross the square. I think tenderly of my soul and make my way lazily towards the main street. The square is bathed in sunlight. I walk slowly as in a dream (I see myself as a giraffe in slow motion). I turn down the sound: I feel I'm walking through cotton wool. Beside me floats a café. I go in. I order a coffee. I stand by the window. A flash in the mirror. My mother's face. The same grimace. The same two wrinkles, steadily advancing, the same way of putting a cigarette in the mouth. It's me. Time has passed through me.

Through the glass I see Miša (Which Miša? Danja's. Oh.). I smirk seductively, purse my lips, bare my white teeth. Miša is disconcerted. He presses his nose to the glass. Flirtatiously. I call him. He nods. Come in! Quick, my darling, quick! Another coffee, please! How are you? (Coffee. Sugar. Spoon. Kiss. Kiss.) Fine. And you? Fine.

Thank goodness it's beginning, I think, smirking as I stir my coffee, with a cryptic expression on my face.

authenticity or a knife in the back

Bublik read my stories carefully. I had no doubt that he would understand what I meant to say. And I meant to say something about:
a) the tragic impossibility of love (as such);
b) the fantastic dimension of reality and the realism of the fantastic;
c) the disastrous effect of the everyday on the human soul.

Reacting from a position of authenticity, Bublik solemnly asked me three fundamental questions:
a) Who is Arsen? (Who's that fool?)
b) Who is Vanja? (Where did you find that idiot?)
c) Who is Levi? (Who's that cretin?)

a live model

I didn't answer Bublik's questions, but my crazy lift began operating. Questions are a good sign. Bublik governed my soul completely. I looked at him with a moist, pleading gaze, full of doe-like yearning. Then Bublik took advantage of the moment to say something that made me tremble. 'Listen, maybe we ought to have a real live character as a model?'

Behind Bublik's idea lay something terrible, unknown; his eyes shone with a mysterious, vampire-like gleam. In my struggle to win over Bublik I was prepared to do anything. I would do this too. This was my last trump! A live character! I was gripped by fear, as one about to commit a premeditated murder.

Bublik hugged me tenderly and I sank into the demonic darkness of his eyes, lost in the warm wool of his hair, his beard. Oh Bublik,

Bublik. Then, just as tenderly, Bublik pushed me away from him, and I set off home dejectedly again.

Irena's stories

Irena was my best friend. According to Bublik's typology, Irena was somewhere between a bird-woman and a knight-woman. She had a carnal attitude to the world. Irena sniffed the world, handled it, licked it. For Irena the world was a kind of marvellous jelly, a trembling aspic out of which she drew tastes according to need. Irena experienced her men as exotic animals, and she herself was an eel, a seal, a jelly-fish, an amoeba.

For me, Irena was a kind of eternal female, a female mythical beast.

I sat down and wrote three stories about Irena. The first was my fantasy on the theme of the eternal female, the other two – experiences of Irena's which she liked to tell me over long, female coffees.

In the evening I took a taxi, went to Bublik's flat and thrust a thick envelope into Bublik's letter-box. Then I went back home, 'phoned him and told him I'd call back in an hour or two.

Bublik was reading my stories. I was with him in my thoughts, stroking his hair longingly.

Irena: a charming portrait
or the birth of the same out of a coffee cup

Irena says: I never drink coffee with cream. There's something disgusting about it. I know an old lady who's been going to the same restaurant at the same time for years, drinking coffee with cream. For years. That's what Irena said. Irena's wonderful.

Irena says: The whole sea was imprisoned in a labyrinth of dark-red bricks. I heard it splashing helplessly. It was captured! That's what Irena said. Irena's wonderful.

We were walking in town. It was summer and very late. A thin jet of water gleamed on the pavement. A drunken woman was urinating in her sleep. I was so frightened. That's what Irena said. I was so frightened. Irena's wonderful.

I like my fingers best. The fact that I can touch things. Fruit. The rind of an orange. It's so bumpy and smooth! And the soft skin behind his ear. That's what Irena said. Irena's wonderful.

Irena says: When potatoes get old, they shrink and their skin shrivels. Then those amazing dirty-pink shoots grow out of them. They're a wonderful colour. I'll make myself a dress in dirty-pink. That's what Irena said. Dirty-pink. Irena's wonderful.

And a nightdress covered with thousands of little zebras. That's what Irena said. Thousands of little zebras. Irena's wonderful.

Then a taxi-driver told me about an exciting experience he had had with a strange woman. She had let him put the cherries from her cherry brandy on her and he did, and one after the other the cherries rolled over the white sheet. That's what Irena said. Over the white sheet. Irena's wonderful.

Irena says: I'm very narrow. The only thing I can give birth to is a slug. I'm sure of it. I'll give birth to a slug. Or a cuttle fish. That's what Irena said. A slug or a cuttle fish. Irena's wonderful.

Suddenly the sea dried up. Something had drunk it. There were only two little puddles of sea left and a silt of pink worms. It seethed, smooth and gelatinous, and then up rose a red-haired woman with heavy make-up, wearing a circus costume, riding in a carriage drawn by vast sand-coloured crabs. That's what Irena said. Vast sand-coloured crabs. Irena's wonderful.

Irena says: I'm always surprised when I see people eating – shoving food into a hole. How senseless! That's what Irena said. How senseless. Irena's wonderful.

Suddenly little grasses started sprouting in me – little green snakes. I could feel them wriggling. It was nice. It tickled. That's what Irena said. It was nice. It tickled. Irena's wonderful.

I don't like her, because she's dark and greasy. She's always talking about food. She screws non-stop for days on end. She's got something dirty under her skin. That's what Irena said. Something dirty under her skin. Irena's wonderful.

Then he let me float down the river and I floated for a long, long time. Then I got caught on something and stopped. It was a child with an old man's face. Dead, with living eyes. I don't remember anything else because a hand dragged me to the bottom. I was quite calm. Perhaps I was amused by the little bubbles rising to the surface, but I'm not sure about that detail. That's what Irena said. I'm not sure. Irena's wonderful.

Irena says: I have always had pocket-sized, stunted men around me . . . I do so like nice skin! And I'd like someone like St Sebastian in those little satin pants of his. You know. That's what Irena said. You know. Irena's wonderful.

Then I'd like to be a seal, smooth and wet. I'd like everything, all the dirt, to slide down me like water. That's what Irena said. Like water. Irena's wonderful.

And I'd put on a white hat with lots of fruit on it. I'd walk through town, flirting with the prettiest dresses in the shop-windows. That's what Irena said. Flirting with the prettiest dresses in the shop-windows. Irena's wonderful.

Irena says: Once I dreamed of a church. It was dark and high. There were shoals of glistening piranhas swimming under the dark arches. A flock of white doves fluttered up from somewhere. The piranhas snapped up the doves with lightning speed. I stood there with white dove skeletons falling slowly on to me. It was quiet. Like when it's snowing. That's what Irena said. Like when it's snowing. Irena's wonderful.

Irena says: I don't like coffee dregs. Maybe because of that old lady. And I don't like days like today when the sky hangs on the town like a rag. Days like this are the death of me. They smoke me up like a cigarette.

There she is: long and white, born out of a coffee cup, gills below the neck, narrow and naked, a cuttle fish between her legs, in the dark space of a church. I see a heap of brittle dove bones pouring soundlessly over her like snow, while she opens her mouth and whispers; and that's that . . . Or perhaps something else. Who knows. The rest is bubbles.

the afternoon of a peahen

She really looked forward to the afternoon; she was glad her husband was at work, she'd take the afternoon for herself, just for herself, though she didn't yet know where she'd go, maybe to the cinema, or round the shops. Two or three grimaces in front of the mirror make very good exercises; pulling faces is recommended by beauticians, though it was more a preventative measure: she has virtually no wrinkles, just two little tiny ones, under the eyes. She put shadow on her eyelids, green – went well with her green eyes – then a little powder on the bags under her eyes; she had been getting bags lately, which wasn't good, though it gave her face an aura of experience. Everything was fine, in fact, even her bust was nice and firm, though that was usually the first thing to start sagging. That and the skin on the neck. The skin on the neck showed your age first.

Out in the street she felt how wonderful it was to have a free afternoon, to walk through the town, look at the shop-windows, peer at things, touch them. That's what she liked best. Touching things. Even if it wasn't good manners. Then she went into a café and ordered a coffee, it was great to be drinking coffee, watching the people going by, smoking and thinking about all kinds of things. Nothing in particular. And then she saw him. Through the glass. He noticed her too, he came over to her at once, his lips stretched into a kind of half-ironic smile, the kind of grin that people with no confidence use to protect themselves – she knew it well, knew it from experience. She thought how terribly old he'd become and how good it was she'd never agreed to a more serious relationship with him; if she had, who knows, they could have ended up married and now she'd have an old husband; you can never predict this business of a person suddenly ageing. But now they began flirting in a mechanical sort of way, a conditioned reflex, an obligation to the past. They talked about nothing in particular and she was a bit surprised he didn't ask her anything more serious, where she was working, for instance, whether she was married and the like. And since he didn't ask her, she didn't ask him. Maybe it was better like that, with old acquaintances who didn't mean anything to you any more.

He invited her to a cake shop and she was thrilled, what a lovely idea, she adored going to cake shops, they were so romantic and sweet, and so nice and small and white and full of sticky, sugary smells and then the rows of multi-coloured, quivering, gelatinous sweets, garnished with the eyes of the little assistants behind the glass counter. She ordered a lot of cakes and sweets and she liked that too, it felt youthful, to hell with her waistline, she glanced at herself in the mirror, her mouth full of white cream, and she laughed and it was lovely that they were laughing together for no reason and that they found these sweets so entertaining. Then she wondered whether it was good, after five whole years, not to ask a person about some basic things like whether he was married or not, but she was overcome by a sense of dull, sweet pleasure and she desisted, and maybe it was just as well.

When they came out of the cake shop, she thought of the zoo, it would be nice if he invited her to the zoo, it would fit in with their romantic, youthful flirtation, and she would enjoy it; she hadn't been to the zoo for years, it was a real shame; those animals were so nice, especially the tiger, so erotic, though she didn't quite know why.

She knew that he was going to suggest a drink now and so he did. They went on having a fine time: he told jokes, she had to laugh, and only occasionally noticed that she was laughing too loudly, shrilly, it sounded hysterical, he would think she felt threatened, that's what men always thought if a woman laughed too loudly, so she lowered her tone a bit and that was better.

The martini was already taking effect, and they served it nicely: with an olive; the olive looked good with the yellowish martini. She was certain he would invite her to his place for coffee, but not until he'd noticed she was flushed and that's how it was, after the second martini.

Perhaps she'd enjoy seeing where he lived, she'd never been to his place, they had only been acquaintances after all, with a slight tinge of flirtation, true, but nothing more. She had been too young then. She had never liked him all that much, but now she knew she would go, she was surprised at herself, she didn't feel like going, she could have refused, but she went.

The flat was dark, cold, filled with old, dusty furniture; no one had dusted it for ages. The shelves were crammed with ugly white china figurines and she asked him where they came from. He said his parents had had a china factory before the war, he'd been left with that rubbish, what could he do with it, it might as well stay.

They sat down on the bed, and he immediately began fumbling with her clothes. She felt quite indifferent, but she let him, without knowing why. Her skin felt sticky from the sweets they had eaten. What disgusted her most was his big, slimy tongue. She remained indifferent the whole time, concentrating on the rows of white china figurines. They seemed to be shaking and smiling insolent, sugary smiles.

When it was all over, she asked where the bathroom was. The bathroom was big and dusty. She was afraid of getting pregnant, that was all she needed, she thought in horror, that stupid afternoon, the revolting sweets, the martinis with that stupid olive, and those white china figures shaking and grinning. There was no shower or hot water, only a dirty rubber pipe. She turned the tap on hard. She felt sick.

She left without saying goodbye, he muttered something about meeting again, she reached home at a run, thinking she'd be bound to catch a chill from the cold water.

At home, in bed, she lay awake for a while glad her husband was already asleep. The afternoon had ended all right after all, and she surely couldn't be pregnant, though she was still a bit afraid of a chill, and she should have taken off her make-up, well, she'd do it in the morning. Then she thought that she'd like to try one of those marzipan cakes again, she'd go back tomorrow, she'd bring her husband one to try, and then she thought about how, naked in the dark like this, she and her husband were like huge white slugs, and then she wondered how slugs did those things, those real, little, white, those real, little, slimy . . .

Salome, to hell

The whole way, the taxi driver talked about himself, his acquaintances, about smugglers, prostitutes and the night life of the city. He struck her as fairly intelligent: he measured out his tales in doses just right for her consumption. Then she thought about how the driver would behave when they arrived: it was late, her husband was away . . . He would probably suggest they have a drink. She felt unsure of herself. The driver must know that her husband was away, otherwise why would she be going home so late alone. She glanced at her watch. It was two in the morning.

He pulled up. She asked how much she owed him, but the driver suggested they sit and have a cigarette and she agreed. It was pleasant to sit smoking in the dark; she could see his face, he was handsome, too handsome for an ordinary taxi driver.

'Which floor are you on?'

'The ninth.'

'Would you like to come and have a drink with me? I know a bar nearby.'

'No, thanks, I have to go.' She was angry because she felt flustered, even though she had been expecting the question.

'Your husband's not at home, then?'

'No, no . . . he's waiting for me. That's why I have to go.'

'Hang on. I'm not interested anyway. Let's just have another cigarette.'

He seemed reasonable and she agreed. She agreed, in fact, because it tickled her to think that she was alone, at two in the morning, with a strange man, a taxi driver, that he might, after all, attack her, because you could never predict these things, and that it was neither decent nor normal to be sitting here smoking, in front of her own house at two in the morning.

She went on sitting there, thinking he was very nice for a taxi driver. They were usually quarrelsome, they cheated you, they were rough, you didn't dare question the price. This one was perfectly nice. Then he said something about her eyes, how beautiful they were, and some other flattering remarks which she already knew by heart and suddenly she remembered a film in which an emancipated woman used to hire a taxi from time to time to rape, literally rape, the poor drivers. Poor, like hell!

He tried to embrace her, but she immediately made it clear that she was getting out, asked the price again and went on sitting there. Could he really tell that her husband was away and who did he think he was, honestly, people took such liberties . . . She thought of the myth of Persephone; she had read somewhere that the myth of Persephone could be applied today to a situation in which a taxi driver attacked his customer, female, of course. Then she thought how stupid it all was and that he was nothing but a little night-time taxi gigolo and if anything happened fine, and if not – well, that was fine too. She felt more confident. He offered her a third cigarette.

Then he resumed his little driver's monologue. He talked about women. He stressed how refined she was, he was sorry about a moment ago, but you never really could tell with women, so you always had to offer. He talked about his wife whom he adored, about the pretty little tram conductor he had a date with the next day when his wife was at work, about how he loved women and how well he knew them, there were all kinds, and he drove them all in his taxi and they were all equally lovely in bed: doctors and tram conductors. As long as they were young, of course.

Still, there'd been one special one who'd given him the best time of his life. He had met her on a bus actually, she was on her way back from the seaside like him, they'd sat next to each other and chatted. He suggested they meet again. She agreed, though he was afraid she wouldn't. She was quite a bit older than him and seemed quite the lady. He took her to his room, by the time he had poured the cherry brandy (the only alcohol he happened to have in the house), the woman had already undressed. She had a big, mature, well-preserved body. They drank the brandy and got a bit drunk, she let him put cherries on her, and he placed them on her one by one, then they kissed and the cherries fell off her one by one and rolled over the white sheet. He added that she was famous and happily married and that they had never met again, but he was proud he'd had an unusual woman like her.

When she touched his hands, the light from the ninth floor seemed to beam down like a floodlight; when she touched his head, she was overcome with fear. Through his sticky hair she felt the hollows of his head, the head breathing and rocking between her breasts. As her fingers grasped his head like a hoop, she saw the image of the woman with the red cherries rolling over the white sheet one by one. The light on the ninth floor was burning indifferently. The sticky head rocked in the hollow between her breasts. Salome! Salome, damn it! Then the head moved, and the body. She pushed it away energetically and rushed out of the taxi with an expression of triumph and disgust on her face.

thematic poverty

Two hours later I phoned Bublik again. He was already in bed, like me.

'Hello, Bublik?' I said in a voice full of expectation.

'What is it?'

'Well, what do you think?'

'Oh, that! My overall impression is one of thematic poverty! Emptiness. What exactly are you writing about? There's no sex! No meaning! No philosophy! Or destiny! Or politics! Or action! It's all so petty and boring! Always the same themes! A Salome complex! You obviously haven't got anything to write about. Where's your childhood? Life? Experience? There's nothing there, understand, nothing! As though you didn't exist!!!'

I heard Bublik's voice flapping somewhere in the depths of the receiver, and, crushed, I let it fall (the dull thud of a dead bird). Bublik had told me I didn't exist, so I didn't exist.

A few minutes later the telephone rang.

'Hey, don't be mad! I was only joking! Listen, who's that stupid Irena?'

'A friend of mine,' I said quietly.

'Can we get together tomorrow? Bring her round for a coffee; sorry – I mean for a description. It'll be fun!'

'Okay.'

'You're a doll. Goodnight, sunshine.'

Bublik, oh Bublik! I rang Irena straight away and told her I was coming over for coffee the next day. Alone? No, Irena, with Buuub-liiiik! I said, pouring all my joy into her ear. 'Well, good, what's all the fuss about!' she said spreading dread in my own.

In the dark, under the covers, alone in the world, I thought about Bublik's words. Thematic poverty. Emptiness. Bublik was right. I really didn't have any experience, life, continuity. All I remembered were details. The emotional garbage of details.

I thought about where I came from, my childhood, for instance. Nothing but details planted in my mind through oral transmission.

My great-grandfather, for instance. A drunk and a lecher, a failed capitalist, and consequently a great egoist, he loved only one thing all his life – his horse. One night the latter (the horse) dragged my great-grandfather up to the house dead drunk. Two days later my great-grandfather was dead as a doornail. My great-grandmother lived to be ninety-nine, and at ninety-nine she could still thread a needle. Details. I always associate 'threading a needle' with my great-grandmother and 'the beloved horse' with my great-grandfather.

My grandmother was seduced and carried off in her sixteenth year by a young communist, a railway worker, a handsome fellow – my future grandfather. My great-grandfather (who was not yet dead as a doornail) went after them with the police, partly out of self-interest (he intended grandmother to marry a rich husband), partly out of class-hatred. Grandfather threatened not only to take his own and grandmother's life if they were not allowed to marry, he threatened to start a revolution. Great-grandfather gave in and gave his permission. And so my grandmother was married and had my mother.

In addition to the hereditary connection Mother also had a railway worker suitor in her youth. He brought her bunches of fresh lilac every morning. Then one day, as a token of his absolute devotion, the railway worker gave her a picture – of his horse. History repeats itself. But soon my mother abandoned the railway-equine connection, met my father and had me.

Detail. In my early childhood my mother used to print kisses for me. On white paper. With lipstick. From the prints of lips on white paper I remember kisses.

Detail. I had a girl cousin who lifted weights. Nothing unusual in that. Other people have girl cousins who lift weights. One day my cousin the weight-lifter tried to drown me in the sea. Without any motive. She just grabbed my head and shoved it under the water. I think (I'm not sure) that from the shore she looked like a child trying to hide something stolen, a piece of bread and jam, for instance, behind its back. But a person's head is not a piece of bread and jam. They dragged me out. I got artificial respiration, and she got a beating. Nothing unusual in that. The attempted murder didn't leave me the deep scars it left, say, Beckett. I took it in the natural order of things.

I don't remember my childhood. I always had thin hair. Feathery. Almost downy. Other little girls had plaits. So I had a 'no-plaits' complex. My mother hastily intervened. She bought me a huge ribbon tied into a bow bigger than my head. From a distance it looked like an aeroplane. The other little girls wore plaits on their heads, and I wore an aeroplane. Hence all my complexes, attempts at compensation, camouflage, beautifying cruel reality. Perhaps it was the aeroplane-ribbon in my early childhood that made me a writer.

I don't remember anything. Except that I was forever stumbling and falling over. Once, wearing a little American dress bought in the market (an historical post-war event: we had just emerged from rationing) I fell into a ditch. Perhaps it was that detail which gave me my ideological orientation. Had it not been an American dress, I might not have fallen into the ditch. No, that's not true actually. I used to fall anyway. Once I fell into a stream. It was a life and death struggle. I wasn't beaten as a child.

I don't remember sex or my attitude to sex either. Just a detail. I used to read at night, like Maxim Gorky. The book was called *Sexual Life*. A pre-war edition. I don't remember the content. I remember the epigraph. It went: 'For an instant of pleasure, don't forget – there could be a thousand days of regret!' It sounded traumatic. I don't remember traumas.

I don't remember my attitude to literature either. All I remember are damned details. My response to my first book was decidedly nasal. I was excited by the mysterious smell of the printer's ink. I sniffed that first book of mine relentlessly – right up until I started school. Then I read it. It was boring. Something about the seasons. I've kept my detailistic attitude to books to this very day. Take a line from a poem I read two days ago. The line goes like this: 'Snow was falling, mauling the violets.' I don't remember anything else.

Details, details. Nothing unusual, important, decisive. Maybe as a child I swallowed a key, a bracelet or a coin; maybe like all children I shoved a dried bean up my nose, and it never sprouted a wondrous . . . but all children do that. I never fell out of a window, for instance. My mother once accidentally poured a bowl of hot soup over my head, but that's nothing unusual either: lots of mothers pour hot soup over their children's heads.

Bublik's right. A limited thematic range. It's all so damned orderly and ordinary. So shabby, fragmentary and unrealised. My father, for instance, was an unrealised genius. Once there were no toothpicks to be had anywhere in the country – I don't remember the year – so my father constructed a toothpick machine. But just as the machine was ready, they started making toothpicks again, and so the flame of genius in my father was wantonly extinguished.

Perhaps it was my mother's paper kisses that determined my career. My mother was, in fact, an unrealised writer. And her impulse was, evidently, the same. A yearning to be loved. My writing was genetically conditioned. Bublik was right.

Bublik, Bublik! Why can't you understand? My stories are paper kisses meant for you. Made of lipstick. From the imprint of lips on white paper . . . Oh, Bublik!

thursday, or the chinese snails

'I had intended to spend New Year's Eve alone. My husband was on a business trip. But I so dreaded holiday solitude in front of the T.V. set I decided to invite him over. I knew that he was alone and that he had nowhere to go. The fact that I did have somewhere to go, but didn't want to go there and that he was the one I had decided to invite gave me a feeling of confidence, a vague sense of advantage.'

Irena knew she had invited him because of her violent desire to get inside him, to break him up and take over the warmth that belonged to her by rights because of all those months of meeting. And although her desire had now lost its aim, the same, undiminished force of inertia remained.

It was the same inertia that had brought him to her with the same inexplicable willingness all these months.

They sat shut up in her flat, aware that no one was going to come and that they would never summon the energy to go out themselves. They felt that the same strange hypnotism which prevented them from moving was beginning all over again.

The statutory candles were lit, the festive dinner on the table; they drank and talked. Irena was overwhelmed by a feeling of nausea. Why this relationship? Who was this man, actually? They met from time to time, indifferently, they slept together just as indifferently, they didn't need each other, but on it went, over and over. Irena always felt a mild disgust with him. She knew the relationship was frozen and that it would never develop in any direction. So why all this, then? Why had she invited him? Was it only to feel this same nausea, boredom, desire to be free of him as quickly as possible?

'He brought me a little bottle of perfume as a New Year gift. He brought a tin of Chinese snails as well. He excused himself: he wouldn't have the dinner, just a few snails and some white wine. I opened the tin and shook the wrinkled brown Chinese snails out onto a white plate. In the silence, by the candlelight, I watched him swallow the snails, savour them. I felt sick. I drank more and more.'

In the morning Irena woke up and saw him sitting at the table, the dinner virtually untouched. There was one dry brown snail left on the white plate. He picked it up carefully with two fingers, raised it to his mouth, pressed it into the opening between his lips and chewed it slowly and indifferently. In the grey morning light his lined face looked like the brown, lined skin of a Chinese snail. She closed her eyes. She heard the door open and close quietly and felt a vague sense of relief mixed with a strong sense of loneliness.

'Fantastic! Fantastic! What a metaphor!' said Bublik, enthusiastically. I didn't know what was so 'fantastic' about it, but, just in case, I nodded gratefully to Irena.

'It's not a metaphor. You've obviously missed the point,' said Irena calmly. 'The point is that he's a snail-man!'

I gazed at Irena's lovely, mysterious face and, trembling with a vague presentiment, I pulled Bublik by the sleeve and said quickly that I was sorry we couldn't stay but we had tickets for *Chinatown*, we were in a hurry, sorry, give me a ring 'bye!

Instead of going to the cinema, Bublik and I went for a coffee. I could sense clearly that Bublik was like a New Year sparkler longing for a match. But he didn't need a match. He exploded of his own accord.

'Ive had enough! I'm absolutely fed up with the hoards of unscrewed women crawling all over your fiction! I've had enough of your Tanias, Ružas, Melitas, Irenas! I'm sick of your cheap symbols, your gherkins, your snails, the whole slimy bestiary! Your woman's prose makes me puke, it's as boring as knitting, dry as a spinster, unimaginative as a Wiener Schnitzel, defensive as an Englishman in the underground secretly pinching someone's behind, superficial and synthetic and taste-less as battery chicken, empty as watching TV shshshshshshsh shsh . . . !'

Like a sparkler Bublik came to the end of his wire. He sighed deeply and swallowed a mouthful of coffee. I was far away by then. I was thinking. Bublik was right. But where could I come by real life? On credit? Destiny on credit? What could I write about? Nothing. I stole the garbage of other people's experiences, the rags of their everyday life, and then I patched them together and added bits . . . I intensified the emptiness. I fed my prose with the cheap vitamins of 'real-life' details, I suffered from a chronic lack of imagination. I tried to restore the elasticity of old, chewed gum that someone had stuck under the table for the next day. Instant-soup prose. I'm tired. You're right, Bublik. I'm nothing but the jettisoned dry bouquet of Chekhov's three sisters.

I went on thinking. After a while I realised I was in fact imitating Bublik's rhythm. I realised once again that Bublik had complete con-trol of my soul. But I had a body as well.

friday – goodbyeday

On Friday I blew my last cash on the hairdresser. While I watched the hairdresser's hands, armed with deadly scissors, hovering round my head, it occurred to me that that would be a good description for Bublik. Then I forgot. That is the last I thought about it. Bublik and I were shut in his room listening to music. Tender, soft music.

My little inner lift was going crazily up and down the whole time. I thought it must be audible that it must be disturbing Bublik's appreci-ation of the music. Bublik had complete control of my soul and it was now becoming clear that he ought also to control the rest of me.

With that aim in view – not that I know how it happened – Bublik and I found ourselves naked under the bed covers.

'Bublik,' I said caressingly.

'Yes,' said Bublik, staring darkly at a point on the ceiling.

'Bublik,' I said more softly.

'I'd like another smoke,' said Bublik seductively, intimating that after the cigarette there would be something more alluring.

'I'll have one too,' I said readily.

We smoked without touching.

'Bublik,' I said tenderly, putting out my cigarette.

'Yes,' said Bublik, still staring at the same point.

'Nothing,' I said meaningfully.

'How about another smoke,' said Bublik.

'All right,' I said.

We smoked.

'Bublik, look, I've come to the conclusion that hyperrealism makes special demands on a writer,' I said as intelligently as I could.

'How do you mean?'

'I mean,' I chirped, 'that a hyperrealist must have real experience of life!'

'That's not important now,' said Bublik in an icy tone.

'You're right, Bublik,' I said, full of hope.

Bublik went on darkly concentrating on the point in question, the aforementioned point on the ceiling and we smoked a third, fourth, fifth, sixth and who knows how many cigarettes. When I was sick of smoking, I got up and began to dress in that deliberate way women use to convey things tacitly, bring them home. Bublik was as silent as the grave the whole time. Before I left I carefully lifted the covers and said, 'A little snail, Bublik!'

And added, 'Chinese, at that!'

I was on my way down the stairs when I heard Bublik's furious shriek: 'Foooooool!'

saturday or yearning overcome

I pass the café on the square. There he is in the café. With Irena at his side smiling her most gifted of smiles. I maintain enough presence of mind and writer's dignity not to go in. I observe the scene with a look full of understanding and dispassionate professional curiosity.

Bublik wears an authentic frown, an expression of tragic concern for modern literature, now long dead, while people go on and on reading memoirs, detective stories, and pornography, and art has plunged headlong into kitsch! Anyway, the British have proved it conclusively, statistically. Irena is evidently impressed by this detail – her smile grows still more gifted.

And what do you know! Bublik suddenly turns round. I wink at him. He is embarrassed. I wink at him again (though the effect is reduced by repetition) and walk away with a sense of miraculous strength. Liberated! There's a taste of warm dough in my mouth. I am chewing mercilessly on Bublik's face. I chew my still warm Bublik ('No! That fantastic dimension again!' shouts Bublik) and feel the urge to spit him out. I roll him into a little warm ball with my tongue – and finally manage to swallow him. I go into a neighbouring café and, waiting for my coffee, I wash him down with a glass of water. Gulp! There.

EPILOGUE

(*one Monday, ten years later*)

There are mornings when the threads of sleep hang treacherously out of us in all directions. Before we've managed to shut ourselves up, cover ourselves, pull up an imaginary zip, disguise ourselves, like a chameleon, to draw the patterns of our surroundings onto our skin. I take a lot of trouble disguising myself every morning. From Monday to Friday I begin by putting moisturising cream on my face, followed by foundation, then shadow on my eyelids, mascara on my lashes, a thin layer of powder on my nose and forehead, rouge on my cheeks; I rub pale lipstick over my lips, pull a silk blouse and grey suit over my body, step into high-heeled shoes; I check everything several times, taking care that I'm TIDILY made up, combed and dressed; everything is designed to conform to the accepted notion of a woman between thirty-five and forty, college-educated; occupation: editor; department: cookery, textbooks on baby-care, embroidery, knitting and dress-making, food preservation and freezing, acupuncture, macrobiotics, diets, healthy eating in middle and old age, growing flowers on balconies and terraces, indoor plants, beauty, make-up and fashion, edible and inedible mushrooms, fresh and saltwater fish . . . Every morning from Monday to Friday, I put on a mask expressing a slight aloofness (rather than coldness), reliability and dedication to my work.

Emerging that Monday into the grey September morning, the grey street with its peeling façades, I bumped into someone on the pavement. We stood for a second, muttering a few words of apology (sorry, not at all, not at all, my fault), and there wouldn't have been anything unusual about it had I not felt a strong urge to press myself against the stranger, bury my head in his chest, inhale the warmth of his body. The urge was so violent and sudden that I stood stock still, as though hypnotised, staring at the stranger as he walked round me with an apologetic expression, took a few steps, looked back in surprise, then went on his way. I remained rooted to the spot, transfixed by a mysterious longing. Then I stood up straight, took a deep breath of fresh September air and set off along a familiar path, through the city park, where an occasional pensioner was already sitting on one of the benches and dog owners were walking their pets. The short walk across the park soothed me, but when I came to the end, to the street I had to cross, I suddenly became conscious of a new restlessness, a twinge, a thirst, a neglected and forgotten feeling. I sought anxiously for that imaginary zip, but the picture that flashed into my mind interrupted me. I saw a tropical marshland, steaming, monstrous, rank, with islands, morasses and alluvial channels; I saw hairy palm-trunks rise near and far out of lush brakes of fern, there were mis-shapen trees that dropped their naked roots through the air into the ground or into water that was stagnant and shadowy and glassy-green; I saw mammoth milk-white blossoms floating, and strange high-shouldered birds, I saw that among the knotted joints of a bamboo thicket the eyes of a crouching tiger gleamed – and I felt my heart throb with terror, yet with longing inexplicable.

The image vanished and I found myself standing hesitant and alarmed, not knowing which way to turn. Then I caught sight of a life-saving cafeteria on the other side of the street and decided to slip in there for a moment.

The cafeteria was dirty, run down and permeated with the smell of canteen food. I ordered a coffee, settled myself in the most secluded corner and lit a cigarette. I stood there facing the mirror that lined the whole wall. There was a similar mirror behind me, and on my right a glass wall looking onto the street. I felt uncomfortable: first people came up from behind me, next they seemed to be coming towards me, and then I could see them, walking away, but in the wrong direction. I tried to find that imaginary zip again. In my vulnerable state, those stupid mirrors could shatter me to bits. There I stood, as though in some mythic space, drinking my coffee, caught in a vice between present, past and future, feeling that at any moment I could conjure up one or the other, that everything existed simultaneously or nothing existed at all.

Suddenly there in the mirror was a face that seemed familiar for a moment but that immediately disappeared. I turned to look at the street, and saw a man's figure moving away with his back towards me. I turned round to the mirror and saw the figure coming into the cafeteria. I couldn't see any more: my view of the entrance was blocked by a wall and the cash desk.

A few seconds later the whole jumbled space spat Bublik out in front of me, as a public telephone would a coin. There he was standing in front of me like a coin, like a fact, and all at once I felt myself subside, felt that imaginary protective zip closing of own accord. I blew out a puff of cigarette smoke and directed my gaze at Bublik with the composure of a chameleon.

'Hi. How are you?' he said.

'Fine, and you?'

'Fine. I haven't seen you for centuries,' he said.

'Well, a decade at any rate,' I said.

'Want another coffee?' he said.

'Why not?' I said.

As Bublik made his way towards the cash desk, I noticed he'd begun to go bald and looked smaller. He was carrying a black briefcase. The image of a man with a briefcase filled me with a feeling of vague shame. Bublik turned and came back, put his briefcase down and went back for the coffees. That worn, old-fashioned, black leather briefcase aroused a vague sense of compassion in me and for a moment completely engulfed Bublik, as though he had merged with it, disappeared into it, into that stupid, ugly object . . .

'So, tell me,' I said, as brightly as I could, attempting to conceal my disquiet.

'There's nothing to tell,' he said evasively.

'How's life?'

'Okay,' he said with a shrug.

'Got a job?'

'Near here. A big company.'

'Are you on your way to work?'

He nodded.

'Married?'

'Divorced.'

'Children?'

'Two. What about you?'

'Happily divorced. No children.'

The telegraphic summary of our lives only increased my disquiet.

'Are you still in the same flat?' I asked cautiously.

'No . . .'

Bublik fell silent. I noticed that he smiled often; a smile would appear on his lips, like beer froth, and he would quickly wipe it away, licking his lips. Right now his hands are sweating, I thought. Somehow I didn't have the heart to continue the conversation. I said nothing. Bublik drank his coffee without a word, then suddenly reached for his briefcase. The abrupt movement unnerved me; I hadn't thought he would decide to leave so soon. Bublik opened his briefcase, rummaged nervously and awkwardly through his papers, and finally took out a thin folder.

'I hear you're working for a publisher,' he began.

'Yes,' I said, somewhat too decisively and, foreseeing danger, took hold of my bag.

'Have a look at this,' he said, putting the folder down on the table. 'Read it if you feel like it. No obligation. And call me if you like. I'm sorry, I'll have to go. I've got a meeting at nine . . .'

'But my line is threads and needles, babies and nutrition,' I was going to say, but didn't because Bublik, closing his comical briefcase, had vanished as though he'd never existed. I glanced at both mirrors. No more Bublik. I didn't even have a chance to give in to the pity that all bearers of manuscripts arouse in me like a conditioned reflex. I opened the folder cautiously. Bublik's visiting card was pasted on the cover. The first page bore the unenticing title 'A Winter Story'.

I finished my coffee quickly, stuck Bublik's sad folder under my arm and set off to work. God, how much in love with Bublik I had once been! But nature must have ordained that the greatest passions, once past, were covered over by a thick layer of dust. I could not conjure up *that feeling*. I could remember events, of course, but there is nothing more dead and irretrievable than feelings which have once been. That flavour (what was it like, actually?) remains forever obliterated. As I walked, it occurred to me that Bublik must have been carrying his pathetic folder about with him all the time. (Fate could not have been so imaginative as to drive Bublik and me together, ten years on, just as the one thing he happened to have with him was his manuscript.) This thought aroused a new wave of pity in me. And then I forgot about it.

It was not until I got home from work that I opened Bublik's folder again and resolved to read the first story, the one with the unenticing title.

A Winter Story

'I'm Mario,' said the man hesitantly, offering the woman his hand. The woman smiled, returned his firm grip, then hunched her shoulders and bowed her head as though apologising for something. Thick snow was falling. The woman shifted from foot to foot and glanced at the man.

'Shall we go somewhere for a coffee?' the man asked indecisively. 'Perhaps over there, across the road.' The woman nodded and took his arm eagerly. The man gave a barely perceptible shudder.

The man watched the woman as they took off their coats, shaking off the snow. She must have been between thirty-five and forty. She was heavily built and blonde.

'What would you like?' he asked when they had sat down.

'I don't know . . . What are you going to have?' the woman asked, smoothing her hair with her hand. There was something very old-fashioned in that movement.

'A brandy.'

'Well, then, I'll have a brandy too,' said the woman, smoothing her hair again. 'I don't drink really, but I will now, with you, to keep you company. I sometimes have a beer. Beer's the only thing I like . . .' She glanced at the man and bowed her head. 'Have you got a job?' she asked suddenly.

'Yes. I work for a big company,' said the man briefly.

'Jan didn't want to tell me anything about you. Find out for yourself, he said . . . Incidentally, I . . . I mean . . . I'm not in the habit of going out with someone I don't know . . . but Jan and I have known each other for a long time at work and it see . . .' the woman swallowed the end of the word.

'It seemed what?'

'Nothing. I mean . . . I felt confident . . . Do you come here often?'

'No. This is the first time.'

'It's nice.'

The woman lowered her eyes again, then raised them to look at the man. The man thought she might be going to cry. She pressed her lips together like a child and smoothed her hair again.

'Do you want another brandy?' asked the man.

'Are you going to have one?'

'No.'

'Then I won't either.'

'Shall we go somewhere?'

'Yes, let's,' the woman said, brightening.

They went out into the street. The man stopped indecisively, thrusting his hands into his pockets.

'It's still snowing,' he said.

'It hasn't snowed so much for ages,' said the woman.

'Where shall we go?' asked the man indecisively.

'I don't know.'

'Shall we go for a meal?'

'I'm not really hungry. I ate at home. But if you . . .'

'Not really, but it's hardly the weather for a stroll.'

'No, indeed,' said the woman, shifting from foot to foot. 'How about going to my place for coffee. I could mull some wine. I live quite close, I don't know whether Jan men . . .' the woman swallowed the last syllable again.

'Why not. I'll see you home,' said the man, setting off. The woman took his arm.

'It's so slippery,' she said. 'Are you going skiing this year?'

'No. I don't ski.'

'Nor do I. But I'm sorry I don't. It strikes me as the nicest sport. I always wanted to go to the mountains in winter. But I never did. I always go to the sea. What about you?'

'I always go to the sea, too.'

'Here we are. We're here,' said the woman. 'We met at the corner of my street. I thought it best to meet nearby. Then if you didn't come, I'd be near ho . . .' The woman swallowed the end of the word again.

'Did you think I wasn't going to come?'

'No, but, you know . . .' She was embarrassed.

The woman fumbled for her keys in her handbag.

'At last,' she said, taking out the key. 'Does that happen to you?'

'Always,' said the man, following the woman into the flat.

'This was my grandmother's place. I'd never have got a flat through my firm. As a single person, I mean . . . Married people, with children, always come first,' said the woman, taking off her coat. 'Won't you take your coat off?'

The man took off his coat. The woman went briskly into the kitchen.

'So, what'll it be? Coffee or mulled wine?'

'Mulled wine,' said the man, looking around. The flat was small, very tidy, like a box for dolls.

'Your place is so tidy,' the man observed.

'Do you live alone as well?' the woman called from the kitchen.

'I do now.'

'And your wife?'

The man did not reply. He drummed his fingers on a glass bowl with two little goldfish swimming in it.

'You've got fish?'

'I wanted a cat, but it turned out I'm allergic to them, and the flat's too small for a dog, so I thought . . . it's something at least,' said the woman coming out of the kitchen carrying a tray with two glasses wrapped in napkins.

'Just like a restaurant,' said the man, taking a glass.

'Well, yes . . . I've noticed that's how they do it in restaurants.' She smiled, took a sip of her wine and went over to the television. 'Do you watch television?'

'Sometimes.'

'I do. Films and serials. I always follow them. Then we discuss what happened in the office. I'll turn down the sound.'

'That's better,' said the man. 'Do you mind if I smoke?'

The woman immediately produced an ashtray.

'I don't smoke myself. I never have. Some of the other girls in the office, they smoke like chimneys, they smoke half their wages. And it isn't nice. For a woman, I mean . . .'

'This wine's really good,' said the man.

'I put both cloves and cinnamon in – so as not to get it wrong.'

'How do you mean?'

'I always forget which goes in red and which in white wine. So I always put both in . . .'

'Quite right,' smiled the man.

'That's the only time I'm not petty-minded,' said the woman.

'What do you mean?'

'Jan keeps telling me I'm petty-minded. Because I like order. I like to know where things are. I want everything to be in its proper place. And I don't think that's petty-minded. I live alone and if I don't take care of things, who will? Although my girl-friends envy me . . . Bitch!'

'What did you say?'

'I told her she's a bitch. Have you been following this story?'

'No. You mean the redhead?'

'Yes. She's the blonde's sister. The blonde's good, but the redhead's nasty. She's always got it in for the blonde.'

'Interesting,' said the man, putting down his glass and making a move to get up.

'Did you see what she did to her?'

'Well, I'll be going,' said the man, looking at his watch. 'I've got some things to attend to.'

'We can turn off the TV if you li . . .' The woman swallowed the end of the word and smoothed her hair.

'No, no, go on watching . . .' said the man, standing up.

'Won't you have another glass? For the road?'

'No, thank you. I really must be going . . .'

'All ri . . .' mumbled the woman. 'I'll see you to the door.'

While the man put on his coat, the woman hunched her shoulders, her arms crossed on her chest as though she were cold.

'People are often better than we think at first si . . . ,' the woman stuttered, slowly bowing her head.

'Goodbye,' said the man, and then turned and added, 'I'll call you . . .'

'Really?'

'The Saturday after next perhaps. And thanks for the wine.'

'Thank you,' the woman muttered. The man turned up his collar, thrust his hands into his pockets and went out into the street.

Thick snow was falling.

That was how Bublik's story ended. With nothing. Just as it had begun. It came out of nothing and came to nothing. Bublik's pages upset me. They smelled of mould and loneliness; they had slipped through a chink of terrible emptiness. This is it, Bublik! ONCE AND FOR ALL I WANT ORDINARY URBANISED LANGUAGE, THE TRANSPOSITION OF TEDIOUS, SENSELESS, EVERYDAY LIFE IN THE SMALLEST DETAIL, I WANT THE TEDIUM WE LIVE, I WANT THE AUTHENTICITY OF TEDIUM, ITS PHOTOGRAPHIC REPRO- DUCTION. DO YOU UNDERSTAND? So here we are then! *Your* heart has been stirred as well, Bublik! You too want love! And now you're acting out what you asked in vain of me ten years ago!

Nevertheless, Bublik's pages touched me: they set something in motion, something clicked, something shifted – I felt the sudden urge to sit down at my typewriter. The last time I had written anything was exactly ten years earlier, for Bublik. And then I forgot all about it.

Time had covered everything, time and an everyday filled with other people's pages about embroidery, dressmaking and breast-feeding. So my writing had been nothing but a weapon in the struggle for Bublik's heart, and I never thought it could be used for anything else. Ah Bublik! Life has spat you out at me like a coin from a public telephone, and I shall pick you up. True you're small change, but more often than not that's all life offers us. So, take what you can. I shall play with you, like a fat cat with a hungry mouse, a game in which there is no winner and no loser, a game without passion or provocation. You've slipped by chance, out of a little metal opening in the everyday and I'm going to . . . pick you up.

I sat down at the typewriter and wrote fast, practically without drawing breath, and when I had typed the last word, I quickly put the pages together, attached them with a paper clip without looking at them again and went into the bathroom.

I had a shower, rubbed my body with fragrant oil, put on lacy knickers, a lacy bra and black silk stockings with suspenders, combed my hair, put on a silk housecoat, applied foundation to my face, shadow to my eyes, mascara to my lashes, shiny lipstick to my lips, rouge to my cheeks, powder to the bridge of my nose and forehead and sprinkled perfume behind my ears. Then I opened my housecoat and sat down in front of the mirror, parting my knees. MY WAR MASK flashed in the mirror and with it the same picture of the tropical landscape I had seen that morning on my way to work. This time it was made of paper, crêpe paper in various bright colours. It was all lush and monstrously huge: the flowers and the birds and the trunks of the hairy palms and the glassy-green, shadowy water, even the tiger, hidden in the knotted joints of the bamboo thicket, swayed like a vast dead butterfly. I was made of paper too and my war mask was of paper and the bitterness which had driven me to put it on was of paper.

I did up my housecoat decisively, stood and went over to the phone. I dialled Bublik's number and when I heard his voice, I said, 'You can come for the folder now, Bublik.'

I put down the telephone, walked over to the desk, took the story I had just written (leaving the same, unenticing title) and put it in an envelope. I wrote the name of a literary journal slowly and carefully on the envelope and put my name on the back.

An impatient ring came from the door at the precise moment I was running my tongue over the sticky strip on the envelope and – stuck it down.

A Winter Story
'Mario?'

That was the name the man with the turned-up collar used to address the woman who had emerged out of the thick curtain of snowflakes and paused indecisively at the corner. The woman nodded, went up to him and held out her hand without a word. The man cast an inquisitive glance at the woman's face.

'Shall we go somewhere for a coffee?' he suggested. 'Over there perhaps?' The woman nodded without a word and they set off. On the way the man glanced at the woman's face, but immediately turned away and stared straight ahead, thrusting his hands into his pockets and stamping his feet a little, as though he were cold.

While they took off their coats and shook the snow from them, the man looked at the woman with evident satisfaction. He looked about forty. He was balding and had broad shoulders and strong muscles visible under a slightly overtight pullover.

'What would you like?' he asked the woman when they had sat down. A spontaneous smile spread across his face.

'Umm . . . coffee,' said the woman.

'I won't have anything,' the man said serenely, smiling again. 'I don't drink coffee. Or alcohol. I don't smoke either.' He crossed his arms on his chest, observing the woman carefully.

'Some men look at a woman from behind first, you know what I mean. Not me, I look into her eyes.'

The woman gave a barely perceptible start and pursed her lips.

'Do you mind my saying that?'

'No.'

'I thought you looked offended.'

'I'm not.'

The man smiled with satisfaction, rubbing his hands and nodding in disbelief.

'I wasn't expecting . . . you know . . .'

'What?'

'Well . . . when I asked Jan to introduce me to a friend of his, I didn't expect you to look like this . . . You've no idea what women can be like! I don't know whether Jan mentioned . . .'

'What?'

'That I tried through personal columns.'

'No.'

'Well, I did. I'm not ashamed. I had lots of offers. I went on several dates. Then I gave up.'

'Why?'

'So as not to lose all hope! One was a hunchback, a real hunchback. Another was so ugly you wouldn't believe it. And they were all better than me. I mean . . . they were college graduates, financially independent – terrible!'

'What is?'

'Why women on their own!' said the man, frowning. Then he shrugged. 'What about you? Have you ever advertised?'

'No . . .'

The man fixed his gaze on the woman, and the spontaneous smile spread over his face again.

'Of course not. You don't need to . . . Did Jan tell you anything about me?'

'No.'

'I mean . . . I told him, I was really specific. I said a woman who weighs less than a hundred and fifty pounds was out of the question. How much do you weigh?'

'A hundred and forty,' said the woman drily, pursing her lips.

'I like substantial women, you see. I've spent my whole life training for something or other! First wrestling, then body-building, then judo, then weight-lifting. But now I've had enough of iron. I'd be better off lifting a woman! Don't you agree!' Suddenly the serene smile vanished from his face. 'I used to be terrifically strong. I'm strong now, too, but not like before. I trained ever since I could remember . . . Until I was thirty and until I got ill.'

'What was wrong with you?' asked the woman. The man waved his hand dismissively and looked away.

'I'm all right now. They said I wasn't going to make it, but I did. Strength of will and a healthy psyche can overcome anything. I used to worry only about my body; now I think about my mind as well. It's important, that balance . . .'

The man turned to the woman. A smile spread over his lips like beer froth.

'Have you got a car?' he asked suddenly.

'No,' said the woman awkwardly.

'Of course not, Jan told me. I asked him first thing whether you had a car. No, he said. So what can I fix, I said. I really like fixing things. Not just cars. Everything in the house . . .'

The woman smiled.

'Shall we go?' she asked hesitantly.

'Sure, I mean, if you want to. Have you finished your coffee?'

The woman swallowed a mouthful of coffee and stood up. The man followed her with a smile on his face.

'You know,' he said, holding the woman's coat, 'I really can't believe it!'

'What?'

'That Jan gave me your 'phone number just like that.'

The man and the woman went out into the street. The woman stopped indecisively.

'It's still snowing,' she said.

The man thrust his hands into his pockets, turned up his collar and, shifting from foot to foot, asked, 'Well, what shall we do now?'

'I'd really like to go home,' the woman said indecisively.

'Out of the question! We've only just met. I won't let you go! It's too late for a film,' said the man, glancing at his watch. 'Listen, how about going somewhere for a meal?'

'I'm not hungry.'

'A walk?'

'In this weather!'

'Then let's go to my place for a drink and the T.V. I live right near here, round the corner . . .'

'I'm not sure,' said the woman.

'I don't know what else I could . . .'

'Neither do I . . .'

'Let's go to my place then, okay?'

'Okay . . .' said the woman.

The man set off briskly, holding the woman by the elbow.

'Only I must warn you, it's not tidy. Did Jan tell you I live with my mother?'

'No.'

'Unfortunately we won't be able to watch the colour T.V.,' he apologised. 'It's in Mother's room.'

'It doesn't matter.'

'Of course, you're right.'

The froth of a smile spread over the man's face again.

'Look at this snow,' said the woman. 'There hasn't been so much snow for ages.'

'Hey, do you skate?'

'No. Why do you ask?' the woman was a little disconcerted.

'No reason. I skate. Now that it's winter, I go to the ice-rink every day, take a turn or two and come back home. Didn't you go skating even when you were a kid?'

'No,' said the woman absently.

'I like skating. It's a way of keeping fit, and it's company: there's music and so on. A good atmosphere. Here we are, this is me.' He turned into a dark passage. The woman paused for a moment, as though hesitating, then followed him.

They went into a corridor. The man pointed to a closed door.

'That's Mother,' he said softly. 'We'll go in here.' He opened the door of another room. 'Come in, take off your coat. Would you like a drink?'

'Okay,' said the woman, taking off her coat.

'I don't drink, so there's not much choice,' said the man, looking through the sideboard. 'Port?'

'Okay . . .' said the woman.

'Here, help yourself,' said the man, taking off his coat, 'and I'll get the T.V.' He shut the door behind him.

The woman sat down in an armchair, sipped her drink and looked round the room. It was quite large, untidy and crammed with things. On one wall was a collection of old weapons: sabres, swords, knives, daggers, on another four enormous, identical oil paintings. Three models of old sailing ships, stood one next to the other on top of a glass case. Two colour postcards were propped against one of them: one a picture of a white angora cat, the other a large, naked, blonde.

The man came back, carrying the T.V.

'We've got five in the house, believe it or not, but only Mother's and this one work.'

The man put the set on a small table and switched it on.

'Shall I turn the sound up? It doesn't matter to me. I read the subtitles anyway. What do you think?'

'I don't mind,' said the woman, finishing her drink.

'I don't suppose you like it here, do you?' the man remarked cheerfully, adjusting the aerial.

'No, it's fine. Why do you say that?'

'I don't like it either. We haven't done anything to it since '68, since my father died. There, it's begun. Do you like this serial?'

'Sort of. I mean, I've been watching it.'

'I like all war films and series,' said the man, sitting down in the armchair next to the woman. 'Are you looking at the boats?' he asked, noticing the woman's gaze.

'Yes. Where do they come from?'

'I made them myself! It isn't at all difficult. You just buy a book and do what it says. I told you that until I was thirty I only cared about my body. Now I'm taking care of this as well.' The man smiled, tapping his forehead with his finger. 'Making a ship like that increases your concentration and will-power.'

The man got up, took down one of the models from the case and placed it in front of the woman.

'It's lovely,' said the woman, touching a sail with her finger.

'That's the foresail,' said the man softly.

The woman smiled and touched another.

'The mainsail . . .'

The man took the woman's hand.

'Topsail, spinnaker, jib . . .'

The woman moved her hand away.

'Here I am, I make ships, but I've never sailed. Only in my imagination. How about you?'

'A bit. To the Adriatic islands. Krk, Lošinj and so on.'

'That doesn't count. I meant a long trip.'

'No,' said the woman, smiling.

'I'd like to,' said the man thoughtfully, picking up the model carefully and putting it back on the case.

'Do you collect weapons as well?' asked the woman.

'Weapons are wonderful things,' the man livened up. 'I've got a catalogue. See this book? I order things from Germany.'

The man stood up again, took down a sabre from a nail on the wall, wiped the dust off it with his sleeve and took the sabre out of its sheath.

'The pearl of my collection: a Turkish sabre,' said the man, pointing it at the woman, then making a swift slice through the air. 'I'd only have to touch you with this and you'd be done for! It's a dangerous thing,' he said, smiling, sliding the sabre back in the sheath and returning it to its place. He sat down in the armchair next to the woman again. 'Hey, I frightened you!'

'No, you didn't,' said the woman, looking at the T.V. screen.

'I did, I can see it in your face.'

The woman stared at the screen without a word. The man smiled broadly and, crossing his arms on his chest, kept glancing at the woman.

'I'm not afraid of anything. Not illness, not death. The only thing that can defeat me is a woman . . .'

'Why do you keep smiling?' asked the woman a little sharply, turning to the man.

'I don't know. I can't believe it. You're too good looking. I wasn't expecting this. It's sort of thrown me . . .' said the man, looking at the woman eagerly. The woman turned away and looked back at the T.V. screen.

'I've lost weight. I'm not eating well. Mother's getting old, she doesn't feel like cooking, and I can't be bothered myself. Maybe, if there was a woman here . . . I used to be terrifically strong. Are you sure you don't weigh a hundred and fifty?'

'A hundred and forty,' said the woman, without shifting her gaze from the screen.

The man's eyes swept wistfully over the woman's profile.

'And you're blonde,' he said ruefully.

'What do you mean?'

'You've got blonde hair. I was specific about that as well. I said she should be blonde and not weigh less than a hundred and fifty.'

'I dye my hair,' said the woman drily.

'That doesn't matter. You look like a natural blonde.'

'Robert Mitchum,' said the woman nodding in the direction of the T.V.

'I'm not watching. I do watch that series as a rule, but I don't feel like it right now. Does this room seem too big to you?'

'No.'

'It's too big for my taste. I want a small room, with just enough space for a bed, a table and nothing else. Would you like some more?'

'Okay,' said the woman handing him her glass.

'But we haven't changed a thing,' went on the man, pouring the drink. 'I've no idea why . . . since Dad died. Mind you, we didn't alter anything before either . . .'

'You must have loved your father, that's why,' said the woman.

The man got up, went to the cupboard, opened a drawer and spent a long time rummaging. Then he came back and sat down by the woman again.

'Here, this is him,' he said, handing the woman a small photograph.

'Was he in some kind of army?'

'Uh-huh, Volksdeutscher. During the war he was in the German navy, in a submarine. Why he went to Germany I don't know. They probably had to, I don't know. When he came back, he was thrown into prison. He worked in minesweeping after the war. Mother told me that. How should I know? But he taught me German and all about electricity. I spent some time in Germany myself. Two years. Did Jan tell you?'

'Why did you come back?'

'I don't know. I was doing well there. Really well. And I liked it. You know, some people are always leaders, the Germans, for instance, and some always fail, no matter what. Perhaps that's what Hitler meant when he talked about the übermensch. I like their precision. In everything! If I sent in an order for a dagger like that tomorrow, it'd be here in two days. That's the way they are.'

'You can turn it off,' said the woman. 'We're not watching.' The man got up and switched off the television.

'I keep rambling on and you don't say anything. Jan didn't want to tell me anything about you. Find out for yourself, he said.'

The woman stood up, poured another drink and walked around the room with the glass in her hand.

'What are these paintings of?'

'They're left over from Dad. He really liked this painting, so he had copies made. He wasn't satisfied with any of them. There's another in the cellar, but it's not finished.'

'And who is the man in the picture?'

' "The Old Sea Dog", by Haerendel.' The man paused and then added thoughtfully, 'We all have a dream. I do. You must have one, too.'

He stood up. 'We all dream about something, and it's gone in a flash! The minute you're born you're dead.'

The man waved his hand dismissively, smiled again for no reason, went up to the glass case, took down the postcard of the cat and handed it to the woman.

'See this postcard?'

'Yes.'

'That's exactly what my cat was like. That's why I bought the postcard. To remind me.'

'What happened to the cat?'

'It died. I may get another though,' said the man.

The woman put her glass down on the table, walked over to the window and opened the curtains a little.

'It's still snowing,' she said.

'You like silence, don't you?'

'Yes.'

'I'd noticed. Not me, I can't stand it. I'm frightened when it's quiet. I always turn on everything in the house. The radio and the T.V., I like there to be noise around me. If you weren't here, everything would be on. Especially the radio. And maybe I'll buy a VCR machine. They're really something!'

The woman shrugged.

'I'll have to be getting home.'

The man bowed his head, thrust his hands into his pockets and smiled.

'Maybe I talk too much and you're bored . . .'

'I really must go,' said the woman, taking her coat. 'It's late.'

'I'll see you home.'

'Don't bother. I live quite near here.'

'I know. Because of your phone number. I'll see you home anyway.'

'Okay. As far as the corner.'

The man and the woman went out. The man turned up his collar. The woman covered her head with a woollen scarf.

'You look like Kim Novak,' said the man.

The woman walked on in silence.

The man followed her. The smile melted from his lips. All at once he stopped.

'You know what bothers me most?'

'What?' asked the woman.

'The fact that people disappear. I don't know where, but they disappear. When I was young I had lots of friends. And they've all disappeared.'

'Really disappeared?' asked the woman, increasing her pace.

'No, they're here somewhere, in flats . . . Wife, job, children, you know. Now there are different people in the streets.'

'Here we are,' said the woman.

'Shall I see you to the door?'

'No,' said the woman. The man shrugged his shoulders and smiled. The woman walked away. The man watched her go, shifting from one foot to the other.

'Can I 'phone you?' he called after the woman. 'I mean, we could go skating?' The man's voice reached the woman dully, as through cotton wool. The woman turned, stopped, then continued down the street at a faster pace. The man stood at the corner, watching the woman until she disappeared in the darkness. He looked around. The streets were empty, the snow was falling harder and harder. The man stamped his feet, drew his head into his collar, thrust his hands deep into his pockets and walked away . . .

C. H.

LIFE IS A FAIRY TALE

....

(Metaterxies)

'The power of a country road is different if one walks
along it or flies over it in an aeroplane. Likewise the
power of a text is one thing if one reads it and another
if one copies it. When one flies, one sees only the road
stretching through the landscape, unwinding before
one's eyes according to the rules of the surrounding
terrain. Only when one walks along the road does one
come to know something of its dominion and how, from
a terrain that for the flier is nothing but a long, flat
plain, it calls forth distances, belvederes, clearings,
perspectives at every turn like the word of the
commander calls soldiers forth out of rank. Only a
copied text can command the soul of the person who
copies it. A mere reader never recognises the new
horizons of his inner being or how the text that opens
up a path through the ever denser primeval forest within
us, prepares them, for the reader obeys the movement
of his ego in the unrestricted air space of the dream
while the copier commands it. That is why the Chinese
art of copying books was an incomparable guarantee of
literary culture, and the copy – a key to the riddle of
China.'

Walter Benjamin, *One Way Street*

'A wonderful turnip has grown in the garden; it is more
like a potato than a turnip.'

N. V. Gogol

A Hot Dog in a Warm Bun

On the twenty-fifth of March a truly unbelievable thing took place in Zagreb. Nada Matić, a young doctor specialising in plastic surgery, awoke in her room and looked at the clock. It was 6.15. Nada jumped out of bed, jumped into the shower, squatted under the stream of water, then, lighting a cigarette, jumped into a terry cloth robe. It was 6.25. She pulled on her grey spring suit, daubed some rouge on her cheeks, and grabbed her bag. It was 6.30. She locked the door, finished the cigarette in the lift, and hurried off to catch her tram.

By the time Nada Matić stepped off the tram, it was 6.50. And just then, right in the middle of the square, Nada Matić was overcome by a sudden, unusually intense hunger. She rushed over to the Skyscraper Cafeteria, which served hot dogs in warm buns, nervously called out to the waitress, 'More mustard, please!' greedily grabbed the hot dog, and impatiently threw away the napkin. (That is what Nada Matić did. That is what I do too: I always dispose of those unnecessary and shamefully tiny scraps of paper waitresses use for wrapping hot dogs.)

Then she set off across the square. She was about to bring the hot dog to her lips, when – was it some dark sense of foreboding or a ray of the March morning sun alighting on the object in question, illuminating it with its own special radiance? In either case and to make a long story short, she glanced down at the fresh pink hot dog and her face convulsed in horror. For what did she see peering through the longish bun and ocherish mustard foam but a genuine, bona fide . . . ! Nada came to a complete and utter halt. No, there could be no doubt. 'Glans, corpus, radix, corpora cavernosa, corpora spongiosa, praeputium, frenulum, scrotum,' our heroine, Nada Matić, thought, running through her totally useless anatomy class knowledge and still not believing her eyes. No, that thing in the bun was most definitely not a hot dog!

Utterly shaken, Nada resumed her journey to the Municipal Hospital at a much slower pace. It had all come together in a single moment: the anatomy lesson, plastic surgery, the desire to specialise in aesthetic prosthetics – it had all flashed before her eyes like a mystical sign, a warning, the finger of fate, a finger which, if we may be forgiven the crudeness of our metaphor, peered out of the bun in so tangible, firm, fresh, and pink a state as to be anything but an illusion.

Nada Matić decided to give the 'hot dog' issue top priority. Taking the 'hot dog' to the laboratory and dropping it in a bottle of Formalin would have been the simplest solution, of course, but what would her colleagues have said? Nada looked here and there for a litter basket; there were none in sight. As she'd thrown the napkin away and had no paper tissues, she tried to hide the 'hot dog' by coaxing it into the bun with her finger, but smooth, slippery, and springy as it was, it kept sliding out, the head gleaming almost maliciously in Nada's direction.

It then occurred to Nada that she might stop off at a café and just happen to leave the 'hot dog' on the lower shelf of one of the tables she often stood beside – she had said good-bye to three umbrellas that way – but in the end she lost her nerve. For the first time in her life Nada felt what it was like to be a criminal . . .

Oh, before I forget, I ought to tell you a few things about our heroine. Nada Matić is the kind of shortish, plumpish blonde that men find attractive. But her generous, amicable, amorous character kept getting in her way, and men disappeared from her life, poor thing, without her ever quite understanding why. Abandoned by no fault of her own, she naturally and periodically found herself involved in hot and heavy escapades with married medical personnel of the male sex.

Suddenly Nada felt terribly sorry for herself: her whole life seemed to have shrunk into that grotesque symbol of bun-*cum*-relay-race-baton. No, she'd better take care of it at once. She gave the bun an unconscious squeeze and the hot dog peeked out at her again, turning her self-pity to despair. And just as she noticed a broken basement window and was about to toss it away, bun and all, who should pass by with a cold nod but one of the surgeons, Otto Waldinger. Quick as lightning, Nada stuffed the 'hot dog' into her pocket, smearing gooey mustard all over her fingers . . . The bastard! Scarcely even acknowledging her, while not so long ago . . . !

And then she spied a mercifully open drain. She removed the 'hot dog' from her pocket with great care and flung it into the orifice. It got stuck in the grating. She nudged it with her foot, but it refused to budge. It was too fat.

At that point up sauntered a good-looking, young policeman.

'Identity papers, please.'

'What for?' Nada mumbled.

'Jaywalking.'

'Oh,' said Nada, rummaging frenetically through her bag.

'What's the matter?' asked the policeman, looking down at the grating. 'Lost your appetite?' A good inch and a half of the 'hot dog' was sticking out of the bun. Nada Matić went pale . . .

But at this point everything becomes so enveloped in mist that we cannot tell what happened next.

Mato Kovalić, a writer (or, to be more specific, a novelist and short story writer), awoke rather early and smacked his lips, which he always did when he awoke though he could not for the life of him explain why. Kovalić stretched, moved his hand along the floor next to the bed until it found his cigarettes, lit one, inhaled, and settled back. There was a full-length mirror on the opposite wall, and Kovalić could see his bloated gray face in it.

During his habitual morning wallow in bed he was wont to run through the events of the previous day. The thought of the evening's activities and Maja, that she-devil of an invoice clerk, called forth a blissful smile on his face, and his hand willy-nilly slid under the covers . . . Unbelievable! No, absolutely impossible!

Kovalić flung back the blanket and leaped up as if scalded. *There* he felt only a perfectly smooth surface. Kovalić rushed over to the mirror. He was right. *There* he saw only an empty, smooth space. He looked like one of those naked, plastic dummies in the shop windows. He pinched and pulled at himself several times, he slapped his face to see whether he was awake, he jumped in place once or twice; and again he placed his hand on the spot where only the night before there had been a bulge . . . No, *it* was gone!

But here we must say a few words about Kovalić and show the reader what sort of man our hero is. We shall not go into his character, because the moment one says something about a writer all other writers take offence. And to point out that Kovalić was a writer who divided all prose into two categories, prose *with balls* and prose *without* (he was for the former), would be quite out of place in these circumstances and might even prompt the reader to give a completely erroneous and vulgar interpretation to the whole incident. Let us therefore say instead that Kovalić greatly valued – and wished to write – novels that were true to life, down to earth. What he despised more than anything was symbols, metaphors, allusions, ambiguities, literary frills; what he admired was authenticity, a razor-edged quality where every word meant what it meant and not God knows what else! He was especially put off by intellectualising, attitudinising, high-blown flights of fancy, genres of all kinds (life is too varied and unpredictable to be forced into prefabricated moulds, damn it!) and – naturally – critics! Who but critics, force-fed on the pap of theory, turned works of literature into paper monsters teeming with hidden meanings?

Kovalić happened to be working on a book of stories called *Meat*, the kingpin of which was going to be about his neighbour, a retired butcher positively in love with his trade. Kovalić went on frequent drinking bouts with the man for the purpose of gathering material: nouns (brisket, chuck, flank, knuckle, round, rump, saddle, shank, loin, wienerwurst, weisswurst, liverwurst, bratwurst, blood pudding, etc.), verbs (pound, hack, gash, slash, gut, etc.), and whole sentences. 'You shoulda seen me go through them – the slaughterhouse ain't got nothing on me!'; 'A beautiful way to live a life – and earn a pile!'; 'My knives go with me to the grave.' Kovalić intended to use the latter, which the old man would say with great pathos, to end the story with a wallop.

We might add that Kovalić was a good-looking man and much loved by the women, about a situation he took completely for granted.

Well, dear readers, now you can judge for yourselves the state our hero was in when instead of his far from ugly bulge he found a smooth, even space.

Looking in the mirror, Kovalić saw a broken man. God, he thought, why me? And why not my arms or legs? Why not my ears or nose, unbearable as it would have been.

What good am I now? . . . Good for the dump, that's what! If somebody had chopped it off, I wouldn't have made a peep. But to up and disappear on me, vanish into thin air . . . ?! No, it's impossible! I must be dreaming, hallucinating. And in his despair he started pinching the empty space again.

Suddenly, as if recalling something important, Kovalić pulled on his shoes and ran out into the street. It was a sunny day, and he soon slowed his pace and began to stroll. In the street he saw a child peeling a banana, in a bar he saw a man pouring beer from a bottle down his gullet, in a doorway he saw a boy with a plastic pistol in his hand come running straight at him; he saw a jet cross the sky, a fountain in a park start to spurt, a blue tram come round a bend, some workers block traffic dragging long rubber pipes across the road, two men walking towards him, one of whom was saying to the other, 'But for that you really need balls . . .'

God! thought Kovalić, compulsively eyeing the man's trousers. Can't life be cruel!

Queer! the cocky trousers sneered, brushing past him.

I must, I really must do something, thought Kovalić, sinking even deeper into despair. And then he had a lifesaver of a thought . . . Lidija! Of course! He'd go and see Lidija.

You never know what's going to happen next, thought Vinko K., the good-looking young policeman, as he jaywalked across the square. Pausing in front of a shop window, he saw the outline of his lean figure and the shadow of his stick dangling at his side. Through the glass he saw a young woman with dark, shining eyes making hot dogs. First she pierced one half of a long roll with a heated metal stake and twisted it several times; then she poured some mustard into the hollow and stuffed a pink hot dog into it. Vinko K. was much taken with her dexterity. He went in and pretended to be waiting his turn, while in fact he was watching the girl's pudgy hands and absentmindedly twirling his stick.

'Next!' her voice rang out.

'Me?! Oh, then I might as well have one,' said a flustered Vinko K., 'as long as . . .'

'Twenty!' her voice rang out like a cash register.

Vinko K. moved over to the side. He subjected the bun to a close inspection: it contained a fresh hot dog. Meanwhile, two more girls had come out of a small door, and soon all three were busy piercing rolls and filling them with mustard and hot dogs.

Vinko K. polished off his hot dog with obvious relish and then walked over to the girls.

'Care to take a break, girls?' he said in a low voice. 'Can we move over here?' he added, even more softly.

Squeezed together between cases of beverages and boxes of hot dogs, a sink, a bin, and a broom, Vinko K. and the waitresses could scarcely breathe.

'I want you to show me all the hot dogs you have on the premises,' said a calm Vinko K.

The girl opened all the hot dog boxes without a murmur. The hot dogs were neatly packed in cellophane wrappers.

'Hm!' said Vinko K. 'Tell me, are they all vacuum-packed?'

'Oh, yes!' all three voices rang out as a team. 'They're all vacuum-packed!'

A long, uncomfortable silence ensued. Vinko K. was thinking. You never knew what would happen next in his line. You could never tell what human nature had in store.

Meanwhile the girls just stood there, huddled together like hot dogs in a cellophane wrapper. All at once Vinko K.'s fingers broke into a resolute riff on one of the cardboard boxes and, taking a deep breath, he said, as if giving a password, 'Fellatio?'

'Aaaaah?!' the girls replied, shaking their heads, and though they did not seem to have understood the question they kept up a soft titter.

'Never heard of it?' asked Vinko K.

'Teehee! Teehee! Teehee!' they tittered on.

'Slurp, slurp?' Vinko K. tried, sounding them out as best he could.

'Teehee! Teehee! Teehee!' they laughed, pleasantly, like the Chinese.

Vinko K. was momentarily nonplussed. He thought of using another word with the same meaning, but it was so rude he decided against it.

'Hm!' he said instead.

'Hm!' said the girls, rolling their eyes and bobbing their heads.

Vinko K. realised his case was lost. He sighed. The girls sighed back compassionately.

By this time there was quite a crowd waiting for hot dogs. Vinko K. went outside. He stole one last glance at the first girl. She glanced back, tittered, and licked her lips. Vinko K. smiled and unconsciously bobbed his stick. She too smiled and vaguely nodded. Then she took a roll and resolutely rammed it onto the metal stake.

But at this point everything becomes so enveloped in mist again that we cannot tell what happened next.

'*Entrez!*' Lidija called out unaffectedly, and Kovalić collapsed in her enormous, commodious armchair with a sigh of relief.

Lidija was Kovalić's best friend: she was completely, unhesitatingly devoted to him. Oh, he went to bed with her all right, but out of friendship: she went to bed with *him* out of friendship too. They didn't do it often, but they had stuck with it for ages – ten years by now. Kovalić knew everything there was to know about Lidija; Lidija knew everything there was to know about Kovalić. And they were never jealous. But Kovalić the writer – much as he valued sincerity in life and prose – refused to admit to himself that he had once seen their kind of relationship in a film and found it highly appealing, an example (or so he thought) of a new, more humane type of rapport between a man and a woman. It was in the name of this ideal that he gave his all to her in bed even when he was not particularly up to it.

They had not seen each other for quite some time, and Lidija started in blithely about all the things that had happened since their last meeting. She had a tendency to end each sentence with a puff, as if what she had just produced was less a sentence than a hot potato.

Lidija had soon trotted out the relevant items from the pantry of her daily life, and following a short silence – and a silent signal they had hit upon long before – the two of them began to undress.

'Christ!' cried Lidija, who in other circumstances was a translator to and from the French.

'Yesterday . . .' said Kovalić, crestfallen, apologetic. 'Completely disappeared . . .'

For a while Lidija simply stood there, staring wide-eyed at Kovalić's empty space; then she assumed a serious and energetic expression, went over to her bookcase, and took down the encyclopedia.

'Why bother?' asked Kovalić as she riffled the pages. 'Castration, castration complex, coital trophy – it's all beside the point! It's just disappeared, understand? Dis-ap-peared!'

'*Bon Dieu de Bon Dieu . . . !*' Lidija muttered. 'And what are you going to do now?'

'I don't know,' Kovalić whimpered.

'Who were you with last?'

'Girl named Maja . . . But that's beside the point.'

'Just wondering,' said Lidija, and said no more.

As a literary person in her own right, Lidija had often cheered Kovalić up and on with her gift for the apt image. But now her sugar-sweet sugarbeet, her pickle in the middle, her poor withered mushroom, her very own Tom Thumb, her fig behind the leaf, her tingaling dingaling, her Jack-in-the-box had given way to – a blank space!

All of a sudden Lidija had a divine inspiration. She threw herself on Kovalić and for all the insulted, humiliated, oppressed, for all the ugly, impotent, and sterile, for all the poor in body, hunched in back, and ill in health – for every last one she gave him her tenderest treatment, polishing, honing him like a recalcitrant translation, fondling, caressing, her tongue as adroit as a key punch, kneading his skin with her long, skilful fingers, moving lower and lower, seeking out her Jack's mislaid cudgel, picking and pecking at the empty space, fully expecting the firm little rod to pop out and give her cheek a love tap. Kovalić was a bit stunned by Lidija's abrupt show of passion, and even after he began to feel signs of arousal he remained prostrate, keeping close tabs on the pulsations within as they proceeded from pitapat to rat-tat-tat to boomety-boom, waiting for his Jack to jump, his Tom to thump, he didn't care who, as long as he came out into the open . . . !

Kovalić held his breath. He felt the blank space ticking off the seconds like an infernal machine; felt it about to erupt like a geyser, a volcano, an oil well; felt himself swelling like soaked peas, like a tulip bulb, like a cocoon; felt it coming, any time now, any second now, any – pow! boo-oo-oom! cra-a-a-sh-sh-sh!

Moaning with pleasure, Kovalić climaxed, climaxed to his great surprise – in the big toe of his left foot!

Utterly shaken, Kovalić gave Lidija a slight shove and peered down at his foot. Then, still refusing to believe that what happened had happened, he fingered the toe. It gave him a combination of pleasure and mild pain – and just sat there, potato-like, indifferent. Kovalić stared at it, mildly offended by its lack of response.

'*Idiot!*' said Lidija bilingually, and stood up, stalked out, and slammed the door.

Kovalić stretched. The smooth space was still hideously smooth. He wiggled his left toe, then his right . . . The left one struck him as perceptibly fatter and longer.

It did happen, thought Kovalić. There's no doubt about it. It actually happened. Suddenly he felt grateful to Lidija. The only thing was, did he really climax in his toe or was his mind playing tricks on him? Kovalić leaned over and felt the toe again, then went back to the smooth space, and finally, heaving a worried sigh, lit a cigarette.

'Anyone for a nice homemade sausage?' asked a conciliatory Lidija, peeking in from the kitchen.

Kovalić felt all the air go out of him: Lidija's proposition was like a blow to the solar plexus; it turned him into the butt of a dirty joke.

Kovalić was especially sensitive to clichés; he avoided them in both literature and life. And now he was terribly upset. By some absurd concatenation of events his life had assumed the contours of a well-established genre (a joke of which he was the punch line). How could life, which he had always thought of as vast – no, boundless – how could life give in to the laws of a genre? And with nary a deviation! Kovalić was so distressed he felt tears welling in his eyes. How he loved – literature! It was so much better, more humane, less predictable, more fanciful . . . In a well-written story Lidija would have offered him nothing less than a veal cutlet; in the low genre of life, Lidija, she gives him – a sausage!

But suddenly Kovalić felt hungry . . .

On Saturday, the seventh of April, Nada Matić awoke from a nightmare she had had for many nights. She would dream she was working in her office at Plastic Surgery. It was crammed with anatomical sketches, plaster moulds, and plastic models – all of 'hot dogs' of the most varied dimensions. Suddenly in trooped a band of students who tore them all to pieces, laughing and pointing at her all the while. Nada thought she would die of shame, and to make matters worse she felt something sprouting on her nose – an honest to goodness sausage! At that point the scene would shift to the operating room, where she – Nada – and Dr Waldinger were performing a complex procedure. But there was a round hole in the white sheet covering the patient, and she couldn't stop staring through it at his hideous smooth space. Then the scene would shift again, and she and Otto Waldinger were in a field pulling out a gigantic beet. She was holding Otto around the waist when suddenly she was attacked by a gigantic mouse! She could feel its claws on her thighs.

Nada Matić was drinking her morning coffee, smoking a cigarette, and leafing through the evening paper. She would seem to have acquired the fine habit of perusing the Saturday classifieds. Suddenly an item in the 'Lost and Found' column caught her eye. She did a double take, stunned by a wild but logical thought: if someone were to lose something like that, it would only be natural for him to try to find it!

On the twenty-fifth of March, I left a collapsable umbrella in the Skyscraper Cafeteria. Would the finder please return it. No questions asked. Phone xyz and ask for Milan.

Nada jumped out of her seat. The ad was perfectly clear! The umbrella was obviously a respectable substitution for *that*. The fact that it was collapsable made the whole thing absolutely unambiguous!

Nada grabbed the telephone and dialled the number. The conversation was to the point: That's right. Five o'clock. See you there. Good-bye.

At five o'clock that afternoon Nada Matić rang the doorbell of a Dalmatinska Street apartment. A dark man of about thirty opened the door.

He could well be the one, thought Nada and said, 'Hello, my name is Nada Matić.'

'And mine is Milan Miško. Come in.'

'Are you the one who lost his umbrella?'

'That's right.'

'At the cafeteria?'

'The Skyscraper.'

'Collapsable?'

'Yes, yes,' said Milan Miško, the owner of the lost umbrella, in an amiable voice. 'Do come in.' Nada went in.

They sat down. The owner of the collapsable umbrella brought out a bottle of wine and two glasses.

'So, you're the one who lost it,' Nada said tellingly and took a sip of the wine.

'That's right.'

'God, how thick can he be?' thought Nada, beginning to feel

annoyed. She took a long look at *that* place, but could make nothing out. She had to put it into words! But how?

'It must have been hard for you . . .' she said, trying a more direct approach.

'With all the spring showers, you mean? I'd have picked up another one, but you do get attached to your own . . .'

'What was it like? Your umbrella, I mean,' she asked its owner nonchalantly.

'Oh, nothing special . . . You mean, what colour, how long?'

'Yes,' said Nada, swallowing hard, 'how long . . . ?'

'Oh, standard size,' he said, as calm as could be. 'You know – collapsable.' And he looked over at Nada serenely. 'The kind that goes in and out.'

Now there could be no doubt. Nada resolved to take the plunge and call a spade a spade, even if it meant humiliating herself. After all, she had played her own bitter part in the affair. So she took the sort of deep breath she would have taken before a dive, half-shut her eyes, stretched out her arms in a sleepwalker's pose, and – jumped! I'm wrong, she thought as she flew mentally through the air, terribly, shamefully wrong. But it was too late to retreat.

And though at this point everything becomes enveloped in mist again, we can guess exactly what happened.

The waitress switched off the light and shut the door after the other girls. For some reason she didn't feel like going with them. She sat down for a short rest and looked through the window at the passersby and the brand names atop the buildings. As she bent over to take off the slippers she wore at work, her hand happened to graze her knee. She let her hand rest on the knee and froze in that position as if listening for something. Then, heaven knows why, she thought of the dark handsome guy who'd left his umbrella in the cafeteria a week or so before and that good-looking young policeman with the funny, kinky questions – both of them so attractive and somehow connected . . . Or had she noticed them and had they registered with her mainly because they had – of that she was sure – noticed *her*?

Sheltered by the darkness, the cartons, and the glass, the girl sat with her legs slightly parted, relaxed, peering out of the window at the passersby, when suddenly her hands reached by themselves for one of the cardboard boxes, pulled out a few packages of hot dogs, and started tugging feverishly at the cellophane wrappers. God, what was she doing? What was she doing? What if somebody saw her . . . ? Nobody saw her.

She slowly brought a raw hot dog to her lips and quickly stuffed it into her mouth. The hot dog slid down her throat, leaving practically no taste behind. She grabbed a second and quickly chewed it up. Then a third, a fourth, a fifth . . .

There in the heart of the city, enslaved by the darkness, the cartons and the glass, sat a waitress with her legs slightly parted and her dark, shining eyes peering out at the passersby while she gobbled hot dog after hot dog. At one point the image of a gigantic, ravenous female mouse flashed through her mind, but she immediately forgot it. She was following the movements of her jaws and listening in on her gullet.

In the afternoon of the seventh of April there was a nervous ring at Kovalić's door. Kovalić was a bit taken aback to see a good-looking young policeman carrying an unusual-looking bundle.

'Are you Mato Kovalić the writer? Or, rather, the novelist and short story writer?'

'I am,' said Kovalić with a tremor in his voice.

'Well, this is yours. Sign here.'

'But . . .' Kovalić muttered.

'Good-bye,' said the policeman and, with a knowing wink, added, 'and good luck!'

'But officer . . . !' Kovalić cried out. It was too late. The policeman had disappeared into the lift.

Kovalić unwrapped the bundle with trembling hands. Out of the paper fell a bottle filled with a clear liquid, and floating in that liquid was his very own . . . ! Unbelievable! Kovalić was beside himself. For several moments he stood stock still; then he went back and cautiously removed the object from the bottle and started inspecting it.

That's it, all right – the real thing! Kovalić thought aloud. He'd have recognised it anywhere! And he jumped for joy – though carefully clutching it in his hands.

Since, however, it is a well-known fact that nothing on this earth lasts for very long, our hero suddenly frowned. He had had a terrifying thought. What if it wouldn't go back on?

With indescribable terror in his heart Kovalić walked over to the mirror. His hands were trembling. He carefully returned the object to its former place. Panic! It refused to stick! He brought it up to his lips, warmed it with his breath, and tried again. No luck!

'Come on, damn you!' Kovalić grumbled. 'Stick! Stick, you stupid fool!' But the object fell to the floor with a strange, dull, cork-like thud. 'Why won't it take?' Kovalić wondered nervously. And though he tried again and again, his efforts were in vain.

Crushed, Kovalić was left holding his own, his very own and now, very useless part. And much as Kovalić stared at it, it clearly remained indifferent to his despair and lay there in his hand like a dead fish.

'Ba-a-a-astard!' Kovalić screamed in a bloodcurdling voice and flung the object into a corner and himself onto his bed. 'No, I'm not dreaming,' Kovalić whispered into his pillow. 'This can't be a dream. This is madness, lunacy . . .' And with that he fell asleep.

Lidija typed out the word *maladie* and paused. She was still on page one. The translation of the report was due on Monday morning at the Department of Veterinary Medicine.

She stood up, stretched, and switched on the light. She glanced out of the window. It was still day, but the street was grey and empty and smooth from the rain.

She went into the kitchen and opened the refrigerator door out of habit. She peered in without interest and slammed it shut.

Then she went into the bathroom, turned on the tap, and put her wrist under a jet of cold water. It felt good. She glanced up at the mirror. All at once she felt like licking it. She moved in close to its smooth surface. Her face with tongue hanging out flashed into sight. She drew back slowly. A smooth and empty gesture. Like her life. 'Smooth, empty, empty, smooth . . .' she murmured on her way back to the kitchen.

On the kitchen table Lidija noticed a few dried-out bits of bread. She touched them. She liked the way dry crumbs pricked the pulp of her fingers. She moistened her finger with saliva, gathered up the crumbs, and went into the combined bedroom and living room. Again she looked out at the street, preoccupied, nibbling on the crumbs from her finger and on the finger itself. The street was empty.

And then she noticed a good-looking young policeman. He had a limber way about him and was crossing the smooth street, or so it seemed to Lidija, as if it were water. Suddenly she opened the window, breathed deeply, pursed her lips for a whistle, and stopped . . . What was she doing, for Heaven's sake? What had got into her . . . ?

The policeman looked up. In a well-lit window he saw an unusual-looking young woman standing stock still and staring at him. His glance came to rest on her full, slightly parted lips. He noticed a crumb on the lower one . . . Or was he just imagining it? Suddenly he had a desire to remove that real or imagined crumb with his own lips.

'What if she really . . .' flashed through his mind as he noiselessly slipped into the main door. But what happened next we really have no idea.

Kovalić awoke with a vague premonition. His head felt fuzzy, his body leaden. He lay completely motionless for a while when all at once he felt an odd throbbing sensation. He tore off the blanket, and lo and behold! – *it* was back in place.

Kovalić couldn't believe his eyes. He reached down and fingered it – yes, it was his, all right! He gave it a tug just to make sure – yes, it popped out of his hand, straight, taut, elastic. Kovalić jumped for joy and leaped out of bed, rushing over to the mirror for a look. No doubt about it: there it stood, rosy, shiny, and erect – and just where it had been before. Kovalić cast a worried glance at the bottle. He saw a little black catfish swimming about as merrily as you please. Intent on engineering clever turns within its narrow confines, it paid him no heed.

'Oh!' Kovalić cried out in amazement.

Then he looked back down below. Situation normal: stiff and erect! Trembling with excitement, Kovalić raced to the phone.

At this point, however, the events are temporarily misted over by censorship, and the reader will have to deduce what happened from the following lines.

Exhausted and depressed, her eyes circled in black, her mouth dry, Maja the invoice clerk lay on her back apathetically staring at that horrid black fish. It was making its two-thousand-one-hundred-and-fifty-first turn in the bottle. At last she picked herself up slowly and started gathering her clothes the way an animal licks its wounds. Suddenly her eyes lit on a slip of paper lying next to her left shoe.

The paper contained a list of names in Kovalić's handwriting. *Vesna, Branka, Iris, Goga, Ljerka, Višnja, Maja, Lidija*. All the names but Lidija's (hers too!) had lines through them.

'Monster!' she said in a hoarse, weary voice, and slammed the door.

Kovalić stared apathetically at the lower half of his body. *It* was in place, sprightly and erect as ever. He flew into a rage, bounded out of bed, bolted to the bottle, and smashed it to the floor. The catfish flipped and flopped for a while, then calmed down. Kovalić gleefully watched the gill contractions subside. But *it* was still erect.

'Down, monster!' Kovalić shouted and gave it a mean thwack. It swayed and reddened, but then spryly, with a rubber-like elasticity, sprang back into place and raised its head at Kovalić almost sheepishly.

'Off with you, beast!' Kovalić screamed. The object refused to budge.

'I'll strangle you!' Kovalić bellowed. The object stared straight ahead, curtly indifferent.

'I wish you'd never been found,' Kovalić whimpered, and flung himself onto the bed in despair. 'You bastard, you! I'll get you yet . . . !' And he burst into sobs, mumbling incoherent threats into the pillow. Then, wiping his tears, he raised his fist into the air, Heaven knows why, and muttered, 'I'll put you through the meatgrinder!' And all of a sudden the old butcher's saying went off like an alarm in his brain: *My knives go with me to the grave!*

And the fear and trembling caused by this new piece of data sent Kovalić reeling – and into a dead faint.

Well, dear readers, now you see the sort of thing that happens in our city! And only now, after much reflection, do I realise how much in it is unbelievable – starting from the alienation of the object in question from its rightful owner. Nor is it believable that authors should choose such things to write stories about. First, they are of no use either to literature or to the population, the reading population, and secondly, they are of no use . . . well, either. And yet, when all is said and done, there is hardly a place you won't find similar incongruities. No, say what you will, these things do happen – rarely, but they do.

For my part, I have a clear conscience. I have stuck to the plot. Had I given myself free rein, well, I don't know where things would have ended! And even so, what happened to Nada Matić? Who is

Milan Miško? What became of Vinko K.? And Lidija and the waitress and the butcher? To say nothing of our hero Mato Kovalić? Is he doomed to spend his life getting it – down?!

But I repeat: I have stuck to the plot. Though if the truth be told, I did insert two nightmares from my own childhood, to wit: 1) the sausage dream ('Watch out or a sausage will spout on your nose,' my grandfather used to say when he got angry with me), and 2) the beet dream (I can recall no more terrifying story from my childhood than the one in which a whole family gathered to pull out a big, beautiful, and completely innocent beet!).

In connection with said plot may I suggest the following points as worthy of further consideration:

1. How did the object alienated from its owner, Mato Kovalić, find its way into the bun?

2. How did Vinko K. discover its owner?

3. Miscellaneous.

All that is merely by the by, of course, in passing. I myself have no intention of taking things any further . . . But if you, honoured readers, decide to do so, I wish you a merry time of it and a hearty appetite!

M. H. H.

Life is a Fairy Tale

···

An ample young lady in a state of constant hunger

'There, you see!' Barbara sighed sadly, reaching for a stale *Ginger Nut* biscuit, popping it into her mouth and sucking her chubby index finger. 'That's how it began. The moment he slammed the door behind him and left me for good, I felt this terrible hunger. And I've been eating, eating, eating ever since. I hardly sleep at night, so I can eat. It's awful!' Her plump shoulders shook in a brief, violent fit of weeping. Then she wiped her tears and bit into a *Lemon Puff* as though nothing had happened.

'Excuse me,' said Jozo politely, taking a little calculator out of his pocket. 'But when did this, how shall I put it, emotionally stressful incident occur?'

'Hmm, just a sec . . .' Barbara began to think, chewing a *Choc Chip Cookie*. 'The thirteenth of July, I think it was. Yes, the thirteenth!'

'And, today is . . . What's today's date?'

'You can't have forgotten! New Year's Eve!'

'Oh, yes, sorry! That means you've been like this for exactly 202 days!'

'Really!'

'That is 4,848 hours!'

'Incredible!'

'Or 290,880 minutes!'

'Awful!'

'You've been, how shall I put it, in a state of constant hunger for exactly 17,452,800 seconds!'

'Dreadful! There's only one thing left for someone like me to do – kill herself!'

'No, Barbara, don't even say it.'

An incomplete personality reduced to a mouth

'Do you know how many kids that guy had?' Barbara asked, leaning confidingly towards Jozo.

'I wouldn't know,' Jozo said modestly.

'Five of his own, legitimate, and three illegitimate!' Barbara managed to say before shoving a *Melting Moment* biscuit into her mouth to stifle a sob.

'That's eight altogether!' Jozo said, automatically reaching for the calculator.

'But ever since he left me, I haven't been really alive. I'm not a person any more, I feel empty!' She thumped her chest. 'I feel I don't really exist! I'm an incomplete personality, that's what I am. An incomplete personality! I'm reduced to nothing but a mouth, a gaping mouth . . .'

'You're right,' said Jozo sadly, nibbling a piece of broken wafer. 'I know the feeling.'

The author who feels incomplete (as an author) affirms a timorous authorial presence which may be necessary, though maybe not

Maybe shd mention that convers tkg plce in modstly furn'shd room. Snowing outside, big flakes stick to windw. Bttle of plonk on table, 2 glsses + heap cakes, etc. Half-open door into corridor, in c'rdr: tlphone – to be mentioned in story once more. Clock heard tckng.

A second incomplete personality and his (the afore-mentioned personality's) mother

'I know the feeling. I'm, how shall I put it, an incomplete personality myself . . .' began Jozo.

'You too!' said Barbara in surprise, swallowing a bite of *Kit-Kat*.

'Yes. It all began the day father left us. That day, or a day or two later, my mother made a vow that she'd never allow life's troubles in general to get her down, particularly loneliness and that dangerous melancholy abandoned women usually succumb to.' He added quietly, 'My mother is, how shall I put it, a very strong personality!'

'How old is your mother?'

'My mother? Eighty.'

'Oh! She's getting on, isn't she?'

'She doesn't mind. You see, how shall I put it, a long time ago she worked out a system for resisting melancholy, or, to put it another way, depression. At this very moment, for instance,' he said looking at his watch, 'she is probably standing on her head, doing star jumps or learning Spanish. Mother thinks learning Spanish is a specially good cure for depression.'

'Incredible! At her age . . .'

'Yes,' said Jozo in a crushed tone. 'And I'm the exact opposite.'

An incomplete personality as the exact opposite

'Wait a moment,' Barbara livened up, shoving three *Garibaldis* into her mouth at the same time. 'I don't see the problem. It's wonderful to have a mother and one with such a strong personality as well. I haven't got anyone.'

'You mean they're all . . . ?'

'Mmm.'

'I'm sorry, how can I put, I'm really . . .'

'Never mind! Go on.'

'You said you didn't see the problem, didn't you? The problem, how shall I put it, is with people of the opposite sex, that is, women. They keep leaving. Twice I even tried . . .'

'Tried what?' Barbara smacked her lips and broke a piece off a *Tea Time Assorted* biscuit.

'Marriage.'

'What of it?'

'Well, you know, it's my melancholy,' said Jozo agitatedly. 'For instance, I never dared shut myself in my room because Mother would keep bursting in and shouting: Hurraaah! You see, how shall I put it, she thought shock therapy was the best cure for depression. And I was what mother called a fundamental melancholic.'

'A what?' Barbara asked sympathetically, licking a chocolate-covered *Hob Nob*.

'A fundamental melancholic. Mother thought that shock would change a person's mood, for the better of course, that it could bring to life the vital inner forces atrophied by melancholy. Sometimes she'd be waiting for me after school round a corner, she'd suddenly leap out, shouting: "Hurraaah!"'

'You don't have to keep doing that!' said Barbara, coughing on a piece of *Fruit Shortcake*.

'Sorry,' said Jozo, crushed.

'Never mind, never mind, carry on. Just give me a glass of milk. There, on the sideboard.'

'There were sudden Tarzan cries in the shock-therapy as well,' Jozo went on, pouring Barbara a glass of milk. 'Mother thought they were the best way of dispelling my moods. She'd go: Aaaaaaaaaaaaaaaa!'

'Hey, not so loud!' said Barbara, searching with her finger in her glass of milk for a piece of *Bounty* bar that had fallen to the bottom.

'Sorry,' Jozo blushed. 'Mother had other methods in her battle against depression. Education, for instance. "Education is a beacon, a guiding light," she would say, because it dispels gloomy states of mind.'

'And?' asked Barbarba, dunking a *Custard Cream* and her own finger in the milk.

When there is a healthy mind in a healthy body, knowledge is power

'Every morning we'd read the great classics,' said Jozo. 'I know the opening sentences of many great novels. "At about nine o'clock in the morning, at the end of November, during a thaw, the Warsaw train was approaching Petersburg at full speed." Do you know where that's from?'

'No,' Barbara smacked her lips decisively.

'Dostoevsky. *The Idiot*,' said Jozo modestly. 'Maybe you know this one: "The sun had not yet risen. The sea was indistinguishable from the sky . . ."'

Jozo looked enquiringly at Barbara. Barbara munched on indifferently.

'Virginia Woolf, *The Waves*,' Jozo announced solemnly.

'You don't say,' said Barbara, for the sake of saying something.

'There was only one novel we couldn't read,' said Jozo.

'Which?'

'Camus' *The Outsider*!'

'Never heard of it. Why that one?'

'Because the first sentence goes: "My mother died today."'

'I see.'

'I'm sorry, I'm boring you . . .' Jozo said politely.

'No, but get to the point. I haven't got a clue about those novels of yours.'

'Mother had worked out, how shall I put it, an integrated system for fighting melancholy. The HMHB system. A healthy mind in a healthy body. We lifted weights, repeating newly-learned English words, stood on our heads rattling off chemical formulae, did press-ups to lists of loan words . . . Would you have any objection to my demonstrating?'

'Well, as you've already . . .'

'What letter?'

'What do you mean?'

'What letter shall I start with?'

'Um, "z"!'

'Zareba, zebu, zeitgeist, zemindar, zenana, zeta, zeugma, zibet, zloty, zoetrope . . .' mumbled Jozo doing press-ups.

'And do you know what those words mean?'

'Not all of them,' said Jozo modestly, getting up from the floor and wiping his forehead with a handkerchief. 'There!' he said with a sigh.

Although life buzzes like a bustling hive, there's something the incomplete personality lacks

'I really don't understand why you call yourself an incomplete personality,' said Barbara. 'You're so knowledgeable, so well-rounded.'

'Well, how shall I put it, it has to do with people of the opposite sex, that is, with women. My wives had to practise mother's HMHB system as well. The first held out for two months, the second only five days.'

'How ungrateful of them!' said Barbara, opening a jar of jam.

'That, how shall I put it, isn't all,' Jozo began hesitantly.

'What do you mean?'

'Well, for instance, when I got into bed with my wife, my mother would barge into the room shouting Hurrraaaah! And I would immediately go . . . limp . . . You understand?'

'You mean . . . ? Oh, you mean your whatsit?' Barbara choked. 'It would, er, go limp?'

'That's right. And even so, it's, how shall I put it, small.'

'How small?'

'Three and a half inches!'

'Not much, I admit.'

'There, now you know.'

'Ah well, what can you do!' sighed Barbara, scooping up jam with her finger and licking it.

'Nothing,' sighed Jozo, shrugging his shoulders and added, as though he had just remembered it, 'And do you know my mother doesn't sleep at all for fear that melancholy might catch her with her eyes closed?'

'What does she do all night then? At least I eat when I'm not asleep.'

'She sends out messages to me . . .'

'What sort of messages?'

'Well, the kind that can cheer a person up. For instance: "A smile a day keeps your cares at bay." Mother makes them up herself. Or: "Life is a fairy tale, my friend, and soon there'll be a happy end!" *La vida es fabula!*'

'What does that last one mean?'

'The same. Life is a fairy tale in Spanish. Mother most liked sending those messages just as my wife and I . . . You understand . . .'

'Yes.'

'Because, actually, there weren't any other opportunities. Our little flat was always full of people. Mother's friends from the mountaineering, cycling, and fishing clubs, The Firemen's Society, miscellaneous itinerants, cardplayers, mother's lonely women friends, thieves . . . "Life in our little flat buzzes like a bustling hive!" mother would often say.

'But, why don't you move out?' asked Barbara, dunking a digestive into the jar of jam.

'Why? I love my mother! Besides, I've given up all hope of becoming a complete personality.'

'So what's the problem actually?'

'Well that . . . How shall I put it . . . Don't you see? It's as though I didn't have anything down below! You said yourself . . . Three and a half inches is nothing! Particularly if they're not used! Do you see? Somehow I'm, well, basically – sexless!'

'I see!' said Barbara compassionately, falling on a box of *Penguin* bars.

The author who feels not only incomplete
but superfluous (as an author)
draws attention to his presence again

Outside snow is falling. Snow is falling. Outside snow is falling in large flakes. Snow is falling in large flakes. Large flakes of snow are silently falling. Outside . . .

If there were no rejects
the ample young lady could never manage

'Tell me, how much weight have you put on?'

'A hundred and twenty pounds.'

'That would be monthly . . . Would you like me to calculate it exactly?' asked Jozo, taking the calculator out of his pocket again.

'Why do you keep calculating things?'

'Habit. Mother bought me the calculator. For my campaign against melancholy. She said it was better for me to calculate things than to sit doing nothing and staring into space. How much did you weigh when this all began?'

'Average. A hundred and forty-five. But, you can see for yourself. Since you've been here, I've eaten at least four pounds of sweets and biscuits. Luckily I work in a chocolate, sweets and biscuits factory. Everyone employed there has a discount on rejects. I bring these rejects home, close the door and eat, eat, eat . . . And how could I do it otherwise? I get £80 a week. I pay £35 for this room, plus electricity. And what's left for me to live on? Work it out yourself!'

'£45, not counting electricity.'

'There, you see!'

'I see.'

'If it weren't for those rejects, I don't know how I'd manage.'

'You couldn't manage at all.'

'Quite! Take these wafer biscuits for instance. Do you know what they cost in the shops?'

'No.'

'70p.'

'That's a lot.'

'And the rejects are only 35p!'

'Really!'

'For the same biscuits!'
'They certainly look the same.'
'The fact that they're broken doesn't matter at all!'
'You'd have broken them yourself.'
'There's no difference, is there?'
'None, really.'
'There, you see!'

Some personalities unravel,
others just don't get involved
– everyone has his cross to bear

Barbara got up from the table with an effort. She waddled over to the sideboard, took out a plastic bag full of biscuits and emptied it into a dish. Then she sat down, put an alarm clock on the table and said, quite out of breath, 'Everyone has his cross to bear.'

'That's well put,' agreed Jozo.

'Take you, for instance. Or Katica and Branka. They're no better off.'

'Who are Katica and Branka?'

'My friends. We work together in the filling department. I used to work in chewing gum. That's where I met my boyfriend. Afterwards I asked to be transferred.'

'Interesting,' said Jozo kindly.

'Yes it is. Katica, now, unlike me, went down to ninety-eight pounds. It's terrible. She's unravelling!'

'What do you mean . . . she's unravelling?'

'You know why her boyfriend left her?'

'No, why?'

'Because she couldn't pronounce the word Popocatapetl!'

'That's a volcano in Mexico!'

'Right, it's some volcano or other. He tormented her for days. Say Popocatapetl, say Popocatapetl. And all she could say was Popopate-cetl, Popopatecetl and Popopatecetl! She couldn't get it right. So he left her. He said you're a fool, you can't even pronounce Popocatapetl, and besides you've got pathetically small tits. Can you believe it? Brankahetically small tits!'

'But why is she "unravelling" now?'

'Because she doesn't eat anything! And everything she wears is knitted and keeps unravelling. She's a fantastic knitter! She's knitted all sorts of things for me! It's much cheaper. You buy wool by the pound and you can knit yourself everything you need. So . . . anyway, lately Katica's just been sitting, silently unpicking wool and fraying. The other day she was at my place, and while I chattered on about something she unravelled her long woollen skirt up to her thighs. She didn't even notice what she was doing, poor thing. It's awful. She's just vanishing before our eyes!'

'What about the other one?'

'Who? Branka?'

'Yes.'

'She's nearly six feet tall.'

'So?'

'Life's not easy for a woman if she's nearly six feet tall!'

'I suppose not.'

'That's why there's no man in her life.'

'Hard luck.'

'There, you see!'

Closed up people
can't expect anything

'It's terrible!' said Barbara, banging the table with her fist. 'May I be completely frank with you, Jozo?'

'Completely,' said Jozo.

'You know, I feel just the same as you. As though I didn't have anything down below. As though I were a plastic doll! or as though someone had cemented me up! As though I had closed up! And I do so want a baaaabyyyy!' Barbara began to sob again.

'Don't cry, Barbara, don't cry!' said Jozo tapping Barbara on the shoulder. 'Is there anything I can do?'

'Give me those biscuits!' said Barbara through her tears and then calmed down a little. 'Nothing. Admit it yourself. With your three inches?'

'Three and a half.'

'With your three and a half inches it's hopeless!'

Although still feeling superfluous,
the author boldly interrupts the dialogue
with a brief lyrical passage

Barbara and Jozo sighed mournfully. Outside the snow was falling in large flakes. There were cries of merriment from neighbouring houses. An unopened bottle of wine stood on the table. The clock said five minutes to midnight.

Life is not a fairy tale even though it's midnight

'Shall I tell you about filling?' Barbara asked suddenly changing the subject.

'What do you mean?' Jozo asked startled out of a profound reverie.

'Why, filling sweets! Just a few days ago we launched a new product. *Sweet Dreams* chocolate creams! We'll try them now. I bought a packet from the factory. Hey! It's nearly midnight!' She was more cheerful now.

The clock showed one minute to midnight. Jozo opened the bottle of wine and filled their glasses. They stood up and toasted each other. It was exactly midnight.

'Happy New Year, Barbara!' said Jozo. 'This is the happiest New Year's Eve I've ever spent. Do you know this is the first time in my life I've ever talked so frankly to anyone. You are, how shall I put it, the most fulfilled person I've ever met.'

'All the best, Jozo! It's nice of you to say that. Still, we must face facts. Life's not a fairy tale. You may still find a decent girl; I've lost all hope. Anyway, cheers! Come on, let's try our chocolate creams!'

'No thanks. I don't like sweets.'

'Go on, just one . . .'

Barbara and Jozo nibbled the new product – *Sweet Dreams* – soft centred chocolates, filled with a mysterious snow-white cream.

The ample-bodied personality melts,
the other is at least partially filled out
(while the dialogues get thinner, the descriptions gain in weight)

'They're delicious!' said Jozo and was going to say something else, but the chocolate cream suddenly stuck in his throat.

'What is it, Jozo?' asked Barbara, alarmed. Jozo stared at Barbara in absolute astonishment as she swallowed her third chocolate. 'Barbara, something's happening to you!' he stammered.

Barbara went over to the mirror. She couldn't believe her eyes! In the mirror she saw her thick double chin slowly melting away, her huge cheeks drawing in, her eyes growing larger; she saw light blue eyes with almost white lashes looking back at her and a pleasing face framed in fair curly hair. For a moment she stood stock still. Then forgetting Jozo, she tore off her blouse and revealed smooth shoulders, full breasts and a slender waist. She waited to see what would happen next.

Nothing happened.

Barbara saw a body composed of two halves. The lower half belonged to the old Barbara and was twice the size of the upper half.

'Jozo!' screamed Barbara. 'Jozo! The chocolates! Quick!'

Completely bewildered, Jozo grabbed the plate of chocolate creams. Without taking her eyes off the picture, Barbara snatched three *Sweet Dreams* from the plates and stuffed then into her mouth. Her skirt slipped to the ground of its own accord. Slim hips appeared. Barbara tore off the last remnant of her clothing and saw her triangle covered with fair silky hair.

'Jozo!' Barbara sobbed with emotion, flinging herself into his arms. 'Jozo, Jozo!', she repeated, weeping. Suddenly she broke off. She looked at Jozo as though she had remembered something and started fumbling with his buttons.

'Quick! Quick,' she mumbled, thrusting a chocolate cream into his mouth. At last the two of them stood naked in front of the mirror waiting to see what would happen. Once again, nothing happened.

Jozo sorrowfully contemplated his thin, pale body, the spots on his shoulders, that pathetic little appendage . . .

'What's this!' Barbara wept. 'Something's wrong! Why only me! Something's wrong!'

Then slowly, like a timid snail putting out its horns, the pathetic appendage began to grow. Barbara rushed off to get a ruler.

'Seven! A whole seven inches!' she cried clapping joyfully. Then she turned out the light and dragged Jozo towards the bed in a frenzy. Stumbling in the dark, Jozo managed to find the *Sweet Dreams* and surreptitiously shoved another into his mouth.

A little later, there was a whisper in the darkness:

'You're wonderful, you smell of cocoa!'

In the meantime the incomplete author practises the description of a sponge finger

– *shape: stress particularly the appropriateness of its shape (like that of a telephone receiver, a spoon, etc.)*

– *consistency (the little sponge body): a communion wafer! just made for the cushions of the fingers and the tongue*

– *feel: a rough smoothness, barely visible floury (flowery) grains*

– *character: brittle, pliable, impermanent (one minute . . . the next . . .): it absorbs, swells, softens, dissolves (blotting paper) – a blotting paper-sponge finger!*

– *sound:* sp–, *that's the hard part of it;* –nge, *that's the soluble bit; sense: innumerable possible anagrams*

– *what is the opposite of a sponge cake? Probably, in a way, a coconut ring . . .*

Joys never come singly

There was a soft knock at the door.

'Who is it?' asked Barbara.

'It's us, Katica and Branka. We've come to wish you a Happy New Year.'

'Come in,' said Barbara.

Two shapes appeared in the darkness, one small, the other tall.

Two smiling faces with a blanket up to their chins, peeped out at them from the bed.

'You could have told us you had someone here, we wouldn't have come!' the shapes said, somewhat put out.

'Come on, don't be silly, this is Jozo,' said Barbara in a friendly voice. Jozo timidly stretched his hand out from under the blanket. The shapes approached the bed, embarrassed, and shook hands.

'Katica,' said the thin one, in a woollen coat.

'Branka,' said the tall one, in trousers and windcheater.

All at once the two heads dived under the blanket.

'Let's not tell them anything,' whispered one. 'Maybe something will happen to them too. Okay?'

'Okay,' whispered the other, giving the first one a kiss on the lips. The heads reappeared above the blanket.

'Come on, girls,' said Barbara. 'Take off your coats, sit down, pour yourselves some wine and try the chocolate creams.'

'No, we're going home!' they both said with one voice, frowning.

'No way!' said Barbara, in mock anger. 'First a glass of wine and then a chocolate!'

The girls poured out some wine and took a chocolate cream each.

Suddenly the woollen jumper Katica was wearing began to stretch and swell, the threads snapping one after the other, and before she knew what was happening out leapt two magnificent breasts with big brown nipples like chocolate pralines.

'Popocatapetl!' shrieked Katica, fainting and falling off her chair. Branka hurried to catch her, but suddenly stopped, groaning, and rushed to the corner of the room. There she turned to the wall, peered into her trousers and gasped: 'Iiiiimpossssible!'

Barbara and Jozo threw off the blanket and got up. For some time the four of them stared at one another, astounded. Katica squinted up from the floor, cupping her huge, beautiful breasts in her hands. Branka was holding onto the zip of her trousers, and Jozo had evidently forgotten about that pathetic little appendage, which was now swinging back and forth to the tune of nine inches.

Barbara was the first to speak. 'Keep calm, everybody! Don't panic! These seem to be some sort of magic chocolate creams. None of us knows how it all happened, why it happened or whether the chocolates really are magic, but the simple truth is that tonight we've all got what we always wanted. Katica, you've got big, beautiful breasts and that's what you wanted; you, Branka, are on the way to becoming a normal man; Jozo has acquired his desperately needed and eminently usable inches – because I get the feeling that in nine months' time we're going to have a baby – and I've lost weight and my all-consuming hunger. We have all gone from being unfulfilled to becoming fulfilled personalities. And now let's get dressed, and throw away the chocolate creams, whether they're magic or not, before any of us thinks up any more wishes.'

Barbara hurled the remaining *Sweet Dreams* chocolate creams into the rubbish bin, put on her dress and tightened her belt several holes. Katica draped a blouse of Barbara's round her shoulders, Jozo pulled on his trousers, Branka did hers up – and they all sat down at the table.

'Hey,' shouted Branka, 'hey, I've still got tits!'

'But they're so small they're not going to bother you,' said Barbara sensibly. 'Besides you'll soon be growing a beard.'

'Hmm,' said Branka, looking at Katica with a strange new look that made Katica blush.

They all raised their glasses and clinked them.

'What a magical night,' said Barbara softly.

When they write,
writers (complete and incomplete)
feel rather lonely
and need to be encouraged

Illuminated with a soft light they all turned their gaze towards the window. Large snowflakes were softly thudding against the window pane and bursting into thousands of magical twinkling stars. For an instant the clock refrained from ticking, all that could be heard was the silken settling of the snow.

The end comes when the magic dictates

'Come on,' said Barbara gaily, 'let's finish this wine and go to bed. It's nearly morning!' She poured herself another glass of wine and following her old habit, dipped her forefinger into the glass of wine and licked it. Suddenly she cried out in pain. Her finger had begun to grow with terrifying speed.

'What's this! Good heavens!' Barbara screamed, her face was contorting with pain. Jozo, Katica and Branka stared helplessly at the finger. When it reached the size of a melon, it suddenly turned red. Barbara shrieked. Just then it burst and out fell a tiny wrinkled male child.

'Quick! A sheet!' cried Barbara regaining control of herself and snapping the invisible little umbilical cord with her teeth, as though she had just sewn on a button.

The girls found a sheet and placed the tiny child on the table. Barbara's finger abruptly shrank and flattened; the split closed up as though it had never been there.

Meanwhile, the little child began growing with the same terrifying speed as Barbara's finger. Katica brought over the kitchen scales and placed the baby on it: 8lbs. Jozo picked the ruler up from the floor and measured his son.

'How shall I put it . . .' he murmured. 'Twenty six inches!'

'It's not thinking of growing any more, is it?' Barbara asked in alarm. At that moment the child began to cry loudly. Barbara unbuttoned her dress and laid the baby against her breast.

'There, it's stopped,' Barbara sighed happily.

'Wow!' Only now did Jozo, Katica and Branka let out a sigh of amazement.

'He's fallen asleep,' whispered Barbara. 'Let's put him on the bed!'

And that's why they need to be encouraged

- *consider the simile: 'The story rolls like a snowball down the snowy slope.' Alternative: 'The story rolls like a chocolate ball down the creamy slope.'*
- *reinforce the symbolic-metaphorical connections between all the elements of the story:*
  1. visual
      (a) geometric: circle – line (melon, breasts, snowball – Barbara's finger, sponge finger, etc.)
      (b) colour: white – black, brown (snow, cream, Barbara – brownies, chocolate, gingernuts, etc.)

  2. cultural: (New Year's Eve)

  3. genre: (Christmas Story, fairy tale, etc.)

  4. check who said: 'One man's sweet is another man's poison'.

  5. other dimensions . . .

Life is a fairy tale after all!

'This is the last miracle we could have wished for. How lovely it is not to have to wait nine months!' concluded Barbara.

'Yes,' said Katica and Branka a little enviously.

'Everything has turned out just right. Jozo can get a job with us in the packing department. With his pay of £75 and mine of £80, minus £35 rent, not counting electricity, we'll have . . .'

'We'll have £120 a month to live on!' came a deep, cheerful, confident voice from the corridor.

'Mother,' the voice continued into the telephone receiver, 'Life *is* a fairy tale!' He hung up.

The author feels something is cracking inside him:
an incomplete (writer)
becoming a complete one

The author finished the last sentence with great difficulty. A shiver ran through him. It was cold in the room. Outside the day was breaking, the snow had stopped. The author took out a cigarette.

He smoked and stared sadly at the snow-covered window. No, it was all in vain. Everything eluded him, characters, words, rhythm. The story (the story he had in mind?) was rolling like a snowball down a snowy slope. He would never, never, become a good writer . . .

Suddenly the flame in the cigarette came to a splinter in the tobacco and flared up. The writer jumped. He felt something creaking, cracking, splitting like a primeval ice floe, then something swelling, bursting, flooding him . . .

The writer quickly rolled a clean sheet of paper into the typewriter and began typing feverishly:

There was a depression over the Atlantic. It was travelling eastwards towards an area of high pressure over Russia, and still showed no tendency to move northwards around it. The isotherms and isotheres were fulfilling their functions . . .

C. H.

Who Am I?

....

Every day I ask myself at least three times who I am. Partly because I'm a very absent-minded person, but not only because of that. I'll be walking through my room, for instance, and knock on the desk three times and ask; Who is it? Then I'll look carefully round me before replying resolutely: Me! Or I'll be cleaning my teeth. The brush gives my gums an intimate tickle and I feel both tender and confident enough to ask it: Toothbrush, toothbrush, whose toothbrush are you? And the toothbrush whispers: Yours. Which yours? I ask irritably, and it mumbles something, half-drowned in toothpaste, so I don't understand. That's how things go during the day.

At night I sleep badly. Tonight I've been tossing and turning, grinding my teeth, chewing sleeping pills, stuffing pink wax balls into my ears, my thoughts bumping against the arch of my skull like fish in an aquarium. Bloop. Bloop. Bloop. I take the wax balls out of my ears and knead them thoughtfully. I make little balls of the little balls.

Then I give up all hope of sleeping and take down a small blue book from the shelf. Only five of my books have blue covers. They are the ones I re-read and know by heart. The green ones, now, I never even open. That's why I've covered them in green so as not to make a mistake.

Anyway, I take a small blue book down from the shelf and I've just started leafing through it when what should come bursting into my room, with a screech of brakes and without so much as a by-your-leave, but – a truck! By mistake, obviously. That is, I do live right beside the road so it isn't impossible for vehicles to turn up in my flat.

Anyway, I'm lying in bed with the covers up to my chin, motionless, staring at the driver's rather stupid face. He winds the window down, sticks his neck out like a tortoise and beckons me with his finger.

'Hey you! Come up here!'

'I'd really like to know who I am. Tell me that first, and then we'll see. If I like being that person I'll come up, if not, I'll stay down here till I'm somebody else!'

The driver looks at me in amazement.

'What is it?' I ask impudently. 'What's wrong?'

'Baaaaaaaa!' The driver sticks out his tongue at me, evidently pleased to have thought of it and charges out of the room with his foot hard on the pedal.

For a moment the room disappears in a cloud of dust. Then through a little hole in the cover I watch with interest as the firm, familiar shapes surface again. I get up, go into the bathroom, take a bottle of face cleansing milk and some blue cotton wool balls and go back to bed.

I remove the dust from my face (dust must grow here while I'm asleep) and I feel my skin soaking up the moisture thirstily. I think about how the face (like the soul) needs moisture, lots and lots of moisture – and how good it would be to go to Ireland. Ireland is very wet. I know. I've seen a film about Ireland, and the moisture came right through the screen! Ireland is saturated with moisture like a sponge, Ireland is as moist as moss, Ireland soaks up moisture like a blotter, Ireland spreads moisture in milky mists, Ireland is as moist as longing, Ireland, ah, Irrrrrelaaaaaand . . .

Forget it, I think. How can I go to Ireland if I don't know who I am? How can anyone go anywhere if they don't know who they are?

Soon I'm relaxed and feel as though I'm about to fall asleep. But then through my half-closed lashes what do I suddenly see floating into my room but a tram! I'm annoyed at the repetition and I throw off my covers and jump out of bed. The tram driver jumps out of the cab, pats me lightly on the shoulder and says, 'Sorry, Nik, give me a glass of water and I'll move on!'

I go to the kitchen and turn on the tap as though hypnotised. I fill a glass of water and hand it to the tram driver. 'There you are! Only, I'm not Nik!'

The tram driver wipes his mouth with a blue sleeve, and stretches his hand out towards my shoulder. At that moment the passengers poke their heads out of the windows, shouting, 'Me too, Nik, me too!'

So I fill the one and only glass I have and pass it, fill it, spill it, over and over, desperately, persistently, as though in a dream. On the kitchen floor threatening pools are already beginning to form.

Innumerable hands dash and dart from the tram windows. Me too, Nik, me tooooo! The tram driver looks anxiously at his watch, gives me a final pat on the shoulder and says, 'Thanks a lot, Nik!'

'Thanks a lot, Nik!' the passengers call out in unison.

I get angry, I throw the glass at one of the tram windows and scream: 'I'm not Nik! You all make me sick!'

That's what I scream: You make me sick. Then I push the tram out of the room and shut the windows.

And then I go back to bed, pull the covers over my head and look for the little hole. Whenever I'm miserable, I look for the little hole (a cigarette burn) and peer out through it. I peer through it for a long time. Until slowly, out of the terrible, unknown depths what should emerge but a little church! I look at the church through the little hole. And there, in the terrible depths and the still more terrible silence, a mysterious brownish light shines. The church is small and pudgy with round blue cupolas. I often wonder where exactly that church is: at the bottom of some ravine, in the heart of some mountain. Sometimes I'm afraid it might disappear, but it's always there. And I can never make out whether the church is in that hole or on the other side of my eye. I wonder. If I patch up the hole, will I sew up the church as well?

I carefully move my eye away from the hole in the cover and the little church vanishes. I emerge from under the covers and strange, I think, something's happening to me, I think, I must be shutting up . . . Like a telescope.

This thought seems important and just as I am in the process of deciding that I must give it further thought, I hear a light tapping on the window pane. Who could that be, I wonder. My curiosity overcomes my annoyance and I go over to the window and open it. A Pigeon flies into the room.

'Hey there, duckie!' says the Pigeon.

'Hey there!' I reply, confused and a little frightened. The Pigeon is two whole inches taller than me, and I'm 5 foot 7, except that I always lie about the last half inch or so.

The Pigeon goes straight to the fridge, pulls open the door and says, 'Empty again!'

I peer in. It's true. The fridge is empty again.

The Pigeon struts irritably round the room, rummaging through my books and picking through an ashtray full of stubs. He finds a fairly large one and lights it.

'Haven't even got any cigarettes, I see!'

I nod my head apathetically.

'What's the matter, duckie?' the Pigeon says kindly. 'Don't know who you are again?'

I nod my head more vigorously. The Pigeon takes a green book down from the shelf and reads:

I . . . i . . . identity! Here we are! So: identity, term with various connotations according as it relates to questions of logic or of metaphysics. The logical law of identity is usually expressed by the formula $A=A$, or A is A. It is a necessary law of self-conscious thought, being, in fact, merely the positive expression of the law of contradiction, which states that a judgment cannot be true and untrue at the same time. Without such a law no thinking would be possible.

*The question of personal identity, that is to say, 'of the continuity of personal experience in the exercise of intelligent causal energy, the results being associated in memory', was first brought into prominence by Locke (*Essay on the Human Understanding*), and soon occupied the attention of Hume and Butler. The fact of identity is that which distinguishes each person from other thinking beings, and with which the preservation of sanity is closely bound up.*

At this point the Pigeon puts the book down and asks me sternly, 'You don't get a word of that, do you, duckie?'

I don't respond. I merely stare at the Pigeon and blush with a sense of guilt. Of course I didn't understand it. I go quietly back to bed, pick up my little blue book and clutch it to my chest like a prayer-book. The Pigeon grabs the book from me, leafs through it and says, 'Balls!'

I blush even more and wonder what it is that makes me blush. I shall certainly have to give that more careful thought. The Pigeon opens the window, flaps its wings as though shaking off dust, climbs onto the window sill, spits contemptuously on the floor of my (my!) room and says, 'Get rid of that inferiority complex, will you? It's messing up your outlook on life. I could ask you which way is south from here, but I won't, because I'm afraid you wouldn't have a clue!'

I nod my head dejectedly and smile faintly with one corner of my mouth. The Pigeon flies away. I go over to the window. I'd be glad to shut it forever. But the Pigeon suddenly reappears on the window sill.

'And will you fill up that fridge, for goodness' sake!'

I mumble something like – yes, yes, of course, I will, certainly – and wave for a long time. I wave tenderly, absently, so that for a moment I forget where I am – at some railway station? an airport? – I even forget who I'm waving to so long and tenderly. And then I remember and think angrily, 'What do you want to go south for, you mythological monster!'

And finally I shut the window! There! Now nobody else comes in. It wouldn't be a bad idea to change my flat, I think, go away to some other, more peaceful place. With a landscape. Landscapes are very important in a person's life. Grass, flowers, plants altogether are very important. So are animals. Ants, for instance. I'd have no objection whatever to opening the window in the morning and seeing the afore-mentioned plants, the sun, of course, and – an ant walking along the window sill. I'd take a sugar lump out of the box and block its path.

Though, come to think of it, a more exotic ambiance would suit me better. A water-melon, say, or a honeydew! Now there's a proper little house! An egg! An archetypal egg. Take a maggot, for example. It crawls into a fresh little house and proceeds to devour it. Once it has devoured it completely, it looks for a new one. They say that the maggots in cherries move in at the flower stage. From the very start, that is. Every maggot is born with its own little house. Every cherry gives birth to its own death. Every little maggot breath its own little cherry death; every maggot breathlet. Its own cherry deathlet.

I go on thinking like that for a while longer; then I climb back into bed and pull the covers over my head. My own breath warms me. I stretch my hand out lazily and what do I feel but a lump! The lump moves. I let my hand wander further: soft curves, smooth skin, curly hair. The lump comes to life, breathes, grows! I hear a gentle grunting under the covers.

'Don't you grunt at me!' I chide the lump. 'That's not at all a proper way to address me!'

'Good morning!' says the head of the Temporary Lover, emerging from the covers.

'Who are you talking to?' I ask.

'You!' says the head of the Temporary Lover, pressing itself warmly against mine. You, say his hands entwining with mine. You, say his legs rubbing against mine, you, say his lips clinging to mine . . .

'I love you,' I whisper and out of the corner of my eye notice that I am kissing my own hand. 'Oh, sorry!' I say, embarrassed, but carry on kissing.

I feel a strange pulsation. Plink! Plonk! Plank! I'm growing! Where are my hands? I stretch my arms out as wide as I can and embrace the Temporary Lover. The next moment I feel a violent blow underneath my chin. My head suddenly falls, it has struck my foot. My chin is now so closely pressed against my foot that there is hardly room to open my mouth. I wiggle my jaw. That's it! My head's free again! I look down, I look right, left, but there's no shoulder to be seen! All I can see is an immense length of neck, stretching endlessly up and up. Goodbye, feet! Where are you, and where am I! And where *have* my shoulders got to? And oh, my poor hands, where are you! How shall I find you!

As I have no longer the slightest hope of reaching my head with my hands, I decide to look for my hands with my head. Incredible! My hands are opening the windows of a flat in the building across the road! Look, they're going into the kitchen, opening the fridge and taking out four eggs, milk, and a piece of bread. Then the left hand goes back for butter. Someone comes in. My arms stop moving and pretend to be electric wires. They are helped by some naive birds which calmly settle on the space between my wrist and my elbow. Then the person goes out and the hands quietly close the fridge. The left one (oh, you little thief!) goes back, takes another egg and a few cigarettes from a box on the table. Then they both quietly close up like a telescope.

I hear the frightened fluttering of the birds. On my table there are five eggs, milk, butter, a piece of bread and a few cigarettes. I feel myself coming home. I smile at the Temporary Lover. He smiles back and says, 'I could eat a horse!'

'Me too!'

I go into the bathroom. I take a long shower, first with hot then with cold water. The cold water congeals my form. I'm whole. I hear sounds and the voice of the Temporary Lover coming from the kitchen.

'I am not going to lie, I sentence you to die! Lie I shall not just, die I say you must! Just not lie, just must die! I'll not lie! You must die! Must die!'

Five hysterical eggs stare at me from the dish. Their indifferent, empty shells gape out of the rubbish bin. The sun comes into the room. The froth of the day. The Temporary Lover and I sit at the table and have breakfast.

'How handsome you are!' I say and watch him a) slicing bread, b) spreading butter on the bread, c) eating bread and butter. How bright he is! Lit up from inside! My lover is eating bread and butter.

I make coffee. The sun shines more and more brightly. I watch the Temporary Lover pouring coffee into his cup, pouring milk into the cup of coffee, pouring sugar into the cup of milky coffee, stirring it with a little spoon, drinking the milky coffee, putting down the cup, not saying anything, lighting a cigarette, making little rings with its smoke, tipping ash into the ashtray. How bright he is! Lit up from inside. I move closer to him and kiss the smooth skin of his lips. He grows tender, warm and soft. Softer and softer. Smaller and smaller. The sun beats relentlessly on the windows. He grows thinner and thinner. He is going, vanishing, melting. I hear a rustling that has the tone of his voice:

'Ah, love . . . love is a sweet sound that makes the world go round!'

All that is left of the Temporary Lover is a little pool of tepid water. I weep, my tears falling on the remains of the omelette and melted butter. Why, I think, it's not fair, I think. Who am I after all? And can I know whether I've been changed in the night? Let me think: *was* I the same when I got up this morning? I almost think I can remember feeling a little different. But if I wasn't the same then, the next question is 'Who in the world am I now?'

I stare helplessly at the little pool of tepid water. The sun is sparkling in it. I cry and cry. Then I happen to glance at my watch, realise that it is midday and time to stop crying. Which I do.

I take a rag. The rag soaks up the little pool of tepid water (he really was handsome!), I wipe my eyes and light a cigarette. I put the cigarette out straight away and look for firm, unambiguous words and carry out similarly firm, unambiguous actions: I take another shower, clean my teeth, brush my hair, get dressed and sit down at my desk to give some thought to what I'm going to do today.

I think I could devote myself to affairs of the spirit. I could go for a walk, enrich my soul and perhaps my vocabulary, which my extreme absentmindedness is making ever poorer. Though I might also translate something from a foreign language. I immediately decide that I will translate something, only I don't know from what language or what. I translate a sentence off the top of my head. *The magician was tall.* I like that sentence; I like the fact that the magician was tall. I don't like short magicians, and I absolutely can't stand tiny ones.

Then I think I might start work on a novel entitled *The Paginated Dog*, though I'm not actually a novelist. Only I can't seem to decide whether the novel should be called *The Paginated Dog* or *The Paginated Horse*. It's a mythological creature, half-horse, half-dog, something like a centaur, only a centaur was half-man, half-horse. The trouble is I don't know which half to make the main part, which is important if one has decided to write a novel about it.

I think a bit along those lines and decide against working on the novel, the more so since I'm not a novelist. I wonder what else I should do.

Then I suddenly remember that I ought to be at work and immediately phone the number of the office.

'Hello? Good afternoon!'

'Good afternoon! Who's that?'

'That's the problem! If I knew, I'd come to work! But I don't know so there's no point. That's logical, isn't it?'

'Hello? Who is this? Who are you trying to kid?'

'No one. I only wanted to tell you I can't come to work today, because I don't know who I am. If I knew I'd come right away! Can't you see?'

'You're crazy!' the receiver hisses.

'Pray don't trouble yourself to say it any longer than that,' I say politely to the receiver, giving it a little shake, and hang up.

Then I take a pencil and write the magic formula *Buy buttons!* on a scrap of paper. The words focus me and give the day meaning. You can't be completely lost if you have shopping to do. Then I write *Buy a zip* – not because I need a zip, but to reinforce the words *Buy buttons*, that is, to emphasise if indirectly my intention to go shopping.

'There!' I say with satisfaction, picking up the scrap of paper and dropping it in my bag. And then for some reason I go over to the window. On the way I stumble on something round.

Heavens, now this! There is an enormous, ugly egg on the floor. Furious I pick up the egg and put it on the table. That deceitful pigeon! Whenever it comes, it always lays an egg secretly in the hope that I'll take care of it! But no! Not this time! One of these days, you mythological creep, one of these days I'll make an omelette of your offspring! And I shake my fist in the vague direction of the window. But then I soften, I stroke the egg, put it to my ear. All right, I think peaceably, I'll take care of you, I'll give you to someone as a present. I wrap the egg in foil and put it in a plastic bag. Then I pick up the telephone and dial a number.

'Hello, Philip?'

'Yes.'

'It's me.'

'Oh, it's you! What are you up to?'

'Nothing. I'm angry with an egg, or rather with a pigeon, although actually I'm not angry any more. Philip, I have to buy buttons in view of the zip or rather a zip in view of . . . and I wondered if we could meet because . . . There's something wrong with me, Philip . . .'

'OK, I'll meet you at The Golden Egg.'

'No! Not the Golden Egg!'

'At The Gold Fish then?'

'All right.'

'In half an hour.'

'In half an hour.'

In half an hour's time I see Philip outside The Gold Fish. No, I think, it's no use speaking to him till I see his two ears or at least one of them. And then I see one, the left one, and run to meet him.

We go into the restaurant.

'Your hair wants cutting,' says Philip tenderly.

'Philip,' I whisper, leaning confidentially across the table, 'something's happening to me, I've changed.'

'Hmm,' says Philip thoughtfully, 'so, you think you've changed?'

'Yes, Philip,' I say excitedly. 'I'm afraid I won't be able to explain it to you, because I'm not me any more!'

At that moment the waiter comes up and Philip asks me, 'What shall we have?'

And immediately orders, 'Two grilled trout, a bottle of white wine, two coffees. All right?'

I wait for the waiter to go and then I carry on. 'It's not all right Philip!' I say dejectedly. 'I can't remember a lot of things as I used to, and the worst thing is . . . I don't know, it's as though I was shutting up. Like a telescope. I feel small. I'm hardly here. I never was so small as this before, never in my life! And it's gone beyond a joke now! It's gone too far.' I suddenly remember the egg in the bag, and shout, 'It's gone so far that people are dumping eggs on me! I'm mad, Philip. We're all mad here!'

'Hey, calm down,' says Philip. 'How do you know you're mad?'

'I just know,' I say stubbornly. 'A dog growls when it's angry and wags its tail when it's pleased. *I* growl when I'm pleased, Philip, and wag my tail when I'm angry. Now, tell me, am I or am I not mad?'

'Hang on a moment,' Philip says soothingly. 'Begin at the beginning and go on till you come to the end, then stop.'

'I can't,' I say wearily. 'All my words have scattered.'

'Hey,' says Philip gently, stroking my hand. 'It's not as bad as all that. Just be what you would seem to be or, more simply: never imagine yourself not to be other than what it might appear to others that what you were or might have been was not other than what you had been would have appeared to them to be otherwise.'

I feel dizzy, I want to tell Philip I'm about to faint. At that moment the waiter arrives bringing two trout on a dish. The trout look strangely flat, as though made of cardboard, the head of one laid alongside the other's tail. Suddenly Philip turns pale.

'Off with their heads! Off with their heads, at once!' he says sharply to the waiter. Calmly, with routine movements, the waiter makes a slit round the heads of the trout. I watch Philip and all at once before my very eyes I see his left ear disappearing, then his right, then his nose. The waiter begins to remove one of the trout's heads. Gradually Philip's mouth disappears, his moustache, his beard . . . Oh no, for god's sake, no!

'I'm going to faint! I'm going to faint!' I whisper in a feeble voice. The last thing I hear is the waiter's voice saying, 'Their heads are gone, sir!'

I come round in a narrow room beside the restaurant kitchen. The waiters are waving white napkins and squirting me with agreeable jets of soda water.

'Philip, Philip!' I say feverishly, 'get me out of here! Now!'

Philip and I leave the restaurant quickly and go out into the street.

'You're hungry. You haven't eaten anything,' says Philip concerned, taking a crust of bread out of his pocket. We gnaw the bread as we walk. The air is soft and pink from the setting sun and I take Philip's arm tenderly. Then it occurs to me that perhaps Philip isn't the real Philip but someone else, a Mock Philip, and I stop in alarm.

'I'm sorry,' I say, 'I'm in a hurry! I've got to buy some buttons, today!'

I dash off towards the tram stop with all the strength I can muster. In the tram I begin to think I was wrong. For if I don't know who I am, how can I know that Philip is a Mock Philip? Never mind, I think, I'll 'phone him and apologise . . .

I wonder where to go next. I remember Honeybun. That's it. I'll visit Honeybun, I haven't seen her for two days.

I ring at the door of Honeybun's flat. She opens the door, all round, all smiles, all curls, all freckles – a Honeybun, in a word.

'Happy birthday, Bunny,' I say.

'How did you know it's my birthday?' Honeybun asked amazed.

'I didn't, but I've got a wonderful egg with me and I thought: wouldn't it be good if it was Bunny's birthday today and I could give her this wonderful egg! Here!' I say, shoving the egg into her hand.

She takes the egg without enthusiasm.

'Come in,' she says. 'It's my birthday.'

I go in, temporarily put out that Bunny is not more impressed with the size of my present, but I soon forget that. I find three of Bunny's friends at the kitchen table. The table is a large one, but the three are all crowded together at one corner of it while the other places are empty.

'No room! No room!' they cry out at the top of their voices when they see me coming.

'There's *plenty* of room!' I say indignantly and sit down on a chair at the opposite side of the table.

'Have some wine!' the redhead who reminds one irresistibly of a doughnut suggests in an encouraging tone. I look in front of me, but I can't see anything but coffee.

'I don't see any wine,' I say.

'There isn't any!' says Doughnut.

'Then it isn't very civil of you to offer it!'

'It isn't very civil of you to sit down at someone else's table without being invited!' says the second one, of indeterminate, though slightly dotty appearance.

'I didn't know it was *your* table!'

'She's right!' says the third, dressed entirely in checks. 'It's Bunny's table.'

'That's right!' I say. 'As far as I know it's Bunny's table in Bunny's flat.'

'You don't know much,' says Dotty crushingly, 'and when you don't know one thing, you usually don't know anything else either.'

'Buunnnneeeee!' I shout. Bunny rushes in from somewhere quite flushed. 'Bunny, these three friends of yours are insulting me!' I say.

'Which three?'

'These three!' I point to Doughnut, Dotty and Checks and hold up three fingers by way of confirmation.

'Leave me alone,' says Bunny sharply, 'you know I never could abide figures!'

Goodness, goodness, I think, everything's curious today! I shan't open my mouth again. I'll sit here for another moment or two and then I'm off. Actually, who knows what the time is by now?

'What's the time?' I ask politely.

'Six!' says Dotty. 'It's always six o'clock here!'

'How come?'

'Simple. We're killing time and we began at six.'

'Oh do talk sense!' I say angrily. 'I don't understand what you mean by these words, and I don't believe you do either!'

'Now, now,' says Bunny soothingly. 'Take some more coffee!'

'Mind what you're saying! I've had nothing yet,' I reply in an offended tone, 'so I can't take more!'

'All right,' says Bunny again. 'I'll just make some coffee, and in the meantime have some bread and jam.'

Bunny brings a jar of jam and some bread and dumps it all roughly on the table.

'Plum?' guesses Doughnut.

'Apricot?' says Dotty.

'Cherry?' says Checks.

And just as I'm about to say – apple – Bunny gets in first and says: 'Apple.'

'Ooooooh!' say all three in surprise at the same moment.

No, it's best if I keep quiet. I'll wait for the coffee and then go. Meanwhile Doughnut, Dotty and Checks chatter, chatter and chatter on . . . It's really dreadful, I think, the amount these creatures chatter! No, it's best if I say nothing. The coffee will be here soon, I'll have some and then go in a dignified manner.

'I think you might do something better with the time,' I say to

Doughnut, Dotty and Checks, 'because it really hasn't deserved to be wasted in meaningless chatter.'

'If you had grown up in a house, you would have made a dreadfully ugly child, this way at least you're rather a handsome pig!' Doughnut says to me.

'Buuuunnnneeeee!' I shout, getting up from the table.

Bunny appears from somewhere all flushed again.

'Would you tell me, please, which way I ought to go from here?'

'That depends a good deal on where you want to get to,' says Bunny calmly.

'I don't much care where –'

'Then it doesn't matter which way you go!'

'So long as I get somewhere!' I say, more to myself than anyone else.

'Oh, I'm prepared to bet you'll succeed in that!'

'Oh, we're prepared to bet you'll succeed in that!' Doughnut, Dotty and Checks guffaw.

By then, I've slammed the door and am running outside. No matter what happens, I'll never go *there* again! That's the stupidest birthday party I ever was at in all my life, I think, and make my way slowly towards the tram stop.

On the way home I try to think about the day that's just gone by, but I can't remember anything. Then I remember the egg and think, maybe it all began with the egg I meant to give somebody as a present? It's a good thing I left it with Honeybun, because if I'd gone on carrying it, who knows where I'd have ended up!

Of course, I know that what I'm saying about the egg is plain silly and that everything would have happened as it did in any case. Though I can't remember exactly what did happen. At Honeybun's it was horrible and strange – I do remember that – yet somehow familiar, as though I had been there before, and sort of tight, like in a hole, like in a jam jar. Oh, that apple jam! Now an apple, for instance! An apple is so round, so whole, so peaceful, and hasn't the remotest idea it's an apple!

I arrive home. I open the door, turn on the light, take off my coat and go straight to the bathroom. I stand in front of the mirror and suddenly feel drawn to it with miraculous force. I press my nose and forehead to the glass and feel a moist coldness. There are eyes watching me out of the mirror. Strange, I think. What frightening depths they have. Maybe there, in the pupil, is that secret hole that shows you something else . . .

I go into the bedroom and start looking for paper and a pencil so I can write down the words *Buy buttons* for tomorrow. My eyes suddenly meet the two large blue eyes of an unknown man who is sitting thoughtfully on my bed, leisurely smoking a long cigar. I stand there stupidly holding the scrap of paper and pencil in my hand. The Stranger and I stare at each other for a long time. Finally the Stranger takes the cigar out of his mouth and asks me lazily, 'Who are you?'

Really now, this is too much! A stranger! Where am I? In someone else's flat! Someone else's country? Who am I? And what can I tell him: that I hardly know, that I knew who I was when I got up this morning, of course I knew, but I must have been changed several times since then.

'Who are you?' the stranger asks me contemptuously.

I wave my hands in confusion, I try to get my breath, I blush, the words stick in my throat and finally I stammer:

'I think you ought to tell me who *you* are first!'

'Why?' the stranger asks calmly.

I stand there flabbergasted, I don't know what I'm saying.

'Who are you?' the stranger repeats the question puffing smoke out of his cigar.

And in an instant I feel that I am whole and peaceful as an apple and that I am simply me. I walk decisively towards the door, lock it, wind my clock, put on my nightdress, turn out the light and get into bed.

And in the darkness I hear my own calm and confident voice say, 'I'm Alice! Move over a little. I'm sleepy!'

C. H.

The Kreutzer Sonata

Arise, O Sophocles, and recount my tragedy, my conjugal woes!

From Zagreb to Dugo Selo

One day in October I was waiting for the Belgrade train to start – the express was full, so I had to take the local – when a man carrying several nylon bags and an enormous wooden cannon joined me in the compartment. He hoisted the bags into the net above the seat by the door – I had a window seat – and placed the cannon carefully in his lap. Shortly thereafter a restless-looking man with dishevelled hair and unusually luminous eyes burst in. He scanned the compartment, then mumbled a few words and took the seat opposite me, fixing his gaze on a point outside the window.

The train was under way when a fourth passenger entered. She was a blonde. She had messy, oily hair and was wearing a loose jacket and jeans. She plonked herself into a seat, dropped her plastic British Airways bag on the floor, and, stuffing a stick of gum in her mouth, settled in to chew.

The man sitting opposite me emitted occasional noises that sounded like a throat being cleared or a laugh sputtering on and off. At first their strange quality attracted our attention, but we soon grew as used to it as to the tedious clatter of the train. Since I had forgotten to buy a newspaper before boarding, I didn't know what to do with myself and alternated between staring out of the window and staring at my fellow travellers. But eventually, true to genre (train, four basic characters, length of action unknown, because one never does know with our trains), I opened a conversation with a gambit that struck me as exemplary.

'Nice cannon you've got there,' I said to the fellow in the corner.

'Bought it in Germany,' said the fellow, clearly relieved the silence had been broken.

'What is it anyway? A toy?'

'Hell no . . . See this hole here? Well, you stick a bottle in the hole. You know, when you have people over? It gives some class to the drinks and all. Looks great too . . . I always bring back a gadget or two from Germany. For the missus. Hell, you know the ladies, how they go for those things!'

'Right . . .'

'Damn right I'm right!' said the cannon man, getting into the swing of things.

The blonde pulled the gum out of her mouth, pushed it back in, made a smacking sound, scratched her thigh, and looked the man up and down.

'Damn right!' the man repeated, but mildly enough to keep the conversation going.

'How about your other cannon?' the blonde inserted. 'You keep that for the missus too?' Her leer revealed a gap in the upper jaw.

The cannon man perked up and was about to respond when the man sitting opposite me said pompously, 'Disgusting!'

'What was that?' the blonde asked, tugging at her gum.

'I said, *Disgusting!*' the man repeated nervously.

'Well!' the blonde snapped, and, grabbing her bag, stalked out of the compartment. The nervous man came out with a noise like hysterical laughter, then gave me a questioning look and said softly, 'Please accept my apologies.'

'But I really don't . . .'

'It's just that I . . .'

'Yes?'

'Nothing,' he said with a wave of the hand and went back to gazing out of the window.

An uneasy silence descended upon the compartment.

'Keep an eye on my cannon, will you?' the cannon man said to me.

'Fine,' I said willingly.

The man laid his cannon on the seat and stumbled out of the compartment in a fog.

As soon as the door closed behind him, the nervous man glanced over at me and said thoughtfully, 'Women . . .'

'Hm . . .'

'Women are awful. They don't understand a thing.'

'What do you mean?'

'Don't you see? That woman can't understand a man's going all that distance to bring his wife a nice gift; all she can do is make fun of him and allude to something completely irrelevant.'

'But she didn't mean anything . . .'

'Oh, yes she did,' the nervous man interrupted. 'That's exactly what she meant. Women have a one-track mind.'

'But . . .'

'But me no buts! Women! If you knew what one did to me . . . But why am I telling you this?' And with another wave of the hand he went back to his window.

'No, go ahead, really,' I said. 'I'm interested.'

'Well, one of them did me in completely, made a total wreck out of me.'

'You don't look like a . . .'

'True, it doesn't show. You can't understand unless I tell you the whole story.'

'Well then, do,' I said.

Out of the corner of my eye I saw Dugo Selo fly by. By the time I'd made myself comfortable and lit a cigarette, my nervous neighbour had embarked upon his tale.

From Dugo Selo to Ivanić Grad

'My initial encounter with what at first glance seemed merely a pleasant girl produced so enigmatic a reaction within me that – walking down a side street and going against my custom and the rules of propriety – I turned for a second glance. You can imagine my consternation when I saw her standing and gazing at me, and I moved on immediately, yet I admit I was glad, because there was something vaguely attractive and sensitive about the girl, something spiritual, something to do with the soul. That was what made me notice her, I who till then had deemed women the least important part of my life.

'Several months went by before I saw her again, but then I began to run into her on the outskirts of town walking arm in arm with soldiers of varying rank. Clearly she felt the predilection for the uniform so common among women of inferior upbringing, the sort that forms attachments on the basis of clothes, faces, and elegance, and ignores a person's privileges and intellectual capabilities. Thus, like many others of her sex, she calibrated the intelligence of a man by the cut of his suit or the last of his boot, excluding the possibility of a dandy being a snob or a pretty-boy an idiot.

'One day we met. Her name was Anka. We met under the boughs of a chestnut grove with the sun setting and autumn rustling all around us – it was, if I do say so myself, a perfectly splendid setting. From then on we saw each other every day, always in the lap of nature, preferably by a pond or a stream.

'Unfolding one by one the events of her wretched life, Anka told me she had become the object of everyone's hatred after her mother died and she was forced to live with her step-mother. The trials that woman put the poor girl through! Here is one example for many. When as a young girl she called her step-mother "mother", the cruel woman would stuff her mouth with hot peppers, beat her black and blue, and throw her into the cellar, threatening to bury her there if she dared repeat her crime. Uneducated and unfeeling, she would torture the poor, defenceless Anka at every opportunity.

'The child was thus continuously and systematically mistreated until one day she ran away from home and slashed her wrists in a park. A week later she was found in the bushes by some soldiers, who took her home, half dead. They are to be commended.

'In any case, Anka and I met regularly at dusk. I would see her home. She listened to my theories with delight, laughed whole-heartedly at my burlesques. As an orphan she had never known a parent's love, and I tried to fill the gap with my own.

'Before long I came to feel that Anka was as much a part of me as the church was of the Middle Ages. I loved her as a bedouin his oasis or a nightingale its freedom. I was, I admit, so intoxicated by my purely Platonic and profound feelings that I would kneel before her at her door like a slave and beg her to stamp upon my heart and shatter it to pieces.

'I must also mention that even though the most outlandish things were said about her – that she suffered from a number of venereal diseases, for example – I never stopped loving her; I maintained my own, autonomous view.

'And then she confessed the terrible, painful truth. In Dubrovnik, where she had gone for her apparently frail health, she spent an evening in the company of a certain heartless young man, a cynic – or, as she called him, a student – who in his unbridled profligacy held forth frivolously on the low incidence of virginity in the modern woman. The lewd discussion, revolving entirely around bestial sexuality, dragged on late into the night. At one point Anka stood and returned to her hotel room, leaving the door unlocked. Before long there was a knock on it, and a voice from within bade the visitor enter. It was the frivolous profligate! He sat on her bed, and she, looking him straight in the eye, said, "I give you leave to verify my virginity."

'On the morning following that cursed night of defloration she came to me with a disingenuous announcement of the fact and implored my noble heart to bear her no malice. In a frenzied rush of love I forgave her her sin and begged her to be my lawfully wedded wife. I forgave her for the sake of my love and her bitter fate, forgave the orphan who sought protection in me and lived in the belief she had found it. How could I shatter her hopes, how could I dash her on the grave of her ideals!

'And how it pains me that the name of that perfidious seaside profligate will ever remain a mystery to me, the Dubrovnik caper being nothing but a fairy tale begotten of false naïveté, fabricated to hide her early depravities, for as I have said: the most outlandish things were said about her!'

From Ivanić Grad to Kutina

My nervous neighbour again came out with his strange hybrid of throat clearing and sputter.

'A deplorable fate,' I muttered, but he convulsively clenched his fist, pounded his chest, and cried, 'And what about mine! What about mine!'

'You *will* tell me the whole story, won't you?' I said compassionately, fearing he would go back on his word.

'Do you mind if I eat some sunflower seeds?' he asked, taking a small newspaper packet of them out of his pocket. 'Here, have a few. I find them calming.'

I declined the offer and lit up again. He continued his tale.

'In any case, Anka and I were married. I recall a minor detail that will show how much I loved her. Not long after our wedding there was a terrible epidemic of influenza in our town. Even many doctors were afflicted. When Anka fell ill, I took fright and moved from my bed to hers so that I might contract the strain and we might die together. What was life to me without my Anka, after all? For eight days I rubbed her with garlic and wine vinegar and poured Jamaican rum down her throat; for eight days she lay at my right hand. On the ninth day she rose. Life was like the sun on a spring morning. And there was a child on the way . . .

'To make a long story short, one morning I woke to find Anka gone! Yes. Here today, gone tomorrow. She took everything I owned and left me with a new-born baby. Next day she returned to demand we sever all relations. I was terribly hurt by the sudden, inscrutable announcement, I was cut to the quick. Then, of course, came the tears. On all sides. She wept, I wept, the child wept. A madhouse, an inferno, a purgatory.

'Whereupon life took up where it had left off. Though not for long. One morning I woke, still weary with woes and obligations, to find her gone yet again! And with her the bedclothes, my new suit, my shoes, socks, hat, and numerous other items. There I was in a state of nature with only my baby to cover my shame. For Anka had taken what even the man who robbed jolly Demosthenes left behind!

'I somehow managed to procure a suit of clothes, though even then I had to drag myself to work. The outside world meant nothing to me. All I cared about was my child. I was like a dog whose brain has been removed for experimentation. And suddenly there she was again, lips trembling, eyes shining. "Tell me, Anka," I said gently, compassionately, "how long will things go on like this?" She vouchsafed no reply. I pleaded with her to tell me the cause of her repeated decampments, but all she could do was shrug her shoulders and weep.

'Of course within a few days she was gone. And this time for a much longer interval. Thinking she had perhaps paid for her inconstancy with her life, I wept like a child over its mother's grave; I lamented more than Orpheus when he lost his Eurydice, because he was not alone in his grief – he had animals standing over him, he had Furies crying over him – while I was completely and utterly alone!

'For days and nights I roamed the streets half-naked, half-insane, scouring the gutters and streams, the parks and bushes. In the end I locked myself in my room and mourned for two whole weeks. My neighbours were afraid of me: my eyes had something terrifying in them; they made people's blood run cold. At last I ran across her in the street; I fell before her as if she were the Madonna. "Come with me, Anka, come home," I said to her. "Think of the baby! You haven't forgotten our little angel, have you?" Whereupon she looked me up and down and answered, "I have."

'The moment I heard her sarcastic reply – the reply of a mother and a wife – my legs buckled, my temperature plummeted, and my soul, invisible yet in pain, sobbed as only a soul knows how. I thought I would kill myself. For two days I prayed for her and wept at her psycho-intellectual savagery, her moral decadence, but in the end she relented and we went on together.'

From Kutina to Banova Jaruga

'Unbelievable,' I said.

'What was that?' asked my nervous neighbour, clearly chagrined at having been interrupted. He spat out a sunflower seed; it stuck to the top of my left shoe.

'Oh, nothing. Nothing at all,' I said apologetically. 'Do go on.' And I lit up again.

'Our life together was less than stable,' he continued. 'Anka made friends with a washerwoman, a frivolous blonde who thought of her maidenhead in terms of this or that popular ballad, and although her disgusting blather turned my stomach and made my gorge rise, I was forced to countenance her so as not to offend my Anka.

'Then one day Anka's father died and she had to leave me for several days. Just before she set off, I said to her, "Be careful, son (I always called her "son"). Avoid all strangers, have a good night's rest when you arrive, and remember that your baby and your husband are awaiting you here at home." Such were the words I chose to send her on her way.

'She did not return. Not after a week, not after two. I would go to the station and wait for her train, but she was never on it. I went to five different stations, waited for days on end, but in vain; in my desperation I even waited for goods trains, but in vain . . .'

Suddenly silent, my nervous neighbour stared mournfully out of the window, recalling those days of frustration.

'And did you ever find her?' I asked.

'Did I ever find her?' he repeated, coming to.

'Anka. Did you ever find her?'

'Oh, of course,' he said with a frown. 'One day I collected my wits and went to see Milica the washerwoman. And there she was, asleep in a hovel, without a care in the world, as if she had no husband, no child, no heart, no soul. I woke her charily. What could I do? When honour and sincerity fail, one turns to diplomacy. But she responded with stories from the streets and ditties from the cafés. I invited her home with me, but her eyes clouded over and she refused. I cursed her heart and soul with what was left of mine. We parted for good. I did not know then what I later learnt, namely, that the fellow from Dubrovnik was behind the door all the time. Though as a man of intelligence and experience I should have known, for while the sun takes only ten minutes to set in nature, it takes ten years in a woman's heart. Or as the Germans say, *"Schwer ist die Vergangenheit der alten Liebe."* Yes, I should have known that the twentieth century would give us no new Lucrece!'

Banova Jaruga – Novska

My nervous neighbour gave a theatrical wave of the hand and turned his mournful gaze to the yellow-grey fields gliding past. When after a time he emerged from his meditation, he fixed the gaze back on me and asked, 'Forgive me, but what do you do?'

'What do I do?'

'For a living, I mean.'

'I'm a . . . typist.'

'Strange occupation for a man.'

He was right. Mine *was* a strange occupation, though I had lied about it – well, fibbed. I was embarrassed to admit I was – a writer. Amazed at the ease with which my chance companion, my perfectly ordinary fellow traveller had told his story, I suddenly felt terribly inferior. The time it would have taken me (a professional!) to invent such a story or even imitate the manner in which he told it! Was it merely a matter of chance that I'd ended up in this compartment, or was the encounter with my nervous neighbour preordained by an ironic muse to rub my nose in business I had refused to face? Being creative is no easy matter. I was sick of the anaemic, lifeless prose I kept chewing and rechewing. It had lost its pleasant, indefinable sweetness the way a fresh stick of chewing gum loses its flavour, but I chewed on, lacking the courage to spit it out, on and on, the same old stick, pushing, pulling, blowing bubbles, always the same, rewriting myself. And the saddest part of it was that my colleagues did no better! Though *they* knew how to make virtues of their faults, and I kept losing ground because of my old-fashioned feeling that the whole undertaking was dishonest. I was simply behind the times. I had discovered the rules of the game, but could no longer bring myself to join the senseless, third-division heat around the literary track. That's why I told my nervous neighbour I was a typist. It wasn't even a fib, really. It was the way I felt.

Novska – Nova Gradiška

'Maybe that's why you're so depressed!' said my nervous neighbour. 'Believe me, it's not what a man *does*, it's what he *is* that counts!' He took another packet of sunflower seeds from his pocket. 'Anka certainly proves that.'

'Yes, well, tell me how things turned out,' I said.

'Whenever I thought of that cursed night in Dubrovnik when she so frivolously, so improvidently gambled and lost the lily of her valley, her *virgo intacta* virtue, I knew she was doomed to a life of erotic excess. The moral anguish of it all! To think that while I slept the sleep of the just with my innocent child, that inveterate sinner and her latest cretin flame were indulging in orgiastic practices in my nuptial bed, perverting the psychic functions of sexual behaviour!

'I was on the point of taking poison, killing myself, for I was no longer a human being, I was all *fluidum amoris* and emotion, all pain as deadly as arsenic and my fallen wife's phariseeism. Wandering in the regions of ardent love and despair, my diseased soul would keen in paroxysms of melancholy and compose epistles to Anka, epistles in which I did not choose my thoughts or formulate them, give them words, as I was wont, but simply stated with no poetic frills that I loved her and wished her to return. She sent them back unopened. Insulted and injured, I suffered a bout of melancholia and like René Descartes I took to doubting everything but doubt itself, everything but the doubt that my wife lay in the unbridled embrace of an idiot, cynic, or swine, who by dint of his status or wealth had engaged her for a single, callous, sinful night. That I could not doubt, for she had an absolute prerogative on moral depravity! Yet much as she tortured me and tortures me still, vivisecting my soul, resecting my brain, I could not forget her. I had all but breathed my last for her, for that dissolute, degenerate woman. "Take me to the madhouse!" I felt like shouting with Friedrich Nietzsche. "Let me forget what she was to me and I to her!" Yet I swallowed my pride and hid my subjectivity beneath the pathological emotions born of love spurned and clinically dangerous depression. I, a child of logical thought, sent her one last missive to the effect that I was fed up with everything but most of all with life, which missive, though she refused to read it, I wrote out of unspeakable pain: I still loved her, loved her with a love that bordered on fetishism, no, went beyond it, for in the frenzy of that love I spoke of the no-more-than-average intelligence of a basically coarse woman in absurdly inflated, hyperbolic terms – an egregious error on my part, because she began to believe me. Psychologists agree that praise spoils a woman, inflames her vanity, and produces a highly deleterious effect on her psychic and emotional make-up. Supremely confident of my clearly unnatural love, Anka trampled on her duties as a mother and on the feelings of a sensitive soul. Only now do I see how sterile her conception of maternal and uxorial obligations actually was. What love she felt for her child and me was more coercive than noble or sincere. In her petty, sick, feminine mind she assumed that the prodigious love and burning heart of a demigod would mask her crass cruelty and that in my despair I would stain our barren nuptial bed with my blood and the blood of our offspring! But as a child of reason and light, a Gnostic, and a self-respecting human being, I was far from giving in to the perverse instincts of a woman. I sensed from the outset that she was vain enough to hope our marriage would end in the obituary column. Well then, her will be done: I would raise the veil of my married life and show it in all its Edenic state of nature, though minus the sensational blood-spattered tragic incidents she might have wished to see included.'

Nova Gradiška – Slavonski Brod

'I'm not boring you, am I?' my nervous neighbour asked, interrupting his monologue.

'Not in the least.'

'I've got to see a man about a dog,' he said and left the compartment.

I opened the window and took a breath of fresh air. My neighbour hadn't bored me; he'd worn me out. Without realising it, he'd been a constant stimulus. As he sat there embellishing his sad, bare tale with verbiage, I conceived a desire to write a story about him. That's right – about him. So I wasn't washed up after all. And this time I'd avoid the trap we contemporary writers had fallen into. How right our predecessors were to let their curiosity run wild and put *life* down on paper! But then copying from life lost its appeal, came to be seen as shameful, passé. Literature was drowning in itself, when in fact it was as easy as pie. All you had to do was take the first train and wait for a story to come your way. Putting it down on paper was like copying from life. The way our predecessors did. All you needed was a decent memory . . .

My nervous neighbour returned. The compartment was quite cold and I tried to close the window, but it was stuck and he jumped up to help me. Just then the train jerked to a halt and we flew into each other's arms.

'Terribly sorry,' said my neighbour.

'It's nothing really,' I said.

We took our seats. The train started up again, and my neighbour went on with his story.

'You know, those five years my wife kept me in her thrall with addictive love and fictive fidelity left a gaping wound in my life. Her dark past and general debauched nature left no room for doubt about her promiscuity, though I did not receive proof positive of it until the end of those five purblind years, when she revealed the secret of her sinful night in Dubrovnik and the fee she earned not only from that *bon vivant* but from his brother as well.

'And that wasn't all. Her depravity demanded ever new sacrifices of me. Among the myriad vices she harboured within her much tarnished soul was the perverse pleasure she took in making me jealous. Did you know that when the wife of none other than Fyodor Dostoevsky told him she had deceived him he leapt at her like a madman, tore the chain from her throat, and drew a gun on her. And when he learnt it was merely a bad joke, he said coldly but sternly, "Never do that again! Do you hear me? I won't vouch for myself." If that is how the great philosopher of the steppes reacted, how could I react otherwise?

'Only now do I see that Anka did not even deserve a normal intelligent man, to say nothing of a man like me! She certainly did not deserve a man who lives a pure, spiritual life and lacks all contact with brutal reality. That is why she took such parasitic advantage of my mind and my soul. That is why I was both "god" and "louse" to her. Even Napoleon, whose genius is beyond dispute, was a "louse" vis-à-vis the sexual imperative of his wife, Marie Louise. Why, had I been Socrates, John Chrysostom, or Kant, to say nothing of Edgar Allan Poe, Oscar Wilde, Byron, Baudelaire, and Knut Hamsun, she would have despised me still, because she lacked intelligence of the soul and wallowed in moral and intellectual decadence.

'Anka so underestimated the ideal and reduced everything to the most material of bases, her platform for human existence, that she would rather I sold shoe-laces, padlocks, or candles than took to market the loftiest commodity man can produce: his literary efforts, that is, his intellect plus bits and pieces of his heart, drops of his tears! I bitterly regret that my wife cared more for the coin of the realm, that she preferred *Wiener Schnitzel* to the music of my pen and *Schweineschnitzel* to my *exercises de style.*'

'Excuse me,' I broke in.

'What is it?' he said, frowning again at the interruption.

'Excuse me, but what do you do?'

'What do I do?'

'For a living, I mean.'

'I'm a writer,' he shot back, 'or rather I plan to be one.'

'Ah,' I said, my mouth falling open.

'Now where did I leave off?' he said without a smile.

'At the point where your Anka preferred *Wiener Schnitzel* to the music of your pen.'

'Oh, yes . . . How was she to know that laurel wreaths are only for the deceased and that Spinoza lived for fifty years on a few farthings a day? That is why Nietzsche says, "One pays dearly for immortality." That is why one dies many times in a life.

'By the way, vice had put down such deep roots in her soul that she lost her self-image as both woman and mother. Not that she had ever been impressed by moral adages. If I had told her what Nietzsche said about woman being a riddle whose answer is motherhood, she would surely have stuck out her tongue at me. Even the sage of Yasnaya Polyana would have wept at the moral dissipation and maternal dereliction of my very derelict wife.

'I feel certain she will pay for indulging in debauchery and jeopardising the sanctity of her womanhood. She is a beast and deserves only derision! I feel that every woman who falls into erotic excess should be deprived of her civil rights and, if she is a mother, of the right to bring up her children. For how can a morally impaired mother bring up a morally healthy child? Her behaviour is bound to stimulate a kind of erotic haemotropism, and she will fall victim to her own flirtations.

'Psychologists assure us that forgiving one's wife her sins requires true heroism. Well, I say that if our society continues to tolerate current moral practices, every bachelor will need to turn hero the day after he marries. Thus I would, with Lenin, legalise free love – as long as legitimate marriage was punishable by fine or imprisonment. It would make for a good deal less pain and tragedy.

'And even though, following Nietzsche, I wash my hands after coming into contact with people who consider themselves believers, I heartily subscribe to at least one tenet of Christianity: Thou shalt not commit adultery! I would, however, propound and propagate the Platonic concept of love and apply it to marital relations, for is it not Plato who says, "Woman exercises such an influence on man that she determines his character"? Yes, I agree with Plato and admit that with her I was no better than a rake. But now that she is gone, I am a new man. A sure sign that Plato was right.'

Slavonski Brod – Vinkovci

My nervous neighbour raised a finger as if to make a point, and I took advantage of the pause to rise and say, 'I've got to see a man about a dog.'

'Go on, then. I'll be here.'

I was glad I had to wait for the toilet. My fellow traveller was tired; his story had lost its rhythm. I wished the blonde would come back, and the cannon man. My nervous neighbour was getting on my nerves, smothering me with his palaver. I dawdled as long as I could, I took an aspirin for my headache, but in the end I had to return to the compartment.

'Here I am,' I mumbled.

'You certainly took long enough.'

I didn't like his tone. My plan to write a story about him popped like a balloon. In fact, I couldn't wait to get rid of him. 'How far are you going?' I asked, lighting another cigarette.

'To Šid.'

'Well, what happened next?' I asked gingerly, wondering whether I could withstand the verbal torture as far as Šid.

'Where did I leave off?'

'At Plato, if I'm not mistaken.'

'Yes, well, if you really want to know what happened next, all I can say is – nothing. While I was struggling body and soul to find my way out of the labyrinth of thoughts and obligations arising from her departure, I received a letter from her announcing that she had been proposed to by a butcher! Unable to find spiritual sustenance in my literary endeavours, she sought it in pigs' entrails and cows' hoofs. Et tu, Brute? You too, Anka?

'Only now do I realise that instead of raising a savage woman from the depths of crime and depravity I should have followed Maestro Paganini's precedent and used a stiletto on her, my *amata*. I should have done so regardless of whether the darkest of dungeons awaited me as the galleys of Genoa awaited him. I should have done so to rid society of a hotbed of crime.

'On the other hand, poor Byron did not become Byron until he broke with his cynical and hypocritical wife, and Oscar Wilde did not become the demiurge of style and sensitivity until his sinner woman left him as my Anka left me. So no matter how unbearable, how abhorrent – abhorrent to the point of banality – I found the sufferings that resulted from her deed, no matter how they deadened my ambition and my will to indulge in any sort of creative labour, I resolved nonetheless to write, to offer the public "pieces of my heart, drops of my tears". And given the fact that, as Lorand has pointed out, brilliant people are not always lucky in love, indeed, are often unhappily married (that is, they can impress the world but not their wives), I resolved to take up my pen and write the death notice of my once beloved bride and pride of my heart, who, though still very much alive and well, was now dead for me. The only way I could quell my blistering, agonising emotions was to lay my love in its grave and tell the world to scorn the mother who abandons her own flesh and blood!

'Oh, I know that a cynic will come forth and say that the sincerity with which I profess my marital problems is abnormal. Well, what do you expect from literary pigmies or, rather, literary idiots, morons, moral robbers and confidence men! For a cool-headed Gnostic, however, any attempt at concealment is a vice, and he says what he must from a position far above the mentally incompetent attacks of your literary "Praetorians" (read "ignoramuses").

'No, I thought, that *femme fatale* is not going to turn a Gnostic into a mental patient. And my heart, my feelings gave way to common sense. Hard, cold reason told me Anka was now dead for me, and I, like a lion, who never looks back at a victim it has missed, I can say once and for all, "Get thee gone, and never darken my door again!"'

Vinkovci – Šid

At that, my nervous neighbour stood up and gave me his hand. He took me by surprise.

'Good-bye. I must be on my way.'

'But we haven't come to your station.'

'I've got to get my things ready.'

I took his hand. He cleared his throat one last time and left the compartment. I didn't know what to think. He'd left so quickly, unexpectedly. Now that he was gone, I started toying again with the idea of writing a story about him. I liked the old-fashioned device of the train setting. I'd have to find ways of breaking up the long monologues, giving it a rhythm of its own. Maybe I should come up with a social angle as well. It's not a particularly attractive topic, but if I brought in a few more characters, chance passengers, I could hold a mini-symposium on marriage. Right there in the compartment. Yes, I might be able to make something of my nervous neighbour after all. As material. Raw material.

When the train stopped in Šid, I opened the window to catch one last glance of him. He looked up at me as he stepped off the train, and waved. I waved back, lit a cigarette, and sat down. When I stood up to close the window, I saw his arms fluttering in the air. He was rushing towards the exit with – no! the blonde at his heels! Well, well. I certainly never thought it would end like that! The train lurched forward, and I sat and stared at the picture postcard in the frame just above the place where my nervous neighbour had sat. It might as well have read 'Greetings from the Back of Beyond'. Now there was a story for you! The kind you'd pick up at a railway kiosk.

Šid – Stara Pazova

Suddenly the door opened and in came the man who had left his cannon with me.

'Where'd she go?' he growled.

'Who?' I asked.

'The blonde, damn it!'

'I think she got out at Šid. Why?'

The cannon man collapsed on the seat. He was breathing hard, plainly drunk.

'Fleeced me, the bitch.'

'Really? How much did she get?'

'I don't want to talk about it. Everything I had on me.'

He spread his arms, shrugged his shoulders, and shook his head. I didn't know what to say.

'You should have known! You should have known by the looks of her.'

He kept shaking his head and breathing hard.

'It – how shall I say – it comes with the image. It had to happen.'

Judging from the look he gave me, he did not take well to my attempt at consolation.

'So it had to happen, eh? It had to happen. Five hundred deutsch-marks! Five hundred fucking marks! Not counting the drinks I bought her at the bar.'

His eyes bored into me.

'And a ham omelette.'

I no longer tried to comfort him. I just made a sober suggestion.

'Why not go to the police?'

'Oh, come off it. It's a lost cause.'

We didn't exchange a word until Stara Pazova, when he stood up and I said, 'Good luck.'

'Oh, come off it,' he said, slamming the door.

I was alone again. Only then did I notice he'd forgotten his cannon. The train was under way, but I tried to stick it out of the window. It wouldn't go.

'Your caaannon!' I shouted. 'Your forgot your caaannon!'

He turned, paused, then said something and made a dismissive gesture.

'What was that?' I shouted, still trying to shove the cannon through the window. As luck would have it, the window got stuck.

'Fuck the cannon!' I heard my second neighbour's angry voice cry out, but by then I could no longer see him. The train clattered on towards Belgrade.

Stara Pazova – Belgrade

I was upset. I felt sorry for the man who'd lost not only his five hundred marks but his cannon as well. I needed a cigarette, but the packet was empty. I reached into my pocket – my left pocket, my right pocket, my left breast pocket . . . My wallet was gone! I checked again: left pocket, right pocket, breast pockets . . . No, not a sign of it! Then I came upon a scrap of paper in the left breast pocket and removed it as if it were a dead mouse. It contained the following typed (I seemed to have received the fifth carbon copy) message:

Dear Fellow Traveller,

I take the liberty of charging whatever sum you may have had in your wallet for my free interpretation of excerpts from the as yet to be published novel *The Sinner Woman*. Do not worry about your personal documents: I shall return them to you C.O.D. Many thanks for your lyrical understanding. As a prospective member of the literary community I found our trip, *inter alia*, an artistically rewarding experience.

Yours sincerely,
'Tolstoy'

And so, satisfying one of the givens of the railway novel, I sat in an empty compartment staring at the black husks decorating my left shoe. When I raised my foot in the direction of the window, the shoe took the form of a shiny, phantasmagoric fossil. One hand held the scrap of paper – the proof of my active participation in the journey genre, third class – while the other inadvertently stroked the cannon. Suddenly someone in the neighbouring compartment struck up a folk song . . .

There I sat – clattering on to Belgrade one fine October day, with a cannon, a spotted shoe, a scrap of paper, and an empty cigarette packet – freshly fleeced of all my documents and three hundred and fifty dinars, my eyes fixed on the view of 'The Back of Beyond', and suddenly I was overcome by a vague feeling of ecstasy: The world was full of fellow writers!

M. H. H.

The Kharms Case

2nd December 1978
To the Editor, Petar Petrović.

Dear Sir,

I am extremely impressed with your publishing programme which shows excellent, surprisingly fresh and unconventional editorial taste. I am therefore taking the liberty of offering you the work of a virtually unknown writer (equally unknown in his own country). I am speaking of the Russian writer Daniil Ivanovich Kharms (1905–1942).

I began to take an interest in Daniil Kharms and the 'Oberiu' group in 1976 during a trip to Moscow and Leningrad, where I collected what material was available, and spoke with one of the remaining living members of the group Alexander Razumovsky. Razumovsky showed his experimental film 'The Mincing Machine' ('Miasorubka') at the first joint appearance of the 'Oberiu' in 1928. I also had a useful conversation with Gennady Gor, a writer who was active at that time, and with Anatoly Alexandrov, the curator of the Kharms Archive and collector of his papers.

The material I have gathered includes George Gibian's first (and, for the time being, only) edition of Kharms' oeuvre (Daniil Kharms, *Izbrannoe*, Würzburg 1974), those few texts which have appeared in Soviet and Western literary periodicals, a modicum of biographical material, several articles about Kharms and the 'Oberiu' group, and the first published study on Kharms and his collaborator Vvedensky by B. Müller [*Absurde Literatur in Russland*, Munich 1978]. This material forms the basis for this selection of Kharms' fiction.

Now a few words about Kharms himself. Daniil Kharms (real name: Daniil Ivanovich Iuyachev) made his literary début with a group of poems published in 1926. In the autumn of that year Kazimir Malevich founded a theatrical group at the Institute of Visual Art (Institut khudozhestvennoi kul'tury) called Radix. Their production *My Mama Is Decked Out in Watches* (*Moya mama vsia v chasakh*), which consisted of a collage of poems by Kharms and Vvedensky was unfortunately never performed. The Oberiu group (Ob'edinenie real'nogo iskusstva) or the Association for Real Art was founded at the end of 1927. Its members were: Daniil Kharms, Nikolai Zabolotsky, Alexander Vvedensky, Konstantin Vaginov, Igor' Bakhterev and Boris Levin. At their first joint appearance (in January 1928), under the title of 'Three Left Hours' (Tri levykh chasa) the 'Oberiu' read their texts, published a manifesto and performed Kharms' play *Elizaveta Bam*. They later made several more appearances, but after a vicious attack on them in the periodical *Smena* (Shift) they disbanded and the miscellany they had planned, *Archimedes' Bath* (*Vanna Arkhimeda*) failed to appear. In their manifesto they declared themselves 'a new detachment of left revolutionary art'. Kharms is portrayed as follows: 'Daniil Kharms, poet and playwright, is concerned less with the static figure than with the collision of a series of objects and their mutual relations. At the moment of action the object acquires a new, concrete contour, full of authentic meaning. The action, now different, contains both a classical stamp and the broad sweep of the Oberiu world view.'

It is difficult to speak of Kharms and the 'Oberiu' outside the context of Russian literature. The 'Oberiu' are the last important avant-garde grouping within that context and, in many ways close to European Dadaism and Surrealism, whose 'vision of the world' belongs to a line that begins with the poet Koz'ma Prutkov, the Russian popular theatre and Gogol, continuing with Khlebnikov, Kruchonykh (that is Tufanov), the painters Malevich, Filonov, Sokolov, the poet and theatre director Terentiev and many others. Vvedensky and Kharms are therefore consistent 'Oberiu' artists in their absurdism, illogicality and black humour, while the best known of them, Nikolai Zabolotsky, subscribes to their 'vision of the world' only in his first collection of poems *Columns* (Stolbtsy), and Konstantin Vaginov both as prose writer and particularly as a poet follows a completely different stylistic model.

At the invitation of the noted children's writer Samuil Marshak, Kharms and Vvedensky worked on the periodicals *Jezh* (Hedgehog) and *Chizh* (Siskin), and it is as children's writers that both of them are not only published but almost exclusively known in the Soviet

Union. Working with Marshak, Shvarts and Oleinikov only fuelled Kharms' avant-gardist infantilism. It was during this period that he wrote *Cases* (Sluchâi).

Kharms died in a Leningrad prison in 1942 and his work was covered in dust. His slow rehabilitation began in the sixties: unpublished texts appeared sporadically, arousing great interest in scholarly circles.

Such are the broad outlines of Kharms' life. I am convinced that his short, absurdist, black-humorous prose with its numerous parodic elements is more in tune with the sensibility of the modern reader than any other recently discovered work of Russian avant-garde literature.

I leave you now to read the manuscript.

Warmest wishes,

Vavka Ušić

P.S. You may remember, we met several months ago at the launch of Krleža's *Collected Works*. I very much hope we shall meet soon in connection with Kharms.

5th May 1979

Dear Sir,

I should like most respectfully to remind you of Kharms, and should be interested to know whether you have read him. Please let me know by phone or letter. I have given my translation of Kharms' story 'The Old Woman' (Staruha) to the magazine *Off* and sent some of his short pieces to 'The Literary Word'. All this will serve as advance publicity (I'm thinking only of Kharms, of course) should you decide to publish him.

As I write these lines I recall a dream I had last night. I dreamed I was in Leningrad, on the corner of Nadezhdinskaia and Kovenskaia Streets, looking up at a house, and there, looking out of a window, stood Kharms. He had a round cap on his head and a small green dog drawn on his cheek. From time to time he would pick up a book, place it on his head, put it down, and then, with unusual seriousness, pick his nose. Although the distance was considerable, I could clearly see the title of the book. It was Knut Hamsun's *Mysterier*. 'Yes,' said Kharms, 'I should so like to be like Goethe!'

I remember being astonished in my dream by the fact that I could hear perfectly though the distance would have made it impossible.

I am eagerly looking forward to your reply.

Best wishes,
Vavka Ušić

1st June 1980
Dear Sir,

It is more than a year and a half that you have had my translation of Daniil Kharms in your possession, and I have as yet to receive a response (positive or negative) from you.

I have recently published translations of the short stories of the contemporary Russian writer Vladimir Kazakov in the periodical *Fields*. Kazakov is interesting as one of the few writers continuing the 'Oberiu' tradition in contemporary Russian literature. He writes short stories and plays in a radically absurdist spirit, though without any humour, like all imitators. Everything can be imitated apart from humour.

If you come across a *Fields*, I would be pleased if you took a look at it. I hope I shall soon have the opportunity of learning your decision in connection with Kharms.

Greetings,
Vavka Ušić

17th June 1981
Sir,

I can hardly believe that my manuscript of Kharms has been with you (I assume untouched) since December 1978! Such behaviour is totally unacceptable. Incidentally, several of my translations have recently been published in the periodical *Scope*. Others seem to have a feeling for Kharms' irresistible charm. If I were you, I would give him some serious thought.

V. Ušić

21st February 1982

I received your message informing me that you are reading my translation of Kharms. What can I say? I'm at a loss for words . . .

V. Ušić

25.5.1982

Dear Mr Petrović,

I had a strange dream: I was lying in bed and beside me (with a cap on his head) lay Daniil Kharms, smoking a pipe. 'Naturally,' I thought in my dream, 'he smoked a pipe in life as well.'

'Pleased to meet you, Garfunkel,' said Kharms, offering me his hand politely.

I remember feeling rather uncomfortable about the fact that he was smoking in bed, that he had got into bed in his climbing boots, and that he had been dead for forty years. Somehow I didn't feel like shaking hands with him. Sensitive as he was (in my dream I was certain he was sensitive, although everything pointed to the contrary), Kharms realised I was upset so he took off his cap and, clearly in a desire to amuse me, began to pull out white rabbits, which were little Pushkins (!), pigeons which were actually Gogols and silk handkerchiefs, which were simply silk handkerchiefs. I remember clearly that one of them fell onto the floor, crumpled up and began to cough. I did not know why I was so frightened. And then I realised that Kharms wasn't lying beside me but sitting beside me and that it wasn't Kharms at all but you! You were sitting like that on my (!) bed, damn you!

I am still waiting for your answer. For your information, some of my texts have been published in 'The Literary Word'.

V. U.

P.S. I wonder what the dream means and how I should interpret that damn you!

28th June 1982

Mr Petrović,

A new book about the work of Daniil Kharms and Alexander Vvedensky has recently appeared. It is *Laughter in the Void* (Vienna, 1982) by Alice Stone Nakhimovsky. There is a translation of several of Kharms' prose pieces in the student periodical *Junk* accompanied by an exhaustive introduction and translator's notes.

Now it is absolutely clear that I misdirected my enthusiasm and that there is nothing more to discuss. I hope that you will at least have the decency to return my manuscript.

V. U.

21.10.1983

I hope that you have seen *The Book*, a translation of Kharms' short stories, in the bookshops. I don't know how much time has elapsed since I asked you to return my manuscript to me. If you fail to do so immediately, I shall be obliged to seek the assistance of a lawyer.

Vavka Ušić

25.11.1983

Hideous, sweaty monster! Sniveller! Idiot! Bone head! Cur! Swine! Loathsome, shameless creature! Insolent fool! Peasant! Dolt! Turd! Filthy beast! Nonentity! Lunatic! Wash your feet!

As you see, the number of insults D. Kharms mentions in his fiction is not very great. I would point out that some of them – idiot, fool and swine – recur and at the same time remind you that you have still not returned my manuscript!!!

V. U.

28th November 1983

Dear Mr Petrović,

I was extremely surprised to receive your letter informing me that you have included Kharms in your list for 1984, especially as it will now be the third volume of Kharms in our small market. I am, of course, willing to add to my selection and write an Afterword. I must also say that your letter has rather thrown me, because I had long since reconciled myself to the fact that my Kharms was not going to appear.

Still, I am glad that you have finally become an admirer and lover of the unique charm of Kharms' humour.

Yours sincerely,

Vavka U.

P.S. I apologise for the ugly physical incident in your office, but had we known each other better you would have known that you should not have used that word with me.

P.P.S. How is your ear? I hope that it has healed. I apologise, really, yet again . . .

15.12.83

Mr Petrović,

I don't know whether you keep up with the youth magazines but I was recently leafing through the literary section of *Swoop* and was furious to discover that 50% of the selections were directly copied from Kharms, 20% were crude imitations, and 30% were more or less attempts to write in his style. As a translator and, I might say, a close follower of the literary scene, I am extremely surprised at the resurrection of a writer who belonged to quite a different age and literary environment. I wonder whether the young are imitating Kharms simply because he lends himself to imitation (short stories close in structure to the joke) or because they like his destructive (in respect of traditional literature) attitude. Or could it be that everyday life (I dare not say this too loud) has begun to resemble the 'life' in Kharms' stories? Namely, if our shops are selling big cucumbers, then . . . See what I mean?

Perhaps the theme of Kharms and 'Kharmsists' would make an interesting afterword?

Best wishes,

Vavka U.

14.1.1984

Dear Petar Petrović,

According to Boris Semenov, Kharms was once in merry company and suggested that everyone write down on a scrap of paper 'what each of them liked and what each of them hated'. Kharms' paper looked like this: I REALLY LIKE: Gogol, Chekhov, Rabelais, Bach, Mozart, Koz'ma Prutkov, Zoshchenko, alley cats, Grosz, walnuts, the colours of Konashevich and Vasnetsov, baked potatoes, long-haired dogs, old books.

I CAN'T BEAR: the statue of Laocoon, Wagner's loud music, soya sausages, Maiakovsky's pictures, fake bow ties, the smell of carbolic acid, playing cards, the poems of Bal'mont and Shchepkin-Kupernik, rattlesnakes, vegetarian cooking and filthy record-players.

With all good wishes,

V. U.

P.S. I absolutely agree with Kharms' opinion of vegetarian cooking and in passing would like to remind you that we need to discuss the Afterword.

24.2.84

Dear Petar Petrović,

Leafing through the Vienna Slavists' *Almanach* the other day, I came upon the interesting fact that Mikhail Kuzmin, well known as a Symbolist poet, wrote a series of fourteen mini-stories of a pornographic nature. They date from 1928. In the same year Kharms, Vvedensky and Malevich used often to call on Kuzmin, and there is some evidence that Kuzmin, a homosexual and paedophile, read his stories to Kharms. Curiously enough, avant-garde art, which questions all aesthetic conventions and thematic taboos, did not remove erotic barriers in its Russian variant. It seems that the Russian avant-garde was not interested in sex. In this sense, Kharms is a puritan. In a 1932 letter to friends he writes he has read a 'very interesting book about a young man who fell in love with a young person, and that young person was another young man, and that young man loved another young person, who loved another young man, who did not love him but another young person. One day that young person slipped and fell through the opening of a sewer and broke his back, and just as he fully recovered, he caught a chill and died. Then the young man who was in love with him shot himself and the young person who loved that young man threw himself under a train. Then the young man who was in love with that young man climbed up a tram cable pole and was electrocuted. Then the young person who loved that young man swallowed some powdered glass and died of damage to his intestines. Then the young man who loved that young person ran away to America, where he drank up all his money and had to sell his clothes, and as he had no clothes he was obliged to stay in bed, where he developed bed sores and died.' Kharms clearly invented the book, but the description of its contents represents the peak of his connection with the theme of love. If we were to consider Kharms' psycho-poetics, we could confirm that his attitude to sexuality remains on the anal-oral level, that is, Kharms often mentions food, particularly porridge.

Having no intention of bothering you further with porridge and the possible symbolism thereof, I send you warm greetings.

Vavka U.

1st March 1984

Dear Mr Petrović,

May I respectfully remind you that we have not yet come to any agreement. At the same time I am sending two little stories. Read them and see if you can tell me who the author is.

1. Once upon a time, in the town of Leningrad, there lived a most ordinary Ivan Ivanovich, who drank beer, worked as a cashier and knew how to walk through walls. He didn't particularly boast about it, he simply knew how to do it, full stop . . . He used to lay bets he could, and his friends in the pub would say, 'Rubbish, Vania, you can't', and he would go ahead and do it! Once he had an accident; walking through a wall, he got stuck, or his leg did, and they had to call the chairman of the Residents' Council and the police, put together a file and break down the wall. Ivan Ivanovich came to a very bad end. He walked through a wall without taking account of what floor he was on, fell and smashed himself to bits.

2. Once upon a time in the town of Leningrad there lived a very learned dog. It knew how to turn itself into anything and everything. Once its master had company.

'Turn yourself into central heating,' said its master and the dog obediently turned itself into a heater.

'It's warm,' said the guests, not at all surprised.

Answer: I knew I wouldn't be able to fool you. The author of these two stories is obviously not Kharms but his friend and collaborator Yury Vladimirov.

14th May 1984

Mr Petrović,

You have still not contacted me about Kharms. I have been wondering about what would make a sufficiently attractive afterword, or indeed foreword. The most interesting thing for the general public would certainly be anecdotes connected with Kharms' life. They occur in numerous memoirs (S. Marshak, V. Trenin, K. Chukovskaia, L. Panteleev, N. Khalatov, M. Petrovsky, I. Rakhtanov, B. Semenov, G. Gor, M. V. Iudina, L. Zhukova, I. Bakhterev, V. Kaverin, et al.) so there is plenty of material. And while we are on the subject, Kharms also surfaces in literature. In his novel *The Harpagoniad* Konstantin Vaginov describes a German who doffs his hat politely and bows whenever he meets a dog. I am convinced that the German's prototype was Kharms. Moreover, Kharms included his own person in his concept of artistic action. A person as a work of art transforming everyday life into an artistic concept is not rare in the art of avant-garde groups in the twentieth century. Kharms played with the notion of authorship, signing his works with various pseudonyms: Daniil Khaarmst, Khkharms, Daniil Dandan, Charms, Harmonius, Ivan Toporishkin, Kharms-Shardam, the writer Kolpakov, Karl Ivanovich Schusterling, etc. The same concept governed his strange clothes, the strange letters he sent his friends, the way he greeted telegraph poles in the street and the like. We must take into account not only literary influences (Maiakovsky, Khlebnikov) but also members of the group in which Kharms was active and which inspired him. The children's writer Nikolai Oleinikov, for example. Oleinikov is supposed to have appeared in Leningrad with a certified declaration stating that Nikolai Oleinikov is a handsome man. In her *Epilogues* (New York 1983) L. Zhukova writes that she once went into a shop on Nevskii Prospect with Oleinikov and he said, 'Give me something blue. I need something blue to eat.' The salesman replied in some confusion, 'I'm sorry, but we're out of blue at the moment.' Oleinikov wrote numerous *vers d'occasion* and letters (attacking the wearing of suits or long skirts, approving haircuts, wishing his typist well on the occasion of her buying a new shawl, etc.) and dedicated them to his friends, not taking account of their artistic value. The poems were published relatively recently and show Oleinikov to be an excellent, even inspired poet and confirm the thesis of the individual as a living artistic concept.

One of my favourite poems is entitled 'Happiness is a full stomach' a comic account of the dramatic struggle between two passions: love of the body and love of food. 'Without bread and butter/I can no longer love/Lest my ardour stutter/Put some stew on the stove!' And so on and so forth . . .

Forgive me for getting carried away with Oleinikov. It is only because I find him closest to the 'Oberiu' spirit and feel that he influenced Kharms far more than can be proved today.

I do not intend to bother you any further so I'll stop now. If you think that the above-mentioned theme could make an interesting afterword to Kharms, let me know in good time.

Yours,
Vavka Ušić

1.11.84.

Sir,

Now it's November, and I still don't know where I am with Kharms! A few days ago I was thinking about a (possible) foreword again. Namely, I am reading the novels of Konstantin Vaginov for a third time, and it occurred to me that one could make a good parallel between Vaginov and Kharms. I do not wish to burden you with excess information, but I have translated a very short vignette of the kind Vaginov interpolates into his novels, this one is from the novel *The Life and Work of Svistonov* (Trudy i dni Svistonova) and it is reminiscent of Kharms' stories. At the same time may I remind you that I am eagerly awaiting your reply.

Best wishes,

Vavka U.

The Experimental Novelist

'Before I put anything on paper, I must experience the phenomenon I am describing.' Such was the principle of the tailor Dmitry Shchelin. For two years now he had been writing a 'novel of everyday life' with all its horrors.

Two months ago Shchelin intended to complete a chapter of his novel with the main character's attempted suicide by poison. Naturally, Shchelin wanted to experience the sufferings of a suicide who tries to poison himself. He got hold of some poison, drank it and lost consciousness. He was taken to the Mary Magdalene Hospital where he spent two months.

As soon as he recovered, he started working on the novel. Now he had to experience the sufferings of a suicide who tries to drown himself.

Just after midnight the following night, Shchelin jumped from Tuchkov Bridge into the Little Neva. Guards from the bridge saw him in time, rowed out to him and dragged him out of the water.

He was taken back to the Mary Magdalene Hospital in an unconscious state. In the morning he came round but that was not all. Now he had to experience the sufferings of a suicide who flings himself under a train.

'Only thus will all the phenomena in my novel be real and deeply permeated with emotion . . .'

The lot of the novelist-tailor is a difficult one.

1.12.1984.
Dear Petar Petrović,

I am sending you an extract from L. Nilvich's article 'Reactionary Juggling'. The article was published in the paper *Smena* in 1930 after an 'Oberiu' reading. The article did its job: the group held no more readings . . . By the way, what news is there of Kharms?

' . . . All the discussants, to the wild applause of the audience, unanimously and resolutely rejected the Oberiu. It was observed with disapproval that in the period of the most strenuous efforts of the proletariat in the forefront of socialist renewal, in the period of decisive class struggles, the Oberiu stand outside social life, outside the social reality of the Soviet Union. They seem to feel one should bury oneself as far as possible from that tedious reality, from insupportable po-li-tics, and indulge in one's own crude insolence and hooliganism! The Oberiu are far from renewal. They hate the struggle being waged by the proletariat. Their rejection of life, their senseless poetry, their artificial juggling is a protest against the dictatorship of the proletariat. Theirs is a poetry alien to us, the poetry of the class enemy, as the student proletariat has declared.

What could the Oberiu say to that?

With unheard of temerity Vladimirov likened the assembled company to a bunch of primitives who, on their first visit to a European city, had seen their first motor car. Levin announced that 'for the time being' (!) few people understood them, but that they were the only representatives (!) of a genuinely new art and were constructing a great new edifice.

When asked who it was for, he gave the classic reply: 'The whole of Russia.'

The student proletariat responded to the provocation of the famous Oberiu in a dignified manner. They decided to record their opinion in the form of a resolution and send it to the writers' union.

Incidentally, why does the writers' union tolerate such trash in its ranks? Is it not a gathering of Soviet writers?

6th January 1985
Mr Petrović,

Leafing through Kharms again, I am struck by the fact that nowhere are there so many deaths as among the 'Oberiu'. Vvedensky's play

Christmas at the Ivanovs (*Ëlka u Ivanovykh*) is surely unique in Russian literature: in the last scene alone nine characters die!

Death in Kharms' texts may be divided into two categories: intentional (70 percent of the cases) and unintentional (the remaining 30 percent). Unintentional (chance, accidental) death (or injury) generally results from unusual circumstances. One may divide the causes by frequency into three groups: a) falls; b) food; c) other. One may further divide falls as a cause of death according to frequency into:

> falling through windows (5)
> falling from cupboards (2)
> falling under a car (1)
> falling under a train (1)
> falling into a sewer (1).

Food as a cause of accidental death occurs on three occasions:

> excessive intake of peas
> tomatoes
> powdered glass.

The other causes of accidental death are the following:

> drowning in a lake
> receiving an electric shock
> suffocating in rubbish
> over-extending the neck as a result of throwing the head backwards
> decubitus
> tetanus
> chill.

I have noted only two cases of sudden physical distress: sudden hair loss and sudden blindness.

Far more frequent is intentional death (or mutilation, physical injury, etc.). Intentional death (or physical injury) in Kharms' fiction is generally carried out:

> a) by mechanical means

b) by non-mechanical means
c) by a combination of the two.

Mechanical means include: a poker, a sugar bowl, a beer tankard, an iron (or bone) rod, a primus stove, an iron, a branch, a croquet mallet, a hammer, a chisel, tongs, a trough, a crutch, a spade, a stone, a table leg. Kharms also brings literature two highly original instruments for physically injuring one's adversary: a set of false teeth (!) and a cucumber (!).

Non-mechanical means of mutilation or killing are limited to brute strength, that is, roughly the following repertoire: punching (the head, body); tearing off (members: arms, legs, head, etc.); spitting (on the victim); snotting (at the victim); beating up; breaking (jaws); chopping off (ears, head, arms); trampling; raping; throwing (the victim against a wall; living people into a pit); rubbing (a child's face against a wall); standing (on the victim's stomach with one's full weight); banging (a head against a wall); wrenching (a live child from its mother's womb).

Particularly perverse is the act of licking blood stains (belonging to the victim) from the floor. Burying as a means of death is mentioned only once in Kharms' writings. It is interesting that animals are never hurt (he liked them), indeed, they are rarely mentioned at all. Only in one text do we find a character rubbing a dead dog over the floor with his foot. It is also indicative that Kharms' most frequent victims are old women and children. The dead are mentioned for the purpose of terrorising others on several occasions.

I have made this brief statistical analysis of death, crime and perversion in Kharms' writings as I consider it a possible afterword for his works. The title could be roughly: 'The Relationship of Murderer to Victim: A Typology of Black Humour in Kharms' Work'. In fact, a great deal could be written about Kharms' black humour in connection with Freud, the European tradition (Jarry, de Sade, Swift and others), the Russian tradition (Gogol, Dostoevsky) and the poetics of Surrealism and the avant-garde's negation of the rationality of the world. However, I have no desire to drag out the problem artificially, I would stress two other key features. The first would be the influence of the *chastushka*, or street ditty, a traditional form of Russian oral literature and certainly the largest and most vital storehouse of black humour. Oleinikov's blackly humorous poems are nothing but 'artistic' *chastushki*. There are various kinds of *chastushka*: political, labour camp, erotic, pornographic, young Pioneer . . .

The other important point as I see it is what might be called the humour of the 'gang'. Kharms, Vvedensky and Oleinikov were children's writers, meeting day after day in the editorial offices of *Hedgehog* and *Siskin*, and you can imagine that together they developed a similar black humour sensibility. Kharms' famous children's poem, written for the first issue of *Siskin*, looks like this in Oleinikov's parodic version:

> *In a flat there lived*
> *Forty four*
> *Forty four sad siskins*
> *A siskin with paralysis*
> *A siskin with syphilis*
> *A siskin who was paranoid*
> *A siskin who had adenoids*

I would suggest that Kharms' black humour (hatred of children, etc.) results more from the fact that he was a children's writer than from a desire to parody Dostoevsky). I shan't bore you. I'm simply throwing out ideas, leaving you to decide for yourself what will best suit the afterword to the Kharms book.

I am looking forward to hearing from you.

Warm greetings,
Vavka U.

1.2.1985
Dear Mr Petrović,

I called in at your office today, but was told you were at a Workers' Council meeting. I was going to wait for you, but when your secretary said you had a meeting after that with the Commission for Systematising Appointments, I gave up. Let me know how things stand with Kharms.

Vavka U.

15th February 1985
Mr Petrović,

I am sending this Vvedensky text for your amusement and as a reminder of you know who! Incidentally, I'm beginning to lose patience. I feel as though I were giving you free lessons at an adult evening class.

Yours,

V. U.

Why Does My Stomach Rumble When I Declare My Love?

Why is it, I wonder that when I declare love to a new woman, my stomach almost always, or at least very often, rumbles? Or my nose gets blocked. It's a good sign actually. As soon as it starts I know everything will be all right. Of course, it is extremely important to cough at the right moment. One should not breathe in, because the rumbling will in any case reach her ears. A blocked nose too has its characteristic sounds. I think it's the excitement. What excitement? The sexual act is an event. An event is something new, not everyday. Doubly illuminated. As we enter it we enter eternity. But we quickly leave it as well. So we experience the event as life. And its end as death. After its end everything goes back to its place again, there is no life or death. Excitement before the act – a rumbling in the stomach, a blocked nose – is excitement in the face of the promised land. So what's it about? Why, the fact that we have a partner in the event, a woman. We are two. Otherwise, we are always alone. Though we're alone here as well, in fact, but at that moment or more precisely, up to that moment, it seems that we are two, it seems that as long as we are with the woman we shall not die, that in her is eternal life.

2nd March 1985
Sir,

I can see that Kharms is not coming out although it is now 1985. I am also surprised not to have heard from you, although I have written you a considerable number of letters. Let me know once and for all what is happening with Kharms and the afterword; in fact, it is the afterword that concerns me most at the moment. I really do want to come to an arrangement in good time, not at the last minute.

Thinking about the afterword I have been leafing through the Kharms literature again. As early as 1981, M. Jovanović in his article 'Daniil Kharms as Parodist' analyses Kharms' story 'The Old Woman' as a parody of Dostoevsky's *Crime and Punishment* and in a way anticipates all those articles which examine the parodic aspect of Kharms' insubstantial opus. Thus, Jovanović is joined by Ellen B. Chances who analyses Kharms' 'Old Woman' as a parody of Pushkin's 'Queen of Spades' and finds obvious parallels, without of course ignoring Dostoevsky who made reference to 'The Queen of Spades' in *Crime and Punishment*. Chances also links Kharms with Gogol ('The Nose', 'The Overcoat') and Chekhov.

A second line of research in Kharms' scholarship points towards the European drama of the absurd (Jarry, Beckett, Ionesco, Genet), a third towards the Russian avant-garde context (Khlebnikov, Malevich, Tufanov, Kruchonykh).

I have found nothing in the existing research on the structure of Kharms' short story (which closely resembles the anecdote, the joke) that does not recur in a surprising way in relation to the work of all short story writers. Have you read Kafka and Borges? Have you read Michaux's stories about Plim? Have you read Cortasar? If you have, and I presume you have, you will know what I mean. I also feel there is a possibility for research which at first glance looks not only bizarre but absurd: Kharms and Krleža. I'm thinking, of course, of Krleža's *Ballads of Petrica Kerempuh*. The Ballads were published in 1936, which is when Kharms' *Chances* (1933–1939) date from as well. Both Krleža and Kharms are characterised by a tragic sense of life: the former is struck by the absurdity of the past and approaching war, the latter by the terrible reality of Stalin's purges. Though taking completely different paths – one exploiting the effect of hypertrophied expressive means, the other the effect of the absence of same – they arrive at a similar, black-humour vision of the world.

I would base my comparative analysis chiefly on Krleža's ballads 'Old Woman Sobbing by the Gallows' and 'Sectio anatomica' and on Kharms' *Chances*.

I won't bore you any longer. Please let me know whether to concen-

trate on these suggestions or on some other theme for the afterword
to the forthcoming Kharms book.

Best wishes,
Vavka U.

23.6.85
Sir,
    I came to look for you again today. Your secretary told me you
were at the dentist, so I decided not to wait. For some reason I have
the feeling you are avoiding me. If that is the case I don't see why.

V. U.

23 January 1986
My dear Mr Petrović,
    I went to the hospital today, but they didn't let me see you, though
they were kind enough (only after my fervent insistence, I must admit)
to show me your diagnosis. Terrible, really terrible, I'm extremely
sorry . . .
    I simply can't understand why after finding the Kharms folder in the
cabinet, you pulled down a pile of other manuscripts, which then
brought the whole cupboard down with them. True, it looked pretty
wobbly and had weak, or, rather, non-existent legs but who would
have thought that an old worm-eaten cabinet could cause contusions
of the head (*contusio capitis*), concussion (*commotio cerebri*) and frac-
ture the parietal bone of the skull (*fractura ossis parietalis lat sin*)?
Though I suppose it is only logical: the cabinet did hit your head first.
All the rest, *fractura claviculae lat sin, ruptura lienis and fractura
femoris sin cum dilocationem* occurred when the cupboard had already
fallen onto you with its full weight. The contusions of the rib cage and
the rib fractures (*contusio thoracis cum fracturam costarum IV–VII lat
sin, fractura costae V lat dex*) probably also resulted from the cupboard's fall, although I do not rule out the possibility that their cause
was the understandable clumsiness your secretary and I displayed as
we lifted the cupboard off you, trying to drag you out as fast as
possible. Only the *vulnera icta manus dex* is an inexplicable riddle.
What was the cause of the gaping wound in your right hand when all
the objects with which you came into contact may be said to be blunt,

or at least far from sharp? There's no way a cupboard can make a wound so deep, anyone can see that!

I can't tell you how sorry I am that it all happened just as you were taking out the Kharms manuscript. Believe me, it would have been far easier on me had it been some other manuscript.

I send my very best wishes, trusting in medicine which can do wonders these days, and hoping you will make a very speedy recovery.

Yours ever,
Vavka Ušić

25th February 1986
Dear Petar,

I telephoned the hospital today, and the nurse's kindly voice told me you are much better, so I'm writing this letter to drag you out of the gloomy hospital atmosphere and bring you back at least for a moment to your job, which you like so much and where your return is impatiently awaited, as I had the opportunity to verify yesterday, when I made a brief visit to your office.

Your secretary told me that the unfortunate Kharms had been sent to the printer with the speed of a torpedo, which made me feel really awkward, because I had gone to the office with the intention of – withdrawing the manuscript. This will come as a surprise to you, I imagine. How can it be, you are surely wondering, that someone who has waited patiently for eight years should give up just like that? I hasten to answer your question, though I am not sure that you will approve of my reasons.

The whole thing came about, as always, by the ill-fated work of doubt. Whether it was the old editorial cabinet which so unexpectedly collapsed on your body that was to blame or something else, I don't know. I only know that that day (the day the cabinet fell) I began to be preoccupied with the evil and intrusive thought that all Kharms' texts, which various people had published in various periodicals might have been falsifications or semi-falsifications, or – at best – badly copied.

Let me recount, for example, the fate of the writings of A. Vvedensky, Kharms' inseparable friend, so you will understand the basis of my conviction.

I. S. Druskin, a musicologist and close friend of Kharms and Vvedensky records having seen in the early thirties, a notebook of Vvedensky's poems, written before 1922. Today we have only two poems from that period. Another notebook – of poems written between 1925–27 – shared a similar fate. The contents of that notebook were copied down by Kharms himself. Of 36 poems only 5 had been preserved in toto, and a further 5 in fragments. In 1928 the painter Pavel Mansurov emigrated to the West taking with him a few sheets of Vvedensky's writings. It is not known where they ended up. In 1926 Kharms and Vvedensky sent Pasternak a selection of poems and a cover letter. The letter has been preserved; the poems have disappeared! Vvedensky's poems, which otherwise ended up in the official garbage, were kept until the beginning of the war by N. I. Khardziev, but at the request of the author himself he returned them in 1940. They too disappeared without trace! The manuscripts from the mid-thirties were burnt: A. S. Ivanter, Vvedensky's wife at the time, set fire to the existing manuscripts when she learned of her husband's imprisonment. The manuscript of the play *My Mama Is Decked Out in Watches*, though written out for the actors in multiple copies, has not come down to us. When Kharms was arrested, I. S. Druskin went to Kharms' flat (it was the autumn of 1941 . . . V. V. Petrov and Kharms' wife M. V. Malich were with him) with the intention of hiding the manuscript archive. As they were unable to take all the manuscripts at once, they left Kharms' *Grass* (Trava), Vvedensky's novel *Murderers, You are Fools* (Ubyci vy duraki) and certain other papers for later.

When they returned to the flat, all they found were ashes: the remaining manuscripts had been 'successfully' burnt.

How is it possible now – after this story about Vvedensky, whose literary destiny and life are inextricably linked with Kharms – to believe without a vestige of doubt in texts that have risen to the literary surface after so many years?

A few days ago I received a letter from a friend in Moscow including a short piece by Kharms:

> *I was born among rushes. Like a mouse. My mother gave birth to me and placed me in the water. I began to swim. There was a fish with four whiskers on his nose circling round me. I began to cry. The fish cried too. Suddenly we noticed some porridge floating on the water. We ate it and began to laugh. We thought it was very funny . . .*

I've been troubled for several days by the question of whether that is an original Kharms or not. Everything would suggest that it is. It's his style, his kind of subject. The mouse (it's a play on words: Russian *kamish* means rushes; *kak mish* – like a mouse) is the key word, because it is also used by Vvedensky in the fragment 'The Grey Note-book' (*The mouse began to twinkle. Turn round: the world is twinkling like a mouse.*). Still . . . My suspicions are fanned by the fact that Kharms' short story model lends itself to imitation. Recall the whole crowd of young short story writers who are now mercilessly imitating Kharms.

All in all the thought is infectious. It goes further and deeper, finds more and more reasons, even broaches the ultimate question: what if Kharms is everything and nothing? And what if . . . No I don't dare even think of that.

In the end, I think the most reasonable thing to do is to trust one edition, in our case that of Meilakh and V. Erl' who are preparing Kharms' collected works in nine volumes. Three have appeared so far, and all three contain poems. Judging by the speed with which the volumes are coming out, the remaining six could appear within, say, the next ten years. You must admit, ten years is not much when literary-historical truth is at stake, that is, the truth we have decided to accept as valid.

I have already translated the first volume and shall soon send it to you. I hope it will help to pass the time. We can discuss the whole project when you come out. Warm greetings and my very best wishes for a speedy recovery.

Yours ever,
Vavka U.

P.S. Please don't forget to stop the printing of Kharms. I have heard that your secretary is intending to visit you tomorrow. Incidentally, I have been reconstructing the fall of the cabinet again in my memory and have worked out where you got that inexplicable *vulnera icta manus dex*. As your secretary was lifting the cabinet, she must have stepped on your arm with her high-heeled shoe. The pressure of the stiletto (combined with that weight!) could easily have caused a deep wound. I wear flat-soled shoes, by the way.

25 March 1986

My dear love, my world twinkling-like-a-mouse, my own little mouse, my Mickey.

I have just got back and have sat down at my desk at once. I want you to get this letter tomorrow. In the bus I kept thinking about the sweet blindness we've been living in (like two stupid mice) for eight (is it really eight?) whole years, I persistently clutching Kharms in my hands (like a compass, yet with no idea where he would lead me) and you persistently rejecting same, not knowing why yourself (for God's sake, it was only a book after all). And all the time Fate, wearing Kharms' mischievous mask, was toying with us. For I am certain it was fate that raised your hand from the armrest of the hospital wheelchair and placed it on my knee.

You are almost better, my love, my little mouse. And we're not pastries (*My ne pirogi!*) as Kharms' avant-garde friends were wont to shout. So keep exercising and keep your eyes off the nurses.

Your Vavka. Vav-ka. Your Ka.

P.S. I hope you're not angry that I keep hanging on to Kharms like a slender thread, like a silken fishing line, like a soft lassoo, like crumbs scattered on the path which led me to you. Kharms once said that he knew four 'oral machines', poems, prayers, charms and chanting. I'm your oral machine: I pray, I cast spells, I chant. I am your Ka. Your reed.

30.3.86

Dear Love,

Yesterday when I saw you in the convalescent home foyer, I felt my heart leap with joy for the first time in ages. You've made a wonderful recovery, you are getting better before my very eyes, day by day. That slight limp you're so worried about – it won't last. I'm sure it won't. If nothing else, we'll do the same as in Kharms' 'Incredible Cat'. In that poem a cat hurts its paw, so they tie a balloon to it and then the little cat half-walks, half-floats above the ground. My love, I imagine you floating above me, you come close, you kiss me tenderly and lift off like a balloon, and I have to reach out my hands to catch you.

I'll see you on Wednesday, I'll get a lift with a colleague this time and bring the books you wanted.

Always yours,
Ka.

Mousey,

Don't forget to phone the plumber about the washing machine and the carpenter. I'm at the university library. Luv, Ka.

Mousey,

I've taken the meat out of the fridge to thaw. We've got company tonight. I met a Swedish Slavist, a 'Kharmsologist', at the Summer School here and have invited him and his wife to dinner. I just rushed home to change and am going out now to show them a bit of the town. You buy some wine and peel the potatoes. Lots of love, Ka.

München, 14.5.87.

Mousey, it's wonderful here, I've met some really interesting new people. The symposium goes on till Saturday. Lars is here as well. He's left his wife. Remember her? The silly cow who got hiccups at dinner. Lars gave a paper yesterday on the meaning of zero in Kharms. It was a great success. I've seen Masha M. from Moscow, too. She's given me an unpublished poem by Kharms, probably because I told her I did some translating. I'm sending you the poem in Russian. You'll get the gist of it.

P.S. I bought you a wonderful cashmere scarf at a sale.

Hugs 'n' kisses
Ka (ka as in 'kashmere'!)

Stockholm 3.12.87

On 31 October 1937 Daniil Kharms wrote: 'All I care about is what is senseless, what has no practical sense. I care about life in its absurd form. Heroism, pathos, fearlessness, refinement, hygiene, morality, charm and risk – these are words and feelings I despise. On the other hand I fully understand and respect thrill and rapture, inspiration and despair, passion and reserve, debauchery and modesty, sadness and misery, joy and laughter.'

For some time now, Mousey, our life together has been less than stimulating. I've decided to stay with Lars. He's written a wonderful book on Kharms.

You take care of the practical matters as you think best. I really don't care about that kind of thing. Life must be useless, like a gift, said Kharms.

I wish you all the best,

Ka.

P.S. The only thing I claim is that portrait of Kharms, which Vladek did for me in any case.

Moscow, 10.11.1988

I'm writing from Moscow, from the Slavists' Congress, where Lars and I are at the moment. I've met some acquaintances from the old days when I was first here. I was shaken to learn that lots of wonderful old people I knew then are no longer with us – G. G. for example, who told me so much about Kharms.

Next year we'll be in the States, Lars has been invited to the University of Connecticut to give a seminar on Kharms. This year Kharms appeared here, in the Soviet Union, for the first time. I'm sending you a copy. I think A. A., the editor, chose a fine title. *Polet v nebesa. Flight to the Skies.*

Ka.

C. H.

Lend Me Your Character

···

Is a pen a metaphorical penis?

1

You shouldn't get involved with writers. That's just what happened to me, though. One day I bumped into Petar, a writer. He gave me a matey pat on the shoulder and invited me for a coffee.

'I read that story of yours, you know,' he said.

'Really?'

'It's good.'

'You liked it?'

'Yeah, specially that female character of yours, and I was just wondering . . .'

'What?'

'I was wondering . . .'

'What were you wondering?'

'I happen to be writing an erotic story and I was wondering . . .'

'What, for heaven's sake!' My patience gave out.

'I wondered whether you would lend me your character, I mean that female character of yours for my story!'

'Whaaat!' I was horrified.

'I need her for coital purposes,' he said, 'I mean, for a screw.'

'Hang on! You want my female character to be screwed by your male character, is that what you mean?'

'Right,' said Petar frankly.

'And who is he?'

'Who?'

'Your character.'

'Nothing special. Sexy, though.'

I stopped, took a deep breath and said, 'No!'

'Why not?'

'Because I'm not letting my character be screwed by a maniac!'

'Hey, wait a minute. First of all a published literary work is public property; besides it's not so much erotic as fantastic prose, that is, well, actually, it is rather erotic . . .'

'Absolutely not!'

I sipped my coffee, offended, then lit a cigarette and stared at Petar. He looked at me calmly, openly, as though his proposal were the most natural thing in the world.

'Listen,' I said, more gently, 'why doesn't your character screw, say, Anna Karenina? After all, what's my character compared to one of such substance?'

'Come on now. It's selling well,' the flatterer interrupted.

'Okay, it doesn't have to be Karenina! What about Joan of Arc or . . .'

'I don't write historical novels,' Petar observed reasonably.

'Well, find yourself someone else then!'

'Why can't you understand,' said Petar. 'An ordinary little home-grown character is just what I need! Besides, if you don't mind my saying so, in your story she's left, how shall I put it, unscrewed!'

'What d'you mean?'

'Just that! Unscrewed. And someone really ought . . .'

'Huh!' I said disparagingly. 'And that someone should be your little hero, of course!'

'Sure,' he said self-assuredly. 'He's not that bad!'

I said nothing. But perhaps I should have done a bit of thinking. Then I might have noticed the signal – the little red light that comes on whenever I meet a person of the opposite sex. This time the little light was sending out panic signals that Petar was 'a person with whom something could happen', but (as usual) I failed to notice it.

'Oh, okay! Take her . . . and screw her, pal!' I gave in so quickly that I surprised myself. That's exactly what I said, '*pal*', thumping Petar on the left shoulder. Then he thumped me. I never do that. I've no idea why I did it then. But, anyway, we thumped each other.

And then we parted. The things he came up with! Actually, I was sorry I hadn't come up with something like it myself. So on the way home I pondered a possible boy-friend for my heroine. Tom Sawyer? Winnie the Pooh? Of course the names that occurred to me were all the sort of names that ought never to have occurred to a serious writer. Maybe it was because I myself had often wished I had a boy-friend as sweet and gentle as Winnie the Pooh. And then I thought how frivolous I was, because how could a serious woman ever consider a brainless bear over Hermann Broch, or at least Robert Redford.

No, clearly I wasn't a serious writer. I had written a little book entitled *Alice Comes Home To Otranto* and the only thing that really appealed to me about it was the title. I was terribly proud of the title. I kept pestering people to guess how many other titles it contained. Basically, I wasn't a serious writer. Things might have been better had I been a serious woman. But, as I say, that was by no means certain.

2

On Saturday I ran out to the nearest kiosk and bought the *Evening News*. I could hardly wait to get home and settle down to reading Petar's story.

It had the promising title of 'The Hot Tongue', and its main characters were called Pierre and Ulla. I read the story right through. It took my breath away.

I phoned Petar immediately.

'Terrible!' I hissed into the receiver.

'Oh, it's you! You've read the story?'

'Yes. Crap!' I said telegraphically.

'You don't like it?'

'No! It's terrible!'

'Can you develop that a bit?'

'Crap,' I repeated.

'Listen, can I come and see you?'

'If you lie,' I breathed into the receiver instead of 'like' and hung up.

While I was waiting for Petar, I set my own offended appearance aright. I put on a respectable little black dress, as though dressing for a night out at the theatre rather than an ordinary conversation, and positioned the *Evening News* in my left hand like a truncheon. Petar appeared at the door with a bunch of flowers. I deliberately didn't put the flowers in a vase. I offered Petar a drink and, still holding the *Evening News* in my hand, sat down.

'You didn't need to borrow her for a mean trick like this,' I said, thinking of my character.

'Why do you think it's a mean trick?' asked Petar calmly.

'For a start, my character gives herself to that character of yours on the basis of just one single . . . Hang on, just a minute . . .'

I opened the *Evening News* and announced, like a verdict: 'On the basis of "a single *moist glance* . . ."' Really! What a male fantasy! Whoever heard of such a thing! What is she? A woman or a wild animal? And *Pierre*! Come on, we're not children, are we?'

'Wait a second,' Petar said blushing.

'Male writers always write in some female character, a secondary one of course, just so their male character can end up with her on the floor, behind the counter, rolling in a pool of beer! Naturally, all they need is one *moist glance*!'

'Hang on. What particular work do you have in mind?'

'It doesn't matter!' I said waving the *Evening News* and slurping Petar's drink. 'You'd all like to be rolling in pools of beer!'

'All this fuss over an ordinary erotic story,' said Petar in a conciliatory tone.

'Pornographic,' I specified.

'Why pornographic now?'

I opened the *Evening News* again, as evidence.

'In the course of a mere five pages, Pierre and Ulla "moan" fifteen times, they are "dazed" three times, he "cries out with passion" twice, she "groans with pleasure" twice. Then, he "enters" her three times, she "surrenders to his caresses" once. "Hardness" is mentioned four times, "moist, moistening" three times, "sweat" and everything connected with that is mentioned a whole eight times, "gushing" and "flowing" three times, "animal" is mentioned only once and then connected with "biting". Then "ecstasy", "rapture" twice, "salivate" twice, "pleasure" a whole seven times, and parts of the body, i.e. "lips", "thighs", "loins", "armpit", "belly", "belly-button", "breasts", "tongue", "moles" and "little hairs", all in all thirty-five times!'

I looked at Petar triumphantly, nonchalantly folding up the *Evening News*.

'As the author presumably I have the right to imagine my characters the way I want,' Petar flared.

'No, you haven't, at least not as far as my female character is

concerned. Because I lent her to you! And besides, how come my
character has two pairs of tits!'

'I told you my story has fantastic elements. Anyway, I have the right
to exaggerate as much as I want!'

'Precisely, it's male exaggeration like yours that makes sex what it
is!' I said, rolling the *Evening News* up into a trumpet and waving it
in the air in accusation of my non-existent audience.

'And what is it?' Petar asked offended.

'Shabby! That's what!' I said, thumping the bed dramatically with
the *Evening News*. Petar stared at the spot I had indicated with the
paper as though the solution were to be found there. Following Petar's
gaze myself, I felt something catch in my throat.

'In any case,' I said barely holding back my tears, 'my character
deserved something better than panting and heaving under your
character!'

'Hey, what's this?' said Petar gently and sat down beside me. 'Not
going to cry, are you? Not because of a little story? Besides, it's not
your female character. Didn't you notice that she's called *Ulla*?'

'Really?' I said, looking for a handkerchief.

'And that's not what yours is called, is it?'

'No,' I sniffed.

'There, you see,' said Petar, kissing me on the cheek.

'That's got nothing to do with it. I'm not crying because of an
individual case, I'm crying for all female characters! Universally, liter-
ary-historically, do you understand?' And I burst into tears.

When Petar started collecting them with his lips, I cried harder and
harder and felt warmer and warmer and saltier and moister and softer
and . . .

'*Come,*' *whispered Ulla, giving Pierre a moist glance.*

3

Two days later Petar moved in with me. There were a few more love
scenes between Pierre and Ulla and then Petar gave it up.

'I'm not writing any more erotic stories. They're so boring and
limited!'

We put away the Pierre and Ulla masks, without really having played
with them, and I was left with nothing but a little stick in my hand. I
stood there like a child who has been given a stick without a lollipop
on it by mistake but whom people fail to notice because they assume
she has simply eaten the lollipop. I gazed longingly at that imaginary

stick, thinking how soon everything was over (or how soon everything had begun). It was like a story in which the happy end comes so fast that the reader hasn't had a chance to want it.

Having put away the intention of writing erotic stories Petar turned in an orderly manner to a novel entitled *Anxieties*, about the relationship of a certain individual to a certain authority. Then he abandoned that idea and went on to a novel entitled *Sufferings*, about the relationship of a certain individual to himself.

As for me (unlike Petar) I turned into an emotional blancmange. That is, I fell in love. That is, my creative life developed according to a strange rhythm whose meaning I could never quite grasp. So for the first few days I cooked like a demon. I would get up early in the morning, while Petar was still asleep, and carry out the little ritual of breakfast in the morning quiet with almost holy fervour. In the grey morning light I wrote an anonymous letter on the white lace tablecloth. Every morning I coloured the eggs a different colour (the blue ones were the prettiest!) and painted love messages on them with a fine brush. I made thin, transparent, delicate rings of butter and arranged them each morning a different way for Petar to read their hidden meaning. I cut the bread into thin slices in the shape of hearts. Once I even baked it myself, kneading a love poem into the dough. The poem emerged from the oven as a lumpy, overdone mass: I had pressed beautiful words into the dough, and the bread came out gibberish.

A few days later I threw myself with the same creative zeal into cleaning, washing, ironing. I spent hours and hours ironing. I liked sheets most of all, white sheets – my unwritten pages. Passionately I ironed my impenetrable longing into them, pressed secret messages into them, messages even I did not understand. Then after a few days I took to knitting and I knitted Petar a meaningless scarf ten feet long and – stopped.

Without knowing it, I retraced the abbreviated history of female literacy. Petar did not notice the creative whirlpool spinning behind him: he was calmly developing the idea for a third novel, entitled *Interferences*, about the relationship of a certain individual and certain other individuals.

Next I switched my strong, incomprehensible creative urges to food. But this time it was I who ate, hiding from Petar, ashamed of myself, weeping because of my terrible, treacherous hunger. Sometimes, on the pretext that I had an errand to run, I would sneak into the nearest confectioner's. At night, while Petar slept, I would get up and tiptoe into the kitchen in the dark. There, by the narrow strip of light from the open fridge, I would crouch and eat, and send obscure signals. Only where to? And to whom?

One day, as Petar sat at his desk working on his new novel, I summoned up my courage, went into the room and said simply, 'Petar, I've been thinking about that story of yours in the *Evening News* and I've come to the conclusion it wasn't that bad!'

'Why do you say that all of a sudden?'

'It doesn't matter why,' I said, giving him a moist glance and stroking his hair. 'I just think it was good, very good even.'

'No, no, you were right then. Pornography, it was pornography of the worst kind,' said Petar, not noticing my subtly dropped metaphorical handkerchief. I picked it up myself and used it – to wipe my nose.

4

Yes, I was an emotional blancmange.

'Why don't you write some of that women's prose of yours?' suggested Petar.

I couldn't explain that it was because all a pitiful blancmange in a dish could do was wish somebody would eat it.

Once, plunging into the larder to get something and turning back to the kitchen to fiddle with something there, I happened to catch sight of my smiling face! I was deeply moved by that senseless smile. I stood confused in front of the mirror, with an onion in my hand, trying to turn the film back. I had gone to the larder to fetch an onion and a little net hanging from a nail on the wall had grazed my cheek. My cheek had interpreted the graze of the net as a caress and I'd smiled!

And now, standing transfixed in front of the mirror, Ulla became aware of a silent film running in her consciousness, and for the first time she saw clearly and sharply, those innumerable tiny actions which she carried out each day without being aware of them. She saw herself stroking the edge of the armchair, then holding a tomato in her hand; she saw the dramatic instant when she broke off the stalk, she saw herself watching that act, fascinated, listening to the sound and staring at the pinkish hollow where the stalk had just been like a child who spends hours peeling a scab, intrigued by the new pinkish skin; she saw herself rubbing her hands on the jagged edges of metal bottle-tops, running the tips of her fingers round the edges, pushing her fingers into the hollow trying to break off the bottom, a thin, round leaf of cork; she saw herself standing in the shower under a jet of warm water, collecting the drops on her lips, bending her head, pressing her lips to the back of her own hand and staring at the indifferent, white tiles; she saw herself knocking an onion against the table as she held it by its young, green shoots and staring, enthralled, at the window; she saw herself rinsing cherries, taking one, licking off the drops of water, breaking off the stalk, putting the cherry in her mouth, tensely anticipating the sound of the sweet flesh bursting, caressing the stone with her tongue, rolling it round in the hollow of her lip before spitting it out into the soft pillow of her palm; she saw herself doing the same thing with a peach, licking the stone for a long time, trying to pull off the pinkish-yellow flesh in the furrows with her teeth; she saw herself carefully pulling the pale yellow strings from a peeled banana, pressing the palm of her hand into the fresh flesh; she saw herself lengthily, rapturously feeling the wrinkled skin on warm milk, and with the same emotion tenderly drawing an imaginary line with her finger from the root of her own nose to its tip, holding an egg in the hollow of her hand for a long time before lowering it into boiling water, frequently stroking her index finger with her thumb or her thumb with her index finger, staring for hours into space, rubbing her lower lip; she saw herself stroking the edges of things, especially wooden, sharp ones, the edges of pictures, the edges of wardrobes, feeling for the edges with her fingers, sharp, hard edges everywhere.

The onion fell to the floor with a dull thud, interrupting the series of pictures, and all at once what she saw in the mirror was her naked solitude, her frightening longing for a touch.

'Pierre!' she cried in despair and ran into the room where Pierre was sitting at the table, buried in papers. 'Pierre!'

She began to kiss him wildly, touching all the edges on him; she rubbed the tips of her fingers round his buttons, undoing them; she caressed the edges of his ears, the edge of his nose, the edges of his wrists, lips, chin, eyebrows, then slipped further down until she came to that swollen, finger-like edge . . .

5

Petar and I were spending an afternoon in so-called marital bliss. I was lying reading, while Petar sat at his desk writing. At one point I put down my book and said, 'I had a strange dream last night.'

Petar shifted his chair away from the desk, took off his glasses and looked at me enquiringly.

'I dreamt of something horn-like.'

'So what?' said Petar vacantly.

'I don't know how to describe it to you. I had a little horn down there!'

'That's clear! A phallic symbol. You're simply envious because you haven't got one.'

'No, it was a little horn,' I insisted bitterly.

Petar obviously wasn't interested in my dream, but he got up from the desk, yawned, stretched and sat down beside me.

'What are you reading?'

'A novel.'

'Whose?'

'Stanislav's.'

'Stanislav's written a novel? When did it come out?'

'A few days ago.'

'I didn't know that,' said Petar, hiding his envy with a yawn. 'What's it like?' he asked carelessly.

'It's about a certain individual and a certain authority in the first part and about the relationship of that individual to himself in the second.'

'It sounds boring.'

'Not at all. It's got pace. It's got everything you could ask for.'

'A plot?'

'Yes.'

'Let's have a look.'

Petar leafed idly through the book, yawned again and tossed it into a corner.

'Crap,' he said briefly, and then he put his hand on my bosom, began to unbutton my shirt, undo the zip on my jeans . . .

'I'll write you something better, I'll give you . . .' whispered Petar, kissing me. 'Come close, I'll give you . . .'

He kissed me slowly and strangely. I felt uneasy. I closed my eyes and when I opened them again, they met Petar's cold, interrogating gaze.

'Everything's horn-like,' said Ulla. I pulled down the zip on her jeans. The sound split the air, remained hovering for a moment, then burst like a soap bubble. I unbuttoned her shirt and began running my fingers round her brown nipples. Ulla suddenly seemed thin and small. I didn't know how to approach and enter her. Then she turned her back and her shoulder blade covered with fine skin leapt out in front of me. At first I was afraid, yet I began to gnaw the brittle lump. Still frightened – it didn't belong to Ulla – I kissed it, moistened it a bit with my tongue and bit into it. She cried out. Horn-like, everything's horn-like.

Suddenly she began to grow. She was too big for me to enter her. She was like a vast white she-whale. A strong, dark, fishy smell filled my nostrils. Once more I was frightened. But then she returned to her natural size. I touched her breast and felt a strange stickiness on my palm. I wanted to take my hand away, but her breast came with it. I placed my other hand on the other one. It stuck as well. I kissed her. Our mouths stretched like chewing gum. I heard her say something but couldn't make out what it was. Strange, I thought, it doesn't hurt at all and we can breathe. Horn-like, everything's horn-like.

By now I badly needed to put it into her, but I was afraid of sticking to her and remaining in her forever. Finally I gave in and felt myself melting inside her like a huge tablet in a glass of water. Little bubbles tickled me, it felt good. Only what shall I do now, I thought, what will I do without it? And then in its place I caught sight of a tiny little horn sheathed in silky, soft deer skin . . .

'Let's stop,' I said, extricating myself from Petar's embrace and lighting a cigarette. Petar and I were silent for a time, and then he said dully, 'I'd like to write a novel about a man who had used up his life in advance, without living it, and who was only marking time! That's what I'd call it: *Marking Time*.'

6

Although with time (as a blancmange) I developed a crust, I still couldn't embark on real prose. So I directed all my creative energy to scholarly work. My articles – 'A Revisionist Analysis of "Beauty and the Beast'", 'Pinocchio: Archetype of the Male Erotic Imagination', 'Why Did Anna Karenina and Emma Bovary Kill Themselves?' 'Smothered in Myths or the True Face of Marko the Prince', 'Toad-men and Snake-Women in Yugoslav Folk Tales', 'The Treatment of Woman in Contemporary Prose', were simply a preparation for my great, secret, project: *A Lexicon of Female Literary Characters*. And when I rushed over to my mother's one day to read her my entry on *La Dame aux Camelias* in my scholarly fervour, and when my mother wept for a full fifteen minutes without stopping, I was convinced I was on the right scholarly track.

I had reached the letter 'G' and as I was writing an entry on *The Girl with Green Eyes*, I ran out of paper. Petar wasn't at home – he had gone out to buy cigarettes and I reached into the drawer of his desk . . .

Pierre stood up and stretched. His back ached from sitting at the desk. His writing hadn't gone all that well today either. He looked round for Ulla and saw her through the half-open door of the kitchen bathed in a thick shaft of light coming from the open window. Strange, thought Pierre, with a shiver. It was as though he were seeing her for the first time. Fixed in a still frame, Ulla was bending over the kitchen table, preparing a piece of liver. The liver's bloody skin stuck to her fingers as she tried to remove it. Irritated, she shook it off and cut the liver into thin strips, sticking her tongue out a little and pressing it with her teeth, which made sharp, hard lines appear on her face. Pierre now saw Ulla clearly: sweaty forehead, double chin, protruding tongue, hunched back, bloody hands. The treacherous light, the pitiful frame, the opportunity for spying filled him with shame. He had discovered a stranger, who was not, who could not be Ulla . . . He felt a vague but powerful sense of affront well up in him, felt his love for Ulla slowly dissolve, like huge tablets in a glass of water. All at once he wished that someone would quietly close the door and Ulla would disappear forever, fade like a photograph, vanish quietly, painlessly, as though she had never even existed.

'What's this?' I asked Petar when he appeared at the door.

Petar hung up his coat, took his cigarettes out of his pocket and asked innocently: 'What?'

'This!' I shrieked thrusting the treacherous page into his face.

'You can see for yourself! It's a piece of writing,' said Petar blushing.

'I presume it's the beginning of a new novel about a certain writer and his relationship to . . .'

'Shut up!' said Petar roughly.

I held back my tears; he remained stubbornly silent.

'Can't you see how awful this is?' I said in a husky voice and dropped the page on the floor. 'We're not living, we're describing each other!'

'Whoever said one had to live in life!'

'Then why not dissolve once and for all!' I shouted bitterly. 'Like those stupid metaphorical tablets of yours!'

'Shut up,' Petar repeated.

'Pathetic pen pusher!'

'Limited literary housewife!' he said.

'Third-rate thief!'

'Manipulator of human souls!' he said.

'Prose plumber!' I said.

'Hack!' he said.

'Imitator of life!'

'Sob sister!'

'Impotent plagiariser!'

'Nonentity!'

'Fraud!'

'Female copyist!'

'Silly metaphorist!'

'I hate you!'

'And I hate you!'

'Oh, how I, how I haaate you!'

1. 'The game goes on,' said Ulla in a husky voice, licking her upper lip with her tongue, and giving Pierre a moist glance.

2. 'The game goes on!' shouted Ulla and gave the door a hefty kick. Ulla entered the room with a slim, tanned, broad-shouldered young man in a black leather jacket and tight leather trousers. Ulla tossed the cascade of her long blonde hair. Her eyes shone with a cold gleam, her chest heaved in agitation.

Pierre paled and squinted through his glasses.

'Tie him up!' Ulla ordered. The young man leapt lithely, like a panther, and in an instant tied Pierre up with a washing line.

'Ulla! Ulla! What are you doing?' cried Pierre. 'Have you gone mad!'

'The mincing machine!' Ulla ordered. The young man appeared at once with a strange piece of equipment in his hand.

'That's it,' said Ulla paying Pierre's entreating looks no heed. 'Now for a little torture!'

3. 'The game goes on,' thought Ulla bitterly, rolling a jagged metal bottle-top between her fingers. She tried to peel off the thin round cork lining with her nails, then put down the bottle-top thoughtfully, rolled a sheet of paper into the typewriter and began to type . . .

'You shouldn't get involved with writers . . .'

Epilogue

About five o'clock it began to get cooler. I closed the windows and carried on writing.

At six my friend Adam stopped by, he was going to the Writers' Club.

'Hey! You're working!' he said.

'No, I'm writing.'

'What is it?'

'A story.'

'For me?'

'No.'

'Interesting?'

'Boring.'

'Why are you writing it then?'

'Who else will if I don't?'

'Another confession?'

'No . . .'

'What then?'

'Sit down a moment,' I said.

When he had sat down I went to pull the page out and read him what I had written. From the typewriter, as though from a magician's hat, one after another, I pulled out white silk handkerchiefs, discreetly perfumed with despair.

C. H.

Author's Notes

The author of these stories believes that she owes her readers some background material. By an extraordinary accident (such accidents are always extraordinary), recently she happened upon a small manuscript entitled *Métaterxie escrite de la main d'Adalbéron, vénérable abbé de l'abbaye de Couesnon*. The Abbot Adalbéron's little book is a collection of hand-copied extracts from Latin ecclesiastical works. The only part that comes from the Abbot himself are the few sentences he interposed between the lines as he carried out his unusual penance. These are simple and touching (I hunger; I thirst; God, release me from this penance; my shoulder is numb; God, when will this end; and the like). The charm of reading this booklet is indescribable, consisting as it does in imagining the background for the poor Abbot's scribal contrition.

But what interested the author of these lines most was the meaning of the unusual word *métaterxie*. The author consulted experts in French language and literature but came to no satisfactory conclusion. She will undertake a more detailed investigation later, but meanwhile she has been visited by inspiration of another kind and has translated the word *Métaterxie* into modern parlance as a metatextual-therapeutic tale, which was certainly not remotely like what poor Abbot Adalbéron had in mind.

All in all the author has written six stories by altering other stories, that is, copying someone else's story and interpolating her own text, or writing her own story and interpolating someone else's text, or writing someone else's text and interpolating her own story. The author has sorted out the personal moral dilemmas connected with this choice of method with Titivilus, and she will explain whence, how and what to her readers in the lines that follow.

The first consideration was one of subject matter. Out of patriotic concern for her native literature the author initially intended to write erotic stories. For despite the flood of stories with erotic themes we do not seem to have found our own horse for that course (there you are, as soon as *that kind of thing* is mentioned, we are for some reason drawn into folklore), so in the eyes of the rest of the world we are, in erotic terms, paupers.

After leafing through her native literature the author finds the most erotic passage in a work for children.[1] Afraid that her conception of the erotic might be perverse, she quickly changed her mind and wrote stories that were actually about the same thing, only from a different angle, i.e. about something different but from the same angle. All things considered, the author has incontrovertibly muddled her concepts. At one point she looked upon the very act of copying (*repeating*) as a deeply erotic art. After all, how would the history of literature have evolved over the centuries if it weren't a matter of – pleasure?

A Hot Dog in a Warm Bun

This story is one of numerous reworkings of Gogol's story 'The Nose', just as Gogol's story itself is only the most artistically successful concentration of the literary and extra-literary 'noseology' of the twenties and thirties of the nineteenth century. Interested readers may consult V. V. Vinogradov's exhaustive and intriguing study, 'The Theme and Composition of Gogol's story "The Nose"'.

The note for this story is meant more as an apology, that is, the author has used the most vulgar form of substitution. The idea was

---

1 Here is the passage in question: 'The old woman thought it a miracle that the night could be like this, and she went into the kitchen. At the very moment she opened the door, the kindling in the hearth burst into flame, and a crowd of Little People – all tiny men, barely a foot high – started dancing round the blaze. They wore sheepskin coats and peasant shoes as red as the fire, their hair and beards were grey as ash, and their eyes bright as the glowing coals. More and more of them emerged from the flames, each from his own piece of kindling. As they emerged, they laughed and shrieked, they flung themselves round the fireplace, squealing with merriment and joining the dance. For dance they did – on the hearth, in the ashes, on the chair, round the jug, over the bench! Fast! Faster! Squealing, shrieking, pushing, shoving. They spilt the salt, tipped over the yeast, scattered the flour – all for sheer joy. The fire in the hearth flared and glowed, crackled and leapt, and the old woman watched in wonder. She did not regret the salt or yeast but rejoiced in the jollity God had sent to console her.'

not difficult to come by, just as Gogol's interpreters had no difficulty in seeing all kinds of things in the vanished nose. The author decided on this crude substitution not to hold herself up to Gogol or to hold anything against him; she simply wished to turn some interpretational gossip into literature.

In fact she could have settled for a variant she knows from real life, but was inhibited by too close a relationship of life to literature, that is, she knew (in real life) a person of the male gender who suffered for a whole year from a very awkward and unusual fixation: the person of the male gender in question walked around the whole of that time with a handkerchief pressed to his nose, convinced that instead of a nose he had a you-know-what, and presumably, instead of a you-know-what a nose. Fortunately, the person of the male gender was successfully cured.

Life is a Fairy Tale
For this story the author was inspired by items published in the paper *Zoom-Reporter*, particularly a piece signed 'Jocko' entitled 'How To Prevent the Growth of Your Member'.[1] There was also a most influential article published in the *Evening News*, entitled 'Love and Chocolate'.[2]

The thought that writers are lonely beings and need to be encouraged belongs to Jorge Luis Borges.

And finally, 'The Story of a Complete Gentleman' by the Nigerian Amos Tutuole is one of the author's favourite stories, and the genre of the Christmas tale is certainly one of the most charming literary genres.

---

1 'Dear Doctor, I am writing for advice about a serious problem. I have noticed that my member has begun to grow, leading to unforeseen complications. I hope that you will be able to help me. Will my member continue to grow and exactly what is the matter with it? The current length of my member is 15 ins. I hope that this situation will not get any worse. Jocko.'

2 'Love and the emotions it arouses cause the secretion of pheniletilamines, substances similar to the amphetamines that stimulate the central nervous system. It has been established that this substance is found in large quantities in chocolate. Experts from the New York State Institute of Psychiatry have concluded that the majority of people who treat the pains of love with chocolate in fact do so instinctively in order to compensate for the reduced amount of pheniletilamine in their systems.'

Who Am I?

The model for this story was Lewis Carroll's *Alice in Wonderland*. More than 15.5 per cent of its text is copied from that wonderful book. O.5 per cent hints at certain other texts and the author hopes that readers will reminisce correctly. Perhaps only the sentence 'The magician was tall' requires explanation. It comes from a story by Daniil Kharms entitled 'The Old Woman', and was chosen neither accidentally nor arbitrarily. Kharms' story represents a successful example of the parodic remodelling of F. M. Dostoyevsky's *Crime and Punishment*.

The Kreutzer Sonata

As the title itself suggests, this story stems from the old idea that familiar stories should be written again. Closing the pages of a book, passionate readers often wonder What if it had happened thus and so? The author of these lines, for example, is just such a passionate reader. She has often wondered what would have happened if Tolstoy had written *Anna Karenina* from the perspective of her husband in a novel entitled *Alexei Karenin*. As he did not, the author modestly decided to take the project on herself. But the great Russian writer would not be so great had he not foreseen such things, and he did write something similar himself, of course, under the title of 'The Kreutzer Sonata'. The author of these lines did not consequently abandon her authorial intention; she simply redirected it a little in the direction of 'The Kreutzer Sonata'. Wandering through secondhand bookshops one day, however, she came upon a little book with the exciting title *The Sinner*. After confirming yet again that all great ideas have already occurred to others, the author of these lines was left with no alternative but to roll up her sleeves and embark on a project involving pure – copying.

The Kharms Case

For the requirements of this story the author adopted the narrative mask of the assiduous translator of Daniil Kharms. Kharms, a remarkable Russian avant-garde writer, was published in the Soviet Union for the first time in 1989, in other words, far, far later than the year this story was written, and far later than the year Kharms appeared in Serbo-Croat (the author did actually translate Kharms into Serbo-Croat).

In that same year, 1989, a certain Mr Z., an expert on the work of

Kharms, spent a short time in Zagreb. Mr Z. had also spent some time in a Soviet prison (by chance the same prison in which Kharms had breathed his last). While serving out his sentence, the assiduous Mr Z. undertook the noble task of studying the prison dossiers (with the permission of the prison authorities, of course). He made the estimable discovery that the date customarily assigned to Kharms' death – 4 February 1942 – is incorrect. On that day the prison authorities returned an unopened food parcel to Kharms' wife Marina Malich. Mr Z. maintains that Kharms died somewhat later, in the prison insane asylum, where he is said to have selflessly distributed medals from the Society for the Philosophy of Balance and walked around with his head bandaged to prevent his ideas from escaping. Daniil Kharms had founded the Society for the Philosophy of Balance (before he was imprisoned) with his friend the philosopher Druskin. The author of this story met Druskin's brother, a composer, during a stay in Leningrad.

During his short stay in Zagreb, Mr Z. contacted the author of this story twice: once 'officially' (to tell her of his astounding discovery), then privately, by telephone, late one evening. On this second occasion, Mr Z. asked her to lend him a hundred dollars, assuring her he had just been robbed near the main post-office. The author did not give it to him, although she had no reason not to.

Whether there is any connection or secret balance among these events is not yet clear.

Lend Me Your Character

In addition to the author's love for Gide's *Marshlands*, this story was inspired by the conviction that great literary characters win the right not only to eternity but also to an independent life. In this sense Hamlet lives on without his great creator. That idea gives rise to another: by entering the realm of both eternal and independent life, characters realise the full freedom of their own potential destinies rather than those imposed on them by their creators. The author immediately imagined a field of joyful promiscuity: kisses exchanged by Don Quixote and Emma Bovary, sweet talk between Heathcliffe and Anna Karenina, inadmissible passion between Peter Pan and Faust . . . The idea struck the author as unusually effective, but as every real writer avoids effects, the author staunchly rejected the idea and this time copied – life! Or more precisely, life, which in any case copies – ideas!

C. H.